D0500187

THE RAP✝URE

THE RAPTURE

LIZ JENSEN

DOUBLEDAY
NEW YORK LONDON TORONTO SYDNEY AUCKLAND

ᴅᴅ
DOUBLEDAY

This book is a work of fiction. Names, characters, businesses, organizations, places, events, and incidents either are the product of the author's imagination or are used fictitiously. Any resemblance to actual persons, living or dead, events, or locales is entirely coincidental.

Copyright © 2009 by Liz Jensen

All Rights Reserved

Published in the United States by Doubleday,
a division of Random House, Inc., New York.
www.doubleday.com

Simultaneously published in the United Kingdom by Bloomsbury.

ᴅᴏᴜʙʟᴇᴅᴀʏ and the DD colophon are registered trademarks of Random House, Inc.

Book design by Casey Hampton

LIBRARY OF CONGRESS CATALOGING-IN-PUBLICATION DATA
Jensen, Liz, 1959–
The rapture / Liz Jensen. — 1st ed.
1. Women psychotherapists—Fiction. 2. Teenage girls—Fiction. 3. Mothers—Crimes against—Fiction. 4. Extrasensory perception—Fiction. 5. Psychological fiction. I. Title.
PR6060.E55R37 2009
823'.914—dc22   2008038518

ISBN 978-0-385-52821-4

PRINTED IN THE UNITED STATES OF AMERICA

1 3 5 7 9 10 8 6 4 2

First Edition in the United States of America

For Raphaël

THE RAPTURE

ONE

That summer, the summer all the rules began to change, June seemed to last for a thousand years. The temperature was merciless: ninety-eight, ninety-nine, then a hundred in the shade. It was heat to die, go nuts or spawn in. Old folk collapsed, dogs were cooked alive in cars, lovers couldn't keep their hands off each other. The sky pressed down like a furnace lid, shrinking the subsoil, cracking concrete, killing shrubs from the roots up. In the parched suburbs, ice cream trucks plinked their baby tunes into streets that sweated tar. Down at the harbor, the sea reflected the sun in tiny, barbaric mirrors. Asphyxiated, you longed for rain. It didn't come.

But other things came, seemingly at random. The teenage killer, Bethany Krall, was one of them. If I didn't know, back then, that turbulence obeys specific rules, I know it now. During just about every one of those nights, I'd have dreams that were so vivid they felt digitally enhanced. Sometimes I could do more than just walk and run and jump. I could do cartwheels; I could practically fly. I'd be an acrobat, flinging my body across the empty air, then floating in the stratosphere like a Chagall maiden. Other times I'd find myself with Alex. He'd be throwing his head back to laugh, as if nothing had happened. Or we'd be having urgent sex, in a thrash of limbs. Or engaging in the other thing we'd so quickly become experts at: fighting. Viciously. Also as if nothing had happened.

Then I'd wake. I'd lie there, my upper body still sweating, the mail-order fan strafing the air across my naked skin, and let the new day infiltrate in stages. The last stage, before I rose to wash and dress and fight my tangled hair, like someone emerging from a date-rape drugging, would be the one in which I'd dutifully count my blessings. This folksy little ritual stayed brief because the way I saw it, they didn't add up to much.

When the skies finally broke, it felt biblical, megalomaniacal, as though orchestrated from on high by an irate Jehovah. On the coasts, cliffs subsided, tipping soil and rubble and silt onto the beaches, where they lodged in defiant heaps. Charcoal clouds erupted on the horizon and massed into precarious metropolises of air. Out at sea, beyond the gray stone bulwarks of the port, zigzags of lightning electrocuted the water, bringing poltergeist winds that sucked random objects up to whirl and dump. Passionate gusts punched at the sails of moored boats and then headed inland, flattening corn, uprooting trees, smashing hop silos and storage barns, whisking up torn garbage bags that pirouetted in the sky like the ghostly spirits of retail folly. Maverick weather was becoming the norm across the globe: we'd all learned that by now, and we were already frustrated by its theatrical attention-seeking, the sheer woe of its extremes. Cause and effect. Get used to the way A leads to B. Get used to living in interesting times. Learn that nothing is random. Watch out for tipping point. Look behind you: perhaps it's been and gone.

Psychic revolution, worlds upended, interrogations of the status quo, the eternal proximity of hell: subjects close to my heart at this point. Popular wisdom declares that it's a mistake to make major changes in the wake of a catastrophic event in your personal life. That you should stay close to your loved ones—or, in their absence, to those best placed and most willing to hold your hand through the horror-show of your new, reconfigured life. So why, in the aftermath of my accident, had I so obstinately done the opposite? I was so sure, when I made it, that my decision to quit London was the right one, arrived at after a cool mental listing of the pros and cons. But my Chagall-maiden dreams and the restlessness that infected me seemed evidence of another, less welcome possibility: that once again I had sabotaged my life—as thoroughly and as definitively as only a professional psychologist can. My brain, working overtime with denial, was a sick centrifuge operating at full tilt.

In the mornings, the modest skyline of Hadport fizzes gently with coastal fog that, pierced by the first light, can take on a metaphysical cast. There's a spritz of bright air meeting water, of delicate chemical auras dancing around one another before mingling and ascending to the stratosphere. Conservative-minded angels, conscious of their celestial pension constraints and forced to relocate, might choose a town like this to spend their sunset years. So might my once energetic and cultured father, if he'd kept his marbles long enough to leaf through brochures about retirement complexes, instead of Alzheimering his way into a nursing home to spend his waking hours watching Cartoon Network and drooling onto a plastic bib: as sorry an end for a former diplomat as can be imagined. If you venture out early enough you can taste the sharp tang of ozone in your mouth. "Decent parking," my practical pre-la-la father would have said, if he'd accompanied me on my morning sorties along the gum-studded pavements of my new hometown. "Useful in your situation, Gabrielle." Later in the day, his high opinion might downgrade itself a notch. Hadport, being near the Channel tunnel, has a high quota of illegal immigrants and asylum seekers: the bed-and-breakfast population, the shallow-rooted underclass about which the *Courier* opines on behalf of "heritage citizens" who have graduated from compassion fatigue to a higher realm of pathological resentment that the paper's editorials refer to as justified indignation. As the day rolls itself out, the trash cans fill and then erupt with Starbucks cups, gossip magazines, buckled beer cans, burger cartons gaping open like polystyrene clams: the husks of what nourishes the British soul. With dusk come mangy foxes, slinking out to scavenge in the drilling heat.

In my new life, I spend most weekdays two kilometers outside town, beyond a network of clogged arterial roads and mini-rotaries. Skirt the brownfield site along East Road, past the Sleepeezee warehouse, the Souls Harbour Apostolic Church, the fuel cell plant, and a construction rumored to be generating a pioneer high-rise pig farm, turn right by the giant tower that, from a certain angle, appears to straddle, rodeolike, the World of Leather, and you'll spot a discreet signpost to my place of work.

Somebody should probably have taken a wrecking ball to it long ago. Built in the early twentieth century, the white mansion, seen through the electrified perimeter fence, resembles a decrepit cruise ship marooned among clusters of monkey puzzles, cypress, and spiky palms: Edwardian, Gulf Stream trees. It was once a hotel for convalescents prescribed sea air, but now its white-brick facade and scattered outbuildings are zigzagged with cracks like ancient marzipan. Wisteria and honeysuckle meander up wrought-iron balconies, trellises, and gazebos blistered by rust. You might hope to find Sleeping Beauty in there, on display in a glass case, somewhere just beyond Reception. But instead, you'll be entering a museum display of dados, cornices, and ceiling roses barnacled to peeling plasterwork. The building manufactures its own air, air that has not quite caught up with the scented-candle culture of modern times. Forest Glade room freshener predominates, struggling to mask deeper strata of Toilet Duck, dry rot, and the sad-sweet chemical smell of psychic suffering.

Welcome to Oxsmith Adolescent Secure Psychiatric Hospital, home to a hundred of the most dangerous children in the country.

Among them, Bethany Krall.

From my ground-floor office, you can see a row of white turbines in the distance, rooted in the sea like elegant food mixers. I admire the grace of their engineering, their slim discretion. I have thought about painting them but the urge is too theoretical, too distanced from the part of me that still functions. I often stare out at the horizon, mesmerized by their smoothly industrious response to the wind. Sometimes, when I have a very specific form of cabin fever, I copy their movements, whirling my arms in rhythm—not to capture energy but to release it. Glimpsing myself in a corner of the mirror, I'll notice my hair, my eyes, my mouth, the intense tilt of my face, but I know better than to set any store by my looks, such as they are. They've done me no good.

When I first encounter Bethany Krall I am two weeks into what has been billed as a six-month posting, filling in for Joy McConey, a psychotherapist who has left the institution on a sabbatical that I assume to be a euphemism for some unspoken disgrace. None of my new colleagues seems keen to discuss her. There's a high turnover in places that have a reputation for being human trash cans. Most of us are on flexible contracts. This is not a prestige appointment. There are hints of new cutbacks that could lead to Oxsmith's closing for good. But raw from my enforced exclusion from what rehab called "the cut and thrust," I can't afford to be choosy about my employment. In the absence of a long-term plan, part of my persuasive argument to myself in deciding to resettle is that a short-term strategy in a strange place is better than none in a familiar one.

Amid the broken staplers, the withered spider plant, and the old styrofoam coffee cups of Joy McConey's vacated office is a greeting card, the kind that's "left blank for your personal message." Inside, in small, frantic-looking handwriting, someone has stated, cryptically: "To Joy. Who truly believed." Truly believed in what? God? An end to the grief in the Middle East? An inmate's psychotic fantasies? The signature is illegible. I am no great fan of spider plants. But something—my frail, inconsistent inner Buddha, perhaps—prevents me from taking life in a gratuitous fashion, even if it's low in the food chain. *Let the plant live. But don't encourage the fucking thing.* It seems that mold can grow on coffee despite a plastic lid. I pour the dregs on the pot's asbestoid soil and chuck the cup into the bin to join Joy's card.

I am not a nice person.

I have gleaned this much from my fraught fellow workers: I've been assigned Bethany Krall as one of my main cases because no one else wants to deal with her. As the newcomer, I have no choice in the matter. Bethany has been labeled intractable by everyone who has dealt with her so far, with the exception of Joy McConey, whose notes are not in the file—very possibly because she never wrote any. While I'm not exactly nervous about having Bethany Krall on my list, I am not enthusiastic either. My perspective on physical violence has shifted since my accident. I now want to avoid it at all costs, and have taken every possible measure to do so, with the exception of having my strangulation-length hair cut short, because I'm vain about it. But perhaps with Bethany Krall on my list I'll be visiting the hairdresser after all: according to the case notes, my new charge is something of an extremist in the aggression department.

After ten years of dealing with criminally psychotic minors I am used to stories like Bethany Krall's, but the reports of her mother's murder still manage to stir up a familiar, heart-sinking queasiness, a kind of moral ache. The full-color police photos are shocking enough to make me blink, redirect my gaze out the window, and wonder what sort of person decides to opt for a career in forensic pathology. Apart from the turbines in the distance, there isn't much to comfort the eye. The shimmering tarmac of the deserted basketball court, a line of industrial-sized garbage cans, and beyond the electrified perimeter fence a vista that twangs a country-and-western chord of self-pity in me. For a brief moment, when I first arrived, I thought of putting a photo of Alex—Laughing Alpha Male at Roulette Wheel—next to my computer, alongside my family collection: Late Mother Squinting into Sun on Pebbled Beach, Brother Pierre with Postpartum Wife and Male Twins, and Compos Mentis Father Fighting *Daily Telegraph* Crossword. But I stopped myself. Why give myself a daily reminder of what I have in every other way laid to rest? Besides, there would be curiosity from colleagues, and my responses to their questions would seem either morbid or tasteless or brutal depending on the pitch and roll of my mood. Memories of my past existence, and the future that came with it, can start as benign, Vaselined nostalgia vignettes. But they'll quickly ghost train into malevolent noir shorts backlit by that great worst enemy of all victims of circumstance, hindsight. So for the sake of my own sanity, I apologize silently to Alex before burying him in the desk alongside my emergency bottle of Laphroaig and a little homemade flower press given to me by a former patient who hanged himself with a clothesline.

The happy drawer.

Before taking the lift up to the room christened, with creepy institutional earnestness, the Creativity Workshop, I go through the rest of Bethany Krall's file, setting aside the more detailed notes of her drug regimen and physical checkups to glance at later.

The facts are stark enough. Two years ago, on April 5, during Easter school vacation, Bethany Krall stabbed her mother, Karen, to death with a screwdriver in a frenzied and unexplained attack. At fourteen, Bethany Krall was small and underweight for her age. Remarkable, then, that her mother's savaging should have been so ferocious and sustained: the child had drawn huge strength from somewhere. But there was no question she had committed the murder: the house was locked from the inside and her fingerprints were all over the weapon. Bethany's father, Leonard, an evangelical preacher, was away at a prophecy conference in Birmingham at the time, having left that morning. He had spoken to his wife and daughter separately just an hour before the tragedy and reported that Karen was concerned about Bethany's loss of appetite, while Bethany herself had complained of severe headaches. Karen Krall had put the call on speakerphone and they had all prayed together. This was a family tradition.

At ten thirty that evening a neighbor heard violent screaming and raised the alarm, but by the time the police arrived Karen Krall was dead. They found her daughter curled on the floor next to her in a fetal position. In this photograph, you don't see Bethany's face, but you see the part of her mother's that isn't blood covered. The screwdriver is rammed deep into her left eye, its yellow plastic handle protruding. It has an odd jauntiness, like a dinner fork stuck upright in a joint of meat cooked rare and abandoned midmeal. The pool of blood on the floor has developed the kind of skin that acrylic or emulsion paint will form. Another photograph, taken from above, shows an open trash can containing, according to the notes, "the charred remains of one King James Bible." A physical examination immediately after the tragedy showed recent bruising on Bethany's body, particularly the upper arms, and damage to both wrists. From this it was concluded that a severe physical struggle had taken place.

On the next page is a happier portrait of the Kralls, taken a year before the family imploded. It shows a dark-haired, sharp-faced child and, on either side of her, the parents: a good-looking father and his pale, more meager wife. They are all smiling widely—so widely, in Bethany's case, that the braces on her teeth take center stage. Unhappiness takes many forms, I reflect. But happiness, or the semblance of it, can be as limited and unhelpful as the word *cheese*. Bethany's teachers described her as highly intelligent but disturbed. Reading between the lines I suspect that, like so many kids of her generation, she is a classic product of the last decade, with its food shortages and mass riots and apocalyptically expanded Middle East war, and in her case, more specifically, of the Faith Wave that followed the global economic crash: a preacher's strongheaded daughter who questioned the dominant role of fundamentalist Christianity in her life and rebelled. At school she was self-destructive and had very possibly had sexual relationships with boys, but she paid attention in class, showing a particular aptitude for science, art, and geography. There were no obvious signs of mental illness, though at the end of that spring term, in a staff meeting, concern was expressed that she seemed "more unhappy than usual."

I flick through to the next section, which is the attending police psychiatrist's report. Dr. Waxman's write-up is verbose, but the story it tells is straightforward enough. In the immediate wake of the murder, Bethany's coping mechanism was as brutal and efficient as a field amputation in time of war: she lost her memory. She did not deny committing the crime but claimed to have no recollection of it or of what had provoked her to such drastic action. Nor would she speak to her father when he returned, distraught, from his trip to Birmingham. Her refusal led to distressing scenes. "Elective amnesia as a form of denial, or refuge, is not uncommon among those who have experienced trauma," notes Waxman. "This can be just as applicable to the perpetrator of a crime as to its victim." On committing her to the care of Oxsmith, Waxman pronounced himself hopeful that she would make progress within the next few weeks and months and moved on to his next case.

But Waxman's optimism about the beneficial effects of Oxsmith Adolescent Secure Psychiatric Hospital was misplaced. A year and a half into her institutionalization, Bethany Krall had made four attempts on her own life and seriously attacked another patient. Her memory had returned, but she refused to speak about the murder or what triggered it. She began to starve herself and, after being diagnosed with acute depression, was given a panoply of mood-altering drugs, none of which proved effective in improving her morale. Bethany showed no interest in cooperating in therapy sessions and remained largely mute. When she spoke, it was to express the belief that her heart was shrinking, her blood was poisoned, and she was "rotting from the inside." Increasingly experimental drug combinations were applied, some of which made her state of mind worse and led to side effects such as trembling, drooling, lethargy, and, in one instance, convulsions. She exhibited extreme disturbance, cutting herself frequently and becoming dangerously underweight.

One day, in the wake of a severe thunderstorm during which she mutilated her throat with a plastic fork, Bethany insisted that she was dead and that her body was slowly putrefying. To prove that as a corpse she was unable to digest food, she stopped eating altogether. At this point, Cotard's syndrome—a nihilistic conviction that one's body has expired—was aired as a diagnosis, and after some discussion it was agreed that she should undergo electroconvulsive therapy as a last resort.

The results are described as "dramatic." Bethany began to eat, talk, and respond more positively to therapy. Although she experienced some of the usual aftereffects of ECT, such as short-term memory loss and disorientation in the immediate wake of each session, the psychiatrists judged the treatment to be an unmitigated success. Bethany herself said she felt "more alive" and insisted she experienced the ECT interventions as positive—despite the fact that she was anesthetized throughout and could have no recollection of them. But weirdness is relative in the territory occupied by the mentally deranged. Anything can manifest itself and, with the skewed anti-logic of anxiety dreams, it does: cans of mango slices containing encoded messages from the Office for National Statistics, a conviction that your skeleton will dissolve if you think about sex, a grouting phobia. A junior arsonist I dealt with once, who could cite the chemical compound of every flammable gas known to man, insisted on keeping his mouth open to avoid getting lockjaw. He'd sleep with a wedge of pillow clamped between his teeth as though his life depended on it. "Life's rich tapestry," Dad would have said, in his bridge-and-crossword days, before Cartoon Network and the drool bib took over the show.

Since March, after an initial five weeks of weekly sessions, Bethany's shock therapy has been administered on average once a month, as a maintenance dose, by one Dr. Ehmet, whom I have not yet met, though I once caught sight of the back of his head and noted that he could do with a haircut. But effective though the ECT has been, Bethany's refusal to discuss her parents and the catastrophic event that brought her here continues. What prompted her to attack and murder her mother with a screwdriver one April evening remains a mystery. Therapeutically, I am not sure how much this matters. Psychological principle has it that buried traumas must be exhumed and dealt with before a patient can move on. But I am less and less convinced by this reasoning. If there was a pill that could suppress horror, I would take it myself and wipe out the last two years of my life. The brain is as uncharted and unfathomable as the sea, and as capricious. But it is also wise enough to do what's required to keep a body going. Who says that, for Bethany Krall, forensically analyzing what she did to her mother, and why, will do any good? Sensing this on some level, might she be using the ECT as a means of obliterating a crucial section of autobiographical memory?

· · ·

Aware of the time, I skim quickly through the rest, which includes a further note, added by Oxsmith's principal psychiatrist, Dr. Sheldon-Gray, at a later date: "The patient's father, Leonard Krall, has declined to see Bethany in Oxsmith. Therapeutically speaking, this may be to Bethany's advantage, as his explanation for his wife's murder is that Bethany was 'possessed by evil.'"

I, too, have a problem with words like *evil*. When my mother died, my father sent me to a Catholic girls' boarding school, a place of unshakable Bible certainties—certainties to which a man like Krall, and the millions like him who converted during the Faith Wave, can be no stranger. Living by such certainties, he knows that the only explanation for Bethany's violence is nothing earthly, such as pain or revenge or anger or simply a chemical imbalance in the brain, but a "visit" from a notion. True faith, the kind of faith that is described sometimes as "burning," carries its own aura. A sort of righteous chutzpah. You see them on their mass marches, their faces illuminated from deep within. That conviction, that passion, that energy: you can envy it.

When I arrive in the studio for my meeting with Bethany, a thickset male nurse is already there, talking on his mobile, deep in an elaborate technical discussion about shift schedules. I've heard that Rafik is tough and alert, but his with-you-in-a-minute gesture doesn't inspire confidence. Despite having spent much of the last few months devising and practicing new physical defense strategies involving the grabbing and twisting of vulnerable body parts and the strategic hurling of objects, I feel permanently vulnerable, a moving target. The notes have just told me that last December Bethany Krall bit the ear off a boy who sexually attacked her. She chewed it up so badly it couldn't be reattached.

Marvelous. Bring her on.

Then suddenly—far too suddenly—a huge escorting nurse with tattooed arms has done just that. The door has opened and a dark streak of a girl has walked right up to me. And already she's too close. You never get used to everyone being taller than you, to seeing them from the wrong angle. She should step back a bit. But she doesn't. Rafik exchanges grunts with his mountainous colleague, who nods at me as if to say "package delivered," and leaves. I could shift again, but I don't want to risk it. She'd know what it meant.

Bethany Krall is small, bird-boned, and underdeveloped for a sixteen-year-old. On her head, a tangled mass of dark hair like a child's angry scribble. Self-harm being an ever-popular hobby among the female patients at Oxsmith, her bare arms reveal the usual welter of cigarette burns and crosswise slashes, some old, some more recent.

"Hallelujah. The new psychiatrist." Her voice is babyish for her age but oddly hoarse, as though someone has scrubbed the inside of her throat with a chemical abrasive.

"Good to meet you, Bethany," I say, maneuvring myself to offer a handshake. "I'm actually a therapist rather than a doctor."

"Same shit, different asshole," she declares, not taking my hand. Like me, she's wearing black: the garb of mourning. Does she still believe, on some level, that she has died?

"Gabrielle Fox. I'm new here, I've taken over from Joy McConey."

"I always start by giving you guys the benefit of the doubt. That means ten stars out of ten to begin with," she says, assessing my wheelchair. "But you get an extra one for being a spaz. Positive discrimination, yeah? So you're starting with eleven."

The notes mentioned she was articulate but I'm still surprised. You come across it so little in this kind of place.

"Ten's fine, Bethany. In fact, very generous of you. I specialize in art therapy. Subscribing to the theory that art's a good way of expressing feelings when words fail."

Her eyes are dark, feline, heavily outlined in kohl. Sallow olive skin, a narrow, asymmetrical face. She's what you'd call striking rather than pretty. Or jailbait. Her hair looks matted beyond redemption. She seems a far cry from the girl in the family photo. Has she spent the last two years soaking up the institution's own brand of teen culture, or is this attitude intrinsic? In either case, she behaves like she's up for a fight, and she looks like trouble, and she sounds like trouble—but then most of them do, one way or another. Preliminary assessment: she's more intelligent and more verbal than most but otherwise, so far, so normal.

"The bottom line is, I'm here to help you and encourage you to express whatever you want to express here in the—" I am unable to say Creativity Workshop: it gets stuck in my throat. "Here in this studio. Whatever it is. No limits. It's an exploration. Sometimes it can take you to dark places. But I'm on your side."

"A spaz who patronizes me. Great. Great to have you on my side in *dark places*. Psychobabbling away." .

"I'm just someone to talk to. Or if you don't want to talk, I'm here to supply you with paper and art materials. Not everything works in words. No matter how big your vocabulary."

She waggles two fingers at her opened mouth to indicate disgust. "You're down to five. I can see you don't belong here." She looks at me levelly. "So perhaps you should just wheel yourself off into the sunset in that spazmobile of yours. Before something bad happens." She circles the chair, then stops behind me and leans down to whisper in my ear. "So you've taken over from Joy. Tragic Joy. I guess you've heard all about the distressing way she left?" Her knowing use of cliché strikes me as a possible clue to her inner clockwork. She speaks as though her life is an object held at a distance, a source of amusement—a fiction rather than a reality. "I warned her about what would happen. I warned her."

I'm snared by this, as she intends, but I know better than to show an interest in my predecessor, so I gesture at the walls.

"Is any of this work here yours?"

There is a game you can play: match the artwork to the wacko. But having spent time—more time than I ever intended—in casinos, among roulette wheels and backgammon tables and stacked chips, I know that it's too much like poker, another pastime it's wise not to indulge in.

"Yeah, Joy was tragic but you're tragic too, I guess," she continues, ignoring my question. "I mean, you bother with makeup when no one's going to take a second look, are they, no matter how hot you are, right? Unless they're some sort of perv. No offense. But hey, Spaz. Reality check."

If you show them an abusive word has got to you, they know they've won. And then they can do anything. And they will. "I asked if you'd done any of the work here," I say lightly. "And you can call me Gabrielle."

"You mean these great masterpieces?"

She glances around with disdain. The artwork features the usual range of motifs: flowers, anarchic fuck-the-system graffiti, graveyards, jungle animals, bulging breasts, and engorged phalluses. But there are some oddities too. One of the kids, a skinny twelve-year-old boy who helped his father murder his sister in the name of family honor, has been constructing a huge papier-mâché hot air balloon, striped blue and white, that hangs from the ceiling above us like a big lightbulb. It is an enterprising, ambitious, hopeful, and joyous balloon: a balloon that is more whole in spirit than the boy who made it. It's both consoling and intriguing that art can do that. Look at a pickled brain, and you'll see a putty gray bolus, lumpy and naked as an exposed mollusc. But there's space inside for a thousand worlds, none of which need be remotely compatible.

"Perhaps it's time to try making something in here," I suggest. "Is that something we could schedule in for you?"

It's as though I haven't spoken. I ride out the silence for a while but then realize she's playing a waiting game too. The fixity of her expression—contempt as a default mode—indicates that her mind's lodged somewhere she considers safe. I catch Rafik's eye and he looks at me with what might be sympathy. He's well liked here. He'd be called "a rough diamond" or perhaps even "a devoted family man" in news reports of his violent death at the hands of a psychotic patient. I wonder how many Bethany Krall sessions he has sat through.

"Bethany?" I prompt eventually. "Any thoughts?"

With a sudden movement she perches herself on the central table and lets out a theatrical sigh.

"First I get my ECT. Then Tragic Joy. And now you. So my *thoughts* are that Oxsmith is treating me like a fucking princess. You're down to one star, missus." Turning to the wall mirror, she inspects her teeth, still caged in the same silver braces as in the family photo. "Hey. See anything interesting in there, Uncle Rafik?" she asks, noticing his eye on her. "Fancy a high-risk blow job?" He turns away, and she cackles in triumph.

"If you don't feel like doing any artwork we can just sit together and watch movies if that's what you want," I persevere.

"Porn? Extra star for saying yes."

"Sure," I say, noting how quickly sex has entered the conversation. "Anything for a star on the Bethany Krall Competence Scale. If they have any porn in the DVD library. I haven't investigated. How do you feel about watching hard-core sex?"

She laughs. "You're babbling again. You people are so fucking predictable."

She is right, of course. If Bethany is disturbed minor number three hundred for me, I am probably therapist number thirty for her.

She knows the tricks of the trade, its let's-coax-it-out ploys, its carefully framed "open" questions and neat follow-ups, its awareness of key words and phrases, a set of formulae I've been increasingly inclined to abandon since my accident. It's clear that with a case like Bethany the normal rules do not apply. I can see that, at this rate, we'll soon be going off-road. Gonzo therapy. What's to lose?

But for now I stick to the well-worn track.

"The art group meets here three times a week for sessions. But some people prefer working alone. I'd guess you might be one of them. I've got watercolor equipment, acrylics, inks, clay, or you can do computer imaging, photography, that sort of thing. My only rule is, no homemade tattoos."

"And if I don't want to do any of that shit? Including date stamping myself by decorating my tits with snakes?"

"The content of our sessions is up to you. We could just talk. Or go for a walk."

Her face sparks up meanly. "Go for a *walk,* like how?" Her voice is cross-hatched with elaborate scorn. Exhausting to maintain those levels of anger and yet have no specific target. How tired she must be.

"Around the garden." Just us and five male nurses with shaved heads who pump iron. A smile is quirking the corners of her mouth.

"Yes, you *would* need some physical protection. With my record of violence? Which you've just read about in my file? I've read about it too. And seen the pictures. Gory stuff. Hey, *I'd* be afraid of me."

I wait a beat. But she's used to that: no dice. "Are there ways you *are* afraid of you, Bethany? Having looked at those pictures?"

Her mother's desecrated face barges into my mind like a crude shout.

"You must feel like totally naked in that wheelchair. I mean, someone could just tip you out of it. You'd be like a beetle stuck upside down."

She contemplates the image for a moment. My heart rate has gone up and I'm aware of blinking more than I should. Sweat pricks in my armpits. She has pinpointed a fear, and she knows it.

"But I'm interested in this walking thing. I mean, how would it work? Seeing as you seem to be, excuse me for pointing it out, but *totally fucking disabled,* lower-limb-wise? Do I push you in that thing?"

"No need. I wheel myself. You learn a lot in spaz rehab," I say, defusing the word and tweaking a tiny smile out of her. I've had this chair eighteen months, and my hands have transmogrified into tools, accessories of meat and bone, the skin of the heel calloused despite the gloves. "So how would you feel about a fresh-air session?"

"How would I *feel* about it," she repeats slowly. I immediately regret my choice of phrase. "How would that make you *feel*, Bethany? Bethany, *in terms of feelings*, what's going on at the moment, inside? That's the bottom line for you, right? Look at you. Babble, babble, babble. You're fucking tragic. I can't believe they let you work here. Don't they vet you guys? Filter out the *lame* ones? Whoops—no pun intended. But zero out of ten. And you've got there in record time. I appoint you babble champion of Oxsmith!"

I gaze out at the slowly spinning turbines.

No: I should not be here. And Bethany Krall has swiftly spotted it.

In rehab, they lectured you on the importance of establishing a healthy routine. Hadport Lido opens at seven. In the mornings, I'll often spend an hour there, hoisting myself into the shallow end and doing twenty tepid laps amid the drowned insects. I have come to know the staff there by name; Goran, Chloe, Vishnu, tanned and healthy and sparkle-eyed. They'll say hi, and I'll say hi back. To them, I am the nice lady they feel sorry for and admire for her "courage"— as if she has any choice in the matter. I overheard them once, evoking the pathos of the nice lady's plight, noting her attractiveness, and speculating about her age. The consensus was that the nice lady was "late twenties"—a flattering assessment for a thirty-five-year-old. The nice lady, who is not really a nice lady at all, swam on. Her arm muscles, already well honed by the wheelchair, have developed into features to die for. *Want them?* she feels like asking whenever she receives compliments from well-meaning people, the kind of people who drive her even more insane than she already is. *I'll swap them for your legs.*

Swimming is both good and bad for rage. It can help to dissipate it, but it can also focus and refine it. I was told back in London that if I wanted to work at a senior level again I'd need to deal with my "issues." That, said my employers, would involve more intensive therapy, plus a written self-assessment and analysis. My reaction, when they told me this in the meeting—a warm afternoon, the sun just sinking behind the old Battersea Power Station—was what we in the business call "inappropriate."

"You're talking to a trained psychologist, for fuck's sake!" I said. Or did I shriek?

Yes, I must admit I shrieked. Shrieking is both deeply feminine and deeply unfeminine at the same time. When women imitate pressure cookers, they show their worst selves, the side that men call either "passionate" or "mad," depending on whether or not good looks are involved.

"Don't patronize me with lectures about coming to terms with the new reality. I live with it every day! I *am* the new reality!"

Nor is shrieking a good way to communicate in a psychiatric establishment, if you are not an inmate and indeed if you have been until now classified among the sane and are in charge of others less fortunate.

"Gabrielle, I have enormous sympathy and respect for you, and you have been through what no person should go through. With all your . . . terrible losses. But you work in the field," said Dr. Sulieman when the members of the committee had trooped out, exchanging distressed glances. "See it from an employer's point of view."

If my legs worked, I'd have kicked him. Violent urges came to me very readily back then.

The "negative attitude" I had toward my diminished status as a human being after my accident was unfortunately a "significant problem." As Sulieman spoke, I inspected the print on the wall behind him, the image he had chosen as his own personalized backdrop: Monet's lily pond, with its hypnotic plays of light, its strangely hot greens and blues.

"A problem which, until it's resolved, means we are unable to accept you back as a therapist at the present time."

He's into the classics, so where's Kandinsky? I wondered. Where's Egon Schiele? Where's van Gogh's *Self-Portrait with Bandaged Ear,* where's Rothko, where's *The Scream?*

I'd just spent an hour with my physiotherapist, learning how to hit people where it hurt. A karate chop to the balls. A squirt of vinegar in the eyes. A flung object, aimed at the head. Cripple power. A flicker of pity from my boss, and that expensive Venetian paperweight on his desk—a whirling rhapsody of trapped bubbles and squirls—would make contact with his skull.

"I need to work, Omar. If you can't take me back, then find me somewhere else."

"That's not the best thing for you, Gabrielle. Or the people you're helping."

"Look at this chair. I'm welded to it forever. I'll probably never have another relationship. Or children. Call me melodramatic, but the fact is, every night I lie in bed and hear the clang of doors closing on my future. So if I can't do the thing I know how to do and still can do, the thing you helped train me in, the thing I'm good at by all accounts, how can I even be me? If you can answer that question for me, bravo. Because I can't. If I can't work, I'm done for."

When a job came up at Oxsmith, he recommended me. Then, three months later, I heard that he was dead. Good people drop like flies, I thought. And I never thanked him the way I should have.

Water under the bridge.

In the art studio, Rafik's pager has registered the arrival of a text which he now seems intent on answering. Meanwhile Bethany has switched tack.

"I suppose you could be something the drugs do," she's saying dreamily. "Something in my head. That happens. I've still got a load of psychotropic toxins in my bloodstream. They'll never leave my body. Like saccharine. Did you know that saccharine just builds up forever in your system?" The notion that I might be a hallucination doesn't seem alarming to her. In this moment, it quite appeals to me too. "So what do I call my new savior? Spaz? Saint Gabrielle?"

"Gabrielle's fine."

She thinks for a moment. "Wheels."

"I'd prefer Gabrielle," I say, swiveling again to assess her profile. She closes her eyes. A moment passes.

"You're quite a *fish*, aren't you?" she says, her eyes opening again in unexpected delight. Dark, like night pools. "Quite a *mermaid*. Always in the water! Up and down you go! You like getting out of that chair, don't you. It's like being freed from your cage!" She beams, as if she has solved a puzzle in record time.

As I try to fathom this, I don't reply. But then it occurs to me she can probably simply smell the chlorine.

"If I touched your hand I'd know even more," she says. The delight has gone, replaced by amused menace. "I didn't even have to touch Joy McConey to know things. I saw what she had coming." If she's asking permission, I am not giving it. I'll shake hands on the first meeting but apart from that I don't do physical contact. "I register stuff. But half the time it doesn't mean jack shit to me. It's, like, way over my head."

"Can you tell me more about this 'stuff' you register?"

She smiles. "Seas burning. Sheets of fire. Whole coasts washed away. The glaciers melting like butter in a microwave. You know Greenland? Basically *dissolved*. Like a great big aspirin that says Hazard Warning on it. Empty towns full of human bones, with lizards and coyotes in charge. And trees everywhere, and whales and crocodiles in the underground. The lost continent of Atlantis." Are these drug-induced visions? Daydreams? Or is it metaphorical?

"It sounds like a dangerous world you're describing. Dangerous and chaotic and life threatening. A lot of people worry about climate change. It's not an irrational fear."

The latest projections predict the loss of the Arctic ice cap and a global temperature rise of up to six degrees within Bethany's lifetime, unless drastic measures are taken now. I should be grateful to be childless. Just as the Cold War figures heavily in the fantasies of elderly mental patients, climate-apocalypse paranoia is common among the young. Zeitgeist stuff: the banality of abnormality. Its roots in fact so appalling we turn the other way politely. I'd like to steer Bethany toward the subject of suicide, my main concern, on paper at least, because if she dies on my watch there will be administrative issues that won't look good on my first post-accident job. What is the likelihood of a repeat performance? Apart from the four attempts, according to the notes she is a regular self-harmer. They also label her well informed, manipulative, and prone to dramatic mood swings, as well as psychotic fantasies, biblical outpourings, and sudden extreme violence. Again, unwillingly, I conjure the police photographs. Forty-eight stab wounds. The screwdriver in Karen Krall's eye. The film of skin forming on the blood like antique sealing wax. The photographer's flash stamped in it forever, like a fossil star.

"It *is* a dangerous world. And we're in it. There's no escape, Wheels." She gives a small, mirthless laugh. "All of those people out there. *Decent hardworking folks who ain't never done no one no harm,*" she says, putting on a cartoonish yokel voice. "Dying a horrible death. *All of us* dying a horrible death." This notion seems to cheer rather than frighten her. Suddenly there's an electric energy about her. I sense an immense reservoir of violence and anger, a latent force that I find as compelling as it is alarming. I must watch out of my own perversity. "Have you heard of the Rapture?" she asks.

"Vaguely." I know of it as an element of the Faith Wave creed brought over by the British citizens who abandoned their sunshine homes in Florida and returned to the UK to sit out the slump. Its popularity was expanded by celebrity conversions and a swathe of addictive redemption-themed TV shows. "Tell me about it."

"It's salvation for the righteous. When the shit hits the fan, the true Christians go straight to heaven in, like, a big airlift. The rest get left behind. Mercy for the pure in heart, justice for the rest. It's all in the Bible. Look at Ezekiel, look at Daniel, look at Thessalonians, look at Revelation. All the signs are there. Iran, Jerusalem. Things are going to blow any day. Seven years of tribulation. Coming soon to a planet near you. The heat of hell. The survivors, they'll be trapped in it. It's starting now. You can feel it. Plagues and pestilences and God's wrath and the reign of the Antichrist. Who shall plant the mark of the Beast upon them."

There is a sick logic to the Faith Wave phenomenon, I reflect: in the face of more Islamic terror attacks, why not pit one insane dogma against another? Every week there are mass baptisms, true-story gatherings, commitment marches.

"Do you have faith, Bethany?"

"Faith?" She snorts. "That's a good one. Would I be here if there was a God? I don't think so! But I have the mark of the Beast. Look." She plants a forefinger on each temple. "Invisible, in my case. That's where the electrodes go."

"What did God mean to you, growing up?"

"He never meant me any good. The thing I never get is, who created God? No one can ever answer that one. It's like the universe. It's ever expanding, right? But what's outside it?"

"God never meant you any good in what way?" She shrugs, and looks away. Either she doesn't know or she is withholding. I wait a moment but when I see I'll get nothing I try another tack. "What was it like being a child in your family, Bethany?" She shrugs again. "You can quote the Bible. So I'm wondering what sort of influences you had."

"Are you. Well, wonder on." She looks edgy. "We believe in the universal sinfulness of all men since the Fall, rendering man subject to God's wrath and condemnation."

"Who's we?"

"Them."

"Your parents?"

"Hey, she's hot! How many degrees has she got up her ass?"

"So tell me what else you're thinking about."

She perks up, splaying her hands in front of her and flexing them as if to test their competence as grabbing tools. Her nails are as filthy as animal claws. One scratch, and she'd infect you.

"Half the planet drowns, I can tell you that. Islands sinking, coasts getting eaten up by the sea. The land getting smaller. Water sloshing all over it in these giant tsunamis, the temperature zinging up. The stuff on the way, that's just part of it. I've seen it in the Quiet Room. Earth looks like a gobstopper. You can zoom in. Satellite vision, Wheels. You hear what I'm saying?"

She is nodding so hard that her whole body begins to rock with the movement. She can't seem to agree with herself enough.

"Yeah. I have fucking *satellite vision*. Like the Hubble telescope."

The Quiet Room is a nondescript chamber on the second floor of Virgil Block, where they administer an antispasmodic drug, a general anesthetic, and then electroshock therapy to inmates who have not responded to other treatments. The thought of a sixteen-year-old enjoying it makes me feel queasy.

"It's not weather that's causing it. Weather's a side product," she's telling me, still rocking, a fleck of spit gathering at the corner of her mouth. I try to quell my distaste for this girl and for the unimaginativeness of her cataclysmic visions—visions already shared by half the population, along with a belief in miracles and tarot readings, if the polls are anything to go by. "It's the kind of thing that could land you in a desert of chemical crystals. Or leave you stranded somewhere in a wheelchair." She raises her eyebrows at me meaningfully. "On a black rock with dead trees. It's not just heat, it's geological activity, worse than the worst earthquake." She is alert, flushed, vivid. The stock diagnostic phrase *a danger to herself and others* slides through my mind. The cynicism has given way to manic excitement. "Cracking, not where the tectonic plates meet but in other places, new places." The words are tumbling out in a rush, making the fleck of spit pulse. "Belching out these unbreathable toxic gases. You know why it's so hot at the earth's core? Because this planet's just a chunk of some supernova that exploded, like, eons ago."

I wonder what channels she has been watching. Discovery, BBC World, Cartoon Network, News 24, CNN. But where? When? The TV in the rec room seems permanently fixed on MTV. The Internet. A million Web sites, a zillion images—you can go anywhere, believe in anything, see carnage of every variety, scare yourself to Neptune and back. If global warming is terminal proof that we have fouled our own nest, Bethany is evidence that some human minds can draw energy from the fact.

"You know what I mean by the earth's core," she says, touching her heart with spread fingers. Her father is a preacher: I wonder how much of her presentation comes, unconsciously, from him. Or perhaps it's just an ability to convey conviction that she has picked up, a charisma. "I mean its center. I mean its soul. I saw it when they zapped me. You're not supposed to remember anything about the shock, right? But I do. My whole body wakes up. I came back from the dead, you know. Like Lazarus. Or Jesus Christ. I can see things. Wheels. Disasters. I've made notes. Dates, times, places, everything. Just like a weathergirl. They should employ me. I'd get paid a fucking fortune. I can see stuff happening before it happens. I feel it. Atoms popping about. Vibrations in your blood. These huge fucking wounds. The planet in meltdown. This freezing stuff, pouring from the cracks. Then it heats up, like some kind of magma. And whoosh. The promised land." She smiles, bright eyed, and for a tiny, fleeting fraction of time she looks ecstatically, murderously happy.

Unimaginably atrocious things have surely been done to Bethany to make her do what she did: things that can never be undone. And she has done an unimaginably atrocious thing in return. I doubt I will ever get to the bottom of the trauma that led her to take a Phillips screwdriver to her mother, though I might take a second look at the photo of the father and hazard a guess that some of the damage came from him too. What matters now is Bethany "moving forward," as the jargon goes, on a shiny conveyor belt of psychic progress. People like me are supposed to believe in repair, and I once did, until I became the object of my own clinical trial. After which—

Not anymore. Damage limitation, perhaps. Sometimes. Sometimes not. When you stop being a woman, as I did on May 14 two years ago, there are things you see more clearly. Sexuality confounds matters, insinuating itself into every exchange. Freed of all that, you can see things for what they are, like kids do, and old people. That's my theory. But it's only a theory. And anyway, who says I am free?

"So you see, with all that going on in my head, it's, like, nonstop around here. Things to think about, things to do, that's me," finishes Bethany. But after the rush of information, the burst of energy, she seems suddenly deflated, dissatisfied with herself. Her fantasies are a fertile oasis in the desert of her boredom, and a corner of her consciousness knows it.

"Things in the self-destruction department."

"Things in the self-destruction department." She mimics me well enough to make me wince internally. "Bibble babble, bibble babble, bibble babble."

I let my eyes wander around the room until I catch sight of myself in the mirror and make a swift, stranger's appraisal: *a woman with extravagant brunette hair, who may be skilled at her work, and good-looking in a seriously-damaged-goods sort of way. Who will never walk again, never have sex, never give birth. Who shall remain forever beholden to others.*

Bethany has stopped rocking and is looking at me intently. I don't say anything, but an instinct makes me assess the distance between us. And the angles. When my father moved into the assisted living facility five years ago, my brother, Pierre, came over from Quebec and together we cleared out his bungalow. One of the souvenirs I took with me was a freak of geology known as a thunder egg that Maman kept on her dressing table: a perfect fist-sized sphere of flint that passed down her family, along with the eccentric story that if someone sat on it for long enough it would hatch. Maman was much attached to the thunder egg, and now I am much attached to it, too, though not for the same romantic reasons. In addition to the regulation personal alarm all staff carry, and in defiance of the hospital's strict regulations, I keep the stone ball in a hanging pouch under my seat, in case of emergency, along with my miniature spray can of photographic glue—also illicit—which I've been reliably told is as effective as Mace. But if I can't react fast enough, and Bethany reaches for a sharpened pencil and stabs me, how long will it be before Rafik— still busy—intervenes and activates his alarm? Trapped as I am, I'd be a lot quicker to kill than Ms. K.

Almost as though she has read my thoughts, with a swift movement—too sudden for me to react—Bethany has reached out and grabbed my wrist with her small, surprisingly muscled hand. Her skin is clammy, her grip too tight.

"Let go of me, Bethany." I take care to say it quietly and calmly, to hide the inner scream. Rafik has jumped to intervene but I signal to him that I will deal with this for now. Still gripping my wrist, Bethany turns my hand over so that the palm is facing upward and puts her finger on my pulse. I feel it begin to race under the pad of her skin.

"Let my hand go, please, Bethany."

But she is somewhere else. Her face has a mesmerized look. "So someone *died*," she says, in her baby voice. "Someone died *a horrible death*." My breath catches roughly in my throat. "There's no point telling me he didn't," she continues excitedly. " 'Cause, fuck! I can *feel it in your blood!*" She narrows her eyes. "I died once, so I know. I recognize the symptoms. Death leaves a mark. Did you know that blood has its own memory? It's like rock, and water, and air." I look down at my pinioned wrist. I know my arms are stronger than hers. But when I start to pull away, she tightens her grip and I think with an inner lurch: perhaps they're not.

With a practiced movement, Rafik has grabbed her other arm. "Easy, Bethany. Let go of Miss Fox now." Smoothly, he pulls off the cap of his belt alarm.

"And you never got to know him properly, did you?" Bethany is whispering. A flashing light in the corridor outside indicates the emergency call has worked. They'll be here in seconds. Again I try to pull away and fail. Rafik has a firm hold of her shoulders now but she's gripped a handle of my wheelchair and barnacled herself to it. The fingers of her other hand, which Rafik is trying to prise away, now tighten further on my wrist, pressing deep into the pulse. "It wasn't fair, was it? It was just the beginning of a *beautiful relationship!*"

"Off her now!" mutters Rafik, tugging so fiercely at Bethany's arm that my wheelchair threatens to capsize. I try not to scream, try not to think, *an upturned beetle.*

"Yeah, a beautiful relationship, right? The best ever!" Bethany's head is next to mine now and she's whispering in my ear. I watch the lights flashing outside and listen for footsteps running. I don't hear any. "But you never found out how the two of you would be together. *That's* your problem. You got emptied out. You had two hearts and one was gone. Hey. That sucks. The poor tragic cripple!"

Finally, Rafik has pulled Bethany off the chair, released my wrist, and forced both her hands behind her back. Roughly, he shoves her against the wall and struggles to keep her in position while waiting for backup.

I reach my hand under my seat and flex my fingers round my thunder egg while the pressure swells in my head. For a few seconds I am too disoriented to speak. I look out the window. The turbines spin their slow rotations on the horizon, far out at sea. My heart hurts. No, it aches. *So someone died a horrible death. . . . You never got to know him properly. Two hearts and one was gone.* Then the rage comes in, a big ugly slub of it. She has hurt me, seen things and said things she shouldn't have, and more than anything I want to damage her. Badly. I palm the stone and consider its decisive heft. It's aching to be thrown. Then I realize that if I don't get away from her right now, I'll do it. Or try to. And miss, of course, and fall out of the chair in a ridiculous lunge. And then it will be me whom Rafik is restraining, and I'll lose my job.

At last the door bursts open and six psychiatric nurses pour in: four men and two women, all built like tanks. They swarm onto her and pin her to the floor while Rafik stands back, rubbing his wrist in pain.

"Little bitch bit me," he mutters, wiping at the blood.

"I think we'll call it a day now, Bethany," I breathe, trying to make sure the sob that's hatching in my throat doesn't make it to the surface. "I'll see you next time."

She seems to find this, or something else, unaccountably funny. In any case, as I leave the room she laughs and laughs, like the horrible, crazy little girl she is.

Suppression is easily done. It's a simple matter of choice. My decision to forget what Bethany said—about things she can't possibly know—is a judgment call. I'm fully aware of what I am doing. In the time it takes to hurtle up the corridor to the lift, I have flung the moment from my mind and from my life, like toxic waste down a chute.

TWO

My new home is minimalist. Things like nice cushions once mattered to me. Cushions that match your sofa and perhaps also your curtains, cushions that end up on the floor when you and a certain poker player are doing the deed, with abandon, in front of a winter fire. But since my world got recalibrated overnight, I've stopped caring about interior decoration, and my only cushion-related concern is the quality of the gel pad I sit on to prevent pressure sores. Domestically speaking, my issues are ramps and wheel-in showers and work tops at the right level, and how to apply to the council to get further innovations installed at no cost. Thanks to someone else's misfortune, I have managed to acquire, on short notice, a self-contained ground-floor apartment in Hadport that is already wheelchair adapted. I'm aware that this represents a kind of jackpot in the disability world and feel duly grateful. I feel other, less comfortable things too. The previous occupant, a young quadraplegic called Mikey, succumbed suddenly to "complications." His family's loss has become my gain. The flat was advertised by the owner, Mrs. Zarnac, on a spinal injury Web site. I'm not superstitious. But I've made a point of not inquiring further about Mikey's complications or asking in which room he died or how many hours passed before his care person found him.

It's a ground-floor apartment in the old part of Hadport. I don't see much of Mrs. Zarnac, who lives upstairs. Lonely-looking older men visit her, and when she cooks for them vinegar smells waft down. It crosses my mind she might be pickling them alive, one after another, for some dark embalming project. In a spirit of defiance and also as a perverse comfort, I have acquired a Frida Kahlo print that leans against one wall because I can't reach to hang it up. *Autorretrato con collar de espinas: Self-Portrait with Necklace of Thorns.* Against a backdrop of jungle leaves, Kahlo gazes blankly out from beneath the single eyebrow that, for aesthetically unfathomable reasons, she refused to pluck into a conventional twosome. It's a head-and-shoulders portrait, so you don't see her wheelchair. At her left shoulder is a black cat, eyes wild, ears cocked back, positioning itself to pounce on a dead hummingbird that hangs, wings outstretched, from a mesh of thorns around her neck. In Mexican folklore, the bird is meant to bring good luck or love. To her right, preoccupied with something in its hands, is her pet monkey, a present from her pathologically unfaithful husband, Diego. The same folklore says this creature is a symbol of the devil. Two dragonflies and two butterflies dance above her head. I assume they represent the imagination, and the freedom it offers. Often I'll lie on my bed, trying to psychoanalyze the passionate and deranged Frida, forced to turn herself into a shrine to pain. She painted her own complex torture again and again, obsessively, in different guises, many macabre: the artist hooked to machinery, pierced by nails, surrounded by fetuses in jars, trussed into a surgical corset, as an antlered deer stuck through with arrows. She's an appalling role model. I am a petri dish of nascent manias, many no doubt as poisonous as those that swarmed in Kahlo's head. The notion that medical technology will evolve and I'll walk again in some semibionic way: I'll spend hours finessing that one.

But the fact is there are still times when I just want to die.

I have another Kahlo reproduction, which hangs in my hallway: *Cuando te tengo a ti, vida, cuanto te quiero.* Its title means, When I have you, life, how much I love you. This being too schmaltzy a sentiment to articulate aloud in English, even to myself (my inner cynic balks), I nevertheless find myself rolling the Spanish words around my mouth and finding them, with the distance of foreignness, a comfort. *Cuando te tengo a ti, vida, cuanto te quiero.* Watching TV puts your own hell in a different perspective, if that's what you want. Today I do.

I make coffee, with which I permit myself four squares of dark chocolate, transfer to the sofa, flick through the movies on offer, hesitate between a documentary about famine and *What Ever Happened to Baby Jane?,* and end up plumping for the news. Two more suicide bombings in Jerusalem. Abductions, limbs lost, children orphaned. Black-clad women wailing their grief in Iran. The row about Chinese and American greenhouse gas emissions has ratcheted up a notch, while the heat wave has spread to the whole of Europe, felling old people in precise strokes, like an efficient industry. The morgues are, in the reporter's phrase, "bursting at the seams". Spain, France, and Italy are the worst affected.

Or the lucky ones, according to a spokesman for one of the Planetarian-inspired ecogroups that sprouted after the Copenhagen climate summit failed to deliver. After my father retired and spent more time with his periodicals, he developed a habit of referring to our era as "the age of dogma." He used the growth of the Planetarian movement to prove his point: like the Faith Wave, he saw it as another example of how the moral debate and its proponents had become more extreme, self-righteous, and fanatical. Then his brain turned to Emmental and I heard no more from him on the subject. Which was a shame because he would have had interesting things to say about its more recent manifestations.

"These are natural, organic losses," the spokesman says reassuringly. Although he's a radical, he talks in pastel, like the kind of low-key but efficient salesman who when selling you a product makes sure to tell you that he owns one himself, and that he is more than satisfied with it. "Human culls are not a new phenomenon," he says. "Desperately sad though it is for the families of those elderly people affected, I think there are positive aspects to these deaths, which we have a responsibility to assess."

"Would you also like to see a zero birthrate, to follow that argument to its logical conclusion? As advocated by thinkers like Harish Modak?" asks the interviewer. I have heard of Modak, seen his photo: a strong-faced, elderly Indian with hooded eyes. His name crops up constantly in eco-debates, and he has inspired a thousand survivalist settlements worldwide. A prophet of doom, is the general consensus in the British tabloid press: a fun killer, an eco-bogeyman.

"Of course. As would any rational person who'd like to help ensure minimal human suffering in decades to come. You'll find there's
a groundswell of opinion. The times are changing and we're changing
with them. Adapting. As we've always done. But personally I'm prepared to take the argument further than Harish Modak does, much
as I admire him. Look at the financial resources being pumped into
combating diseases like AIDS and malaria, when logic tells us that
epidemics are simply Gaia's very efficient way of keeping populations
down. And if that's the case, when we intervene to combat organic ill-
nesses, all we're doing is encouraging population growth and therefore exacerbating the—"

I flick off the TV. Only two years ago, when I was in rehab, people
like this man, with his talk of positive shrinkage, were seen as mar-
ginal eccentrics at best and, at worst, ecofascists and eugenecists—a
source of relief to those of us who found themselves at the top of
their waste-of-carbon lists. But now, within a few months, what began as a movement conducted on the blogosphere has found its way
into the mainstream. I have seen enough neglected and damaged
kids to have strong opinions about people's "right" to have children.
But disease is another matter.

Diseases like malaria. Diseases that foreigners get.

Inhaling minimally and pondering the interesting evolution of the
word *organic,* I maneuver myself off the sofa and into my chair. A sin-
gleton weekend looms and I must find ways to fill it.

In my new life as a queen of tragedy I have a classic lightweight
wheelchair, which this afternoon I am using to trundle along the pedestrian area of Hadport, with its tiny boutiques selling candles and
wind chimes and horoscope jewelery and overpackaged soap, then
into the shabbier side streets of kebab outlets and news agents, then
past the cinema, the sports center, the bird-spattered statue of Mar-
garet Thatcher, and the ponytailed, sixty-something New Ager selling
fluffy worm puppets on long strings. Today there's an outdoor market
with fresh fish and ripe fruit on display: the smell of mackerel and
cheeses and sugar-toasted peanuts mingles with the salt ocean air
and the tang of warmed seaweed. After the downpour and the gales,
the sun is back, a relentless fireball. The heat is abrasive, a hair dryer
with no off switch. Surfaces glitter in the shimmering air. Everyone is

wearing sunglasses. I can't think of the last time I saw anyone's eyes in daylight. Or the last time I bared mine.

I head for a café I have discovered whose three crucial attributes I regularly celebrate: disabled bathroom facilities, a view of the waterfront, and good coffee. Here I settle at a corner table near the window and read Bethany Krall's medical report, the first part of which is written by Dr. Ehmet, listing the various drugs she has been administered over the months, before Cotard's syndrome and electroconvulsive therapy entered the equation. Antipsychotics and antidepressants, plus drugs to counteract the side effects: Prozac, Cipramil, Lustral, Risperdal, Zyprexa, Trazodone, Effexor, Zoloft, Tegretol. The next part is written by Hamish Bates, a therapist who worked with Bethany for two months before leaving for the private sector. According to him, the ECT "gave her relief from the delusion of being dead but stimulated a preoccupation with climate change, chemical pollution, weather patterns, geological disturbances, and apocalyptic scenarios." He is interested in Bethany's frequent references to the Rapture, "a concept that is heavily debated in the Faith Wave's Armageddon discussions, along with the belief that the Messiah will return after a seven-year period of 'tribulation' or 'end times,' in which God will punish humankind for its sins, by means of plagues, floods, fire and brimstone, etc. With the spread of war in the Middle East and the fear of biological weaponry further exposing the cultural nerve, it is no surprise that a notion such as the Rapture has seen a resurgence." Having done his Googling and recycled some five-year-old *Guardian* op-eds, Hamish Bates allows himself to wax philosophical in his final paragraph, speculating that Bethany's recurring themes are "classic metaphors for the turmoil of the mind, prompted by the geological disasters and meteorological vagaries of our times: clusters of catastrophes that cry out to fit into a pattern, be it accelerated global heating or divine retribution for man's sins."

I may question Bates's originality, but I agree with his assessment. Bethany's pain is planet-shaped and planet-sized: she has her own vividly imagined earthquakes and hurricanes, her own volcanic eruptions, her own changing atmosphere, her own form of meltdown.

The pool is swarming with kids on weekends, so I spend the rest of the day and Sunday at home with the fan on, surfing the Net for information on electroconvulsive therapy and state-of-the-art wheelchairs I can't afford. My curiosity on those matters satisfied, I move on to a subject that has been at the back of my mind since the TV debate on human cull caused by the heat wave. The Planetarian movement's spiritual leader—though he publicly distances himself from its wilder outpourings—is the Calcutta-born, Paris-based Harish Modak, a geologist and one-time colleague of the late James Lovelock, who came up with the notion of Gaia, the planet as a self-regulating organism with its own "geophysiology". I skim Modak's latest article, which appeared recently in the *Washington Post*. There is "colossal arrogance," he maintains, in the assumption that humans will last forever. If one looks at the planet's life across billions of years, rather than in terms of humankind's meager history as a dominant species, we will see that our presence on Earth has lasted the blink of an eye. "We are the agents of our own destruction—and when we are gone, extinguished by our own heedless quest for expansion, the planet will not mourn us. Indeed, it will have cause to rejoice. Today, the human species stands at the brink of a new mass extinction which will see, if not its disappearance, then its extreme marginalization." Modak cites climate model projections that back him up starkly, and he reproduces the famous table that demonstrates how, if the planet is allowed to heat up by three more degrees, positive feedbacks will force it up to four, then five, then six. "The Chinese curse 'May you live in interesting times' has descended on those of us living in the twenty-first century as never before," Modak concludes. I rather like his grandiloquence. He'd probably object to anyone's saying it, but his sentiments have a biblical as well as a Hindu ring to them. "For the first time in human history, the destruction—already apparent—is global. In times past, children and grandchildren were seen as a blessing, a sign of faith in the future of the gene pool. Now, it would seem that the kindest thing to do for our grandchildren is to refrain from generating them."

Although more conservative and measured than the Planetarian on the TV, Modak's underlying message seems to be that pessimism is the new realism. I do not doubt his projections or his figures or his graphs. But his conclusions depress me.

Once a year Hadport is home to the national British chess championships. Chess players are notorious for both their terrible dress sense and their lack of orientation skills. It was a week ago that I first caught sight of the carrot-haired woman—in her forties, badly dressed, disheveled—opposite my flat. At first I assumed she was one of their strange tribe, stranded in Hadport after her lost match like a misplaced evacuee. She looked off-kilter. But then I had other thoughts, prompted by the fact that she was empty-handed. Every woman—whether or not she plays chess—carries a bag. Her lack of this standard accessory made me think that perhaps she was local after all: local enough to be a neighbor who has popped out on a rare bag-free errand. Or mad. A bag-less woman can look, and feel, almost obscenely naked. Dewombed. The world is increasingly full of distressed people. Every small town has its aimless oddballs, men and women who drift in and out like flotsam.

When I arrive home from the café later that afternoon, I see the woman again. She's standing on the pavement opposite my flat, her hands hanging loosely at her sides. She's wearing a T-shirt and linen trousers. I feel her watching me but I refrain from looking directly back at her. During the whole of my transfer out of the car, she doesn't shift. Once in the house, I glance at her through the window. She is still standing there, motionless, like a mannequin on guard duty.

I close the blind to banish her but I fail. Because whether or not it was her aim, she has succeeded in unsettling me.

That night, I lie awake thinking, unable to sleep. Harish Modak is right, I decide, that humans are short-termists by nature and only far-sighted political vision can halt the damage to the biosphere. But part of me—the part that has got me this far, despite all that has happened—refuses to agree with him that such vision will never come into being. I didn't survive a horrific car accident in order to let a handful of world leaders cook me to death. *Cuando te tengo a ti, vida, cuanto te quiero,* I murmur: my tiny foreign mantra of cheer. I'm normally good at switching off from work, but Bethany Krall pesters her way in. The hoarse grate of her voice in my ear. Her wayward, carefully enunciated menace. *You had two hearts and one was gone. So someone died.*

I keep remembering the feel of her fingers on my pulse. Like a doctor who meant me no good.

My colleague Dr. Hassan Ehmet is a melancholy Turkish Cypriot with sloping shoulders and badly groomed hair whose claim to professional fame is a study of mass hysteria and religious cults in the Far East, soon to be published as an academic book by Oxford University Press. Although he is not the most charming of men, he charms me. I like the way he wears his loneliness and erudition on his sleeve, the way he gives a small "heh" when he's cracked a dry medic's joke.

"Genuine tragedies in the world are not conflicts between right and wrong. They are conflicts between two rights. Heh. Bethany's is the conflicts of two rights. Hers and ours. What puts her into a state approximating to happiness or perhaps even transient bliss, heh, is a regular dose of electricity applied directly to the brain. The interesting thing is, the rather *remarkable* thing is, she now requests it herself," he tells me over an execrable cafeteria lunch. "She can feel its beneficial effects. I suspect that within a few months the suppressed memories will start coming back. Some of these children, they are basically like cats and dogs. You know. Carnivorous animals, sometimes they eat grass to help their digestion. They know what they need when they're sick, heh. It's instinct." It strikes me as a curiously crass thing for a psychiatrist to say, especially one who can quote Hegel at you in the lunch queue, but perhaps he is right. "She's unpopular with the therapists because she's intuitive. She picks up on moods. Her perceptions can seem a little, what is the word, *uncanny* at times. It disturbs people." I try to look surprised, wryly amused, as though I am not implicated. I don't know if I succeed. "Like Joy McConey. Poor woman."

"What was her relationship with Bethany like?" I ask, curious that he has mentioned my predecessor, because her name tends to go unspoken at Oxsmith.

"Understandably troubled," says Dr. Ehmet. But now he looks embarrassed. He regrets having spoken.

"But why?" *I warned her about what would happen.* "Is Joy . . . ill?"

He nudges at a falafel with his fork. "In a manner of speaking. Joy's circumstances were very unfortunate," he mumbles. "She drew, er, unprofessional conclusions about Bethany."

"Such as?"

But he shakes his head, splits his falafel, and contemplates its mild protein steam. "We are all hoping Joy will return, so you will understand if I don't say more."

I nod to acknowledge this. "But what about you? Where do you stand with Bethany?"

"I'm purely on the, er, *electrical* side in this case. Heh. So I don't have to listen to her," he says, squashing the falafel with his fork so that its grains mash up through the tines. "I just give her the volts."

The Quiet Room, where I am about to witness Bethany having ECT, is clinic-white. Dr. Ehmet has been explaining that the procedure, once disturbing, has become fairly banal to watch, thanks to the general anesthetic and antispasmodic drugs.

"Oh yes, the days of high drama are long gone, heh. No more violent fitting. No more patients swallowing their tongues or spitting out their teeth." He sounds a little nostalgic. "It's still controversial because there's memory loss. And the fact is, no one knows why it works. One theory says that the shock stimulates the neuroendocrine system and balances the stress hormones. Then there's another one that says it's not about hormones being rearranged but the chemicals in the brain. Others reckon it's just wiping out brain cells. But I think if they are, they're being renewed. More *constructively.*"

I don't recognize Bethany at first, when a nurse wheels her in on a trolley bed. She's clad in a white hospital gown and her hair is scraped back from her face. Without makeup she looks even younger. Spotting me at the far end of the room, she points at her forehead, sketches a swift lightning bolt in the air, and smiles the triumphant smile of a terrorist whose demands are being fully met.

The ECT machine itself is unspectacular, consisting of a rectangular box with colored wires emerging and a dial.

"It is time for the IV now, Bethany," says Dr. Ehmet. It's matter-of-fact: they have clearly done this many times before. She proffers her skinny little arm. The criss-cross of razor slashes goes all the way up.

"I'm putting in an IV of Brevital," Dr. Ehmet explains, catching my eye and mouthing clearly. "An anesthetic." As it goes in, Bethany's eyelids close like those of certain dolls I had as a child, comatose the moment they horizontalize. Her face, normally volatile, instantly relaxes, as though unconsciousness has forced her features to sign a temporary peace accord with one another. The nurse inserts a new IV. "A muscle relaxant," indicates Dr. Ehmet. "To prevent broken bones and cracked vertebrae. It's a seizure we're giving her, after all."

Dr. Ehmet is one of those men who enjoy conveying information. Since I've already read about the procedure on the Web, he hasn't yet told me anything I don't know, but I'm happy to see the theory put into practice and for him to talk me through it. The nurse wipes Bethany's forehead with a damp cloth, then gently parts her lips and inserts a rubber mouth guard over her teeth—"to prevent tongue damage," Dr. Ehmet explains, as he applies gel to two padded elec- trodes and fits a breathing mask over her nose and mouth. On the anesthetist's nod, he applies the pads to her temples and holds them in place. Nothing visible happens.

"I'm, heh, shooting an electric current into her brain now. A level- two dose, stimulating a grand mal seizure that will last for precisely ten seconds. It's all in the timing."

Although there's still no sign that anything has happened—no convulsions, no twitching, no noise—an unexpected wave of revul- sion brings me close to gagging. It's like watching one of those animal rights campaigns showing grainy footage of a tiny tragic macaque monkey pinned to a slab. Dr. Ehmet has a professional eye on the digital clock. "And then release."

He removes the electrodes: under the sheet, Bethany's toes curl and flex, reminding me of speeded-up footage of bracken unfurling. Dr. Ehmet gestures to me to come closer. Positioning myself next to Bethany's head, I am oddly tempted to touch her brow, where the pads went, but I resist the urge.

"There we are. Logged off," says Dr. Ehmet. "It's only a light anes- thetic so she'll wake in a couple of minutes. 'She won't look a million dollars,' as they say. Or should it be euros? Heh. But she'll feel like new."

Five minutes later Bethany's eyes flick open and she groans, then yawns. Just as Dr. Ehmet predicted, she does not look a million, in any denomination. In fact, she's monstrous: ragged and bleary and punch-drunk, a preview of herself at forty. Her pupils are wildly di- lated and when she sits up, groggily, she holds her head as if her sense of balance is impaired.

"Bethany, do you know my name?" I ask.

Memory loss is the most significant side effect of the procedure. Sure enough, Bethany doesn't recall who I am. It doesn't appear to bother her.

"I saw this giant whirlpool made of wind," she croaks. "It was fucking incredible." The procedure seems to have carried her voice down an octave so that it sounds like it's emerging from a toilet or a cave.

"Where?"

She seems muddled. "The clouds. They start spiraling. And then on a map. The destruction's, like, mega. Write this down. Write down, *the fall of Jesus Christ.*"

"What does that mean to you?"

She shakes her head on the pillow. "*And whosoever was not found written in the book of life was cast into the lake of fire.* But you wait till you see it, man." She blinks. "Behold, the Lord maketh the earth empty, and maketh it waste, and turneth it upside down, and scattereth abroad the inhabitants thereof."

"Where do you remember that from, Bethany?"

"Hey, I know who you are. You're Mrs. Bibble Babble. Mrs. How-does-it-make-you-feel. Listen. This is what you don't get. This isn't about what I'm *feeling.* It's about what's going to happen. Hey. Bring me that."

She points to the wall, where a flimsy paper calendar hangs. I hesitate, then reach for a corner and pull it down.

"Flip through to July," she commands. I do what she asks, then hand it to her. "There," she says, pointing to a square. "The twenty-ninth. It's going to be a big day." She squints into the square as though it's a tiny window through which she is seeing the far distance. "South America. Brazil. Hurricane. Whoosh. Up it goes and then it all comes down. A whole lot of people are going to get wiped out. Kapoom. Along with their scooters and their chicken coops and their crap fencing and their screaming munchkins and their pet dog Fuckface."

"How do you know this is going to happen?"

"Because I saw it, *duh.* Just now."

"It sounds like it might be frightening."

She shrugs. "Whatever."

"What do you mean?"

"For the people who die it is. Not for me. I mean, I don't give a shit about them. Hey. I *want* them to die. The planet's overpopulated, right?" This sounds suspiciously like the dogma I have just spent a large part of my weekend mulling over. *The fewer the merrier. More oxygen for the rest of us. Organic diseases.*

"Have you heard of the Planetarians?" I ask.

"The who?"

"It's an ecomovement."

She looks either baffled or bored, it's hard to tell: she clearly doesn't know who they are, or can't remember, or doesn't care. Instead, on she talks, at high speed—about magma, and trapped gas beneath the earth's crust, and a volcano that's gearing up for an eruption. I nod and say little. I'm remembering there's a word in Russian, *izgoy*, that describes someone with a flaw that makes that person singularly unfit to perform his or her professional role. A blocked writer, a lascivious priest, a drunken chauffeur. As a screwed-up therapist, someone like me should not be working at all. Not yet. It is far too soon. Anyone can tell you that. Bethany, with her Competence Scale, already has. But here I am. An *izgoy*.

Trying to help a girl who has risen from the dead, bursting with ideas.

"October the twelfth, that's when the shit hits the fan," she is saying, flicking through the calendar. "Write that down too. Mark it on the calendar. You got a pen?"

"I'm afraid not."

"Well, remember it then. That's what I do. And write down about the hurricane. Rio, on July 29. It's got to go in the notebook." She grins. The braces on her teeth flash. I can see her moving on to the next stage, an adult facility like St. Denis or Carver Place or, worse, Kiddup Manor and spooling out the rest of her existence there, with the occasional incident of violence and the odd suicide attempt. Yet sometimes you want to help someone, despite yourself and what you have become, even if you know the patient is beyond it, and so are you. No remedy you can invent will change his or her trajectory. The fuse was lit long ago. But you try. Again and again you try, your life on a loop, a wheel. And when you get home you finish the bottle of Australian wine under the blank gaze of Frida Kahlo with her pet monkey and her dead hummingbird and her bad-luck cat and her necklace of thorns, and you leaf through the art books whose images still manage to flood your heart and brain, and drink your way into darkness and dream that you are flying in the stratosphere and having sex with a man you must not think about under any circumstances because the past, and the future it once held in embryo, has been wiped out.

And then you wake.

THREE

S elf-analysis is a bad habit I indulge in regularly, under the guise of "working on myself." It's clear that in moving to the only place that will have me, but where I have no friends, I have been trying to prove something. But what? My independence? My ability to continue business as usual? The fact that I can leave my previous life behind? My own perversity? When I look at what is happening in the world I wonder: am I projecting my own internal dramas on the social landscape, or is there actually an atmosphere of recklessness in these long, overheated summer weeks? A generalized malaise that seems to go above and beyond the norm, not just in Europe but across the whole globe, a globe that is overfreighted, claustrophobic, product mad, too dense for its own mass? I would like to stop reading the papers and watching the TV news but I'm increasingly addicted to knowing the extent of the horror. World preoccupations remain an uneasy, toxic mix: money (too little of it), disease (too much), territorial aggression, racist executions, spiraling gas prices, Web stalkers, Islamist terror, the new fly-borne malaria, melting ice caps, aggressive cults in China, carbon credit fraud, the rise of the Planetarians, the rampant spread of "intelligent design" teaching in schools, overpopulation, and the new, proud-to-be-a-fundamentalist movement. In Britain alone there are now fifty thousand Faith Wave churches of the kind Bethany was raised in; ten years ago, there were five hundred. Meanwhile in Iran and Israel the violence is an open wound on TV, so predictable in its bloodiness that the mutilated children and howling women become a spectacle you shudder at briefly before zapping over to some Japanese game show. The well-meaning optimism of those entertainment programs, with their perky nerdiness and banana-skin tomfoolery, provides a counterpoint to the real-world grief. Their crude hilarities flit through my head while I swim my laps, like my Spanish Kahlo mantra or fragments of some absurd erotic fantasy, poignantly irrelevant.

When I arrive for our next session in the art room, Bethany is in full manic flood, ranting at the thickset female nurse about some snail shells missing from her bedside drawer. Still unsettled by her ability to perceive and target my vulnerabilities, I am on my guard and keen to keep a distance.

"There were twenty-five and now there are only fucking twenty!" she shouts. "Can you explain that? How about this: Heidi's a fucking klepto. She nicks things, everyone knows it, it's her fucking *diagnosis*! Hey, there's this earthquake that's going to *destroy* Istanbul," she says spotting me come in. The stolen shells forgotten, she pursues her theme: the quake measures "seven point blah-blah," and it'll kill "zillions." Oh, and there's a volcano about to blow on an island she can't name somewhere in the Pacific—though if she had a map, she'd show me. A hurricane in the South Atlantic will zap in on the twenty-ninth of this month. "Kapoom! And that tornado that's just attacked the American Midwest, I predicted that, Wheels. And I have documentation to prove it," she says elatedly, waving a large red and black notebook at me. "Yay! Proof positive! Evidence of things not seen!"

"Can I have a look?" She hands it to me. "Shall I start at the beginning?"

She laughs. "You can start anywhere. Hey, hold it upside down for all I care. It's not like you're going to believe it."

I flip the notebook open in the middle and see a jumble of images tattooed onto the page in dark pencil and pen, gouged deep and overlapping one another in a chaotic palimpsest. But despite the unruliness, she draws with confidence and skill. There are cloud formations, waves, and rocky landscapes, vigorous lines with shadows darkly cross-hatched. Leafing through slowly, I also get the impression, from the multiple arrows flying in all directions, that Bethany imagines a scientific basis to these scenes. Her schoolteachers reported that she had an aptitude for science, art, and geography. You sense, in this travesty of her three favorite subjects, the tattered remains of an inquiring mind fed a solid educational diet. The images are annotated with her tiny spider's writing, which stumbles its way across the page haphazardly. *Pressurebuildingeastwestsurge. Likeathiefinthenightthey shallbecaughtup.*

"Can you talk me through what's going on here?"

She chuckles. "Talk you through Armageddon? Talk you through Ezekiel? I like the idea of them naming a city after me one day. Bethanyville. Or even a country. Hey, I like that. Bethanyland."

Grandiosity: worth exploring. Patients are like tangled balls of string. You have to find the end of the string and tease the rest out. Work at it until the ball starts to unwind. Then see where it rolls. Off the edge of something, usually.

"Do you think you're special in some way, Bethany? Do you feel you might have special powers?"

She laughs. "Like I've been saying to everyone all along, duh. I can see the future."

"What do you see there?"

She looks at me sideways, suddenly furtive. "Bethanyland."

"What's Bethanyland like?"

"It sucks. It's a completely fucked-up place. The trees are all burned. Everything's poisonous. There's a lake there."

"Lake Bethany?"

"You wouldn't want to swim in it. All the fish are dead and there are mosquitoes buzzing around everywhere, the kind that give you malaria. You wouldn't exactly be in your element there, Wheels. But you'd have no choice. No one would. You'd be lucky to be alive. You'd have to get used to canned food. Bring a can opener."

"A bleak landscape."

"But you know something? You're so on the wrong track. You're so lost it hurts. I told you, I can feel things happening. Joy McConey knew I was right." I remember my predecessor's good-bye card. *To Joy. Who truly believed.* Although the signature was illegible, it's clear that the handwriting in Bethany's notebook—small, frantic—is the same. I feel a frisson of disgust. Did Joy actually pore through Bethany's scribblings and find method in her madness? If she did, and came to believe in Bethany's so-called predictions, no wonder she has had to take time out.

"How was it for you when Joy left?"

She shrugs. "It was no big deal," she says, flipping through the notebook to reveal several diagrams of what look like cloud movements. "She wouldn't help me to get out of here, so from my point of view she could get fucked. But it was tough on her." She smiles slyly. "You know, losing the pleasure of my company? And between you and me, I think she got a bit paranoid. I know what Joy McConey's thinking now. She's thinking that I've got my revenge."

I wait for more, but she seems absorbed in her papers. There are drawings of volcanoes spewing fire and more sketches of cyclones, with arrows shooting this way and that. It strikes me, not for the first time, that the disturbed imagination has fewer choices of route than one might think. She points to a huge swirl. "I can see the way everything flows. Blood and water and magma and air. I can see everything move. I can feel what's happened to you, from your blood. All of it." Her eyes glitter. "It's only the electricity that's keeping me alive. I've told everyone what's happening. I've told *you*. But Joy *listened*. Hey. Guess how many stars I gave her. Joy McConey, you leave Oxsmith with a grand total of nine out of ten!"

I feel oddly slapped. *"I'm* listening."

"No, you're not. But hey. You will be. There's going to be a tornado in Scotland any day now. Check it out. And the big one's on its way. The Tribulation starts in October. You'll be listening so hard your ears fall off."

Her laugh is like the smashing of bottles.

Wheelchairs have come a long way since the glorified wheelbarrows favored by Roman men. After an orgiastic party—the kind where they'd lie on padded chaise longues and guzzle food from a central trough, stopping only to vomit—a slave would wheel them out into the night, obese, drunk, and sexually glutted. Or so I imagine it as I struggle with my returning-to-the-house routine: chair out of the car, body into chair, body and chair to front door, body and chair back to car to get shopping from trunk, open front door, wish for a slave. In fact, a dough-faced Polish girl called Danuta, from an agency, now comes in once a week to clean: she'll do the heavier shopping for me, too, and the washing. I can do all these things myself but it's too time-consuming. As my visit to the supermarket has just reminded me.

But through it all, up and down the aisles, I thought of Bethany. Odd, the way she has taken up residence in my brain as a permanent fixture—far more than any of the other kids I've been seeing regularly, even little Mesut Farouk, who made the striped hot air balloon, or Lewis O'Malley, who cut off his own hand in a ritual act of self-punishment, or Jake Ball, who bankrupted his father by buying military hardware online by credit card: damaged babies, junior would-be Terminators who bring out the frustrated mother in me. "Intuitive," Dr. Ehmet called her. I never look forward to our sessions but I want to get to the bottom of her. She's like a nagging crossword clue that I can't solve. One that wakes me in the night, sweating.

The evening is still so sun scorched that the air above the pavement shimmers. I don't see the pale-eyed woman at first. She is standing across the road from my flat, her red hair oddly lustrous. Catching my eye, she raises her hand in a salute, like a secret agent using a gestural code we have both learned at spy camp. I have mixed feelings about the mentally ill being cared for in the community.

The following morning, the radio news contains a story about a tornado in Aberdeen. It happened at 6 a.m. Five houses lost their roofs, and half a gas station collapsed. There was no warning. I'd like to dismiss the fact that Bethany alluded to it. But somehow I can't.

Like many other successful doctors, Oxsmith's clinical director, Dr. Sheldon-Gray, is a ferociously keen sportsman. His office, reached through a small antechamber where his PA, Rochelle, presides, is partly a gym, the broad desk sandwiched between two exercise machines, one for rowing and another for running. He is cochairman of the regional Water Ski Association and won championships in his youth. I have learned this from my colleague Marion, who also informs me that the doctor's superathlete weekends are spent with his family—a sport-supportive wife and three boys in their teens, who all don wetsuits and take turns getting towed across a lake at high speed at the end of a rope. I envy them, of course. Perhaps I would like to be a member of their family and experiment with handicapped athletics. They told me in rehabilitation that nothing is physically unachievable if you want it enough: just read the memoir of the young rock climber who crossed China on a hand-propelled bike after a devastating fall or the American quadriplegic who plays a kind of wheelchair rugby called murderball. Perhaps if I stay on the right side of Dr. Sheldon-Gray he will invite me on his speedboat and I will acquire new skills. But perhaps not, once he learns that I have come to question him about Bethany Krall's incomplete dossier.

He has his back to me as I enter. I don't see him at first because it's a large room, and he's at the very far end by the windows, at floor level. I'm not expecting that. He is in a tank top and shorts, rowing on his machine. The room has recently been painted in wipe-down buttermilk: you can still smell the faint anodyne odor.

When I reach him I swivel my chair until our contraptions face each other, almost close enough for their metal to kiss. Or even mate and breed. My boss is veering muscularly back and forth, emitting small masculine stress sounds like "ungk" and "gah," his arm sinews tautened to the maximum. He's sweating like a rutting goat.

"I'd like to discuss Bethany Krall," I say. "There's nothing in the file by Joy McConey. If she made notes, they've gone missing."

Apart from his fanaticism on the physical fitness front, Dr. Sheldon-Gray possesses no obvious tics and no apparent signs that he is one of the walking wounded of which my profession is largely composed. Nevertheless the rowing machine's pace seems to slow at the mention of Bethany. I sense hers is not a name the director wishes to hear. "Gah," he puffs. "Sorry, can't stop until I've done my quota, so if you just talk and bear with me. Ungk."

"I'd like to see what Joy wrote."

"Of course you would."

"So may I?"

"No. Gah."

"Can I ask why not?"

He makes me wait, listening to his intimate noises, until he has done another three strokes: his eye is on his heart-rate reading and the digital clock.

"It would be—gah—unhelpful."

"Unhelpful in what way?"

Abruptly, he stops rowing and starts rubbing at his face and neck with a towel. He looks across at me, still panting. Confidence gives a boom of volume to his voice, as though he's speaking to a crowd. He begins wiping down his arms.

"Well, she's officially on sick leave but there's more to it than that,

I'm afraid. She began to show signs of mental unbalance. The notes reflect that. So I removed them from the file." He flips his towel over his back in a decisive, alpha-male movement.

"I see," I say as he fiddles with the little digital box on the rowing machine, trying to rezero it. "I'm sorry she's ill. I knew she was on a sabbatical, but no one told me the specifics."

"Well, now you know them. So. Is that all?" he asks, when the digits are fully blanked.

I don't reply. Instead, I wait. And wait some more. "I mean, it's fair enough, don't you think?" he justifies finally. I say nothing. "If you, Gabrielle, in a state of extreme personal distress, wrote a report on a patient that reflected badly on your professionalism, you wouldn't like it to remain on record, I imagine?" His striking eyes meet mine. Their astonishing clarity and blueness make them look artificial, like a pair you might pick out for yourself in a glass eye shop. Given my own shaky tenure here, I can't argue with the man. "I'd stick to working out Bethany Krall for yourself, if I were you, Gabrielle. Are you settling in well, by the way?" Without waiting for a reply he starts rubbing down his strangely hairless legs, adding: "We must get you involved in some local stuff. Plenty going on here socially. Big charity bash coming up at the Armada. It'll be a good opportunity for you to meet and mix. Though it's mostly science types," he says with an air of apology.

"What species of science type?" I ask, suddenly interested. The Bethany puzzle is still vibrating.

"The lesser-spotted biologist, the two-toed statistician. I don't know. The usual suspects."

"OK."

"OK what?" The exertion has turned his face as pale as the buttermilk wall behind him.

"OK, I'll come. Thank you. Can you get me an invitation?"

He does a double take. "Of course. Leave it with me. Rochelle will contact you."

Working out Bethany Krall for myself isn't an easy ride. Like extreme weather, her moods vary wildly. Some days she is talkative, while on other occasions she barely acknowledges me, refusing point-blank to enter into a dialogue, even about cloud formations or another favorite topic, plate tectonics. Her artwork is impressive. She works on sev-

eral large and evocative sky paintings and dashes off a series of brooding charcoal drawings of storms spreading over wide, featureless
landscapes. More and more, she doodles rocky surfaces from which
a vertical line emerges, heading skyward but fizzling into nothingness
near the top of the page. Sometimes it takes root underground, its
trajectory veering to the left and then ending in what looks like a cartoon bang. Is it plant or machine? When I ask her about it, she is
noncommittal: the scene is something that keeps "appearing" after
ECT. Perhaps it's on another planet, she offers. But to me it whispers
Freud. I try to draw her out a little on the subject of her religious
background, in the hope that it might lead to some revelations about
her family. She can quote the Bible extensively but is as scathing
about God as she is about doctors, repeating the question she raised
when we first met: what has God ever done for her?

"That presupposes that God exists," I prompt her. But at this, she
falls silent. If Leonard Krall abused his daughter sexually and her
mother colluded in the atrocity, then her need for vengeance would
be easily explained. I work with her patiently, trying to edge toward
the subtle alteration of perception that might one day enable her to
escape the tortured landscape of Planet Bethany and move to a place
of lesser punishment. But if revelations are on the horizon, they are a
long way off, and I'm aware of my failure.

Our next meeting takes place outside. It is still breezeless and so
oppressively hot that I have taken to carrying a little lacquered fan
with me everywhere, like some old-world geisha. Above us the sky is
that intense Hockney blue that seems to almost gag on its own den-
sity. High scatterings of clouds above, like flung chalk dust, and
stripes of darker vapor below. The heat is vengeful. Rafik is shadow-
ing us, a few paces behind: I have told him to make sure that if
Bethany touches me or makes any sudden move he must intervene
immediately. I'm taking no chances. I don't trust her further than I
can spit.

Five years ago, the British seasons made some kind of sense. Not
any more. One side of Oxsmith's facade is set on fire by the hectic
leaves of a Virginia creeper, which blazes like fish scales. Some have
already curled to brown and been shed. A cluster of lilies, withered
and papery, mauve and delicate orange, rears up valiantly from the
drought-struck lawn. In my previous life I would have photographed
distressed, moribund blooms such as these and then taken the im-

ages further in the studio, fast and angry, nudging at them with pastels or brush and ink, reveling in the accidental splatters, the emotional jolts that change the way you think about what you see, because you've seen it anew, transmogrified it, forced it to sing your song. For the first time in months, I feel a spasm of creative desire. Why not begin all that again? Do I have to deprive myself of things I once found good?

Yes. No. Yes. Yes. It seems I do.

"The tornado in Scotland," I begin. "The one that struck Aberdeen—"

"A lucky guess," she interrupts breezily. "Coincidence. That's what you're thinking, right?"

I smile. "But I admit it was odd."

She cackles but says nothing. We move in silence for a while.

"So this car crash you had," Bethany says abruptly. "Fucking spectacular, eh." I am confounded. I haven't told her anything about the accident. How does she know it was a car crash? What does she mean by *spectacular*? "Anyway, tell me something. I'm curious. What's it like being—"

"Disabled?" I offer, to regain control, to buy time, as we round a bend. "*Confined* to a wheelchair?"

"I was going to say *challenged*," she ripostes merrily. "Or *differently abled*, yeah?" It seems that today is a good day.

"I'm fine with 'paralyzed.' "

She stops and closes her eyes. "He was driving, right?" she says, knowledgeably.

My brain jams, then restarts with an internal thud, catapulting me into the offensive. "OK, so tell me more," I say. "Since you know, let's hear the rest." But I immediately regret it. In giving in to my anger, I've betrayed myself.

"I can't see the details. But I know the result."

So do I, and so does everybody, big deal, I think, and move on. But how can she know who was driving? Because men usually drive? Just another "lucky guess?" For a few minutes there's no sound but the crunch of gravel under her feet and the quieter press of my wheels. If I give her something, she might give me something in return.

"OK," I say. "Here's the short version. It's nighttime. He's driving, as you suspected."

"Knew."

"Well, you knew right. Anyway he loses control, the car veers off the road, it rolls over a few times, I land in some mud, and when I wake up in hospital they ask if I'm aware of a loss of feeling anywhere."

My voice has stayed calm but my heart is bashing and I'm unbearably hot and suffused with a feeling of disgust, as though I have rolled over a slug and it's stuck to my wheel and any minute I'll feel the slime of its prolapsed innards against my palm. Next to me, Bethany nods as if recognizing the scenario. Nothing fazes her. On the contrary, what I've said seems to give her nourishment.

"But it was your fault, right?" Like a lot of other disturbed kids, Bethany has a sure instinct for locating one's jugular vein. I shut my eyes and stop the wheelchair. When I open them again, Rafik is at my side. I breathe in and out slowly.

"In a way it was, and in another way it wasn't," I say as evenly as I can, moving on. "Depending on the mood I'm in on the day, Bethany. I wonder if there's anything that feels familiar in that, when you look at your own life?"

But she isn't going to be sidetracked in that direction. Her refusal to countenance the past has shown no signs of erosion. The occasional biblical quotation—usually citing chapter and verse from Ezekiel, Thessalonians, or the book of Revelation—is the closest she comes to revealing influences from her life in the outside world. It could be months, or even years, before Bethany decides she trusts somebody enough to talk about her parents. If she ever does. And why would she? She'd have everything to lose, and precious little to gain. If whatever happened to her was bad enough to prompt her to kill her mother, then convince her that she herself had died—

"So just how paralyzed are you?" she asks. I've recovered now.

"My legs don't function," I answer, pushing my wheels faster. Rafik holds back; she stays alongside. "I can't stand up or walk, but I can still swim. It's my arms that do the work."

"She can still swim," she says, as though pondering it. "But can she have sex?"

I take a breath. It's the question everyone secretly wants to ask, in a normal world. But a maximum-security forensic hospital for criminally insane minors is not a normal world. "I have no feelings below the waist. I'm what's called a T9 paraplegic, complete," I reply.

"Meaning nothing much happening from the belly button down. Or thereabouts." Slowly, and with much experimentation, I discovered in rehab that I can still, just about, experience arousal of sorts—though most of it seems to take place in my head, via my breasts. Not something I feel the need to share with the suddenly inquisitive Bethany Krall. "I'm wondering why you ask," I continue carefully, grateful for once that there's no eye contact. In opening the door to a discussion of her own sexuality and experience, have I launched her on a ghost train? But she seems not to have heard or has chosen not to answer.

"I didn't choose this," I say softly—though in my dark raging moments I fear otherwise. "But I can live with it." Can I? As a vision of making love with Alex on the poker table enters my head, my rib cage tugs inward like I'm wearing a corset that's being tightened by a cruel Elizabethan. "Maybe you can understand that? Spur-of-the-moment random actions that have lifelong consequences?" Her mother hovers between us but Bethany resists the bait. "You've been at Oxsmith for two years now. But do you understand why you're here?"

She laughs, but it's mirthless. "I'm here because of people like you refusing to see what's going on even when it's staring you in the face. Much easier to lock me up than to listen to what I'm saying." Suddenly she's on a furious roll. "You pretend things aren't happening because that's what you want to believe, and by the time you do, it's too fucking late. The tornado in Scotland. You want to think it was a lucky guess. You're welcome to. But I saw it. And then it happened."

"Like you said yourself: a lucky guess." I see Karen Krall's bloodied face in the police photograph: waxy, like a melted doll's. You can't help wondering what sort of force Bethany needed to ram the screwdriver into her eye socket like that. What sort of noise the puncture would make. "But how do you see your future?" I ask, to take my mind off it.

"You mean, do I want to leave Oxsmith one day? Be released into the *community*? Get married, become a mum, lead a normal nine-to-five life—all the things little girls are supposed to want?"

"Little girls?"

"Cut the crap. I mean those moronic teens in your moronic teen group talking about their moronic boyfriends and their moronic sex and their crackhead retard babies."

"Forget about the other girls' ambitions, Bethany, whatever you think they are. What do *you* want?"

She stops, and together we look at the wall of red creeper. "If I had a baby I'd call it Felix. That means happy, right? It would be kind of an ironic name." I wait for more, thinking: the name I always had in mind was Max. "But I won't be having a baby." Me neither. They said I nearly died, there was "no way of saving anything." *Anything*: an interesting euphemism. No Max. Not now, not ever.

"But how can you know you'll never have children?"

"What's the point, when the world's fucked? I'd have to be a sadist." Harish Modak and the Planetarians would agree with her. They're singing from the same hymn sheet.

"I can think of a million reasons," I say. A foolish reflex, because if she were to call me on it I am not sure I could name a single one.

But Bethany's inner whirlwind has moved on. She has leaned down, and I feel her breath on the back of my head. This is her favorite way to threaten me.

"Me getting out of this place all depends on you, Wheels," she whispers, coming so close that her mouth nuzzles the hair by my ear. Her babyish, hoarse voice worms deep into me, insistent as an exotic parasite. "I'd say it depends on how good you are at your so-called job." A familiar sting of pain travels up from my smashed ninth vertebra to my neck. I shudder it away and shift in my chair. I've learned over the past two years that when half of you is dead the other half can come violently, almost malevolently alive. "Joy McConey got nine out of ten but in the end it wasn't enough, she just wasn't up to it. Didn't have the nerve. She's paying for it now. But maybe you'll be the one. Have you ever thought that you were brought here for a purpose?"

"Meaning?"

"Meaning, are you going to help me escape from here or not?"

I look at the wall again, its splash of triumphant, bloody red. A gust of wind strokes it, detaching a slew of brittle leaves. I don't reply, just turn and look at her. Her eyes have gone distant and dreamy, as if she is peering at something beyond the horizon or in a parallel place.

"There's a thunderstorm coming tomorrow. From the west. I like storms from the west. Hey. Tell you what. I'll come and watch it from the Creativity Workshop." She pauses. "You never call it that, do you. Too right-on, yeah?" I fight a smile. "There's a good view. We could eat popcorn together, Wheels. Cuddle up together and share a Coke like at the movies." She pauses and I can feel her grin. "You could pretend to be my mum."

FOUR

have stopped at the swimming pool on my way home from work. Six thirty is a good time, in this heat. Although at over sixty-five degrees, the water is never truly refreshing, you'll get a lane to yourself, if you're lucky. But it seems I'm on a doomed mission. As I'm parking, a blue Renault hybrid pulls up sharply in the disabled space next to me and the woman passenger inside stares at me pleadingly. It's her. The woman with the lustrous red hair and the pale eyes. There's a man with her. He's blond, balding, harassed-looking, and probably what they call time-poor. Older. He looks at me over the steering wheel and gives a helpless, frustrated gesture, as though I should be able to identify and sympathize with his plight. Then, as the woman starts to open the car door, he stops her with a swift movement. And suddenly they're struggling, locked in a graceless, desperate tussle. I picture the dull, bestial unhappiness of a couple shackled to each other by their mortgage and their children's shared DNA. I have no doubt that their fight concerns me in some freakish but unfathomable way. Having secured my parking space, I now hesitate. Although I am getting better at it, maneuvering the wheelchair out of the car is still a hassle. I don't like the idea of this couple being there, fighting, while I do it. I've seen the crazy red-haired woman once too often.

Unwilling to abandon my swim, I decide to drive around the car park in the hope they'll assume I have gone and then leave themselves. Pulling out, in my mirror I see the woman turn to yell at the man again. Her features are stamped with misery. Something is severely, irredeemably wrong. It crosses my mind that they could be the parents of an Oxsmith patient: they seem about the right age to have a teenager. Mental illness in a child can exact a terrible price. Whole families implode. But if the woman wants to speak to me, why not ask for a meeting in the normal way? When I get back to my parking space they have left and I can enjoy the pool. But it takes thirty lengths' worth of hard swimming to eradicate the woman's stare.

The storm has erupted. The thunder's on a spin-and-tumble cycle and the sky is mottled with gray and black clouds. When Bethany arrives in the studio—a bulky, Mohawked female nurse is already sitting in—we watch the sky froth and churn. The view is operatic, the arms of the white windmills revolving intently in the distance, fork lightning cracking over the ink pool of the sea, trees straining at the roots, their canopies stirred up like seaweed, sometimes a filament whipping off to become a missile. As the lightning flashes illuminate the room and plunge it back into shadow, Bethany wanders around turning her head this way and that, as though sensing the air's pulse. She opens the window and thrusts her face out, inhaling the air through the white bars.

"I'd like to climb to the top of a mountain. Just stand there and let the lightning hit me. Kapow. Right into the brain. Or dive into the sea when it's on fire."

"I wonder what other kind of thoughts you have, about death," I say, because it's worth a try. But she pays no attention. Today I'm an irrelevance, a petty distraction from her queen-sized thoughts. When she finally stops pacing, she stands in the middle of the room, her face spattered with raindrops, breathing in deep lungfuls of thunder air, eyes closed.

"Here," I say, shoving some charcoal at her with an aggression I somehow can't quite hide. "You came here to draw, so draw."

Surprisingly, she obeys. I watch her at the work top, her face concentrated, her body bent oddly close to the paper. She works fast, fluidly, intensely, almost tearing at the page. Charcoal dust flies up. Every now and then she wipes the sweat from her face, leaving a dark smear of grime. What she is sketching now—a series of swirls and arabesques—doesn't correspond to the landscape outside. She covers the paper hastily, letting each sheet fall to the floor when she tires of it. In one, there's a human shape: a man diving off a cliff.

"Who's that?" I ask, pointing.

"Ever seen those cliffdivers, on TV? In Acapulco? They spread their arms and they dive off into the sea. Like Christ."

"Would you call yourself a believer?"

"No."

"You used to be. The church you belonged to—"

"His church. Not mine." She points to her temples. "Look. The mark of the Beast. Doctors do that. They put stuff in and they suck other stuff out."

"Tell me what sort of man your father is, Bethany. Even if you have mixed feelings about him, I wonder if there's something you could describe about him?"

She shakes her head.

"Or your mother?"

"Hey. I'll tell you something. Useful fact about electricity. Lightning isn't supposed to strike twice in the same place. But some people have been hit by it three times. It's the metal in their blood. My blood's full of metal."

"Do you feel you attract trouble?" I ask, rolling a piece of chalk between my fingers. I am getting a visceral urge to draw—or more simply just to make a mark on something as proof of my own existence. But something deep and tribal, something with its own arcane emotional rules and rituals, forbids me. Bethany shakes her head and smiles, then tut-tuts.

"Therapy questions will get you nowhere. Try asking some real ones."

"Give me some suggestions. Let's do a role reversal."

"Nice try," she laughs. "But who the fuck would want to swap places with a spaz?"

I begin to tidy up the clay-working area. A minute later, the bell rings for lunch and the nurse comes for her and she is gone.

The clouds are massing outside, unfurling in silent gray waves of vapor. Watching them roll and spread, I realize that I need Bethany.

When I concentrate on her, exquisitely unpleasant though it some-times is, I can forget myself. And forgetting can be addictive, I've learned that by now. Bethany has no love for the world. If you feel that way, and maybe have cause to, if you believe you died at the age of fourteen, there can be worse things than being here, imagining that you house a ghost—a kind of raging electric Gaia—that empow-ers you. Bombarded by cataclysmic predictions about the conse-quences of global warming, and with a childhood forged in the increasingly popular notion of hellfire, why *not* give way to the delu-sion that you have special powers? With the temporary memory loss that comes with ECT, you can be born again every week, to voice ex-travagant threats or, in another mood, to find solace in small, en-closed things, your anxieties and dreams in deep storage. I know about that, I've lived it: the hopes quietly shelved or violently thrown aside, the sustaining beliefs about humanity's importance in the uni-verse rendered absurd, meaningless.

The sky is almost black now. It could be night. The clay corner is a disaster area, so it is only half an hour later, when my next session is due to start, that I roll over to where Bethany has been working and see, next to the charcoal skyscapes and the skydiver, the crude red crayon drawing she has left on the work top. It could have been done by an eight-year-old. It's a stick figure, lying askew. Female, to judge from the triangular breasts and the triangular skirt.

Something is sticking out of her eye.

Strokes among the young are on the rise, according to Mary, my physio at the rehab center: an oddly unpublicized side effect of alco-hol and drug abuse. Many wheelchair users are of my own generation or younger, often accompanied by parents or even grandparents. I see proof on my early morning outings, when I'll find myself doing an un-gainly little swizzle dance in front of another set of wheels, position-ing my chair to leave my *camarade de guerre* enough space on the pavement. As we do this, those of us still blessed with the power of speech commiserate about dog shit and inspect one another's wheel-chairs just as guys eye one another's cars or mums compare baby bug-gies, and we smile ruefully in recognition of our shared knowledge of a world in which practicalities and the subtlest of physical plea-sures—the delicate aftertaste of artichokes, a particular piece of music, not to mention the erogenous zones that emerge to compensate for those we have lost—have come to mean more than we could ever have imagined before. Like it or not, and I do not, I have become a member of a community. Though I would rather saw off my own head than join a club or counsel wheelchair users—something I might be qualified to do. I have enough of my own stuff to deal with.

And look how well I'm doing!

I have a job, along with an office I can call my own, and a spider plant that refuses to die no matter how much coffee I pour on it. I am also in charge of several junior nutcases, including a sixteen-year-old murderess obsessed with the Apocalypse.

Blessings: count them daily, Gabrielle.

Practice what you preach. Cuando te tengo a ti, vida, cuanto te quiero.

Keep a fucking gratitude journal.

When I get home from my morning glide, there's a package waiting for me, and a card. I recognize the erratic handwriting on the parcel as my friend Lily's. She's written a note instructing me to have a wonderful day. Inside the packet is something soft wrapped in scented tissue. Fabric: fabric whose heft indicates it is unashamedly expensive. As I pull the tissue apart, a sudden flood of red silk spills out and collects on my lap. A dress. I hold it out. It has spaghetti straps, a swooping décolletage, sequins on the hem: it's the kind of dress a Brazilian transsexual would kill for. Tears shoot into my eyes when I realize the date and what I have suppressed. Can I really have become so disconnected from myself?

The card is from my brother Pierre and his family in Canada. One of the twins, Joel, the younger by nine minutes, has sent a drawing of me in my wheelchair. I am holding a balloon. I have a wide banana-shaped smile on my face and the long, sharp eyelashes of a beauty queen.

Later that day, four chronically obese girls start fighting in Physical Expression and I have to call in extra backup, so by the time I get the message to come to Dr. Sheldon-Gray's office I'm as miserable as any wheelchair user is allowed to be on her thirty-sixth birthday in a town where she has no friends. But Sheldon-Gray has news for me. As per my spur-of-the-moment request, my boss has engineered my social debut at the charity function at the Armada Hotel tonight.

"Buffet dinner included," he beams, handing me the invitation. "Drinks from seven thirty."

She shall go to the ball!

After the day I've had, it's suddenly a unappealing prospect. When I asked for the invitation, I was in one of those optimistic, inquiring moods that can occasionally overtake me and that I have taught myself to indulge to counteract the darkness. Today, in a different cast of mind, the notion of cornering some hapless scientist and quizzing him or her about the background to Bethany's delusions suddenly feels idiotic, unprofessional, and shamefully naïve.

"Thank you," I tell Sheldon-Gray. "I'd love to come."

No more dramatic entrances in impossibly high stiletto heels for Gabrielle Fox, I think some hours later, as I negotiate a pool of grease on the tiled floor of the Armada Hotel's giant industrial kitchen. She is Cinderella brought low, arriving at the ball via a service entrance because of lack of access front of house. The bang of pots and pans, the sizzle of fat, and the hiss of pressure cooker steam are noises she will come to know well in her new life. Twang that guitar. I trundle my way past churning dishwashers, vast hobs, and sauce-splattered chefs, and out via the kitchen's double swing doors and a bleak corridor into the suddenly gaudy hubbub of the charity reception. Where spread before me is everything I used to enjoy, in an ironic way, in the world of Before but have developed a dread of since the accident: tuxedoed men, women parading the sparklier end of their wardrobes, waiters with drinks and fiddly, experimental-looking things to eat on trays. Later, there will doubtless be speeches by men who praise the untiring efforts of the stalwarts behind the scenes. But I remind myself that, if nothing else, I have a mission: to find someone I can interrogate about natural catastrophes—such as tornados in Aberdeen—and how one predicts them. Hoping to find a guest list without having to enter the throng, I maneuver my way across its perimeter behind a screen of potted plants. But I have been spotted by a tall woman who has laid a manicured hand on my arm and is now bending down, as though on a giant hinge, to clink her necklace in my face.

"Welcome. What a gorgeous dress you're wearing."

"Oh, thank you," I muster a smile. "It's a present from a friend. It's the first time I've worn it."

The fact is, I feel fraudulent, undignified, and inappropriate: a nonwoman pretending to be a real one. The blood-red dress, which would look elegant on an upright woman, feels brash stuffed into a wheelchair, with my boobs popping out like two scoops of vanilla ice cream yelling, Lick me. I am a cleavage on wheels. I am Disabled Barbie Goes to a Party but Does Not Get Laid for Reasons That Escape No One.

"It's so heartening to have some real victims of the condition with us tonight," the woman is telling me conspiratorially, her hand still on my arm. "It brings home the urgency. And it's positive. I'm all for positive. And I bet you are too." And she bats my bare shoulder in a "go, girl!" gesture. "You're *so* brave," she says, expanding on her theme as we make our way through to the main hall, a sea of asses and cummerbunds. "Don't tell me you're not. I know how cruel it can be—my niece Jilly had it. Jilly's father always called it S.B. Short for 'son of a bitch.'"

Finally I am with her. Spina bifida. Oh, Jesus, how do I get rid of her? This town needs a gas chamber.

"I'm sorry. This is from a car accident," I say, patting my chair as if it is my good old friend, which it is not and never will be. "Perhaps those people over there can help you?" I suggest, pointing out three other wheelchair users who I presume to be genuine victims of "S.B." This is their gig: they can do the talking.

"An accident?" she wants to know. Curiosity is an attribute one can applaud in oneself but despise in others.

"Car." I have learned to keep it brief.

"Lord, what a terrible shame. You're so attractive!"

I know, I want to tell her. It should have happened to someone really ugly. And then it wouldn't have mattered.

But people mean well. Flashing her a smile, I execute a fast wheelie and cross the room swiftly. A wheelchair can part crowds like the Red Sea. The white-tuxedoed Dr. Sheldon-Gray is with his wife, Jennifer, whom I recognize from the photo in his office, which flatters her because it doesn't show her porky bottom or her visible panty line. Will I ever get used to the way I am forced to assess crotches whether I wish to or not?

"Is there a guest list?" I ask bluntly.

"In Reception, I think," offers Jennifer. Clearly relieved I have found a project, Sheldon-Gray smiles, winks in a generalized way, and excuses himself: he and Jen are off to work the room. I part the seas again.

The guest list is attached to a notice board on the wall just out of my reach. This feels dangerously like the final straw. After a few attempts at grabbing it I'm about to give up and go home when a large, tall man emerges from the melee of the hall wiping his face with a napkin. Spotting my predicament he strides over, rips the list down, and presents it to me with a comedy flourish.

"Thank you."

"Are you looking for someone on there?" he asks. His accent is Scottish.

He is big and a little overweight, with a soft-featured, pleasant, if unassuming face and an interesting oddity in his left eye—a splotch of green in the hazel brown of the iris.

"Not really. I'm just interested to see who's here."

"Well," he says, pointing at a name. "Members of the great-and-the-good club mostly. But there *I* am. A nonmember." *Dr. Frazer Melville, Department of Physics.* "Pleased to meet you." He thrusts out a hand to shake. "And you?"

"Gabrielle Fox," I tell him. His hand is warm and a little sweaty. "I'm a therapist at Oxsmith."

Dr. Frazer Melville—who I pray is not going to be a weirdo—is studying my face sidelong with forensic interest. "Shall we reenter the fray?" He gestures at an empty table just inside the hall, near the shelter of a large potted plant. When we have made our way to it, he pulls up a chair and sits himself opposite me. "So you're a Londoner."

"You can tell just by looking?" I ask.

"Yes. As it happens."

"Are you some new breed of urban anthropologist?"

"No, but I'm a Scot, and one fish out of water can spot another."

"It's not London that does that. It's the chair." It comes out more grumpily than I intend. "But if you're a physicist, maybe I could pick your brains about something. I have a patient who has a kind of climate-and-geology obsession."

The big Scot smiles. I like the splotch of green in his eye. It's like a tropical fish darted in and set up home. And his teeth. I like Dr.

Frazer Melville's teeth, too, which are white and even and not too small for his face. This matters to me. He is probably—though this is totally irrelevant—about forty.

"Sure. But I'll be honest with you. I'm not planning to stay here long. I hate these functions, and I hate wearing this ridiculous costume. There's an Indian restaurant across the road that won't poison us."

Immediately, the prospect of rejecting a chaotic buffet scrum in favor of a quiet curry has distinct appeal. In addition, Frazer Melville's accent entertains me enough to make me want to hear more of it, and I like his attitude to the charity event.

"But if you'd rather stay here with the thoughtfully assembled, er, *amuse-gueules*—"

I shake my head as a pesto confection glides past on a tray. "My turn to be honest. I can guarantee you that this thing *I'm* wearing is even more uncomfortable than your outfit, if we're having a competition. I'm hitting seven out of ten on the pain scale here."

"Well, it may not be comfortable, but it's flattering," he says, openly surveying my cleavage. "You're a joy to behold if I may say so." Oh well. I have put it on display, so it would be hypocritical to complain. I suppose. But I am on shaky ground.

"My friend sent it. She's a fashion buyer," I say quickly, feeling a radical blush spreading upwards from the flesh in question and blooming on my face like a Rorschach test.

"What you need is food, Gabrielle Fox. I can see you're hungry. May I?"

When he maneuvers me out through the frenzy of the kitchen, I feel like a baby in a buggy kidnapped by its eccentric uncle.

Outside, I take charge of the chair again. The heat from the kitchen is still burning on my skin in the warm air. The blush hasn't quite died down either. As we approach a crosswalk side by side, I wonder whether I should tell him it's my birthday. No: he'd offer to pay for the meal, and I can't allow that. I stay on the pavement but Frazer Melville steps out jauntily, forcing two cars to brake hard. With a burst of inappropriate amusement, I realize that I am in the company of a man who might well turn out to be as dangerous as he is energetic.

. . .

Delhi Dreams, aromatic and low-lit, with flock wallpaper and red fur-
nishings, is classic British Indian in style, with decor untouched
since the 1970s. Ensconced at a quiet corner table, the physicist is
telling me that he moved to Hadport from Inverness six months ago,
having obtained a grant to continue his research at Hadport University. His background is pure and applied physics. He tells me that his
current branch of study, fluid dynamics, covers a wide spectrum but
in the case of his PhD involves the kinetics, pressure, and flow of
ocean currents. "But then I wanted to broaden things out, so I studied meteorology and started investigating air turbulence. Trying to
discover why molecules move the way they do. Did you know that
flocks of birds and shoals of fish and swarms of insects follow similar
kinetic rules? It seems random but there's a logic to it. There are lots
of new theories around at the moment. None of which I can explain
without drawing mathematical equations on a napkin and boring the
pants off you. So tell me about this patient of yours."

Wait! Me first! It's my birthday! I want to blurt. But even if I could
find an unchildish way of telling him it would still sound abrupt, incongruous, and borderline tragic. He'd wonder why I'm not somewhere else, with friends. Which would set me wondering, too, and
reaching dismaying conclusions. We order poppadoms and a comfortingly aggressive house red, and I tell him about Bethany—whom,
in a last-minute nod to professional confidentiality, I refer to as
"Child B." I tell him about Child B.'s Faith Wave background, Child
B.'s nihilistic delusion of being dead, followed by her breakthrough
with ECT, her intelligence, her intractability, her militant cynicism,
her artwork. I can't have spoken at length to anyone for a long time,
because it's like someone has unplugged a cork. I wonder if I sound a
little obsessed with Child B. But if I am, it's still a relief to discuss
her with someone who isn't in the business and will never meet her.
"It's like she's always playing some kind of game with you. She's unsettling. She claims to have the power to predict natural catastrophes."

"Meteorological or geological?"

"Both. Just the other day she said there was going to be a tornado
in Scotland. And sure enough, there was."

"The one in Aberdeen?"

"I have to admit I found it unsettling."

He smiles. "You shouldn't have, because it's emphatically a coincidence. Small tornados happen far more often than anyone realizes. We get a lot in this country. Case dismissed. Go on."

"And she can sense things in people's blood, too, or so she claims. Blood and water and rock."

"They have more in common than you'd think," says Frazer Melville, tearing off his tie and shoving it in his pocket. The poppadoms arrive and he attacks them with verve. "Why not make a note of what she says? Or better still, get her to write it down."

"She already does. She has notebooks full of drawings. But I don't press her on the details. It's best neither to confirm nor to deny a patient's fantasy."

"That's policy?" This also seems to amuse the physicist. "You have a *fantasy policy* at Oxsmith?"

"In a way. And not just at Oxsmith."

"But what if it isn't fantasy?"

"The paranoids really are out to get me? Istanbul really is about to be destroyed by a massive earthquake?"

He pauses midbite. "It's on a fault line. So it's a real possibility. Quite well known."

"And there's going to be a massive hurricane hitting Rio de Janeiro next week? On the twenty-ninth? She gets very specific. And it all seems to be Armageddon-related, one way or another."

"Para-catastrophology." He pulls out reading glasses to survey the menu we've just been handed by the waiter. Not forty, then, I think. A bit older. "A whole new field. Could put experts like me out of a job. There was a bloke in the States, in Vermont, called the Weather Wizard. He's dead now. His real name was Louis D. Rubin. He looked at the clouds and predicted days when there'd be unusual weather. He was mostly right."

"So she might be right about this hurricane, for example? By picking up signs the rest of us can't see? Because that's what she'd claim."

"I'd doubt it. It's still the hurricane season, and they're getting bigger every year because of the increased air temperatures. But super-hurricanes are a complex phenomenon. With global heating, we're seeing all sorts of things we haven't seen before. That's the trouble with trying to model anything on a computer: we only have the parameters of what's already known. But Rio de Janeiro—highly unlikely, I'd say. It's South Atlantic, and typically they're in the north.

The first on record was in 2002. Took a lot of us by surprise. But it may have marked the start of a trend."

"So what are the chances that she's right?"

At this his eyes change shape and you can almost see his brain turn into a calculator. "Off the cuff? A thousand to one." He smiles suddenly. "I'd be happy to bet our next dinner on it." He takes a big bite of poppadom and crunches noisily.

I can't help smiling too. I can't be used to it, because it makes the muscles around my mouth ache. Is it possible that I am enjoying this evening after all? I agree to the bet but insist that this dinner's on me, because it's my birthday. There. I have said it. Delighted, he orders champagne, for which he insists he'll pay. Surprisingly, Delhi Dreams has some, and even more surprisingly, it comes close to being adequately cold. If he thinks it odd that I have nothing better to do on my birthday than have dinner with a physicist I met at a function to which I had to scrounge an invitation from my well-connected boss, he doesn't mention it: he says it's an honor, and he raises his glass in a complex toast that pays tribute to my "fabulous dress and its contents," to Child B., and to the vagaries of high and low pressure uniting us "at this auspicious moment of twenty-first-century history."

Frazer Melville, who is forty-four, who lost his mother to cancer only two months ago, and who is divorced from a Greek geologist called Melina, eats in the same way he orders. He is eager, greedy, unselfconscious, and sure of his taste. Melina couldn't have children, he tells me. But that's not why the marriage failed. It was more complex. "And quite humiliating for me," he confesses. "Knocked me right back." I nod and wait for him to go on. "Irreconcilable differences just about covers it. It was tough, but we're on amicable terms now that she's back in Athens. Our interests overlap, so we run across each other's work from time to time. Exchange the occasional e-mail about marine landslides and whatnot."

"Did you ever make fireworks when you were a boy?" I ask him.

"Only the basic liquid kind with Diet Coke and Mentos. I wasn't a sophisticated pyromaniac. I melted gallons of wax over bonfires and made a million tangerines explode. A normal childhood for someone who ended up as me. OK, my turn. Gabrielle as a kid. You were a miniversion of what you are now. Sharp, and very proud of that amazing hair, even though you knew you shouldn't be. You knew how to empathize but it got you into trouble sometimes. But you weren't so angry back then. Or so beautiful."

The problem with blushes is that once they've started, there's no preventing them from running their course. The champagne is going down well. Giddy after two glasses, I start telling jokes, culminating in the one about the faith healer. I barely recognize myself.

Later, back home, I wonder if I am still able to like people. It isn't something I've properly tested. I let him push my chair when we went through the hotel kitchen—and not just because I wanted to protect my dress from being splattered with sauce by some maniac sous-chef. In the delicate etiquette of wheelchair use, I permitted an intimacy.

A few nights later I am having one of my vertebra dreams. I am operating on my own lower back, fixing the damage with pliers and a monkey wrench. "There," I tell the nurses and medical students who are watching. They are in a semicircle. "If I can do it, you can." I point to the diagram of the spine, the one they first showed me when they explained my injuries. It looks like a bonsai tree. An alarm bell goes off. It is a warning. I must finish the operation because they need the pliers back. And the monkey wrench.

It's actually the phone.

There is light coming through the blinds, but it feels like the middle of the night. I check my alarm clock: it's 7 a.m. The phone is cordless; I have left it on the table by the door, too far to reach in any hurry. So I do not pick up—partly because I suspect it is Lily, who I know from our conversation a few days ago is gearing up to one of her love crises. Vertebra dreams always throw me. I am having trouble getting my mind in order. My head hurts. I had three glasses of wine last night. Alone. Lesson number one of paraplegia: alcohol is bad for you. After six rings, the answering machine kicks in.

"Sorry to ring so early, Gabrielle," he says. "You're probably fast asleep. Dreaming of new ways to—"

"New ways to what?" I ask, picking up. Funny, how a paralyzed woman can shift her butt quite quickly when she wants to.

"New ways to intrigue men from Inverness. But listen here. This is going to sound odd but I have to ask you. That South Atlantic hurricane your psychotic case talked about. Child B." He sounds excited, a bit reckless. "Can you remember when she said it would hit Rio?"

"The twenty-ninth."

There's a grunt on the other end of the line and then a fumbling sound: my Scottish physicist friend is apparently getting dressed, one-handedly, as we speak. I can hear Radio 4 on in the background.

"I thought so. Just had to check."

"Isn't the twenty-ninth today? What is this?"

"I don't know. A weird and amusing coincidence. Look, thanks, Gabrielle, and sorry to wake you, lovely one. I'd like to talk but I'm going to be busy over the next few days. Look at the news and you'll see why. I might just be buying you dinner." And he hangs up, leaving me disturbed and excited. By the phone call, and its content. And by the interesting expression "lovely one."

According to the TV news, a hurricane that has been brewing in the South Atlantic Ocean is now whirling its way down the coast of Brazil. Its name is Stella. Its mass and speed qualify it as a super-hurricane.

And it is heading for Rio. Just as Bethany said.

FIVE

Television is a cruel medium, constantly ushering newsworthy visitors, uninvited, into your living room. After the commercial break, the guest of honor is carnage. The hurricane is busy flattening a sprawl of towns and villages down the coast of Brazil. On the screen, splintered trees and a blur of broken manmade lumber jostle along fast-flowing rivers of mud or spin into the vicious cycle of a whirlpool system where the flotsam of urban catastrophe churns circularly in all its heart-wrenching banality, with sofas, beat-up cars, road signs, office equipment, hoardings, and human bodies bobbing like oversized corks in a brown froth of mud. If Stella hits Rio it will be "a disaster on an unprecedented scale," according to the CNN commentator, who is explaining with a set of rapidly evolving graphs how the vortex of wind is picking up momentum and vibrating its way south. Brazilians struggle in the flooded wreckage of what must once have been their homes—a sheet of corrugated iron here, a door frame there, a child's bed. Desperate people clinging to gas canisters and oil drums. Lives upended in the time it takes for a pan of beans to boil.

Hurricanes can threaten one place and hit another, veering off randomly, says a meteorologist. This is particularly the case with supersizers. The current projection of the computer models is that Hurricane Stella will not hit Rio but head out to the ocean, where it will eventually dissipate. But no one wants to take chances: with a backward glance at the unhealed wounds of New Orleans and Dallas, a mass exodus has begun, bringing with it a new set of crises and panic-induced emergencies. There are three-mile-long backups on the exit roads, and the trains are bursting. *A whole lot of people are going to get wiped out. Along with their . . . scooters and their chicken coops and their crap fencing and their screaming munchkins and their pet dog Fuckface.*

Nightmares of a certain variety can do me in. I have not yet worked out how to avoid succumbing to them. As the TV horror blooms like a pornographic flower, I close my eyes and inhale, and I am back in the stench of my private hell: a sewerish, earthy gasoline stink, the blinding, almost transcendental torture of my neck and chest, the odd blankness of my lower half, the choking smoke, the seemingly endless wait for help as I drift in and out of consciousness. Alex's groaning.

I held on to his elbow, the only part of him I could reach. At least it felt like an elbow. Rain was falling—big, thundery drops, warmish, strangely greasy. It seemed we were outside. I felt soil, or silage, or compost, or mud. We'd been on a minor road. And were they nettles stinging my arm? Or a new, excruciating form of torture, designed to make your brain float out of your head and hover somewhere above you like an alternative moon in a sky filled not with light but with the eiderdown of irradiation that is the twenty-first-century urban night? My atheism forgotten, I mouthed the default prayer of the desperate, like a beached fish gasping its last. Mild concussion tumbled the phrases in a linguistic tombola. *As we forgive those, hallowed be thy name, our father, thy kingdom come, our daily bread, our trespasses, as it is in heaven, deliver us.*

Any port in a storm.

Enough. "I am grateful it was T9 and not C1. I am grateful I am alive not dead, and I am grateful that for my mother it's vice versa, and that Dad doesn't know who the hell I am when I come to visit him. I am grateful, I am grateful, I am grateful. *Cuando te tengo a ti, vida, cuanto te quiero,*" I mumble, moronically, as I leave the room and perform my elaborate bathroom routine, and then return, refocused, to see satellite pictures showing a huge whorl of white vapor whose central vortex, like a celestial plughole, is the hurricane's blind eye. A series of graphics explains the mechanics of supersizers: the warming seas, the greater bulk of moisture and the flux of air above, the drama such combinations can trigger, the fact that with global warming they will become "part of the landscape." *Part of the landscape*.

I try out the odd expression on my tongue as I windmill my arms and watch people I don't know as they panic, improvise, weep, wave, and drown.

When my mind is in turmoil, my stomach needs fuel. Like many other poor cooks, I have learned to scramble eggs to survive. I smash four into some melting butter and start stirring. What I lack in culinary skills I make up for in coffee-brewing expertise: thanks to the benign influence of my first psychoanalyst, I have developed an anally precise morning-beverage-preparation ritual, which involves the grinding of Colombian beans, the careful charging of my small but perfect percolator, filched from my father's flat when he retreated permanently to his private netherworld, and the frothing of hot milk with a special battery-powered gizmo that bears a passing resemblance to a dildo. Ten minutes later, breakfast prepared and consumed, I feel if not a whole woman again (that I'll never be) then three-quarters of one, which is as good as it gets for me on the rehabilitation front. I drive to work. On the radio, there's more news of Stella. At last, it is veering out to sea.

Through the open door of the recreation room at Oxsmith, you can hear the rapid clatter of a Ping-Pong game and the thud of MTV on the big screen that's surrounded by a group of kids. By the far wall a lone boy, prostrate, is chanting tonelessly on one of the scuffed prayer mats while a Tourette's kid shifts from one foot to the other muttering expletives. I wheel my way past a hugely fat girl swaying to the music, her belly spilling over the top of her jeans, her face as smooth and empty as molded plastic. She has wound T-shirts around her head to form a giant multicolored turban. Watching her fixedly, a boy who a month ago removed his own eyeballs and had to have them surgically replaced is gearing up to masturbate. Business as usual.

I find Bethany Krall watching CNN on the small television in an annex off the main room, where two male nurses are talking desultorily and punching at their mobiles. She has made herself comfortable. Perched on a chair with her legs tucked underneath, she's chewing gum furiously, as if there's some kind of speed mastication record she's hoping to beat in the course of her day that is somehow related to the unfolding nightmare on the screen. I can see immediately that she's riding high.

"It's back to the worst-case scenario," says a woman on the TV. "Hurricane Stella's changed course again, and she's now definitely heading for Rio. She'll hit any time in the next hour."

"Yo, Wheels." Bethany grins as she spots me, then fists the air like a triumphant athlete. But with a third coffee inside me, I am back on track, and I refuse to let the latest news shake me. The only sane approach to what's happened is to take it as given that Bethany's prediction of the hurricane is a guess based on something she has gleaned, via the Internet, from some obscure weather station. Or simply coincidence. What did Frazer Melville say? *Case dismissed.* My job as a professional is to manage Bethany's conviction that it isn't a random fluke. And even reverse it. The alternative—the Joy McConey model—doesn't bear thinking about. The trouble is, when you deal on a daily basis with people's fantasies *not* coming true, there's no handbook on how to behave when they actually do. I'll have to run on whatever instincts I have left.

"Yes, you were spot-on, Bethany," I say.

"Well, *duh*," she says through her gum. Her face is still pale, but the cheeks carry a faint, waxy flush, reminding me of those Madonna statues that cry tears of blood on demand in mystically devout pockets of the world. "Well, Wheels? Aren't you going to *say* anything?"

"I am," I say noncommittally. "But I don't imagine it's what you'd most like to hear."

"You're going to say it was just a random coincidence, right? Well, Joy was just like that at first. Back in the days when she was a zero too. So if that's what you want to believe, you go right ahead." I nod slowly but say nothing. "They always give people blankets," she comments, jerking her head at the screen, and rolling her gray green gum around on her tongue and teeth. "Why's that? It's not like it's *cold*."

"Shock makes your body temperature drop," I respond automatically, trying to hide my irritation at the laconic, I-told-you-so way she's watching the drama unfold. She can't seem to imagine what this means for individual lives. For her, they're like tiny pixilated screen beings. Little Sims whose lives you can meddle with and overturn at will. "Especially if you're wet. It's comforting."

It's more than two years ago that I held Alex's elbow and thought that cold flesh needn't always be a bad sign. That if I just kept hold of it, kept squeezing it so he'd know I was there, passing on my warmth, everything would somehow be all right. I thought, too, about his family. Now everything would be out in the open. There'd be no avoiding it, no denying it, no more pretending. Sickness mingled with relief, tempered by the hovering suspicion that I would probably panic later, if I could muster the energy. They would give me a tranquilizer of some kind, I hoped. Perhaps they already had given me one. At that point, it didn't cross my mind that I was badly injured. The fact that I couldn't feel anything seemed like a blessing, a sign that I was intact, that I hadn't lost anything. Yes: I'd been given some kind of tranquilizer. How good of them, how thoughtful, professional, and well-organized. I could close my eyes and sleep.

"My life is over," a weeping Brazilian woman in a floral dress tells the world, via a dubbed American voice. *"Everything has gone. My baby is dead."* Babies have a way of getting to me. I turn away. Through the window bars, the sky is full of popcorn clouds.

"Right. We'll discuss this later. I can't hang around," I tell Bethany.

"Yeah. Anger Management, right?" She smirks, then turns back to the screen, where they have moved briefly to other news: Japan's stock market has gone berserk, an actress who once starred alongside Tom Cruise has taken an overdose, the body count in Iran has reached half a million. I'm just rolling out of the room when a stupid but brutal thought strikes me. I stop in the doorway and turn round.

"What else do you feel you have known about in advance?"

She shrugs. "Lots of stuff. That earthquake in Nepal two weeks ago? I told you about it."

"Did you?" At a recent session in the art studio I recall her reeling off a list of dates, places, and events while drawing a diagram of what might have been a sex act performed by machines. But I was more interested in the artwork than the manic rant that accompanied it.

"Yes. And you didn't listen," she says, catching the nurse's eye and offering him some gum, which he declines. I did listen, I think defensively. But I filtered. The way you have to, to make sense of anything these kids say.

"What else?"

"Try listening next time," she says, yawning. "It's not like it's going to stop happening."

"But this—thousands of people killed or made homeless, and if it hits the city—"

"It will."

"Then thousands more lives about to be ruined—"

"That's OK, it's cool," she interrupts. "Heard of a fait accompli? Anyway, how come *you* suddenly care about all those South Americans? Because you didn't last time I mentioned it." She shakes her head in disbelief. "It's like Dr. Ehmet. *Hassan* to you. He's Turkish, right? But when I tell him about the earthquake destroying Istanbul, it's like talking to the wall."

"An earthquake in Istanbul?" Perhaps the filter needs adjusting. Just as an experiment, of course. My stomach tightens. "Remind me."

"Next month. Put August 22 in your diary, Wheels. It's going to make this thing look like a fun ride at Disneyland Paris. *Ay caramba.*"

When I return two hours later, Bethany is still lounging in her chair, one leg splayed over the armrest, chewing her gum and watching Hurricane Stella whirling through Rio, a mass of roiling water, vapor, and debris.

"Oy!" Bethany greets me with a waved hand in the air. "Come and join me." I maneuver alongside her. On the TV, helicopters pester at the storm's tail like gnats, relaying images of the disaster zone: filthy corpse-bearing torrents that fill valleys and swamp plains, relief trucks blocked by precipices of rubble, and, out at sea, glassy slicks of oil from shattered tankers. As Stella wreaks its worst on Rio, a deeper metropolis is revealed, skewed and ravaged, beneath the flesh of the old: a Hieronymus Bosch landscape of liquid streets and bust-apart shacks and unidentifiable shards that were once part of—what? Playgrounds, schools, bars, hospitals, brothels, homes where children bickered and adults made love and cooked rice and gave birth: the ebb and flow of simple, frustrating, difficult, normal, grief-smudged, passion-fueled human existence. A fierce sunball hangs low over Rio, French-kissing it, upending day and night. Against it, an aerial view of the city blanketed by a swirl of cloud silhouettes the white statue of Christ the Redeemer on the mountain, with his outstretched arms blessing land, ocean, and sky. Absurd, but it has never properly struck me before that the figure itself forms a giant human cross. There's something both terrible and poignant about the scale of it, as if its vastness and grandiosity are in reverse ratio to the economy that raised it, concrete testimony to a grandeur of spiritual ambition not matched on the ground.

"It's a credit to the foresight and expertise of the statue's designer, Heitor da Silva Costa, that Christ has withstood the force of the 300-mile-per-hour winds," says a commentator. "More than ever, in these terrible times, the Redeemer is a symbol of hope—"

"Hey, watch this, Wheels," says Bethany excitedly. "Here comes the good bit."

"What do you mean by *good bit*?" I snap, furious. Sometimes it's a struggle to stay professional. Often you fail. And so what.

"Shhh!" she commands. I watch her sharp little profile. From the attentive, bright-eyed way she's observing the events unfolding on the TV, you might think she'd had a hand on orchestrating them. The picture has flipped to another angle. It's shakier footage this time, live, taken from high above the city, across from the statue. The picture zooms in on the white-robed figure of Christ high above the forest below.

"A figure of eternal peace," says the news commentator. "Standing on the mountaintop of Corcovado, in the world's biggest urban park, encapsulating the spirit of Rio itself and the hopes of a hundred million Brazilians that one day the devastation wrought today by Stella will be—"

The camera seems to jolt, and he hesitates, only to be cut off by a disembodied Portuguese voice that interrupts him in a fast, excited burst. Apart from the camera jolt, or what seemed to be a camera jolt, it's not clear immediately from the image that anything is wrong. Have I missed something? More voices join in, in several languages, all suddenly talking at once, in apparent confusion, as though a hundred TV channels have merged. The image flickers and resettles, the zoom pulls out, then hurtles back in. Technical problems.

Then the knowledge slams in, and my heart misses a beat, leaving a time vacuum in my chest. I say sharply: "Oh, Bethany, no." I can't look at her because I know she'll be grinning. I think, *Bethany, don't do this.*

The figure of Christ, now pictured in profile, sways and tilts forward.

Vertigo. Then a brief, yawning silence.

There are certain moments that you know you will recall for the rest of your life with perfect clarity. They are stamped with the blood's instructions: you will remember because you have no choice. There's a microsecond when the statue seems to do nothing, as if frozen in middecision, before it tips into its long and hallucinatingly beautiful death dive, the white figure falling headfirst in what starts as a slow lunge downwards as it disconnects from the plinth, then surrenders to the terrible grace of physics. I catch my breath. Its operatic scale is at once monstrous and riveting. The commentary has stopped. The only backdrop is a profound quiet. And then, with the stretched momentum of a fantasy or a lucid dream, the figure crashes into the mountainside, bouncing like a giant skittle and shattering into fragments as it goes: first one arm cracks and flies off, then the other; then the torso itself snaps in two, the pieces tumbling at angles to drop into the thick smear of gas below, a mixture of smoke and oil and rain and cloud. A liquidized mirage of a place that might be heaven and might be—

Watching it, and recognizing it, I go hot and cold.

Bethany's skydiver.

"Oh, please, no," whispers a man's voice on the TV. "No, no, no, no, no." The silence broken, they all begin talking at once, shock-stimulated into a babble of disbelief, excitement, and despair.

I belong to a generation that has seen statues and icons and buildings come tumbling down on TV: Lenin in Russia, the Berlin Wall, Saddam in Baghdad, the Twin Towers. But those topplings meant something to those who caused them. What does this mean? Who is to blame? What can one read into a random catastrophe, an out-of-the-blue event, an "act of God"?

Nothing. In place of an explanation, however grotesque, there is a void.

Without a word to Bethany, because I am unable to speak, I swivel round and roll out at high speed, a ball of horror trapped in my throat.

That night, at home, I turn on the TV and they are showing it again, and again and again because they know from experience that we can never get our fill, that it cannot become real until every detail has been absorbed and digested and processed and reimagined. And sure enough, the swell of chatter in the wake of Christ's epic fall has burgeoned into an international, interfaith Babel of opinion and emotion. There are weather experts, structural engineers, geophysicists, stonemasons, religious leaders, psychologists, and even a conceptual artist dissecting the event. It's established that soapstone, from which the statue was made, is highly weather resistant and unlikely to give in to strong winds, even at massive accelerations. But an engineer argues that if the base had been hit by a heavy object—not impossible given the colossal amount of debris sucked into the sky—then the statue could have become dislodged, balancing only by force of its weight. "Just look at where the statue stood: you can't get much more exposed than on a mountaintop. Winds at that speed and at that height. . . ." Another expert weighs in: it was not an accident waiting to happen but "a freak convergence of weather and structural physics." The Net is buzzing with conspiracy theories. Christ's fall was caused by a remotely triggered minibomb, part of a "9/11–style Jewish plot." No, it was executed by Muslims on a hate mission. It was Iran's revenge. Clashing opinions and interpretations vie for dominance in an atmosphere of excitement tipping into mass panic. The statue was slammed into by a flying object. It wasn't struck by anything: it had merely eroded more than anyone realized. The Brazilian government knew the truth but covered it up. It was in extraordinarily good condition. No velocity of wind could wreak that damage on an object weighing a thousand tons. A toddler could have felled it with a single swipe.

Depressingly, the "fall of the Redeemer" debate gathers momentum, obliterating the hurricane story. A radical Islamist cleric has claimed it's "the judgment of Allah," which has set a predictable chain of events—outcry, counterattack, death threats—in motion. Anti-Muslim rioting flares across the world, countered by anti-Christian demonstrations and the burning of crosses: a war of ideologies, sparked by a falling chunk of stone. There are arguments about the dangers of iconography, the dangers of religion, the dangers of literalism, the dangers of scaremongering. Again and again, along with millions, I watch the fall of Christ.

But slowly, as the hours pass, sanity creeps back and the statue's fall—which killed no one—is finally put in the context of the wider destruction the weather has caused. By the time Hurricane Stella concludes its two-day rampage, conservative estimates say that it has wiped out four thousand lives in Rio de Janeiro. The aerial images show acre upon acre of residential suburbs, of industrial estates and sprawling favelas laid waste, littered with slowly drying debris, corpses, and rubble. The disaster relief agencies pour aid in, doing their utmost to prevent the spread of disease. But already there are reports of typhoid. These are images I cannot bear. But I know that Bethany will be watching, chewing her green gum, soaking up the horror like a sunbather who can't catch enough rays.

When I eventually get through to Frazer Melville he assures me that Hurricane Stella hitting Rio on the date Bethany predicted is, to use the jargon, "statistically insignificant." Meteorology, he insists eloquently, is a notoriously inexact science and much of it is simply guesswork. There are plenty of freak forecasts on the Internet: Bethany could well have been trawling those. It's easy enough to be taken unawares—as many were with Stella. But it's just as easy to say you knew it was coming.

"It's like trying to second-guess a bucking bronco. Bethany got lucky, that's all."

"If lucky's the word. But what about your phone call? You sounded excited."

"Coincidences *are* exciting. So exciting I had to wake someone up at an ungodly hour. You were the obvious person. For which my apologies."

"A thousand to one, you said," I persist. "Is that statistically insignificant too?"

He sounds unfazed. "The good news is, I owe you dinner."

Three evenings later Bethany's skydiver drawing, which I have ripped down from the wall of the art studio, lies in a folder at my feet in La Brasserie des Arts. I hate to eat alone only marginally less than I hate to microwave ready-meals or order takeout. But by now I know the staff at La Brasserie well enough to have a favorite table and to be greeted personally by the manager. Who smiles at me encouragingly when he hears that tonight, for once, I will have company other than *Psychiatry Today*.

When Frazer Melville arrives he kisses me on both cheeks and apologizes for being seven and a half minutes late.

"Remind me of the statistics of this not happening?"

"Me being late? Very low." His joviality masks an edginess.

"The hurricane."

"I said a thousand to one. But actually it was more like three."

"So you owe me two more dinners." While he fumbles his jacket off, I pull out Bethany's drawing and place it on the table in front of him. "Can you factor this into the calculations? She showed me this a week before the fall of the Rio Christ."

I have written the date she drew it at the bottom of the page. I watch Frazer Melville absorb the image. The eye always travels left to right and top to bottom—the way Chinese hieroglyphs are drawn. He takes it in three times before speaking.

"Noteworthy," he says finally. But offers no more.

"It makes me feel less sure that it's just coincidence," I say. "I mean, she would argue that she predicted this. And that she's fore-seen other things too. There was an earthquake in Nepal she claims she told me about in advance."

"And did she?"

"She may well have done. I was listening for other things. But when I saw the Rio Christ falling on TV, the connection to this image was obvious." He says nothing. His eyes flit across the drawing again. We order our food and then there is another silence. Frazer Melville keeps glancing at Bethany's drawing propped against the salt cellar. I can see it's irking him.

"I'd like to look at her notebooks, if I may," he says finally. "Out of interest. Check what else she's seen in these so-called visions and see if they correspond to anything."

"Infringement of patients' rights. I'd lose my job."

"If anyone found out," he says matter-of-factly. "But they don't need to."

I feel a flash of anger. Does he really think it's that simple? Logis-tically, it would be easily managed, especially with a wheelchair that already conceals an illicit thunder egg and an even more illicit spray can: he's right about that. But there's a moral issue.

"Are you familiar with a notion we call human rights?"

"Would she mind?" he asks.

"She'd think it was Christmas. But I'm more curious about your reaction. On the one hand the scientist says it's just a coincidence, an *exciting* coincidence, and on the other—"

"The scientist would like to know if there have been any others. Nothing unusual in that."

"How many would you need to see before you stopped thinking

they *were* coincidences? How many correct prophecies does this kid have to make before it goes beyond *noteworthy*? One more? Two? I mean, if she did turn out to be right about Nepal, which I could check—"

But Frazer Melville is shaking his head vehemently. "From where I'm standing—from where any scientist is standing—the answer to that is, more than she can ever provide."

"So why look?"

"Same reason I'm a scientist in the first place. Curiosity about the jigsaw. Seventy years ago no one much believed the theory that a meteor was what wiped out the dinosaurs. Now it's established fact. New theories tend to gain ground slowly. Often because they're heavily resisted: they put careers at stake. There's a cynical saying in science: A professor's eminence is measured by how long he's held up progress in his field. Look how long some scientists hung on to the idea that the current global warming had nothing to do with human-generated carbon emissions. But argument and debate move science along. Doubt is essential. So is going out on a limb. You can't have an inquiring mind and be presented with a puzzle you know no one else has solved, without wanting to solve it."

"But it's not just scientists. Look at the fall of Christ the Redeemer. All those people speculating that it's divine symbolism. Have you heard that the pope's announced he's having a new statue made, twice as big and guaranteed indestructible?"

We agree that the new religious turmoil is showing signs of becoming alarming. Then, as our food arrives, we move on to fundamentalism and atheism, then to the paranormal, and superstition and the way religion is revered, or at least respected, in most cultures, while folkloric superstition is seen as dodgy, cheap, flimsy, medieval.

"I was taught by nuns," I tell him. "They couldn't see how tribalistic they were. Or how pagan. As for the traditions, it seems to me that the Catholic Church enjoys just making things up as it goes along. You could almost admire its creativity. And look at the Faith Wave. Overnight, intelligent design gets credence."

"I like what Ralph Waldo Emerson said. The religion of one age is the literary entertainment of the next. My mum was a Protestant. She'd go to church on Sunday mornings, then get plastered in the afternoon. Toward the end she lost her faith. Just like that. Weird that she stopped praying, right when it might have helped her. She decided she'd wasted too many hours on her knees, for nothing. The vicar came to see her at the hospital and she wouldn't pray with him." He smiles. "She was stubborn, my mum. You know what her last words were? To hell with God, Reverend."

We move on to the selfishness of genes, the phenomenon of altruism, and the categorical imperative. Which, with some twists and turns, leads us on to the Planetarians: I am instinctively more averse to them than Frazer Melville, who agrees with Harish Modak's viewpoint that the Anthropocene era—the reign of man—is hurtling to a close. "Not least because no phase lasts forever," he points out. "And why should it? People who know about rocks see Earth on a different time scale from the rest of us. To them humans are just another species—a species that happens to be dominant for now but won't be in the future. Some people see Harish Modak as monumentally cynical, but in fact he's just stating the obvious. Geologists have been arguing this kind of thing for years. They're the boy who pointed out the emperor was butt naked. But no one listened before."

"Child B.'s father's church believes in the Tribulation."

"The seven years of hell on earth thing?"

"Yes. Before it kicks in, the good guys get whisked to heaven in the Rapture."

"Ah, the deus ex machina divine teleportation system."

"Into the clouds and away. Leaving your clothes behind and a lot of baffled people."

"First time I heard about it must've been back in the Bush era."

"That's when it got properly into its stride. It fitted with the ethic. Heat the earth till you usher in the apocalypse, then get a private plane to airlift you to shelter, and screw the rest of us."

"Well, sinners do need punishment, if you follow the logic."

"And they need to reap what they've sown and be assaulted by locust plagues and earthquakes and what have you. The Faith Wave lot used to see climate change as an anti-oil conspiracy cooked up to boost the power of the UN. But that's evolved. The new thinking is it's a sign we're on the brink of doomsday. Which they're keen on, because it means they'll be raptured. Did you realize that in terms of numbers there are more hard-core Christians today than in medieval times?"

"Does your kid go in for this stuff?"

"She was reared on it. But they found a burned Bible in the trash after she killed her mother."

"She killed her mother? Christ. You didn't tell me that bit." He looks uneasy. "Are you surrounded by murderers in that place?"

I shrug. "I don't think of them that way. They're just disturbed. And it's my job. Anyway, what I'm getting at is that Child B. had—has—religion issues. To put it mildly. The fall of the Rio Christ was to her what 9/11 was to all the anti-Western Muslims we saw dancing for joy that day. And not just because she claims to have predicted it. If her father visited, I'd have a lot of questions for him."

"You can hardly blame him for keeping clear, if she killed his wife."

"Things are always more complex than they look," I say. "I'm wondering about the healthiness of his role in her life. And her mother's." We consider this for a moment and then I point my fork at him. "Eschatology."

"Greek. The doctrine of last things."

"Correct. If you're an eschatologist and you believe the apocalypse is about to happen, you're happy. You're going to be saved. But as a sinner, how would you spend your last moments on the earth as we know it?"

"I'd do exactly what I'm doing now," he says, amused. "Eat *spaghetti alle vongole* in enjoyable and combative and extremely attractive company. No, scrub that. I'd take the said company to its natural psychic habitat, which is probably Paris because I'm guessing you're partly French, with a name like Gabrielle."

"French Canadian."

"OK then, Montreal. Which doesn't have quite the same ring to it. But we'd order ourselves a gastronomic extravaganza in a Michelin-starred restaurant and finish it with industrial doses of Belgian chocolate."

Something about the physicist doesn't add up. "Are you *flirting* with me?"

"Well, if I am, you started it. You invited it. Yes, maybe I am. In a safe kind of way."

I flare. "Right. So being paralyzed from the ninth vertebra down makes me a safe kind of girl? Thanks for the compliment."

"I didn't mean that. I meant . . . I'm flirting in a *nonthreatening* kind of way."

"The way gay men do?" A wild guess.

Interestingly, the physicist looks thoughtful rather than outraged. "How do gay men flirt?"

"They talk a lot and they give compliments but they never follow through on the physical side. Is that what you meant by unthreatening?"

"I read somewhere that 30 percent of people have had at least one homosexual experience, and I must say I was quite surprised the figure was that low. But the trouble is, in my case, I was always far too attached to the mammary gland."

"I noticed," I laugh.

"So you *are* a mind reader."

"No, I've got a pair of eyes, though, and I'm a normal woman. Or I used to be." I stop, appalled that I've just said it aloud. It isn't funny. What am I doing discussing my breasts with a physicist, when nothing works below the belly button?

"The fact is, I've been quite, er, reserved on that front since my marriage broke up," confesses the physicist.

I nod. "How long were you together?"

"Four years. But we were apart for a lot of that time. Melina would do these long field trips, and then I'd go off to China or somewhere. By the time it ended, we exchanged e-mails more than we spoke. But there were other factors. Well. There was *one* other factor."

"An irreconcilable difference?"

He reddens and studies his spaghetti with intense interest. Then he looks up and smiles. "It turned out I wasn't the only one with a thing about mammary glands."

It's too funny not to laugh, but after a moment we both stop ourselves, embarrassed.

"So she was a lesbian before you met?"

He sighs. "I expect you've read case studies about things like this." I nod. "What do they conclude?"

"Well, often what happens is that both partners think the homosexuality is just a phase or something they can overcome. Love conquers all, et cetera. And sometimes it does."

He looks up, relieved. He even musters another laugh. "So go on. I'm interested."

"OK. In your case, perhaps it turned out you were just Melina's heterosexual experiment."

He nods ruefully. "Is it that classic?"

"Fairly. Sorry to tell you. And the turning point?"

"When we learned she couldn't have children. That's when she gave up on the whole idea of men, I think. Or the whole idea of me. Somewhere along the way she met Agnesca."

"And since then you've been wary of forming new relationships."

"Understatement. Everything's been on ice. Physically and emotionally." He looks anxious, then smiles. "Is that classic too?"

"Speaking as your new therapist?" I say. "It's completely understandable. Your manhood took a knock. But it will pass when the right person comes along and if Jupiter's in the ascendant. All shall be well, and all manner of things shall be well. Julian of Norwich. That'll be fifty quid."

He smiles. "Worryingly cheap. But if it doesn't pass? What if I carry on being . . ." "Reserved? Then stick to Belgian chocolate. Industrial doses are fine. A lot more satisfying."

"And you can do it alone."

"There's this expectation that we should all be sexual beings, but the fact is, not all of us are, particularly." For some reason, as I am saying this, I am imagining the physicist's erect penis.

"That's me. Depressed testosterone. I think basically Melina . . ."

"Castrated you? Cliché. But no doubt true. Have you found a substitute passion?"

"I worship increasingly at the shrine of food," he confesses as his dessert arrives, a confection of peaches, meringue, and sorbet.

"Since this," I say, indicating the chair, "sex isn't high on my agenda either."

"You don't miss it?"

"It's been so long I've practically forgotten," I lie. "But the men, they mind a lot."

"I bet they do!" He says gallantly, deliberately misunderstanding, and I laugh again.

"The guys at rehab, they were all obsessed with having sex again. Could they do it, could they give a woman pleasure, how soon could they try Viagra?"

"And the women? How was it for you?"

"There weren't many of us, compared to the men. Men throw

themselves around more, apparently. Congenital recklessness. So anyway, there were only two of us. The thing we wanted most had nothing to do with sex."

"I guess you'd want to stand up? Be your real height again, look people in the eye?"

I take in his slightly anxious brow, his thick, rust-colored hair, his deep-set brown eyes with the green fleck in the left one, and feel immensely touched that he has bothered to imagine. I am not going to put him right. The fact is, not being able to stand up is not the worst thing. Not by a long, long way.

We have reached the coffee stage when the manager, Harry, comes up to me.

"You have a possibly unwelcome visitor. She says she'd like a moment of your time." Discreetly, he nods in the direction of the door. "She seems a bit off. If you don't know her, I don't mind asking her to leave."

Disheveled and defiant, she stands with her hands buried deep inside the pockets of a grubby beige jacket. The red-haired woman.

My guts tilt.

"Who is it?" asks the physicist, looking across.

"My stalker," I say. "Just joking." Then nod reassuringly at Harry. "Yes, let's do it. But take her jacket off her." I'm not taking any chances. As Harry heads over to the woman, I take a big gulp of wine.

"Gabrielle, I don't know what's going on, but is this a good idea?" asks the physicist.

"It's—inevitable. I'm glad it's happened in a public place. It'll be interesting. You'll see." I have taught myself a long time ago not to say no to certain things just because they scare me, so in reality it's an easy decision. But when I reassure him, I sound calmer than I feel.

She shuffles up and I see she's younger than I'd thought. Early forties. She doesn't look threatening: just lonely and deranged. Spotting the picture of the skydiver, still perched against the cruet set, she points. "Bethany drew that."

Immediately, things fall into place. Of course. Who else could she be?

"Yes," I say. "Two weeks ago. Frazer Melville, this is Joy McConey, my predecessor at Oxsmith. She's referring to the female patient I've been calling Child B."

The physicist is clearly unsettled by the turn our evening has taken, but he adjusts quickly: after shaking Joy's hand, he pulls up a chair for her. Waving away the waiter's offer of a glass of mineral water, Joy McConey slides into the chair, leans her arms forward on the table, and begins speaking urgently, her eyes flitting this way and that.

"I can't stay long, he'll come for me. My husband," she explains hastily. "He won't want me talking to you. But you have to listen. Bethany Krall's much more dangerous than you think."

It's an odd assumption, that I find Bethany dangerous. "I'm listening. Tell me what you have to say."

Frazer Melville is looking anxious and a bit resentful.

"You know the reason Bethany gets things right, Gabrielle?" her voice is light, strained, almost girlish. "Can I call you Gabrielle, is that OK, you won't feel it's an intrusion?" Her pale freckled face, tinged yellow by the flickering candlelight, veers at me asymmetrically. There has at some point been an attempt to apply mascara: the area below one eye is smudged with it. "I mean, I know what it must look like, I know you saw I was following you. But I had to warn you about Bethany."

"So *does* Bethany get things right?" I ask, cocking an eyebrow at Frazer Melville. He rearranges his teaspoon.

"Yes. You'll see. I started paying attention after the cyclone that hit Osaka six months ago. She talked about it after her ECT, and then it happened. And then more things did." The physicist is looking at Joy McConey intently. "The Nepal earthquake. Now this hurricane, the fall of Christ—she predicted it, didn't she? I mean, this drawing . . ." She points at it.

"So she claims."

"Well, believe me, that's part of it." I can sense the physicist getting agitated. I shoot him a look that I hope conveys, *Calm down. Therapists have breakdowns too. More than you'd think. Fact.*

"I didn't see your notes on Bethany. But I'd be very interested to hear what you wrote in them."

"She feels things. Blood and minerals. The way things flow." Frazer Melville stiffens. I can see now that Joy is trembling, as though she has just stepped in from a night of snow. "I told Sheldon-Gray and he wouldn't listen. No one would. But her father, Leonard Krall. He knows what she's capable of. I tried to warn people and so

Sheldon-Gray got rid of me. And if you're not careful, they'll do the same to you. Ask Leonard. Ask him what *he* thinks. Ask him why he won't visit his own daughter. She'll try to get you to help her escape. And if you don't, she'll do what she did to me."

"Excuse me," interrupts a man's voice. Then, "Joy." He approaches quickly, and I recognize him as the blond, balding man she argued with in the swimming pool car park. He looks firm and angry. But there's shame in there too. Humiliation. His wife has gone nuts, in public. And he's picking up the pieces. I wonder how often he has done this. "Let's get you home to the kids now, Joy," he says, grabbing her hand and tugging. He is clearly at the end of his tether, beyond embarrassment. "Look, I'm so sorry," he says, addressing me. "I've been trying to prevent this, believe me. Joy's not herself at the moment." She looks at him with contempt.

"My husband," she says with bitterness, "is a great believer in women keeping their mouths shut."

"It's OK," I tell the man. "I'm interested. Please—Joy can stay if she wants. I'd like to hear what she has to say. Joy? What do you think Bethany did to you?"

But he is already steering her off. In the doorway, Joy turns.

"Can't you see what she's doing, Gabrielle?" she calls across the room. "She's not just predicting things! She's making them happen!"

The next morning the physicist arrives at Oxsmith wearing a frayed linen jacket and a tie that doesn't match. He's bearing a large square box wrapped in plain brown paper and strapped with duct tape, which he now plonks on my lap unceremoniously and without explanation.

"Sure, just use me as a shopping trolley," I say, smiling. "I'll spit a coin back at you when you're done. But you'll have to push me because I can't see zilch."

He glances around the reception area nervously as I log him in. It's the first time, he tells me, he's been inside any kind of secure hospital. I can tell he's excited at the prospect of meeting Bethany—but he's wary too.

"It's more hospital than prison, right?"

"Most days," I tell him. "But it can flip the other way."

Bethany is waiting in the interview room, chatting to a female nurse with multiple piercings. When the physicist offers her a handshake, Bethany shoots me a glance of ironic despair: haven't I warned him she only does rude? I look away. I am not helping her out. Finally, flummoxed by the insistence of Frazer Melville's huge, proffered hand, she sighs, grasps it, and shakes it up and down three times—formally, like a mechanized puppet. Duty done.

"Frazer Melville is a scientist from the university," I tell her.

"Uh-huh. I'm honored." She certainly does not intend to sound it.

"Me too," he says, lifting the box from my lap. "So much so that I brought this gift for you."

"It's not my birthday," she says gracelessly, eyeing him sideways, full of mistrust. But I can see curiosity fighting its way through the jaded facade.

He says, "In Japan, it's traditional to bring a present when you visit someone's house or apartment for the first time. I think it's very civilized, so I'm trying to get it to catch on here."

She snorts. "Well, welcome to my charming high-security home. As well as the tasteful color choices, may I point out the bull dyke nurse here, and the bars on the windows, and the total lack of any view of the outside world, and"—she is unpacking the box as she speaks. But when she glimpses what it contains, she stops dead and opens her mouth in an O of shock. She has lifted out a large globe made of light translucent plastic. She places it on the desk. I can see a struggle going on inside her. I know that her instinct is to articulate something positive—perhaps even blurt a thank you. But she can't allow herself. I see her quelling it. Expressing a positive emotion would be against her principles.

"There's a bulb inside," says Frazer Melville, plugging the cord into the socket. The colors light up like the stained glass in a church, but they're more subtle, more mesmerizing and otherworldly. Bethany, still silent, gives the sphere a small push and we watch it spin a slow, elegant rotation. The surfaces of the land masses, corrugated with contours, are tinted brown and shades of green, while the lakes shine a luminous turquoise. The oceans slide from one vivid blue to another according to depth. There are none of the usual demarcations of nations or cities: the only markings that relate in any way to the existence of humans are the Suez and Panama canals and a thin, discreet tracery of lines indicating latitude, longitude, and the Tropics. It's pure geography: an unpeopled Earth.

"If this is some kind of sick joke—" Bethany begins, and then stops. For the first time her vulnerability is not hidden, and I can see its rawness.

"I do jokes," says the physicist jovially. "But it's been a while since I did any sick ones. It's yours to keep."

How often I've returned to that moment. Or more precisely, to the tentative smile that creeps across Bethany's face as she presses her hands to the sphere, her long, thin fingers, nails bitten to the quick, crawling across it like a blind person's. I'm reminded of a vet I once saw, his eyes closed, his head pressed to the flank of a sick horse, prodding with his fingers and listening.

"I'll come and fetch you in twenty minutes and then we'll go over to the art studio," I tell them. Because I still can't bring myself to say "Creativity Workshop." Especially in front of a man who—

A man who.

When I return, the globe is spinning slowly and they are both gazing at it thoughtfully. Lola, the nurse, has been standing near the door; she sends me a look that conveys an unfathomable mix of concern, alarm, and pity and jerks her head in the physicist's direction.

"Everything OK?" I ask. But it's clear from his face that something has gone wrong.

"Cool," says Bethany. She looks sly—perhaps even ashamed. He says nothing and suddenly I'm aware of his freckles. They are standing out like sprinkles of brown sugar because the skin beneath them has paled. When I make a questioning face, he waves his hand dismissively. Lola again tries to communicate something but I can't interpret her gesture. Bethany, on the other hand, is fired up, in the dangerous no-man's-land where energetic becomes manic.

"Bethany's located the site of a forthcoming volcano, as well as an earthquake in Istanbul," says the physicist finally, giving a forced smile. But I sense this is not what he's upset about. What has she said to him?

"A volcano?"

"I told you about it, Wheels," says Bethany eagerly. The physicist looks shocked at my nickname and glances at me questioningly, but I shake my head: let it go. "But I didn't know the name of the island before."

"I identified it as Samoa," says the physicist, stopping the globe and indicating a dot in the ultramarine of the Pacific.

"October 4," says Bethany. "It's in my book. But now I can write down the name."

We transfer to the art studio, with Lola accompanying us. As Frazer Melville inspects Bethany's drawings, which I have pinned to the walls, he seems to recover slightly, making various "uh-huh" and "I'm impressed" and "what's this then" noises, while Bethany paces around the room like a caged creature, picking things up—a clay pot, a handful of brushes, a stub of eraser—and fiddling with them before plonking them down again. Above us, like a striped cocoon, hangs the hot air balloon that Mesut Farouk has now nearly completed.

"Are you familiar with van Gogh at all, Bethany?" blurts the physicist, after a long silence.

"Sure. The sunflowers, everyone knows them. Sold to the Japanese for, like, squillions. Went nuts and sliced off his ear, right? This place'd be home from home."

"I have some art books," I say, pointing at a shelf I can't reach.

Frazer Melville pulls down the relevant book and flips through to van Gogh. Irises. Women bent double picking up cut corn. *Self-Portrait with Bandaged Ear.* "There are three in particular I'm looking for," he murmurs, then stops and points. "That's one of them." *Starry Night*: a hallucinogenic nightscape dotted with luminous orbs of light, each with its own extravagant aura. Instantly, you can see why he has chosen it—not for the huge white-hot stars themselves or the cluster of cypress trees in the foreground or the Provençal landscape below but for the wild churns of cloud between. It's as though an entire skyful of vapor has been shoved in a giant washing machine.

"See what I mean?" The similarity with Bethany's storm arabesques is striking. I feel unobservant for not having noticed it before. "Van Gogh liked turbulence too," says the physicist, eyeing Bethany.

"Yeah, well. Great minds think alike," she says dismissively. There is still something odd about her—a guilt, an uneasiness.

"He captured it in an almost scientific way, without even realizing it. People think of turbulence as being random but in fact it obeys very particular rules, which can be applied to liquids and gases." I wonder what he's getting at. He seems to be expecting Bethany to make a comment—to add to what he has said or know something about it, but she doesn't.

"Can I take these?" he asks. "I'd like to make copies."

"Sure," Bethany says. She's trying to sound blasé but the enthusiasm with which she tears the first one off the wall and shoves it at him tells another story. "Can you sell them to the Japanese?"

His smile is tight and it fades fast. It's clear she has unnerved him in a way I have yet to fathom. And now he's in a hurry to leave. I'm ready to go too. It's nearly three and I have a session with a new kid who arrived yesterday, an arsonist fresh from police custody. Taking his leave of Bethany with another awkward handshake, Frazer Melville says he would like her to do some more drawings for him. Of anything she likes, anything at all.

"Gabrielle showed me your sketch of Christ the Redeemer falling in Rio," he says, hesitantly. "I was impressed by it. Were you aware, when you drew it, what it was?"

She shrugs. "I can't remember. I see lots of stuff, I don't always know what it means."

"I remember you mentioned the fall of Christ," I tell her.

"Whatever," she says, dismissively.

I look from Bethany to the physicist and back again. There's something awry.

"She shouldn't call you Wheels," says Frazer Melville firmly as I am signing him out at Reception. "Why do you let her?"

"Because where Bethany's concerned, verbal abuse is the least of my worries, and frankly, it beats Spaz. Which is what a lot of the others call me. Now let me ask you a question. What was it that she said to you?"

"When?"

"When I left you alone. She said something that got to you."

"No," he says, pretending to look puzzled. "Apart the earthquake and this volcano in Samoa, she didn't say anything specific."

I don't call him on it. But I note, for future reference, that the physicist is an appalling liar.

I am in the art studio with Newton, a schizophrenic sixteen-year-old with gender identity issues. He likes art. For the past hour he has been working in clay, producing squat crocodilian figures with gaping jaws and sharp teeth. Like most of the other kids, he has a history of violence. His entry ticket to Oxsmith last month was his confession to the sexual torture of his two young cousins. He's on a wide panoply of drugs, some of which cause his hands to shake. Pale faced, he dyes his hair white blond and wears badly-applied makeup—today, a gash of red lipstick. Giant fluffy slippers engulf his feet, and he sweats monstrously, malodorously, and with what almost seems like gusto. It's ten in the morning, and Newton is idly spinning Bethany's globe.

"You get the fuck away from that." I haven't been expecting her to come in. Rafik is escorting her, and it's clear from the glow on her face that she's recently received a fresh surge of electricity to the brain.

"Show us your cunt first, girl," he says conversationally. In the youth culture of Oxsmith Secure Adolescent Psychiatric Hospital, it's a mundane enough demand. But Newton's too new here to know about Bethany. No one's warned him that tiny does not mean harmless. Casually, Newton dips his hand in a pot of milky liquid clay and pulls it out, dripping. "Nice and wet," he murmurs. If you could stop time, could you stop disasters, or would terrible things happen anyway, in a parallel world that had no respect for your mental flow charts? "Go on, babes, show us your gash." He holds up his hand and the pale slurry slides down and drips to the floor. "Then I'll stick this up you. Give you a good fist fuck."

Rafik and I exchange a look—a look of agreement that one of them has to go. I silently vote for Bethany. The art studio isn't big enough for her and anyone else. When Newton smiles, the lipstick smears his teeth so he looks like a carnivore after an orgy of raw meat. Before I can intervene, he has slapped Bethany's globe with his clay-whitened hand, smearing it with a wet trail that loops around it like a filthy halo, smudging the equator.

Then: "Show us your cunt. Go on. Let's see what you got, girl."

And now it's escalating. "Get the fuck off it," Bethany says. Her voice has become flat and expressionless and for that reason I'm alarmed.

"Show us your cunt. Then come and suck my big black dick." Newton is enjoying himself.

"Right, Newton," I cut in sharply, motioning to Rafik to move closer. "Step back from the table now, please." I say. "Step right back."

"She means it," says Rafik, bracing his torso menacingly. If you're not brutalized and fundamentally darkened before you come to a place like this, you surely are by the time you leave. No matter what your role.

Newton laughs and shakes his head as though this is the funniest thing he's heard in a long time, then thwacks the globe with the flat of his hand. The ball spins at increasing speed, its colors whirring into one another. Another swipe, harder again, and it teeters drunkenly.

Bethany moves so fast I miss it.

With a deep animal shriek, she has catapulted herself at Newton, grabbing him by the hair and wrenching him off the now toppling globe. It crashes to the floor with an inevitability that's almost hilarious, cartoonlike. It bounces once without breaking, then lands a second time with a bright smash, busting into a skitter of shards. Still shrieking, Bethany begins pummeling Newton with her fists. The giant slippers go flying. Rafik flings himself down and tries to wrestle the two kids apart. Quickly, I pull the cap off my alarm and reach for the spray can under my seat. But events have overtaken me. With a hefty reactive kick, Newton has dislodged the central work top from its trestle, and a tray of half-finished clay figures crashes to the floor, along with a pot of brushes in white spirit. Bethany, Newton, and Rafik are now thrashing around in clay and chemicals and broken plastic. Kicked a second time by Newton's flailing foot, the work top gives up the fight with gravity and tips heavily toward me. I grab the side but it's a bad move: its weight forces my chair onto one wheel so that I am half trapped beneath it, balanced uneasily and askew, while the other wheel spins in thin air. I'm aware of the door bursting open and six male nurses rushing in to overpower Bethany. Trying to break my inevitable fall, I push hard at the tabletop—only to collapse with it, sideways, cracking the side of my head on the floor as I'm thrown right out of the chair.

And then blackness.

When I come to moments later I am still in the art studio and there's blood everywhere. A wide smear leads to Newton, who has rolled over to the side of the room. He's screaming and clutching his groin, which is blossoming with a red stain of blood. Rafik has Bethany pinned to the floor in an armlock. Through half-closed eyes, I watch her get stabbed in the buttock with a syringe. Our therapy session is over. On balance, I would not rate it a success.

The next morning, having been kept in St. Swithin's hospital overnight for supervision, I am taken home in an ambulance. I am lucky not to have been badly injured. There's a wound on the back of my head and another on my thigh, which I can't feel and must therefore take particular care of. Bethany is in isolation. Her hand was cut by the plastic she used to stab Newton with, but the injury was superficial and treated on the spot. Newton was less fortunate. He's still at St. Swithin's, on the operating table, having a plastic shard removed from his scrotum. He will probably lose his right testicle.

I wonder how the loss of Bethany's globe has affected her. How she'll manage on twenty-four-hour assessment for the next two days. The part of me that's still professional cares. But the woman who has just come back from hospital with a head injury that required the nurses to shave ten square centimeters of hair off her scalp wants her to stay locked up in solitary confinement for all eternity. And while they're at it, they can throw away the key. Sometimes it's OK to hate crazy people.

Frazer Melville arrives to cook us dinner. There were delicate telephone negotiations concerning this, at the end of which it was agreed that if I set the table and promise to wear "a killer frock," he would do the rest. After I have told him the story of the fight and the fate of his short-lived gift and my redefinition of the expression *bad hair day,* we agree that the fact Bethany is being kept in isolation until further notice is advantageous. Her lack of access to television or the Internet—not that I've had the impression she is a fan—is a good way of ensuring she doesn't surf for clues or tune in to the weather channel, if that's what she has been doing. Which can't be ruled out. There is also tacit agreement that, having discussed her by phone, we will banish her as a topic of conversation for the rest of the evening. I hope we can stick to it.

Are there any sweeter pleasures in life than seeing a man cooking enticing, unusual food in your kitchen, and enjoying himself so much that he says "oh yes!" and "magnificent" as he chops carrots and grates nutmeg and squeezes lemon juice? If there are, I don't know of them.

"I do envy men their colossal levels of self-belief," I say, watching the physicist at work. For some reason, the killer frock I have chosen (olive green linen, with cream flecks) has a very low neckline and I have taken special care with my makeup. I have even, rather ridiculously, put on a pair of green high heels that I bought in the world of Before. They match my dress so perfectly they could have been designed especially for it. When I left rehab they told me always to wear shoes one size too large to prevent my feet from getting pressure sores, but when the time came to put the green shoes in the box for the charity shop along with all the others, vanity triumphed over reason. So here I sit in my green dress with matching shoes, with my hair arranged to cover the bald patch, hoping it's all worth it but secretly fearing I look like a blow-up sex toy.

"The self-belief is well deserved in my case," he says breezily. "Your taste buds are in for a culinary extravaganza. Those wanky Michelin star chefs in London can eat their hearts out. Here, have a glass of wine. So. Has Bethany sliced off her ear yet? Actually, don't answer that."

While the physicist dices and mixes and tastes, I show him some of my drawings and paintings, my collection of art books, and my thunder egg.

"It's handed down the generations," I say, passing it to him. "Usually at weddings. Very symbolic. The story is that one day it'll hatch."

"A nice specimen," he says, wiping his hands on his apron and examining it. "And it'll crack open one day, of its own accord, you claim?"

"And a dinosaur will emerge. Or a sea monster, according to some versions." He laughs and snips off a stalk from the chive pot and pops the end in his mouth, then puts a strand in mine. We chew on them like two cows considering the merits of a certain type of pasture as he chops the rest with a chef's expertise. "It's a kind of fertility symbol, I guess."

"And are you supposed to—incubate this thing? Sit on it like a hen?"

"Well, if anyone's adapted for that, it's me."

"And if it doesn't hatch in your lifetime?" he asks, a smile playing. "As I am sorry to tell you, I suspect it may not?"

"Well, I'd have to pass it on, I suppose. I could adopt an orphan."

"How about Bethany? Then you and I could get married and we'd be a family."

He doesn't realize what he has said. I draw in my breath, then quickly let out a laugh. "A turbulence expert, a psychotic murderess, and the owner of a magic egg. Sounds like a winning threesome."

"You're a shrink—you could keep us on track." I reach across to slap his backside, an intimacy that gives me a certain thrill. "And I would promise to never, ever patronize you," he adds, patting me condescendingly on the head.

Although I am no cook, I happen to love food. The first course consists of scallops with an artichoke puree and crumbled Italian blood sausage, which I declare to be "mind blowing" because I have never tasted anything quite like it before, even in unusual dreams. Next comes venison with a cranberry and blue cheese sauce and a potato gratin.

"You're a dangerous man and you might well end up killing me," I tell him.

"You have a strange way with compliments. But save room for my pièce de résistance. Three kinds of chocolate. A chocolate-stuffed chocolate blob known as a 'torte' with chocolate sauce and a side serving of chocolate mousse. Garnished with a sprig of mint, so if you decide you're dieting you can eat the foliage and I'll scoff the rest."

Afterwards, replete, we go onto my little terrace, where the air smells of honeysuckle and night stock, and we watch the ridiculously huge sinking orb of the sun, and the physicist talks about his mother, who died two months ago, in Glasgow, of pancreatic cancer. He didn't blame her for drinking herself stupid: the morphine wasn't doing its job properly. He both misses her and feels relief. "Bodies," he concludes. "Great when they work, and terrible when they don't." He reddens. "Oh fuck. What a stupid gaffe."

"It's not a gaffe. I agree with you, as a matter of fact. I won't start telling you I wouldn't have it any other way. It basically sucks."

He shifts in the wicker chair. It's too small for him. If he lived with me, I'd buy him a grandiose armchair that he could spread out in. Something physicist sized. Expensive and expansive. A chair he could lean back in and hold forth from, Scottishly.

"What was life like, before?" he asks. He isn't looking at me, and his big, clumsy freckled hands seem to be comforting each other.

"Since you're being tolerant of my, er, emotional illiteracy, is that what you people call it?"

When our eyes meet, I realize he really does need to know. I've thought about this. How to tell him. But Bethany is needling at me. What does she know about me, or think that she knows? What did she tell him that afternoon at Oxsmith?

"There's a photo album on the lower shelf in the living room. Fetch it and I'll show you."

There are pictures of my parents and of Pierre and his wife and the twins as babies, and then older, and then Dad in the nursing home with one of the carers, and some others of me and Alex. I can see the physicist struggling with what to say when he sees me in the world of Before. I was a woman then. Happy and upright and smiling, with a man's arms around me.

"Well, you were never tall," he comments. I smile. "Who's the lucky guy?"

"Oh, that's all over," I say, trying to sound dismissive. But I fail.

"Were you married?"

Through a gap in the trellis, I see an Ikea delivery van lumbering past. I imagine a child's bunk bed and the diagram of how to assemble it with an Allen key. Someone's asking for trouble. "I wasn't. But he was." A white van. Then a motorcycle. And then a Volkswagen Passat. "Alex had a Saab. They're supposed to be very safe. Dark blue. There was a child seat in the back, with a little built-in rattle gizmo. He had two kids. If you were kissing in the car and you switched on the CD player by accident, out came 'The Wheels of the Bus Go Round and Round.'"

"Oh."

"He'd take off his wedding ring when we were in bed. Very respectful. But she was still there. There was this band where the skin was paler."

You get so used to editing out the painful stuff. There are still things I'm not telling the physicist, but this is enough for now. How can I tell him what I'm not even telling myself? He's looking at me intently, as though he's aware I am leaving out something crucial. As though Bethany has told him.

Told him what?

Alex wasn't my usual type at all, I say quickly, determined not to let my paranoia take charge. He was an entrepreneur, with a chain of clothes shops all over the country. We met in the casino he part owned. He had a passion for poker. My friend Lily dragged me there because she was in between marriages and there was a croupier she fancied. Well. One thing led to another. We all make mistakes. You can't make an omelette, et cetera.

"Only at the end of it all, there was no omelette," I finish lamely, appalled at my own cliché. Broken eggs, empty shells, messes on floors: why can't I just tell the plain truth? Because I can't. I know the next question, the one that usually goes unasked. To get this excruciating stage over with, I answer it anyway.

"He was driving. The weather was terrible. I have no memory of how it happened. But we were arguing at the time." This is a mixture of lies and truth, fact and wishful thinking. I have rewritten this story in my head a thousand times. "We wanted a life together but he just couldn't—bring himself to do what was needed." *He had a problem with commitment.* How I despise that phrase women use to explain why men won't marry them. The phrase that says, *It's not me, it's him.* Another phrase from women's magazines: *He wanted to have his cake and eat it.*

"I loved him. But inevitably, given the situation, I also hated him."

I don't tell him the rest. About the impossibility of it all, and about why I was screaming at Alex when he rounded the corner and why I was still screaming at him—shamefully, uncontrollably, like a woman possessed—when he misjudged the turn. About the slow and quiet way he died.

I don't tell him because I don't tell myself. I've been through enough.

"I used to think about it the whole time." Truth.

"And now?"

"I've cut it down to once a week." Lie. I think about him every day. Every single fucking day.

"Did it make you feel, well, bitter? I mean, not just losing him but losing . . . er . . . having your injuries?" The physicist is looking at me strangely, as though he knows what I'm not saying. How can I give utterance to the thing I can't think about, and can't face, and never will? How can I ever tell anyone?

Finally, to distract us both, I talk about the aftermath of the accident. About my lost month in a coma and how, when I emerged from it into something that passed for consciousness, I discovered myself on an angled bed that they adjusted three times a day like a cooking spit. The morphine prompted extraordinary hallucinatory dreams. I was a mountaineer scaling a white cliff a kilometer high, attached by a thicket of pulleys and ropes. I was the commander of a tiny high-speed submarine, zooming beneath the quilt of the sea, negotiating abysses and sharks and whirlpools and giant octopi like a manic conquistador. Sometimes, surreally, I'd see people in hospital gowns standing upright and gliding about the ward like ghosts. Later I learned these were other patients in stand-up wheelchairs. The drugs ensured that most explanations slid past me. "As soon as you're ready for some physio, we'll put you on a tilt table to help your heart work harder," they said one day. Medical scaffolding, to coax my broken body into mustering muscular life. Could my heart really work any harder? Apparently yes, it would have to, because one day a destroyed woman came to see me. She stood there for a long time. She didn't say a word. I knew who she was. I'd seen photos. She scrutinized me as if I were a pitiful and disgusting and shameful specimen and then she turned and walked away. She could have come and killed me but she didn't. She could see there was no need. That leaving me like this was crueler because I was my own punishment. She was a sociologist, so perhaps she could name the category I'd fit into as a woman with no man, no baby, no feeling below the waist, and no imaginable future. I never saw her again. The morphine made it unreal, like a dream with no beginning or end. But a routine began to emerge. I forgot and remembered things selectively. You can take only so much pain. Every day, three times a day for six weeks, I was pitched at a new angle, to relieve the pressure on my shattered spine and pelvis.

"It's funny, but I was in that spinal injuries unit for at least ten days before I realized I wasn't alone. I thought the other voices I heard were in my head. It turned out there were ten of us. Nine other broken people all sandwiched on their beds at different angles. Or strapped into standing frames. I was the only woman."

The others were young, mostly: three motorcycle accident victims, a builder who had fallen off a ladder, a man who had jumped off the fourth floor of a block of flats in a suicide attempt. A boy—he said he was just sixteen—had the strangest voice: a rasping noise, with each breath emerging heavily, as though at great cost. Evidently he was the worst off of all of us. He was paralyzed from the neck down and on a ventilator. The wheezing that accompanied his speech came from the machine.

"People came and went. The suicide died one night, so at least his wish came true."

We were all very drugged, in the wake of our accidents, so there wasn't a great deal of talking. Instead, there was a lot of dreaming. "I traveled endlessly on that bed, in my head, just taking in what had happened to Alex. I traveled to the moon. I traveled beyond it. In an odd way, it was liberating, being just a brain suspended in space. There was no panic at that stage, because no one had told me I'd never walk again."

"They wanted to spare you?"

"No, it wasn't that. It was because at that point nobody knew. I was in spinal shock. The body just closes down. It can be months before you know what you're stuck with. I was drugged, and I was calm. It was there that I first learned how to disappear into myself. How to squash and stretch time."

He looks fascinated, puzzled, a little excited. Horrified, too, by the image of hell I have sketched. I wonder how much he's understanding. Can anyone who hasn't experienced this imagine what it's like, to watch whole hours spin by in seconds or feel seconds loop into eternity? To go on long, elaborate voyages of the imagination in which you can become whole new people? To realize that there's nothing you can't do, nobody you can't be, if you allow your mind to float? I tell the physicist that it was toward the end of that time that I learned the worst of what had happened to me, and what it meant for my future. I do not tell him that it was then, in those weeks, that I made the decision to eradicate Alex and all that went with him—the wife, the kids, their complex family grief—from my mind. There are limits to human endurance. Something opened up inside me, a new skill that unfurled like a flower, there on that torture bed. I relived my whole life, sometimes in the most elaborate detail, but I also imagined lives that had gone and lives that might have been.

The physicist's look is so unprocessed I can't take it, because other people's pity is unbearable. So is sympathy. And so is moral disapproval. I look away.

I have not told him that most of all, on those long inner journeys, I imagined a boy called Max with blue eyes and brown hair. I saw him first as a baby and then growing up. When he was tiny I gave him crayons to draw with and clay to mush, then later I showed him the work of painters and sculptors, taught him to fry eggs, watched him battling with scuba gear, listened to the story of how he fell in love.

The physicist has taken my hand. He is stroking it. He is looking into my eyes so intently that I have to babble.

"Afterwards, right from the start," I go on quickly, "I wanted two things. I wanted to work again, as soon as possible. And I wanted to walk." He nods again and turns his face away because I suspect there are tears, which he has correctly guessed I would not wish to see, because they'd make me think less of him and perhaps hate him, too, to the point of violence.

"Who wouldn't?" he mutters. He had better be very careful here. Does he realize that if he feels sorry for me, I will get out my thunder egg and smash his head in with it?

"At which point the very nice and well-meaning therapist invited me to 'untangle' what was 'realistic' and what wasn't," I go on, determined to get this over with. I take another swoosh of wine. "Untangle, unravel, unpack, deconstruct. You get to hate the jargon, when you're not the one who's using it. Actually you hate it when you are too. She got me filling in the kind of psychological questionnaires I used to design, right at the beginning of my career."

"Humiliating?" he asks. He's blinking. They told us in rehab to watch out for people who want to help you, who make a beeline for you because you are needy, who want to be your savior. Cripple pervs. If that's what this is about, he can leave.

"It was humiliating to begin with. But then interesting. Denial of reality can be helpful. Something blind and ungracious and determined took over. I made it take over. I realized that if I could work myself into a kind of righteous rage, almost a political rage, I could do things. I became evangelical about life going on as normal. I was going to start again, faster than anyone else, better than anyone else, and what's more, in a new place. I didn't want to be judged against what I was before. I wanted to be among strangers who'd never known me as someone who could walk. I wanted to present this as a fait accompli. I wanted to say, here I am, and this is what I am, so fuck you."

The physicist smiles. "I can see that. And that's one of the reasons—" He stops. "You're cleverer than I am, Gabrielle. And you have a mean streak. So listen. You're not to ridicule me and make me feel like a twat."

"Just please don't tell me you admire me for my courage."

"I wasn't going to," he says, standing up, and moving his chair away from me. "Put your arms round my neck," he says, leaning down. I reach up to him. The physicist's chest is broad, as warm as bread from the oven. I can feel the thump of his heart. Which means he can feel mine too. "Hold on tight." He's clasping my whole torso close to his. "I was going to say," he says, lifting me bodily out of the chair and settling me against him with my knees over the crook of his arm. He is big and I am small but I'm still worried that I must feel like a sack of potatoes though he bears my weight as if it's nothing. Then his face is next to mine and he's rocking us both. We stay like that for a while, swaying together in the warm night air. The sky has darkened and the moon is a pallid crescent. It's absurd. It's romantic. It's ridiculous. I love it and I want to die, but not in the way I usually want to die. "What I was going to say was, it's one of the reasons I keep wanting to do this."

"What, weight training?" Why can't I stop myself?

"Spoil it again and I'll drop you. Just shut up and listen because I'm being romantic here." Yes, I think. You are. And I can't handle it. It will kill me. It will kill my belief that I am no longer a woman. No, worse, it will revive the hope that I am, and then all that can happen is that it will be shredded. I close my eyes. "It's one of the reasons I keep wanting to hold you in my arms," says the physicist. "And then kiss you."

"Did you like that?" he says finally, as our lips part. It was spectacularly potent. I am like a recovering alcoholic going back on the booze. I'd forgotten what kissing was like, what kissing does to the rest of you. But my body—what's left of it—hadn't. Hasn't. Is now in a turmoil of wanting, and not knowing how to get, how to have.

"Frazer Melville." It's as though his name has been trapped inside me and his kiss has released it. He settles me on the sofa, still holding me close. "Frazer Melville, Frazer Melville, Frazer Melville." Like my Spanish mantra, it's similar to rolling a strange taste around on my tongue, a taste I could get addicted to. I want more. Of his name, of everything. Of him.

He pulls back to look at me. "Answer my question." He sounds proud but a little pinch of worry has appeared on the bridge of his nose. "Did you like it?"

When no human being of the opposite sex, public health professionals excepting, has touched you intimately in two years . . .

The feel of another body. The press of lips. It's too much for me. I am done for.

"Well," I say, trying to sound hard-boiled but failing. "The thing is, I'm supposed to have an insight into people's psyches. And an understanding of body language and the human impulse. It's the basic job description."

"Meaning?"

"That if you were giving out any signals, I missed them."

"But your lack of professional skills aside, my question was: did you like it?"

"No. I hated it," I say. I am aware of the muscles around my mouth. They are doing something they're not used to doing. It's not that I don't smile, I realize. It's that I don't normally smile this wide. It's the mad banana smile from my nephew's birthday card. No, I didn't pick up his signals. Not properly. But he picked up mine: the ones I only half knew I was giving. Oh, OK. The cleavage thing, the makeup, the perfume, the straight-out-of-hospital-into-green-stilettos—I know. But. "But just to be sure, why not do it again two or three more times," I say coolly, pulling a swatch of hair across my bald patch. "And I'll let you know my final decision."

In rehab, I read a manual about paralysis and sexuality with a good, self-explanatory title involving a mini-pun. *Sex Matters* recommends that you and your partner take things slowly. That when contemplating sex, you explain to him, if he doesn't know already, what that might involve. What can go wrong, what positions might be favored, what embarrassing accidents might occur. Screw that. Screw taking things slowly. Despite the bandaged wound on my thigh, and the fact I must be extra careful with it, and despite the bald patch on my head, I want to know what it's like. Now. With the physicist. With the physicist Frazer Melville. Whether he is ready for it or not.

"Kiss me again, Frazer Melville," I tell him. "And then take me to bed."

. . .

Later, as I fall asleep next to him, with the fan churning the hot night air across our skin, I know something important. I am still a woman whose body can experience physical delight. A woman who has missed, more than she ever admitted, the intimacy, tenderness, and intensity of sex. And if her lower section can't muster an orgasm, her nipples and brain most certainly can.

SIX

The trouble with the principle of "time out" is that one patient's personal hell is another's idea of a cushy number. Like any bottomless pit, Bethany Krall, freshly ensconced in the peer-free zone referred to as "seclusion," is enjoying the increased attention she is receiving. Therapist contact has been upped to five hours a day in the wake of her attack on Newton, and she is on "one-to-one": twenty-four-hour risk assessment with a nurse in continuous attendance who will be watching for self-harming behavior. We're on a rota basis. Her food is brought in on a tray. "Room service," she calls it: that, too, suits her current narcissistic mood. When she needs the toilet, she is escorted there by Lola or another female nurse, who keeps her in full view at all times. Lola has told me that Bethany makes the most of this and performs scatological running commentaries for the benefit of her audience. We discuss the damage she has inflicted but she is unrepentant. Instead, she is eager to know the gory details. In particular, which part of the globe the surgeon extracted from Newton's scrotum when removing his irretrievably damaged testicle.

"I'm betting it was Scandinavia. As in Norway, Finland, Sweden, and Denmark." If nothing else, it seems her knowledge of geography has expanded, thanks to the atlas she's brought in with her.

"Perhaps if you stay in solitary confinement long enough, you'll eventually get an education and become Bethany Krall, professor of earth sciences," I suggest. She laughs, a dirty, full-throated laugh that is too old for her, and the braces on her teeth flash in the light. Twinkle, twinkle. There has been a lot of gaiety from Bethany since she has been moved to a bare cell in McGrath Wing, where we now find ourselves, with Rafik in attendance. But none of it is of the balanced-member-of-the-community variety.

"I wonder if that episode reminded you of anything that happened two years ago, at home?"

She smiles patronizingly. "Wrong questions again, Wheels. You're one fuck of a slow learner. By the time you get what's going on, you and your spazmobile will be, like, ten meters underwater. Bibble babble, with bubbles. Hey, joke." Oh well, I think. So be it. Nothing can get me down today. I smile benignly at little Bethany Krall because I can afford to.

I am a woman who has had sex.

I could ask for more intensive sessions with Bethany in the wake of her attack on Newton. But resuming our previous arrangement would run *counter to protocol,* as the hospital's bureaucratese has it. Nor am I keen to risk further interrogation from Sheldon-Gray, after my recent debriefing with him, which took the form of questions fired at me from the rowing machine.

"How's Newton doing in hospital? Ungk. Are you sure you have the physical backup you need for this job? Gah. Has your confidence taken a battering in the wake of this? Ungk. Have you done your police statement? Do you need some time off, now that the thing's been paperworked?"

I struggled to answer him coherently and convincingly as he to and fro'd, shoveling his sweaty air from one side of the room to the other, as though it were a task he could later tick off the day's list: transport x molecules of gas from A to B. I stuck to my plan of keeping it short. The tiny digital clock on his exercise device showed me that our entire conversation lasted one minute, forty-eight seconds. At the end of which I showed him the drawing Bethany had made of the stick figure.

He raised his eyebrows. "Good work. Pursue it."

I told him I would and left.

. . .

"That stick figure you did in red crayon," I now ask Bethany. "Which I think was probably your mother. What were you thinking about when you drew it?"

"I don't do stick figures," she says sullenly. I take it out of my folder and show it to her. She squints, frowns, and shoves the drawing back at me with a stumped expression.

"Not mine. Someone else must have done it. Someone who can't draw for shit."

"I was with you. After you drew the fall of Christ, you did this."

"I don't draw like that. That's a kid's drawing."

"I wonder what the kid who drew it was thinking."

We look at each other a moment, and then she turns her face away.

It dawned on me, during the labyrinthine discussions I used to have with my psychoanalyst, that most women carry in their heads an idealized mother. A home-baking, perfect-gravy mother, a waiting-outside-the-school-gates mother, a mother with whom to share lip gloss and T-shirts, a mother to confide in or to laugh with over a TV sitcom. A counterweight to the mother you have in real life—the mother who, in Bethany's case, filled her so unassailably with the urge to kill that she reached for a Phillips screwdriver and made the rest history.

"You just don't get it," she mutters. "Look. This earthquake is right round the corner. It's hitting Istanbul the day after tomorrow. The pressure's building up in the fault line, I can feel it. I'm telling you. I was right about the hurricane. I was right about Jesus tumbling down the mountainside. What happens when you see I'm right about this too?"

"What would you like me to do, Bethany? If you were right?"

"It's just time someone believed me. Don't you get it?"

Our time is up. Rafik opens the door on my nod. Bethany is looking at me intently, as though measuring the angles of my face. Then, fast as a change of wind, her mood has shifted and she's laughing softly to herself.

"What's funny, Bethany?" I ask lightly, pleased that we are back on safer ground. "Can I share the joke?"

"Wow, Wheels," she laughs, delightedly. "*You're* the joke. Congratulations."

"On what?" I ask, uneasy.

She smiles to show the braces on her teeth. She says slowly, savoring it: "On getting laid." I roll an inch back. "Ha! *'A bundle of myrrh is my well-beloved unto me, he shall lie all night betwixt my breasts!'* "

"My private life is my business, Bethany." The words come out too sharply. She has caught me unawares and I have let it show.

"Not anymore." She grins. "Hey. *'My beloved is unto me as a cluster of camphire in the fields of En-gedi.'* He stuck it in you! Rejoice!"

Rafik turns away discreetly. Bidding them both a swift good-bye I roll speedily out.

Since half of my body withdrew from the game, I have learned to notice, relish, and even fetishize life's miniature but extreme delights. Like my Oriental lilies opening in a splash of ghost white petals and filling the flat with their alarming erotic pungency. Or my Bulgarian choral music drifting through from the next room, mingled with homelier elements: a metallic clatter, an air blast of burnt toast, and the muttered cursing of a physicist called Frazer Melville preparing, at my request, a pot of Lapsang souchong tea in an unfamiliar kitchen. It is Saturday, August 21, but I am determined not to let Bethany's catastrophe calendar—which predicts a massive earthquake tomorrow—spoil my day. So far I am succeeding. I am enjoying being myself and no one else. I may even have looked in the mirror and taken pleasure in my own reflection. Frazer Melville and I have been under my duvet for the best part of fourteen hours. We have been "experimenting." We are absurd. We are a woman in her thirties and a man in his forties. And we're behaving like two teenagers discovering sex for the first time. Frazer Melville and I probe, explore, and exchange information—shyly, boldly, teasingly. *What if I do this. That's good. Not there. But there, like this. No, can't feel a thing.* A lot of the focus is on my breasts. Hallelujah: I have landed myself a tit man. Last night, he cautiously entered me again. I felt nothing physically, not even a phantom tweak of something residual in my pelvis. But in my head it was quite another matter. In my head it was explosive. In our different but perhaps not-so-different ways, Frazer Melville and I, now breakfasted and back in bed, appear to be enjoying ourselves.

But it can't last. I can't let it.

I say, "We have to do something."

He sighs, shifts, perches his head on his elbow, looks at me hard, and takes a deep breath before he speaks.

"I agree."

"So if it hits tomorrow—"

"I contact scientist colleagues with the other predictions Bethany's made."

I am more relieved than I care to admit that he has been giving the idea consideration.

"Without mentioning her," I specify. "She can't be named."

"Of course. In any case, it would be scientific suicide."

"How will you go about it?"

He shrugs. "I tell a selected cross-section of scientists whom I know to be open-minded that some predictions have been made by a certain source. That they've proved accurate. That the earthquake's the latest example of this. That there are further predictions that will need testing. That I believe there's a scientific explanation that demands investigation. But more importantly, the regions concerned would benefit from being warned because lives are at stake."

It sounds simple. Too simple. But at least we have a plan.

We lie in bed until midday and then go see a genial, forgettable movie. He is not used to being so close to the screen, and I am not used to being kissed in my wheelchair during a film and attracting whistles from the people in the rows behind us. So it's a new experience for both of us. If either of us has an apprehension that this might be the last day that our world is happily balanced, we hide it well.

Sex is many things, but that night, for us, it is an urgent and elaborate distraction from the subject we are both determined to avoid, now that we've agreed on a strategy. Frazer Melville undresses me and makes me close my eyes. I must promise not to move a centimeter "or it will all go wrong." Intrigued I wait, rigid, smiling. There are noises. Then I feel him come close to me. I smell chocolate. Then he touches my left nipple, but not with his tongue. With something cool and heavy. He works slowly on whatever he is doing. I feel his concentration. Half guessing what he is up to, I focus on the electric pulse that spreads outward from my breasts across my shoulders and spine, along my arms, into the tips of my fingers, across the back of my neck.

"Now this one." He caresses my right nipple, the same cool pressure, and I feel the flesh swell. "Open your eyes."

He has painted my nipples with chocolate paste. Where did the paste, and indeed the idea, come from? They are huge and nearly black. They glisten. I laugh. "Well I knew you were fond of chocolate."

"Two of my favorite things both at once," he murmurs. His voice is thick. Frazer Melville's erect penis sticking out of his fly. I take it in my hand, feel its heft.

"I can't wait anymore," he says. "I'm starving." And then he's sucking my breasts and we are both getting smeared with melting chocolate. He has discovered a way of propping me up using pillows and cushions. Me naked except for the bandage on my leg, he fully clothed. I feel like a greedy queen being worshipped and serviced.

Looking into my eyes, Frazer Melville takes me and takes me and takes me. I can't feel a thing. But as he moves inside me he says my name over and over again. I gasp, utterly confounded. And I think: Perhaps I am still a woman after all. No, not perhaps. Yes, yes, I am. A woman who can make love, and drive a man—

He comes with the raucous, unashamed cry of a caveman.

I'm woken at one by rain slamming against the windows. Outside the trees sigh and creak. I settle my head on Frazer Melville's solid, smooth-skinned shoulder and think about what last night did to my soul. *Cuando te tengo a ti, vida, cuanto te quiero.* But then I remember the date and the ecstasy deflates. I reach out and switch on the radio, turning the sound down low. I get the BBC World Service, stalwart friend of the hardened insomniac. There's a documentary about dwarfism. I learn the word *achondroplasia.* The average height of an adult dwarf is 132 centimeters for men, 123 for women. Voices and more voices. The night ticks on, and Frazer Melville breathes gently beside me. Thunder and wind outside. I fall asleep briefly and reawaken to catch the end of an arts program. Everyone's speaking in the same reasonable tone. There's a discussion about new trends in Bollywood, with clips from classic and contemporary movies. There is nothing on the three o'clock news; relieved, I am just drifting back to sleep with a sports quiz on in the background, when there's a news flash.

I hoist myself up in bed. I try to do so gently, but my movement disturbs Frazer Melville, who sits up, his yawn as wide as a silent shout. I turn up the volume and we take in the news like two parallel shock absorbers. All through the five-minute broadcast, I feel oddly calm and in control. Something inside me refuses to shift. Perhaps I am in denial. I can still smell the chocolate on my skin.

When the news ends, Frazer Melville says, eloquently, "Oh no. Oh Christ. Oh fuck." Like him, I want to start up a litany of swearing, an antiprayer. Or fall asleep again, pretend it's a dream, start life again in the morning, properly, normally, and for real. But when you fall asleep a skeptic and wake to news that makes you a believer, the experience is as fundamental as having your whole skeleton replaced. You can't ignore it. I feed a match to the lamp by the bed, a Moroccan cage of metal that sends angular shafts of candlelight flickering around the room. Outside, the storm has died away and the rain has become sporadic, undecided whether to stay or go.

"Whoever we told, they'd never have believed us," I murmur. We have been lying here for some time. It is the only thought to cling to, under the circumstances. If I am being the rational one, what is Frazer Melville up to? His breathing is overcontrolled. Perhaps he is fighting something. Tears? A heart attack? Men do that. They die in women's beds from sex or shock. Or both.

"Remember—we had this discussion yesterday," I say, raising myself clumsily on one elbow to make eye contact with him and assess his mood. "We had it several times. It was lighthearted, maybe. But we had it. We agreed that if we rang the Turkish embassy and told them they needed to evacuate a city of fifteen million people by the twenty-second of this month because a kid in a maximum-security hospital had a vision—"

But I can't continue. My sudden burst of conviction, if that's what it was, has evaporated as quickly as it arrived. I sink back down on the pillow. Frazer Melville doesn't speak.

At half past three there's an update. Reports about the extent of the damage are confused, but the quake, whose epicenter is in the Sea of Marmara, just outside the city, measured 7.7 on the Richter scale. It struck at fourteen minutes to one local time and triggered a mini-tsunami that swept the south of the conurbation. First estimates say that about 40 percent of the city is affected. At least ten thousand buildings have been destroyed, among them the famous Blue Mosque. Skyscrapers and homes and office blocks and schools have collapsed. I imagine toy building blocks and a pall of cement dust. It's not yet dawn, so there's almost zero visibility and a high risk of aftershocks. First estimates say tens of thousands are likely to be dead or injured and trapped. How many doctors, over the next few days, will be asking those saved from the wreckage whether they're aware of any sensation below the waist? Or the neck?

I feel nothing. Then, just as I am beginning to wonder why I am not reacting, the top half of my body starts to sweat and then shake. Tonight it is a nightmare. But soon it will officially be day. And real.

Frazer Melville and I have not been acquainted long enough to fathom each other's behavior in a crisis, so when he turns his back on me I do not take it personally. He needs space to think. But I wonder nonetheless what is going through his mind. Does he resent me for wanting to pick his brains at the charity event at the hotel, for dragging him into this? Do I resent him for not knowing what to do now, for not comforting me with the reassurance that it's a coincidence, just like the hurricane? Together, we are alone. We cannot help each other, any more than we can help the people of Istanbul. Clumsily, I roll away from him and do battle with my thoughts.

At five he gets up silently and makes us both coffee. We barely speak. We drink it in bed, with the TV news on. Most of Istanbul is razed to the ground. At least three oil tankers have sunk. The Bosphorus is mayhem. On shore, women wail amid the rubble, men storm about with spades. A baby screams hysterically, without seeming to draw breath. A thick eiderdown of dust covers the devastated city. Fires have broken out because of gas leaks. The images are beyond terrible. We watch, transfixed. Frazer Melville barely blinks.

On one comfortingly diminished plane of logic, I am thinking: *Coincidences happen.* But another, more grandiose, legalistic counterthought runs: Frazer Melville and Gabrielle Fox, because they had knowledge they did not disseminate, are responsible for manslaughter on a massive scale and, at worst, are mass murderers by default. Their sins of omission have led to atrocity on the scale of any war crime.

We will go our separate ways. We are not a couple. We are two distinct and very different people on the verge of an abyss we could never have imagined. There's no rule book on how to behave in these circumstances. Frazer Melville leaves the house before me. Feeling foolish but defiant, I go online and donate a thousand pounds to

Merlin, a small but apparently highly effective disaster relief charity that my father became involved with when he retired. But although the indirect provision of tents and doctors and pharmaceuticals to Turkey's victims makes me feel better, it's brief. Within minutes of my logging off, the guilt has swamped me again.

At nine I leave for work as usual. Because I don't know what else to do.

The heat has become so ferocious that venturing outside is an ordeal, something one must gear up to, armed with drinking water, sunglasses, cream, headgear. Items that were once optional accessories are now survival kit. Out on the street, the sky bears down like a low ceiling that will collapse at any moment under the pressure of the sun. It's too hot for the gloves I normally use for the chair, so on the way to the car my hands slip on the wheels. By the time I get to Oxsmith, I'm ready to smash something, which is ironic, given that my morning is taken up by two sessions of Anger Management, in which I must try to pass on advice and wisdom that I am catastrophically failing to heed myself. While I have seventeen teenagers all breathing in rhythm and envisioning serene landscapes, positive energy, and blah blah, I am frantically plotting my next move. Which is a trip in the lift to my boss's office, because saying nothing about Bethany's prediction is no longer an option. I know Sheldon-Gray is going to take this badly, and already I am despising him for it.

No sweaty stuff today, no rowing machines, no towel rubbing, no *ungk* and *gah*. Dr. Sheldon-Gray is fully dressed, in a pink shirt and pink and gray tie. The smooth skin around his clipped goatee looks freshly exfoliated and moisturized. This level of care indicates he has meetings lined up. Real meetings, with real people. I do not count. I realize I have drunk too much coffee. I'm jittery with caffeine.

"So who's the latest problem?" demands my boss as soon as I appear in his line of vision. Since asking for Joy McConey's notes and leaving the charity event early, I have fallen out of favor. I am now officially an annoyance. "I'll take a bet on it's being our little autoasphyxiating Tourette's friend, whatshisname." He drums his fingers on the polished walnut of his desk.

"No. In fact, I wanted to talk about the Istanbul earthquake."

"Terrible tragedy. Appalling. Yes. Hassan Ehmet has family nearby. He's taking time off. No flights going there at the moment, but he's managed to get one to Athens that's leaving around now. He drove up to Gatwick first thing, called me from there." Dr. Ehmet, with his little *heh* and his bad haircut and his PhD thesis waiting at the printer's at Oxford University Press: how will he cope with turmoil on this scale?

"He plans to drive across," Sheldon-Gray is saying. "Frankly, I doubt we'll get him back. Turkey's going to need all the trauma counselors it can get. So we'll be stretched here again, I'm afraid. What's new, eh? Anyway, you wanted to say?"

"Bethany Krall." His face tightens and clouds over. But before he can protest, I get straight to the point. When I explain that Bethany Krall apparently made an accurate prediction about the quake—as lightly as I can, which is not very, because I am actually scared and angry and can't be bothered to hide it—he starts rocking in his chair. When I mention Hurricane Stella, another "prediction," Sheldon-Gray twitches his head like a cow shaking off flies. I realize that he respects me some 60 percent less for having raised the matter. Feels a 40 percent increase in contempt, even. I can't blame him. Most of me feels the same. When I offer to explain in more detail, he declines in a way that brooks no argument. For a psychiatrist used to hiding his emotions, he is unusually transparent. Elaborately adjusting his cuffs, he takes a deep breath.

"Gabrielle, I am shocked and disappointed and—yes, I'll say it—*appalled*. I had thought more highly of you. Look. You can be sure Bethany told Hassan all this nonsense too. The difference is, he's a scientist." But how *has* Dr. Ehmet reacted, I wonder. What does Sheldon-Gray know about it, if Hassan's on a plane? "History is repeating itself here, is it not?" the man in pink continues loudly. His voice has a politician's edge to it. There are times when you feel very alone in your body. This is one of those times. I would like to slide away and replace myself with a clone whose face doesn't redden. "Let me tell you something you should know about your predecessor. We talked before about her notes and why I removed them from the file. The fact is, they show that Joy McConey became disastrously involved in Bethany's fantasies. She ended up convinced that her predictions were coming true. I'm sorry to tell you I'm having déjà vu here. Joy McConey sat right where you are now and made claims about Bethany that clearly showed her to be unbalanced." I nod. "So perhaps you can understand that I am alarmed when you, too, begin to show signs of being *gullible*? Will you also be needing some *time out*?" He spits out the cliché like the hairball it is and nudges at his mouse pad.

"But the earthquake—she predicted it to the day. That's simply a fact. Hurricane Stella too."

"Gabrielle. Have you by any chance heard of the internationally renowned search engine Google?"

I guess it's another rhetorical question so I don't answer. I want to grab him by his pink tie and strangle him but he has somehow succeeded in knocking me back. "Let's just type in 'Istanbul earthquake predictions,' shall we, and then advance our search, *as the technology permits us,* to specify dates preceding the quake." He clicks ostentatiously. "And look what pops up. Aha. Aha. Yes, well. No surprises here, Gabrielle, or at least not to me. Just a quick glance at this screenful of information here is enough to tell me that young Bethany Krall may not be alone in having, er, *foreseen* this tragedy."

I look. There are certainly plenty of listings. "An amateur geologist from Whitstable," murmurs Sheldon-Gray, now determined to enjoy himself. "A woman called Mitzi in Prague quoting the book of Revelation: 'There was a great earthquake and the sun became black as a sackcloth of hair and the moon became as blood and every mountain and island were moved out of their places.' We have entered the seven-year Tribulation, she says, when the Raptured shall ascend to heaven and the sinners burn in hellfire. Well, we're all aware of Pentecostalism being the new European craze . . . Here's another one: someone in Utah who works with crystals calling herself Daughter of the Planet," he reads. "Crystals are also very à la mode nowadays, I understand. We mustn't underestimate them, must we?" He scrolls down. "I am sure that if we were to investigate Nostradamus, we would find a reference there too." I close my eyes and open them again. He is still there. "You've been in this business long enough to know the pitfalls, Gabrielle. We all find ourselves vulnerable around some of these very, er, *intense* young people. The professional response is to recognize that vulnerability and take the appropriate steps to counter these, er, unhelpful impulses."

Bibble babble, says Bethany in my head, and I squash a panic impulse to laugh aloud. "Are you saying I've mishandled Bethany's case?" I say, trying to keep my voice even. But I don't manage it, and my boss's shockingly blue eyes adjust themselves accordingly. Perhaps they are multifunctional, and he will now use them to X-ray the contents of my skull in search of proof that I have a screw loose.

"Well, what do you think?" he asks with a weary sigh. I don't know his age, but suddenly he looks it. A man with a pension plan and a set of discreet escape routes. "Look," he says, gesturing at his screen. "You can see from this that the world is full of people like Bethany Krall. Our job is to free them of their fantasies, not collude in them." He smooths down his pink and gray tie and picks up the phone, indicating that our meeting is over, and begins to dial. I feel instantly uneasy. Whom is he going to call, and what is he going to ask them?"

"And if we can't manage that, Gabrielle," he says, almost as an afterthought, receiver cocked to his ear. "Well. The fact is, if we can't manage that, *we do not have a job.*"

When I drop in on Bethany later that day, it seems that she has heard about the earthquake, despite being in seclusion.

"Jackpot, Wheels," she greets me. Her eyes are woozed, as though she's seeing oncoming headlights, and welcoming them.

"How do you know?"

"It woke me up. I can still feel it," she says, pressing her palm to her almost breastless rib cage. "In here. And all over my skin. Now are you going to tell me I'm wrong?"

"No. It happened."

"And are you going to tell me it's a coincidence?"

Nothing in my training has prepared me for something like this. But it has taught me "solutions"—what Bethany might call babble responses—to certain situations. Like now. "Yes," I say. "I'm going to tell you I think it's a coincidence. So would Dr. Ehmet, who has family in Istanbul."

"Of course he'll say that. Because it's the only thing he can say, because he didn't listen to me when he should've." She lowers her head so it's level with mine. "You've got to get me out of here," she whispers urgently. "Can't you see that, you dumb cow?"

"I can see that's what you want, Bethany," I say. "But you're in here for your own safety. And other people's. You're here to get well."

"You know that's fucking bullshit," says Bethany. Her eyes are darker than usual. "I need to get out of here. This earthquake's, like, *nothing*. There's way worse coming. I can feel it. Seriously. It's fucking mega. On October 12. The big one. I don't want to die in here. I need to get out. You've got to help me."

I feel phantom pins and needles in my legs. Anxiety. "What's happening on October 12?"

Bethany kicks at the floor with her scuffed black trainer. Her expression shifts like the faint jazz of an oncoming storm. "It's something new. No one's seen it before. It starts in one place and it spreads everywhere. Too fast for anyone to do anything about it. Just help me get out of this place, Wheels. I don't want to fucking drown. Not here."

"Is it a flood you're talking about then? A flood in the UK?"

"It's more than that. But I don't know what." Her eyes flicker warily and her voice becomes urgent. She seems scared. "It's your job to help me, right? So help me."

As I make my way to the lift, Frazer Melville calls.

"What time do you finish work?"

"Five thirty."

"Can you come to my office at the university? Bring Bethany's notebooks—all of them. Can you get here by six?"

When is an appropriate moment to tell a man that his existence weakens you? When is an appropriate time to admit that you can no longer control your heart? Not now. Not ever.

"I'll see you there," I tell him casually.

When carrying a body up two flights of stairs, there is only one convenient method, which is that favored by firemen when they rescue people from burning buildings. Hence the ignominious position I find myself in now, slung over Frazer Melville's broad shoulder like a sack, while he puffs his way doggedly up the steps, the bag containing Bethany's notebooks—which I sneaked out of Oxsmith under my gel cushion—swinging off his other arm. If there was any residual coolness between us after this morning, the comedy implicit in this indignity has put an end to it. We stop on each landing so that he can regain his breath and I can laugh—because it's either that or cry, and when there's a choice between humiliation and amusement, I know which response is best in buildings with no decent access. The university's physics department is housed in an ancient block that is undergoing some kind of elaborate reconstruction involving multilayered scaffolding and the removal of asbestos. As soon as I saw the entrance, I recognized it as unfriendly. Not to say actively hostile. "I'm sorry," Frazer Melville apologizes again, still puffing. "I should have thought about it. It's just that I keep forgetting you're disabled."

"I'm not disabled." The words bump out with each step he takes. "And nor am I handicapped, or challenged, or differently abled, or a cripple. My legs don't work. So I'm just paralyzed, OK?"

"OK, Mrs. Paralyzed," he pants. "Let's get your nonworking legs in here." And he bashes his way through a door.

He settles me on a beaten-up sofa, then straightens his back with a series of shucking movements while I look around. I'd imagined clean lines, a certain cerebral minimalism. Instead, there are desks cluttered with cables, computers, compasslike machines with multiple dials, walls plastered with contour maps, computer printouts. And all set in a miniature indoor jungle: tree ferns, orchids, palms, succulents, and even climbers that tangle their feelers around desk legs and lampstands. I think of my own suffering spider plant, Joy McConey's legacy, and feel a stab of remorse. I can't even look after a thing in a pot.

When Frazer Melville closes the door, another wall space is revealed, on which are tacked three van Gogh prints that I recognize at once as paintings from the most disturbed phase of the artist's life, when he was living in Arles. There is *Starry Night,* the painting Frazer Melville showed Bethany at Oxsmith, stamped with constellations and a fierce crescent moon. I remember he expected a reaction from her, some form of recognition, as though the mental disturbance she shared with van Gogh should make them kindred spirits. Below it is *Road with Cypress and Star,* which van Gogh painted before he left the asylum where he spent his last months. A towering tree forms the central image. There's a road to the right, with two figures walking toward the viewer, and to the left a wheat field under a sky in which hang both sun and moon. The third is *Wheat Field with Crows,* executed shortly before van Gogh's suicide. Because of this, much has been made of the three roads offering different routes through a yellow field and of the brooding sky, speckled with crows whose buckled forms are echoed by the menacing black clouds pressing down from above.

"Right," I say, my eyes now accustomed to the sprawl Frazer Melville works in. "You've got me here. So now explain."

He points at the wall next to the van Goghs where there is a large graph dotted with tiny arrows. "It's called the Kolmogorov scaling pattern. It's a formula used by physicists to predict the speed and direction of particles in relation to each other in a fluid. The kind of swirl you get when cream meets coffee or smoke comes out of a chimney. There are even some economists who claim to see its patterns in the fluctuations of the foreign exchange markets. Now do you see the comparison between the Kolmogorov scaling pattern and the van Gogh skies? And between van Gogh's skies and Bethany's?"

"Up to a point. But a swirl's a swirl. Right?"

Apparently not. They have a structure, he tells me, a narrative: they map a complex dance of currents and countercurrents. And van Gogh had epilepsy.

"How's that a factor?"

"Some years ago a Mexican physicist, José Luis Aragón, became interested in van Gogh's skies. He analyzed them mathematically." Frazer Melville is shoving a scientific paper at me. I read through the abstract by Aragón et al.:

We show that some impassioned van Gogh paintings display scaling properties similar to those observed in fluids, suggesting that these paintings reflect the fingerprint of turbulence with a realism consistent with the way that a mathematical model characterizes this phenomenon. Specifically, we show that the probability distribution function (PDF) of luminance fluctuations of points (pixels) separated by a distance R is consistent with the Kolmogorov scaling theory in turbulent fluids. We also show that the most turbulent paintings of van Gogh coincide with periods of prolonged psychotic agitation of this artist.

"These three were printed when he was suffering from prolonged bouts of epilepsy," says Frazer Melville. "In this paper, Aragón shows how they actually map turbulence—*invisible* turbulence—with extreme accuracy. And he goes on to speculate that the delusions accompanying van Gogh's epileptic fits might have given him a unique understanding of the physics of flow."

"And Bethany's ECT—"

"Those currents are giving her a grand mal seizure. A similar experience to an epileptic fit. But it's induced artificially and controlled rather than arriving spontaneously through a brain malfunction."

"You mean there might be some kind of science to explain what she's predicting?"

"There has to be. At least for what she's claiming to feel. But as for how she can pinpoint the location and the date—I have no idea. I'm hoping there's a clue in the notebooks."

I fish them out of the bag and lay them on the desk. Taking the top one, he flips through the pages eagerly, but soon his expression shifts from interest to dismay. "Christ. It's total chaos."

"What were you expecting—rational method? But there's probably a pattern in there somewhere. If we can find it."

"How?" he says, surveying a scrawled-over page despairingly.

"If she writes on consecutive pages, there'd be a chronology to them."

He continues to flick through. Some pages are chockablock with tiny, cramped notes, interrupted by sketches peppered with arrows. Others are devoted to freehand drawings, some of ordinary-looking clouds, others similar to the storm images Bethany made in the studio when she drew the Rio Christ. Ten or twelve pages of the most recent notebook—only a third full—are devoted to a series of what I think of as her "Moonscape with Machinery" drawings. The style of these is more diagrammatic and observational, less emotionally charged than the others. There is a structure to them, an almost architectural formality that gives the impression of something that has been copied to scale, something that actually exists beyond Bethany's imagination and that has its roots in reality. They make no sense to me but Frazer Melville seems struck by them. "Interesting," he murmurs, stroking a page as though it might contain hidden Braille. "No turbulence. Nothing at all, in terms of air flow. I wonder what she'd do if I asked her to imagine it. What it would look like." The scenario is the same in all of them: a rubble-strewn stretch of land and a vertical line, sometimes thin, sometimes thick, descending from the sky to hit a flower-shaped cup or funnel at ground level, which continues underground and then curves, traveling horizontally and ending either in vagueness, or in a wedge shape, or in what appears to be an explosion. On the earth, around the funnel, Bethany has drawn broken rocks or scree.

"What does this represent?" I asked her once.

"I don't know," she said. Edgily, as though I'd cornered her doing something shameful. "But I keep doing it."

"I'll give you my psychologist's take on these," I tell Frazer. "There's no evidence I know of that she's been sexually abused, and she hasn't told me it happened. But I think it did. Or something like it. A violent invasion. Now you tell me your guess."

"I can't. But I think they're too technical to be symbolic. To me they look like some kind of mining operation."

"And what about these ones?" I ask, leafing through to show him another Bethany motif: a collection of geometric-looking five-sided forms packed together in a block.

"A honeycomb? A multistory car park? Stylized coffins?"

"I'm going to run all this by my ex," says Frazer, sighing. "But she'll probably say it's *hyessou*."

"What's *hyessou*?"

"It's Greek for 'a load of bollocks,' " he says miserably. "Knowing Melina, she'll assume that my mother's death has unhinged me."

The routine we now embark on is meticulous. Methodically, for the next two hours, with little talking, we go through the notebooks page by eccentric page, numbering them as we go along, with Frazer Melville making photocopies and taking digital photographs that he transfers to his computer.

"All done," he says finally, setting the last, incomplete book down on the desk. I pick it up and riffle through the pages. She has used different colored pens for her drawings, but all the text is scrawled in black. Then I stop and see that the very last page is covered in handwriting.

"Did you copy this?" I ask Frazer Melville. He looks across, exhausted. "It looks like a list."

"Let's have a look," he says, pulling his chair up next to mine. It's a set of dates, places, and events. Some are written in black and others in green, red, or blue, as though there's a kind of code to it. The first reads, *February 11, volcanic disturbances, Mount Etna, Italy.*

"There was some activity back then," says Frazer Melville. "Before the big eruption in May. Though I'm not sure of the exact date. I could check it."

"She could have written it down afterwards," I say. "Look at the way she's used different colors. This certainly wasn't all written in one go. What's next?"

"*February 24, cyclone, Osaka, Japan,*" I read. The list goes on through March and April: a tornado in southern Spain and a "new geyser" in Iceland, a black cloud formation in Russia, a deadly "methane belch" from a lake in the Congo. One by one, as I read them out, Frazer Melville looks up the events on the Net. In each case, they not only happened but happened on the dates Bethany has noted in her red and black book. The eruption of Mount Etna on March 18. An earthquake in Nepal and a typhoon in Taiwan on April 20 and 29, respectively. They, too, are there. *May 21, rock falls in the Alps:* we both remember that story in the news. A Swiss village was destroyed because of permafrost thawing below the mountain slope and unleashing its grip on the granite. Something churns inside me uneasily as I recall the footage.

"No need to check out this one," murmurs Frazer Melville, pointing to the next entry: *July 29, hurricane in the southern Atlantic, Rio de Janeiro.* "Or the next." *August 16, earth tremors, northern Pakistan and Kashmir.* "That rings a bell," he says. Googling it swiftly, he shoots me a confirming glance.

"Read me the rest."

"*August 22, earthquake, Istanbul. September 5, heavy rains, massive flooding, Bangladesh. September 13, cyclone, Mumbai. September 20, storms leading to fires, Hong Kong. October 4, volcano, Samoa.*"

The next event is dated October 12. It says, simply, *Tribulation.* There's no indication of what this means or how it will be triggered. Or where it will happen.

Frazer Melville doesn't speak for a long time. "For the sake of argument, let's say she *did* predict all these events accurately. Not just Rio and Istanbul but all the previous ones. Which we can have no way of confirming. But let's assume it."

"OK. Then what?"

"Then such a high number of correct predictions—and note, not a single false one. You can't call this coincidence. Or even lucky guessing."

"Which leaves us where?"

"Looking for a scientific explanation." He breathes in deeply and exhales. "It's quite a long shot, but it's a hypothesis. In the absence of anything else . . ."

"Go on," I say, urgently interested. Bethany's list has unnerved me more than I'm prepared to admit.

"None of these events happen out of the blue. The day the volcano erupts, or the hurricane hits, or the earthquake strikes, or the geyser appears, is the climax of a process that will have begun some time before. In some cases, years previously. We have to look at meteorology and geology quite differently, of course, in terms of time scale. Weather can be brewing for a week or more before it becomes violent, for example. Whereas the Istanbul quake has been on the cards for years, with the pressure building up along the fault line. So let's hypothesize that Bethany is picking up otherwise undetectable signals—let's call them vibrations—relating to events that are already on their way to happening. Let's say that in each case she's sensing the beginning of a buildup of pressure, whether it's atmospheric or underground. And then let's hypothesize that she's somehow been able to imagine very accurately the time it will take to develop into an event and where it will manifest itself. She knows the globe pretty well, for someone of her age. But in any case I'd suggest it's more about instinct than knowledge. It's known that the pressure along the fault line that led to the Istanbul quake has been moving steadily east. But it's basically a question of the deeper earth structures shifting along a timeline. And Bethany somehow picking up the pressure changes."

"Just instinctively?"

He shakes his head. "No. There has to be a reason. A physical connection between Bethany and these . . . phenomena. Perhaps a kind of magnetism or even something sonar."

"Go on."

"There's a kind of directional magnetism that enables birds to know which direction to fly in when they migrate. It's well known that animals pick up a lot." I remember Dr. Ehmet using a parallel with cats and dogs to explain Bethany Krall's need for ECT. "If there was an earth tremor fifty kilometers away, many species would sense it. Let's imagine that in Bethany's case the ECT gives her extra sensitivity to energy fluctuations. Or just an awareness of when natural flows are disrupted enough to trigger some radical event."

"It feels quite far-fetched. But as a theory I certainly prefer it to the notion that Bethany's some kind of eco-psychic. The question is, how far does it go? And what's it *for*? And where does this biblical stuff about the Tribulation fit in?"

Frazer Melville shakes his head. My mind's racing. Joy seemed to think Bethany's father held a clue. If I went to one of Leonard Krall's sermons, might I get an insight into the genesis of her visions?

But first there is a question I need to ask Frazer Melville, a question that has been nagging at me since the day he met Bethany. It's delicate. Is now the time to ask it? Maybe we are not ready for personal confessions. But the particular circumstances demand a particular kind of honesty. Frazer Melville takes my hand and squeezes it. A tiny gesture of closeness that reassures me.

"When do we start telling people?"

He says, "Not just when but what. And who. And how. I mean, I announce to the renowned Dutch meteorologist Cees van Haven, in conjunction with no one, that Bangladesh is in for another flood. I can just hear him laughing. And that India is to expect another cyclone—hey. Unprecedented. And I e-mail Melina to tell her that Hong Kong will be hit by storms leading to fires. She'll think I've gone nuts. Then I tell a Chinese vulcanologist colleague about an eruption in Samoa. Well, Samoa's on the Pacific Rim, where there's regular volcanic activity, so no surprises there either."

"The difference is that you give precise dates."

"And the dates come and go, and if Bethany's right, they say it's coincidence, and if she's wrong, I'm stuck with egg on my face. And then just as I'm signing off I say, Oh, P.S., the Tribulation, otherwise known to religious fanatics as seven years of hell on earth, preceded by a celestial airlift of the faithful known as the Rapture, is due on October 12, but we don't know what it is, let alone where it kicks off."

"No need for the P.S. These are scientists. Leave God right out of it."

"OK then, scrub God but mention that this vague but paradoxically cast-iron prediction of a natural disaster emanates from a child psychopath who murdered her own mum and has just stabbed a fellow inmate in the bollocks. But I can't name her for privacy reasons."

"So leave that out of it too."

He sighs. "With no scientific evidence to back it up? Look what happened to Joy McConey." He's doing something origami-like with his notes.

"Are you talking yourself out of this?"

He stops and smiles. The green fish in his eye ignites. "No, my little sex goddess on wheels. This is my way of talking myself in."

We sit for a moment in silence.

"When you met Bethany and I left her alone with you in my office, she said something to you," I begin. "Something that made you miserable."

My remark has an effect more dramatic than anything I could have envisioned. Frazer Melville has leaped to his feet, and suddenly he's offering me coffee, politely, as though we don't know each other, as though we have not been here for two hours, as though we have never made love. "It's no trouble to make some," he says, pointing at a toxic-looking percolator in the corner.

"I seem to have hit a nerve," I say calmly. "Come back and sit."

"It was nothing," he says, returning reluctantly to his chair. But he shifts it slightly away from me as he does so, widening the space between us.

"That's not my feeling. My feeling is she said something you'd rather not face or discuss. But maybe you need to." He looks at his spread hands. I am getting closer now, and he'd rather I wasn't.

"One day after she'd had ECT, Bethany touched my wrist, like she was feeling my pulse," I tell him. "And then she said things about me—about my car accident—that I can't understand her knowing. That I can't explain away." There. I have raised it.

"No need to tell me," he says quickly. "If it's painful." *So someone died. You had two hearts and one was gone. The worst thing was, you never found out how the two of you would be together.*

"Yes, it is. And also very private."

I look at the splotch of green in Frazer Melville's left iris. A tiny tropical fish that has gate-crashed his eye. It makes me long for him.

"Gabrielle, I would never ask you about anything you'd rather not discuss. I hope you'll trust me with that. We have plenty of time."

"I know. But the reason I mention it is because I think she did something similar with you. That's my guess. Am I right? That she knew something personal?"

He nods miserably and looks at me in an unfathomable way, his eyes glassy from—what? Is it fear, confusion, guilt? Or something else?

"You don't have to tell me what it was," I say quickly. "But I want to establish—she unsettled you, didn't she, by coming out with some personal information?"

"Yes," he says. "She did."

I wait for more. I am patient that way.

"But it wasn't about me," he mumbles. "It was about . . . another person. Someone I care about a lot. Who I wouldn't want to hurt for the world."

Despite my belief that it's absurd to be jealous of someone's past, I flush. Frazer Melville hasn't told me a great deal about Melina. I know that when she left him for Agnesca they didn't speak for two years. I also know that later on, when he was working on a paper about marine landslides and wanted her opinion as a geologist, he contacted her professionally and they began an e-mail correspondence that has continued, sporadically, ever since. He speaks of her healthily, in the same affectionate way one speaks of a social misstep one has long since forgiven oneself.

"Don't tell me any more if you'd rather not," I say, taking his hand. "It's just Bethany's way of feeling powerful. I know how her mind works." We sit in silence for a moment, but then my curiosity—no, my jealousy—gets the better of me. "Was it something about you and Melina?"

He looks troubled.

"No, it wasn't."

"Oh." I am more relieved than I should be. And then puzzled. If not Melina, then who?

"I don't know how to say this." I sense exhaustion. Or something beyond it, in another dimension. "Gabrielle. Can't you guess? It was about you." Suddenly I can't find any words. And something's lodged in my throat so I can't tell him to stop, to shut up. Which I want and need him to. Now. Very urgently. "Gabrielle. I'm sorry. Bethany told me that when you had the accident, you were . . ." He stops. He's looking at me in a way that glitters. It's agonizing. For a light moment, I feel nothing except a swelling in my throat. "I'm sorry. You put me in such a difficult— Oh, darling."

A fleeting, almost hallucinatory relief. Then more pain, an exquisitely precise movement inside my rib cage, like the tightening of a
ratchet.

I say, "Oh." And then my mouth shuts and I know it won't open
again, so there's no point trying. When something has been said, even
if the words are spoken silently, it can't be unsaid.

"Gabrielle? Are you OK?"

I nod. He takes both my hands. I know he's looking at my eyes but
I can't meet his. I look at our hands instead—his freckled, mine
olive—and remember my first meeting with Bethany. Something she
said drifts up. *Did you know that blood has its own memory? It's like
rock, and water, and air.*

"Is it true?" he asks, finally. With effort, I shift my gaze to the wall.
There's a brown splotch on it. The shape is reminiscent of France or
Spain. I wonder how it got there. Perhaps someone threw a cup of
coffee. Decaf. Or perhaps tea. If there was sugar in it, there might be
tiny crystals, clinging on.

"Sweetheart. Speak to me."

But I still can't look at him. I stare at the French/Spanish splotch,
wondering about the sugar, imagining the crystals, until its edges
blur. He stands up. He lifts me out of the chair. He holds me to his
chest, squeezing me. I can feel his heart banging, a steady, hard, hurt-
ing thump. My legs dangle like a puppet's. Then he sits in his chair
and takes me onto his lap, his arms straitjacketing me. There's clearly
no escape, either from him or from myself, so I lean my head back.
His body is hot, comforting. I feel a weird kind of shame creep over
me, like a sick desire.

"She had no right to tell you."

"I'm so sorry."

We don't speak for a moment. Outside, a car alarm sets up.
Around it, you can sense the night's dark yawn, the brush of birds'
wings against hot pine needles, the delicate exhalations of tarmac.

I say, "I was going to call him Max."

"How—"

"Twenty-eight weeks. They can be born alive at that stage. But he
wasn't."

If I allow myself to cry, I will never stop.

So I don't, and we sit like that for a while, I don't know how long, and then he carries me down the stairs and drives us back to my home through the warm night, windows open to the hot, scent-laden air. In his arms, in bed, I give in to it. Frazer Melville knows there's nothing to say, so he doesn't try. But he holds me all night. And that is something.

SEVEN

In the morning we watch the news. The pall of dust is clearing to reveal a choked wasteland desolate as a hundred thousand Ground Zeros, dwarfing anything I have seen or could have imagined, a smoking, smoldering bleakness that stretches for kilometer upon kilometer, with odd pockets of normality on which the sun shines: a playing field, a rind of park, a sparkling lake sprinkled with painted paddleboats. Mosques, their domes popped open like puffballs, gape up at the sky. Thousands of people are entombed in rubble. Soldiers in masks search for survivors, picking their way through jagged promontories of reinforced cement with heat detectors and sniffer dogs.

I wonder what goes through Bethany Krall's mind when she watches the aftermath of a horror she so clinically predicted. Does she feel powerful, proud, omniscient, invincible? Or in a corner of her psyche, is she scared out of her wits? And Dr. Ehmet, scouring name lists, tent encampments, homemade posters, and Red Cross centers for his family, one of millions? I do not imagine this man, with his bad haircut and his brave "heh" and his Hegel quotations, being well equipped for the task he has set himself, but he will do it anyway. And his broken heart will join all the other hearts smashed in seconds, for no reason that makes any sense to anyone.

In a few days, there will be stories of freak survivals. A child will crawl unscathed from an impossibly narrow fissure in the ground. An old lady will recount the tale of a jar of mulberry jam that saved her life when she lay with her legs trapped under a beam. Then fast-forward to the time, not so far from now, when the bereaved have trudged away with the objects they hold dear—a photograph, a toy, a cactus, a teapot, a copy of the Koran—leaving the husk of Istanbul to stand and then fall: a ghost city, a modern Angkor Wat. Before long, nature will stake its claim. Insects, pigeons, squirrels, lizards, snakes, and blown sand will overtake the ruins of flats and travel agents' offices and schools and department stores. Morning glory, cyclamen, and all shades of bougainvillea will writhe their way through the remains of tower blocks and climb up the rusted steel reinforcements of hospitals to bloom in bright carpets; poppies and bindweed and rosemary and lemongrass will deck splintered wood and smashed concrete with verdure; acacia trees and chinaberries will colonize the cracks, splitting tarmac to conjure the worst kind of beauty: the kind that celebrates human collapse. When something has been tortured it can never be itself again. Be it a spine or a heart. Nerve endings and longings have died; impulses have changed; sensitivities have found new routes of expression; specific muscle movements and emotional urges have calcified. So although I am beginning to diagnose in myself the rapid growth of a mental symptom, triggered by my recent closeness to the freckled physicist, I do not succumb to the comforts it could offer me. I recognize it for what it is: a false sensation. Like the neurological swarming in my legs, this symptom—some would call it love—is phantom evidence of an emotional indulgence my circumstances deny me.

On my lunch break I surf the Net, following links and refining searches, backtracking and lateral jumping, switching trains of thought on the lightest whim. I skim stories about the Planetarians' latest call to indict ex-president Bush for "Earth crimes." About the Siberian tundra defrosting faster than even the most pessimistic models have predicted, about the outer edges of the Amazon basin being reduced to giant puddles of mud, full of choking fish, about how one day soon the remaining forest will burn and become savannah: one lung gone. About the Gulf Stream absorbing the huge Arctic melt, slowing down, bringing less heat to the Atlantic, and playing havoc with shorelines. "If the warming process cannot be reversed in time, then the near-extinction of the human race is inevitable in the long term," wrote Modak in his *Washington Post* article. But when Bethany refers to "the Tribulation," the cataclysm she cannot name, is she simply speaking of the climatological point of no return, the tipping point that Modak believes has already passed or some other, unidentified catastrophe?

How can you prevent something you can't even name?

I click and click and end up nowhere.

Feniton Acres is one of the brownfield developments that sprung up before the housing crisis. I arrive there later than I had planned, sometime after six. The destination I have programmed into my GPS is part of a mall with a central parking lot. There is a Jacuzzi franchise, a fishing-gear supplier, a vet's, a cinema, a few upmarket clothes stores sporting mannequins in tame leisurewear. Behind it all, there's a golf course. The church itself, vast and pink, is low-slung, with a crablike shell and a Scandinavian architecture–kit feel: a militantly uncombative building in a manufactured community. Amid the carefully spaced rowan trees and Japanese maple, I note with amusement that here, at least, the halt and the lame are welcome: in addition to several disabled parking spaces, there is wheelchair access in the form of a cement ramp leading up to the main entrance.

Like many other people concerned with the impression they make, I tend to hesitate in doorways—a bad habit that has worsened since my accident. But here, I do not have the luxury of preparing myself: the entrance is of the hospital or hypermarket variety, with sensored glass doors that slide open automatically. It must be well soundproofed because wheeling my way in, I'm hit by an unexpected boom of music. A discolike hymn is under way. A sudden rush of conditioned air brings an instant chill and gooseflesh to my bare arms. Inside there is a sea of people swaying to the music. They radiate happiness.

A few heads turn: I'm smiled at encouragingly. Among the five hundred or so worshippers, there's a high proportion of black and brown skin in relation to white—much more than you would expect from Feniton Acres's demographic. The hall is a giant carpeted space in a neutral, pale blue. Near the front, beneath a cement cross that

rises in bas-relief from the whitewashed wall, there's a band with gui-
tars, some timpani, wind instruments, and percussion, all played by
men, apart from the saxophone, which is wielded by a teenaged girl
in jeans. A few more smiles of welcome as I am ushered by a smart-
suited young man to a space near the front of the hall, by an aisle,
with a view of the action. He hands me a white envelope and a pen
and whispers, "This is for your tithe. We all give what we can." On
the front of the envelope are boxes to fill in, with name, address, and
credit card information.

Near me a young woman is facing the congregation and swaying
to the music using elegant arm and hand movements that look
vaguely familiar. Several members of the audience, none of whom are
singing, watch her intently. Then it dawns on me: they are deaf, and
she is translating the hymn into sign language. Though why she
might need to I am not sure, as the words appear on a huge screen at
the back of the hall in blue letters:

I'm going to stand right up and let Jesus in
And heal my soul from mortal sin
I'm going to pray to Him each and every hour
Because the way is His and so is the power.

In front of me, a woman's blocky body sways to the rhythm.
And then I see him.

In real life Leonard Krall is bulkier, more imposing, and somehow
more vital than the suave man in the photos on his Web site. He's
wearing a dove gray suit, very well cut, and has a microphone hooked
over one ear. He doesn't look like someone whose wife has been
stabbed to death with a screwdriver and whose daughter is possessed
by Satan. Catching my eye briefly and giving a nod, he rocks his
whole body as he sings. A happy man, you'd say. A man who knows
who he is and why he is here. A man in his element.

Unsure of the tune, when the chorus starts up again, I mouth the
words. Around me, people are exchanging delighted, almost conspir-
atorial glances, as though they are all in on the same big secret. And
perhaps they are. I think: *The mass production of serotonin. Religion is*
the opiate of the people. Then, as the pulse of energy amplifies around
me, another phrase floats into my head, a phrase from somewhere
else, somewhere contradictory: *if the spirit moves you.* I feel a big,

foolish smile blooming on my face. Acceptance: accept, and you will be accepted. I'm being caught up in it. You can't not be. A man next to me has flung his head back. While the others sing, he has his hands clasped in prayer and is offering up a fast, unbroken babble of words, as though experimenting with the possibilities of his tongue. I envy his freedom. I shut my eyes and sway to the music. With movement denied to my lower half, my upper body craves it. I lift my arms and wave them from side to side as I sing, following the words scrolling across the big screen above the choir. Tears come to my eyes in a Pavlovian reflex. I can't help it. Group singing is like good sex. After the climax, you're exhilarated but winded. I could do this forever. We sing four more hymns, ending with "Stand Up, Stand Up for Jesus," the only one I am familiar with. I am almost disappointed when it's over and the congregation finally sits. Leonard Krall, bulky and energetic, begins pacing the front of the hall.

"Those supermarket loyalty cards. Hands up—who doesn't have one?" A ripple of laughter. "Well, I don't know about you but most of the time I don't give mine a second thought, except when it's time to claim the discounts. But last time when I fed my card into the machine I started to wonder about the word *loyalty* and about the real transaction that's going on here. As in, who's being loyal to who—and why?" He pauses, and as the nods kick in, he moves on to "the wider meaning of loyalty in our globalized society." What kind of loyalty is important: loyalty to a retail provider, or a football team, or to our tribe (he indicates quotation marks), or to all of God's children, whether or not they speak our language and even share our creed? Is it loyalty to a set of Christian principles? He thinks it is. You can see Bethany in him, in the upper part of the face, in the spacing of the eyes. There's a potency. You could find him attractive. "War, famine, disease, catastrophes. The spread of atheism, climate change, the violence in Jerusalem and Iran. You watch. The political world is going to be shaken and shaken. 'Yet once more I will shake not only the earth but also heaven.' Hebrews, chapter 12, verse 26 and verse 27: *'The things that cannot be shaken will remain.'* We will remain. Here, steadfast in the Lord. For we can't be shaken, right? But others can." He raises his voice warningly. There is an epidemic of false religion in our world today. Our nation must turn back to God, the God of today, the God of now!" He is shouting. "May we be drenched in your grace,

O Lord! Drench us, drench us in your eternal love!" Then he softens. "Glory be."

The woman next to me agrees emphatically, joining the chorus of murmurs and amens.

"There's no doubt in my mind that evil forces are at work on Planet Earth. That the devil is gearing up for something. Well here's God's message: the followers of Christ are gearing up for something too!" He stabs the air with his finger, prompting more murmurs and staccato claps of approval from the audience. "We're gearing up for the Rapture!"

Cheers break out, and he's pacing the hall like a panther, making flashes of eye contact.

"There are signs. I see signs and I feel signs. Signs the Bible has spoken of. What did we all feel when we saw Christ come tumbling down the mountainside? Have you really chosen this hour, Lord, at the beginning of the twenty-first century, to rapture us and visit this planet with Ezekiel's war?" Not waiting for an answer, he thumps the air. "It is written, people! It is written! 'Behold, the Lord maketh the earth empty, and maketh it waste, and turneth it upside down, and scattereth abroad the inhabitants thereof. Therefore hath the curse devoured the earth, and they that dwell therein are desolate: therefore the inhabitants of the earth are burned, and few men left.' God is presenting a challenge to us terrestrial beings. But don't expect everyone to understand his ways. John, chapter 3: 'You must be born again to see the kingdom of the Lord.' "

Amen, comes the fervent murmur.

The home life of the Krall family. I want to ask questions. Did Bethany and her parents sit on a leather sofa together and watch inspirational DVDs? Did Karen Krall ensure her daughter consumed five portions of fruit and vegetables a day, as recommended by the Department of Health? Did Bethany come regularly to this church and listen to Leonard's gospel? What role does forgiveness play when your daughter leaves a screwdriver sticking out of your wife's eye?

"When Istanbul was razed to the ground," Krall is saying, "it confirmed a deep knowledge—a knowledge borne on the Faith Wave that we are part of—that the end times are approaching. People, we have nothing to fear. Fear is the devil's weapon against us and we shall not allow him to prevail. We know we are safe and that the Lord will protect us. But what of our loved ones and all those who are not saved, who have not found God's love?"

There's a murmur of assent in the audience. I learned at school, among the nuns, never to underestimate the sheer force of belief. The unshakability of true faith. Leonard Krall has it.

"We have been chosen to live through these times and to interpret these times," he is saying. "So we will stand up to that devil who is destroying this earth that God made and spreading atheism across the globe, and we shall await the return of the Messiah, the great Redeemer. For just as we saw him fall, so shall he rise!" Still pacing the floor energetically, he has slipped seamlessly into song mode: a chord of music erupts from the keyboard in accompaniment.

"So shall he rise, so shall he rise, so shall he rise, rise, rise!"

He lifts his hands and people get to their feet and sing a song about the risen one, the chosen one, the holy one. I clap along in rhythm. Again, that physiological response, that paradox: my heart lifts and a smile blooms and I am enjoying myself. At the end of the song the congregation remains standing, which means my view is blocked. I shift further into the aisle. Krall's head is now bowed and his fist is in the air, revealing a dark-haired wrist, a silver watch, a white cuff. His energy is intimate, almost sexual. His eyes are closed and his body shivers, indicating a mood shift. When he speaks again, tipping his head back in an almost languid gesture, it is with quiet force.

"We shall be among the saved, and we do our best to turn the hearts of all those we know and love who have not yet found his grace toward God so that they, too, shall be saved. Psalms, chapter 25, verse 4: 'Show me thy ways, O Lord, teach me thy paths.' We don't want anyone to suffer on this earth during the end times. Some of them are our friends and our loved ones. We take no joy in their circumstances. We want them to repent their sins and rise and be raptured alongside the righteous, and rejoice in the return of the Messiah. And he shall come for us. Oh yes, make no mistake. He shall come."

Assent ripples across the hall.

After the service, I roll my way past the clusters of men and women and teenagers clad in the uniform of high street fashion chatting animatedly, flush-faced, while the younger kids run out to the mall.

"Welcome," says Krall, pulling up a chair, getting down to my level and shaking my hand with the confident grip of a people person, a gifted speaker who can also listen. "It's great to see new faces. Are you local? Leonard Krall." He's still holding my hand and I begin to wonder when he will release it. "People call me Len. Pleased to meet you."

"I'm Penny," I lie.

"Penny," he repeats. Another squeeze, and I get my hand back. I came up with Penny—an insecure, religious version of my preaccident self—on the journey here. "I'm just passing through. I was driving past and I heard the music, so . . ."

"You couldn't resist. Those old favorites, yeah?"

"Comfort singing."

He chuckles. "Better than comfort eating, right?"

"What you said about the Tribulation and the Rapture struck a chord." This earns me some intensive eye contact and a nod, but no more. It's unnerving to see Bethany's brown eyes shining out intelligently and softly from another face.

"You know something, Penny? I can feel Jesus in you."

I don't quite know how to respond to this, except with paranoia. Has he spotted I'm a fake?

"Can I have a word with you, when you've said your good-byes? The fact is, it wasn't just the music that brought me here," I confess. I have tweaked his interest.

"Sure thing, Penny." He straightens up, ready for the task. "Give me ten minutes," he says, winking at a man walking past. "Clear this righteous mob out of here and we can chat in private."

I wait as he presses more flesh, jokes with more men, listens to more women, mock punches little kids. There's a barbecue atmosphere.

Fifteen minutes later we are alone. "So. Penny. Talk to me."

"The Tribulation. Does it have phases?"

He shakes his head. "Well, you're right in there with the big questions, aren't you? Phases, yes. In fact some Christians believe it's started already. Look around you. Plagues, extreme weather, disasters, globalization, economies collapsing, terrorism, atheism. You could call them symptoms."

"So do you believe it's started?"

"On bad days I do. But a close reading of the scriptures indicates that true believers will be saved before it begins."

"In the Rapture. They'll be caught up in the air."

"So the Bible tells us."

"I take it you believe in evil?"

He laughs. "Too right I do. If you take God seriously, you have to take the bad guy the same way. But above all, I believe in good. I believe in the power of God's will and God's plan first and foremost. Even though terrible things happen. And God seems to let them happen. That confuses people, but it shouldn't. We're always asking ourselves what I call the why question. Lord, why hast thou forsaken me? But God knows what he's doing. He has a plan. It's just, we're like ants, Penny. We're too small to see his plan. Our vision doesn't reach that far. Our problem is arrogance. We need to do away with arrogance. It takes humility to accept that God has it all mapped out, but that we can't always know it. Things that don't make sense to us make sense to him. We see through a glass darkly." A shadow crosses his face but disappears immediately. He grins. "Sorry, Penny. Me, banging on."

"But can evil be innate? I mean, this idea of innocence and corruption. Can a child be naturally evil?"

"She can be visited by the devil."

"She," I say. There is a tiny silence. Leonard Krall stiffens imperceptibly and his gaze withdraws inward.

"The devil is powerful," he murmurs finally, almost to himself, and for the first time there is a hint of sorrow in his features, the sorrow of a man who has lost his wife and child. "The devil is cunning. The devil is malevolent and he finds ways of luring the righteous off the path of good." He looks at me intensely, as though searching for the Jesus that he sensed earlier. "What do you think of that, Penny?"

"The church I belong to doesn't—well. They're all in favor of good. But evil doesn't seem to exist. And I keep thinking, can you really have the one without the other?"

"Political correctness?" His smile is encouraging, complicit. "I'm not going to start knocking other churches or beliefs," he says. "But I'm a Bible man. And if you're a Bible man, you believe what's in the scriptures and you don't edit out the devil just because you don't like the idea of evil. *Trust the text.* Evil's among us. But our faith will deliver us from it. Faith is evidence of things not seen. Hebrews 11. I like that one. *Evidence of things not seen.*" Then he reaches in his pocket and hands me his card. It bears his name, with an e-mail address and a mobile phone number. "Take this, Penny," he says. "In case you'd like a longer chat. I move about a lot, spreading the word, but you're very welcome wherever I'm preaching." The combination of his sincerity and my fraudulence brings on a deep blush. I take his card and thank him. With no pocket to put it in and not wanting to stuff it down the side of my chair, I fumble in my handbag for my wallet, which I promptly drop. Gallantly, he picks it up. And then, less gallantly, and to my shock, he flips it open. My driver's license stares at us both.

And in a split second, everything has changed. "Gabrielle Fox," he reads aloud. The blood drains from my face. "It's a pity it doesn't give your profession on here, Ms. Fox." I want to be sick. "But I would guess journalist."

"I'm not a journalist," I mumble. "Please give me my wallet back."

With a quick head move, his smile has vanished. "They still come sniffing around every once in a while. But none of them's sunk this low before," he says, indicating my wheelchair. *"Penny."*

"I'm paralyzed."

"And I'm Mickey Mouse. Look, Ms. Fox. Most people here know that I suffered a personal tragedy a couple of years back and that the church and God's love have helped me get to a place where I can count my blessings. I don't bother with the why question anymore. Now I don't want to offend you. But I don't like subterfuge. So if a young woman who has clearly suffered in life comes to me seeking counsel over a genuine spiritual concern about the nature of evil, I am happy to help her. But if someone cold-bloodedly gets hold of a wheelchair and cheats her way into God's house to ask me personal questions about a private tragedy concerning my family, that's another matter. I would have to respectfully ask her to leave."

I feel mildly unwell. I would like to teleport myself out of here. Rewind the scene to the bit where we're singing and clapping and I'm enjoying myself. Anything to get out of this—this *this*.

"I have nothing to say to you." His face is white. "Except, who the hell are you?" I was not expecting sudden rage on this scale and it scares me. For a stomach-turning moment I think he's going to hit me. I reach for my thunder egg and I'm ready to swing it at him. But before I can, he has maneuvered his way behind me and snatched the handles of my chair. I grab the wheels to block them, but when he gives a blunt shove my hands aren't strong enough to resist. He is wheeling me out. The automatic doors open. Dusk is gathering. Without a word he pushes my wheelchair—faster than it has ever been pushed—down the ramp.

"We Bible men are fond of miracles, Ms. Fox," he says. He's beginning to tip my chair forward. I cling to my wheels. I want to scream but nothing comes out. I look around wildly for someone to help me, but the parking lot is a deserted prairie. "And I like to think they sometimes happen." He's still rocking me. I grab onto the armrests with all my force, but he doesn't stop. He's strong. He's tipped the chair so far down that I'm staring at the tarmac and losing my grip. I'll have to let go if I want to avoid serious injury.

"So let's see if we can make the lame walk, eh?"

I am too dumbstruck to speak. I need to stay in the chair but I'm losing the fight. Desperate to protect myself, I let go just in time to break my fall with my hands. I'm sprawled on the ground. I may have knocked one of my legs, and there's a searing pain in my left palm. I glance at it and see blood and gravel and chopped-up skin. Pain versus pride: I'm struggling not to sob. And losing.

He laughs. "Nice acting." He flings my wallet down and its contents spill on the gravel. My driver's license stares up at me.

"I'm your daughter's therapist," I blurt, my eyes stinging from the pain. "She's been foreseeing natural disasters. She predicted Istanbul." His body stiffens. He doesn't speak, but I can feel him registering what I've said. "Can you explain that, Mr. Krall?"

"Oh, I can explain it, all right," he says. A shudder runs across his features. Fear, or contempt, or both? "Or rather the devil can. It's him you should be talking to. He's the one in charge of Bethany."

"She's your daughter."

"Not anymore. I pray for her soul every day of my waking life. You're being manipulated, Ms. Fox. And you can't even see it."

By the time I've recovered enough to move, he's gone. As I drag myself back up into my wheelchair, he has returned to his church and closed the door and I am alone.

Swallowing my tears and trying to think of ways I can make the incident sound amusing rather than grotesque, I call Frazer Melville from the car but get no answer. I turn on the radio. In Turkey, there are stories of last-ditch rescues, poignant reunions, tragic miscalculations, the spread of disease, the bungling of aid. I drive, trying not to think.

Frazer Melville is waiting for me at home, with a bottle of champagne and a thin, unhappy smile. "To celebrate the end of my career as a credible scientist," he announces. We clink glasses and he sets about cleaning up my scraped hand. In our different ways, we are in despair.

"You sent the e-mails?"

"I've concentrated on the next four incidents, since the first ones have already happened and we can't make sense of the last entry. I presented them as speculations made by someone who has accurately predicted natural disasters in the past. I kept it neutral and asked for statistical likelihoods of the events happening on the date given, and I sent some of Bethany's 'Moonscape with Machinery' drawings to Melina. She has an ex-colleague with connections to Harish Modak."

I tell him I am proud of him. But I can see that the pressing of the send button has renewed his turmoil. "And you're sure that all these people are open to . . . ideas that you can't prove?"

"Can't be sure in all cases. Melina's not that way inclined, but I'm guessing she'll pay me the compliment of replying seriously and not use it against me. Harish Modak—if Melina's contact takes it seriously and passes it on—is someone who just might take a chance. Out of pure curiosity. He's maverick enough."

"I've read one of his articles. I was impressed. Though I wanted to shoot the messenger."

"He's Lovelock's spiritual successor in some ways. In others not. He doesn't really give a toss what the rest of science thinks of him. But has huge influence."

"So what now?"

"We consume more alcohol and you tell me about Leonard Krall."

The next morning my boss gets straight to the point. He has received a phone call from Bethany's father. A phone call of "justified complaint." There's nothing to say, so I don't.

"Can you deny it?"

"He tipped me out of my wheelchair." It's as weak as it sounds.

"Yes. So he told me. He apologizes for that. Nonetheless. It doesn't exactly cancel out what you did, now does it?"

"Did he ask after Bethany?"

"No. She murdered his wife. He has a right to keep his distance. Anyway, this isn't about Bethany, it's about you. You!" He stands up and bangs his fist on the desk. Instinctively, I flinch. But he doesn't care. "Jesus, Gabrielle. What the hell were you thinking of?" Then he sits down abruptly and slaps his hand on the desk again.

I smooth my skirt. "I was curious," I tell him quietly. That's the closest I can get to the truth. A fuller answer—that I was hoping to find a clue to the daughter's visions in the father's religious beliefs—will damn me further. Not because I wanted answers to my questions but because of the way I went about getting them. "Is curiosity about one's patients a crime?"

"You were curious," he repeats quietly. "*Curious.*" He exhales an infuriated sigh. "Well, I too am *curious*, Gabrielle. And being curious—about you, in this case—I naturally made a call to London and spoke to your previous employers in Hammersmith. And learned that Dr. Omar Sulieman, who gave you such a glowing reference when you applied for this posting, has sadly *died*. So we were unable to have the conversation I would have liked. But I spoke to his successor, Dr. Wyndham. Who hadn't known you but looked you up in the file at my request." I take in a breath but don't speak. There's no point. A seagull settles on the windowsill, tilts its head to observe us for a second, then takes off in a white whir. "It seems from the records that all the other members of the Assessment Committee opposed your reinstatement at the Unit, on the grounds that you weren't ready to go back to work in the wake of your accident and bereavement. Psychologically, they claimed, you were unready to meet the challenges of resuming such a demanding career, and they recommended that you take another six months' sick leave. Dr. Sulieman, however, overrode that decision when he supported your application for the temporary post here at Oxsmith."

A silence. Thinking time for us both. He's looking at me expectantly. The ticking clock on the wall says it's eighteen minutes past ten. As I watch the seconds pass, my mind goes into overdrive. Money—or the lack of it—suddenly looms large. According to my lawyer, my compensation from the accident is a long way off. Has my one misjudgment rendered me unemployable? At nineteen minutes past ten, still aware of his eyes on me, I say, "I'll pack up my office and get out of your hair."

But Sheldon-Gray looks alarmed rather than relieved. "According to your contract, you have another month. Just be grateful I'm not taking immediate disciplinary proceedings."

"These are very serious claims," I say, sensing an advantage. "Therapists who behave unprofessionally are a liability to any establishment. Surely you'd want to expose me officially?" He does the thing with his cuffs. I press on. "Unless perhaps you have a staff shortage due to Dr. Ehmet's having gone? And recruitment at Oxsmith being—*I gather*—a regular problem . . ."

"You have four weeks," he says brusquely. The cuffs now in order, some papers on his desk seem inexplicably to call for his immediate attention. "And please don't ask me for a reference. Because I assure you, there will be no pity factor this time." I am dismissed. I swivel to leave. "In the meantime," he tells my retreating back, "your contact with Bethany Krall is at an end."

With Indian takeout steaming on the passenger seat of my car, I drive over to Frazer Melville's home, where I have rarely been due to its lack of wheelchair-friendliness. It's a rented terraced house not far from the port. Inside, the walls are decorated with huge tattered maps, black-and-white botanical photographs that he has taken himself, and images of nature at its most dramatic: sunsets, rivers of molten lava, thunderous waterfalls. Like his office, it's an erudite, well-educated sprawl: the chaos of a creative and avidly curious individual who has omitted to organize regular home help. He's palefaced and monosyllabic. We pick at the food, straight from the cartons, almost in silence. I do not dare ask the question because I can read the answer on his face.

"I've printed out the replies I got," he says eventually. "Such as they are." He jerks his head in the direction of the side table.

I roll over and take a look. He has printed out seven separate e-mails. "Dear Frazer," begins the first:

> I read your e-mail with great amusement and have passed it on to
> Judy because she's always assuring me we scientists are a humor-
> less bunch. Nice one!! Anyway, I look forward to hearing more

from your mysterious Oracle with interest and will mark up my calendar.

Best wishes, Cees.

P.S. Since you ask, I would estimate the chances of a cyclone hitting Mumbai on the date you mention to be 5,380 to 1.

The second:

Dear Dr. Melville, please accept my deepest condolences on your mother's death last month, which I heard about when I contacted your office this morning. All of us at the center would like to send you our sympathies at this difficult time and hope that you recover your spirits very soon. On a personal note, I recall when my father died I was very shaken and wasn't really myself for some months afterwards . . .

The third:

My dear, dear Frazer,

Hello from the Arctic! If you are serious about these "predictions" being bona fide science (and from the tone of your mail I fear yes, you are) then this is a big professional mistake, whether your "source" is right or not. As your friend as well as your ex-wife, I will now do what I hope you would do for me. I advise you, dear Frazer, to not take this further. You have a wonderful reputation in the field. I know how hard you worked for the name you have, so perhaps you already have second thoughts. In any case, I promise you with hand on my heart I will not pass this on. I'm sure you have been under strain with your mother's death . . .

"The worst are the ones who didn't reply," says Frazer Melville flatly. "Because I know what they're thinking and what they're saying to one another. They're dancing the fucking Schadenfreude polka."

"You're regretting it."

"No. Yes. Not if Bethany's right. But if she's wrong—well, of course. I'll just have to plead insanity. At least I'll have a shrink to back me up."

"An art therapist."

He smiles forlornly. "Beggars can't be choosers."

But a few days later, he rings in triumph. "She predicted heavy flooding in Bangladesh on the fifth and it happened. And now a cyclone's heading for Mumbai, due to hit tomorrow. Just like she wrote in the notebook. September 13. She predicted it over a month ago. Maybe more. No weather forecaster can do that."

"Do you feel vindicated?"

"Don't you?"

"No," I decide. I think of Bethany, chewing her green gum and punching the air like she'd won a prize. "Just sick. And somehow . . . responsible."

"I'm recontacting people about Hong Kong and Samoa. But I'm not hopeful. The people I tell either think I'm nuts or they're jealous because they reckon I've invented a new machine that can detect early warning signals."

Some days after the cyclone has wreaked its worst, killing more than 300 in Mumbai, I drive to Frazer Melville's house.

He opens the door in silence. He has lost weight and his clothes hang loosely. He doesn't bend to kiss me, and this time there's no welcoming touch. I can feel he's withdrawing from me and perhaps even keeping something crucial to himself. BBC World is on. As I had already heard on the news, much of Hong Kong island is on fire. A gas blast caused a high-rise to topple, killing eighty. Elsewhere hundreds more are dead, after lightning struck the boat settlements and the resulting blaze, fanned by tropical breezes, flared upward into the tinder-dry woodland of Peak District. It's evening over there, and Hong Kong seen from the air is a splash of orange in the South China Sea. Across the water in Kowloon, more fires are raging, triggered by gas blasts.

"You have to tell me what's going on," I say eventually, nodding at the screen. "Apart from this."

"I had a call from my head of department yesterday," he says. "He's not happy about the fact I've been making scientifically unfounded statements."

"A few e-mails to colleagues?"

"It's an abuse of my university status, according to him. He's old school."

"So what's the punishment?"

"Oh, just the usual freezing out, I imagine. But I'm not staying to find out. I told him I wanted a six-week sabbatical."

"He agreed to it?"

"With insulting alacrity." His smile is bleak. "No one will speak to me, not even off the record, about these fires," he says, waving at the TV. "I'm persona non grata."

"And Harish Modak?" I ask. There's an uneasy silence, which I take as a no. "And the Web?"

"Oh, it's spreading like bird flu." He doesn't need to say that this is more a curse than a blessing.

"So sooner or later the science and news journalists will pick it up, then." We let this thought hang for a moment. "So what next?"

"We go to London and make the people who can make things happen listen to us."

"Campaigners?" I ask.

He shrugs. "A last resort is a last resort."

"But how will their reaction be any different?"

He reaches for a bottle of whisky and sighs heavily. "I don't know." His face succumbs to gravity. "Now do you want a drink? I'm having one." He sloshes himself a glass, swallows it down in one gulp, and then pours another.

The next morning is gray, and the weather has finally cooled a little. In the fields and hedgerows and on the industry-sponsored round-abouts, the reds and oranges and dark greens stand out like heraldic flags. It's effectively the second autumn of the year. The first shriveled the leaves on the branches and sun-blasted the fruit to ripeness back in May. Now more leaves are falling, horse chestnuts are splitting open, and the hedgerows are studded with the bright red of ripening rosehips, deadly nightshade, and hawthorn. I'm used to driving alone, my wheelchair folded on the passenger seat, and I'm finding it hard to adjust to having a person next to me instead, particularly one as weary-looking and hungover as Frazer Melville is today. Last night I could see he was drinking too much but I didn't steer him away from it any more than I allowed myself to signal a desire for the physical intimacy I was aching for. Was I respecting his space or just being a coward? He'd seemed almost oblivious to my presence, and I was too insecure to initiate anything. In any case, I rationalized, his bedroom is upstairs.

But now, the fact that we did not make love last night has spawned an unease, adding invisibly to the conflicted issue that has dominated the first twenty minutes of our journey: how much should we reveal about Bethany? I have insisted that her anonymity remain sacrosanct. Plus, I've argued, revealing our source as the inmate of a mental institution will hardly credit our case. He acknowledges this but declares himself hamstrung: if he cannot refer to Bethany's insights into turbulence as a product of ECT, then he can offer no scientific evidence to back up his theory about sensitivity to geological and meteorological vibrations. Finally, we reach a fragile accord, but the subsequent wordlessness of our journey up to London bears witness to our misery and stress. After all that's happened, there suddenly doesn't seem much more to say. The bottom line, as he has pointed out repeatedly, is that we have nothing left to lose. And therefore no choice, following our snub from Harish Modak, but to plead our case to environmental pressure organizations unrelated to the Planetarians. Frazer Melville, BA, MA, PhD, and various other acronymic suffixes, has effectively lost his job, and I am on the verge of losing mine. If his silence represents optimism about our current mission, I wish I could share it and be blessed with some inkling as to what the Tribulation might actually involve beyond some vague notion of floods and locust plagues. A nuclear accident, perhaps?

On that cheerful mental note, we enter the capital.

Saving the world from ecological disaster is big, slick business. The organization's funding engine may be fueled by mass collective guilt, but its public face is as confident and forward-thinking as the building that houses it, from its solar-paneled facades and discreet roof windmills to the impressive collection of donated artists' work in the lobby. I'm struck by the scale of the operation, the corporate competence of the administrative machine. Money and conviction make for a potent mix. In the waiting area, dominated by a TV wall showing highlights of public campaigns, we are offered lattes. Ten minutes later we are ushered up to the tenth floor, from where the erratic cubist panorama of London's skyline is on display beneath a thickening lid of cloud. I take in the drab municipal grays, interrupted by green swathes of park, and the landmarks I remember my father pointing out to me on our outing here together six years ago, when his brain and my legs still functioned, in what proved a last, unintended family farewell to the city: the Swiss Re building, the Post Office Tower, the great wheel of the Eye, Nelson's column, and St. Paul's. In between, the snaking lines of red buses. We rode on one that day. Upstairs. We talked and talked.

It's clear from the respectful greeting given to Frazer Melville by the chief ecologist, Karla Fitzgerald, and her team, that my physicist's name carries a certain cachet.

"We came to see you in person because this is an unusual situation," Frazer Melville begins after he has settled on the sofa and introduced me simply as "Gabrielle Fox, a friend who shares my concern." He's nervous. Can Karla Fitzgerald sense it too? She smiles easily, but she's businesslike. She apologizes for not being able to spare us more than ten minutes: she has another meeting at eleven. We have discussed how to pitch our story and where to begin.

"The Istanbul earthquake was very accurately foreseen by someone who we have reason to believe has access to a very specialist predictive system." Frazer Melville's tone is professional, but I can see Karla Fitzgerald's instant, quiet shock. "The same system enabled this individual to pinpoint the date of the hurricane in Rio some weeks in advance," he presses on. There are photographs on her walls of children. Karla Fitzgerald's own perhaps, when she was young. Or her grandchildren. "The same source is now speculating—"

But Karla Fitzgerald has stood up abruptly, her hand raised in an emergency stop gesture. Abandoning her desk she comes across and settles next to Frazer Melville on the sofa. My heart plummets. I've sensed sympathy too often not to recognize it now.

"Look, before you go any further, I must tell you that this information isn't new to us, Dr. Melville," she says gently. She could be talking to one of her grandchildren. "We've already heard about those predictions. And where they come from. We do recognize it's quite a coincidence. But no more than that." Has Bethany contacted them herself? "Several organizations, ours among them, were approached some time ago by a very disturbed woman. She claimed the disasters were being caused by a child in a psychiatric institution where she used to work. Somewhere on the south coast. Hadport, I think." There is nothing to say. Karla Fitzgerald looks apologetic. "The girl's name was . . . Bethany?" Frazer Melville looks down at his hands. "Look. I appreciate your both taking the time to come and see us. A lot of people are very concerned about these issues, and so they should be," Karla finishes diplomatically. "We always tell them that the best way to help is to make a donation or become active in the organization. I have some membership forms here," she says, standing again, returning to her desk, and reaching in a drawer. She fans out some bright papers. "Is that something that might interest either of you?"

Beyond humiliation, we drive home in silence.

Sex is a great healer but once again, the physicist is not interested. He flinches from my touch and I feel spurned, even though I know it means nothing. Might mean nothing. Doesn't necessarily mean anything. I should go home but I make the mistake of not doing so. Instead . . .

Anger management theory, which I have only recently been propounding to a roomful of surly psychotic teenagers, has it that one should not allow irritants and grievances and defeats to accumulate. That one cannot read the minds of others any more than one can make the world accord with one's own vision of how it should be run. But soon the physicist and I have begun a heated argument in which I fail quite spectacularly to practice what I have spent so much time preaching, both to myself and to others. I insist that we must do something more, something that will make a difference. Still smarting from our defeat, he wants to know what, now that we have burned our bridges. Tell new people, I say. People who will believe. He is scathing about who those people might be.

"Internet paranoiacs. Ecofanatics. Psychics. People on the distant margins. The kind of people you give a wide berth to. The kind of people Sheldon-Gray Googled for you. Freaks in Prague and mystics in Yucatán. Apocalypse dot fucking com. Forget it."

But I cannot allow pessimism to prevail. We part on bad terms. He seems to have lost about five kilos in two weeks and doesn't look well for it. I am supposed to have an understanding of the human psyche. But today I do not.

. . .

The next morning when I arrive at work I'm informed at Reception
that Dr. Sheldon-Gray wants to see me immediately to discuss an "incident" involving Bethany Krall. When I get there I discover that today his pomposity is formal, statesmanlike, as though the next step in
his career involves a UN candidacy. He is afraid there is bad news.
Bethany is in St. Swithin's hospital. She is "not doing too well."

"What happened?"

"Electrocution. She got hold of a metal fork and stuck it in a
socket. Passed out, of course. Burns all over her hands and up her
arms. Miracle she's not dead. Rubber soles. Oh, and before all that
she shaved her head."

"Totally?"

"It seemed ritualistic. They're keeping her in hospital." Something's up. I can feel it in the air. He has a plan.

"So what now?" I'm wondering how best to play this.

He places his hands on the desk, spreads his fingers, and eyes me
defiantly. "I'm having her transferred to Kiddup Manor."

Kiddup Manor: modern psychiatry's death row.

In the silence that follows he lifts his hands from the desk and
places them in an attitude of prayer, the middle fingers touching his
lower lip. The blue eyes scroll across my face assessingly. If I speak
now, my voice will tremble and I'll betray myself. So I don't. Instead
I nod, as though Bethany's transferral to one of the most brutal institutions in the country is worth mature consideration and will make
no difference to me.

"Any particular reason?" I manage finally.

"I'm merely following the guidelines. They're very clear when it
comes to repeated self-harm. Another approach is called for."

"You realize what will happen to her there?" I say as calmly as I can.
"That all the progress she's made here in Oxsmith will be undone?
That they'll pump her with drugs until she's practically a vegetable?"

He shrugs. "A safe vegetable. No longer a danger to herself or others. Look, the ECT experiment was a mistake."

"It worked."

"For a while. But she just stuck a fork in an electric socket, knowing it could kill her. Look, I'm prepared to take responsibility for the
ECT decision. I'm the one who signed the forms, and it seemed like
the right treatment at the time. It produced an improvement. But

now it's backfired and I admit defeat. Anyway. Since you've been her most recent therapist, I just thought you should know. As soon as she's free to leave hospital, she's no longer our patient."

"Or our problem."

He smiles. "Semantics. We do the best we can. But there's no dishonor in admitting that Bethany Krall's treatment here has been one of our most spectacular failures."

"How long will they keep her in St. Swithin's?"

"Until the burns heal. Take tomorrow off. You look dreadful."

It's late. I hesitate, then call the physicist. His phone is busy, so I decide to drive over and tell him what's happened, hoping that I'll end up staying the night and that the tension engendered by our disastrous trip to London will dissolve with a session in bed. It's what I need. Sex. Sex with Frazer Melville. To be in his arms.

A late-night jogger thunders up the pavement outside his house, accompanied by three high-stepping dogs on long leashes. There's no space free directly in front, so I park opposite. The lights are on in his living room. I'm just about to dial his number so that he can help me up the steps when I glance at the house again. I don't know why. But that's when I see her. She's tall and wearing jeans. She's standing at his window, looking out. Blond. Trim. Young. She wasn't there when I pulled up. But now, like a horrible jack-in-the-box she has materialized in the physicist's home. Then I see him emerging from the kitchen. Is that where she has come from too? Has he cooked for her? Like a car driven by a reckless drunk, my heart attempts a sickening U-turn. Fails. And stalls.

The woman looks at home.

She moves away from the window and over to the sofa, where the physicist settles next to her, close enough for their bodies to touch. They're looking at something together, heads lowered over the table. He wants to impress her. And she's considering the matter. She has the power.

By now I'm not just trembling. I am shuddering all over. And I can't seem to stop.

His ex, I realize. Melina. Since the e-mail, she's been worried about him. So she's flown over. To take care of him. She doesn't look Greek. Has she stopped being a lesbian? Does she want him back? Does he want her?

Or not Melina. Someone else. A young colleague. One of his students.

Have they fucked yet?

She crosses her legs and I feel a flash of venomous, untamed envy. She can stand on them, she can run with them, she can use them to get up and down, she can spread them when he's entering her. A dry retch hatches in my throat.

It makes sense, the kind of obvious sense a 3-D puzzle makes when you slot the last piece into the right configuration, having wrestled with it for hours.

I am not a real woman anymore, and I was wrong to think I was. My mistake was to assume there were no other women in his life. Women with elegance and slim, fully functioning legs, Melina or someone else, someone who has every right to take a sexual interest and is worth losing weight for. Women who can stand up, and turn on their heel, as she is now doing, and wander across the room to look at the books on the shelves, as though she is contemplating moving in and wondering where hers will fit. Can you die from jealousy? It feels like you can, and that I will.

I am about to start the car and make my getaway. But suddenly, appallingly, I can't—because the physicist has jumped to his feet and is heading directly for the window.

Terrified that he'll spot me, I duck. Not easy. My heart's thumping. Bent double like an ignoble paperclip, I'm having trouble breathing. I am absurd. I am raging. My chest is tight, my upper spine hurts, I am still shuddering. I force myself to stay with my head tucked down by the steering wheel, not daring to look up in case I reveal myself. The blood rushes to my head.

My hands and my mouth and breasts are not enough for him, however alive they are, however greedy for his touch, however responsive. Because when the physicist and I make love, below the waist I am as lifeless as a blow-up doll. And nothing can change that. Ever.

When I finally dare to look up again, there's an almost sick relief in seeing my worst fears confirmed.

I am free to drive home now, because the physicist has done what couples do when they require privacy.

He has closed the blinds and blocked out the world.

EIGHT

What I have learned about psychological survival is that the plan you have for yourself might not be shared by others. That your personal notion of justice is an artificial construct, a luxury and an irrelevance in a world built of cells, minerals, wind, sea, flame, synapses. That the size of a defeat is always in proportion to the size of the ego knocked down. And that all knowledge comes at a price.

Today I am paying it.

Hangovers are a vivid form of vengeance. Last night my apartment became the venue for a small, introverted chardonnay festival. A melancholy choir of Bulgarians provided the entertainment, via a set of headphones that ended up irredeemably tangled beneath the bed. Part of me just watched. The other part was in charge.

Today, pig sick and fallen from life's untrustworthy grace, I will be indulgent toward myself. I will arrange for a mushroom pizza with extra cheese to be delivered to my door by a wordless bike-helmeted Kosovar. I will watch home makeover shows on daytime television. I will drown in unabashed *moi*. I will be my own worst enemy pretending to be my own best friend, tending to my self-inflicted wounds with all the patience and compassion of a committed narcissist. I will recognize passion, sexual fulfilment, and romantic love as mirages that may have fooled me once but never will again. And I will forget that Bethany Krall is being transferred to a maximum-security hospital that will feed her heavy doses of narcotics until the end of what will probably be a short life.

Tomorrow, another story: the sequel. In which I hand in my notice at work, inform my landlady, Mrs. Zarnac, that I'm moving out of her vinegary domain, and ask Lily if I can stay with her in London despite the tricky logistics of a second-floor apartment with no lift, stop caring about the fate of Child B., banish Armageddon, and brainwash myself into erasing the fickle, freckled physicist from my psyche. That, at least, is the agenda I have mapped out for myself before I settle down with a towel to dry my hair and check my phone messages.

Upon which the plan changes.

Not as a result of the first message, an emotional outpouring from Lily—whose predicament bears uncanny parallels to my own. She and Joshua have officially split up, and she's moved out. She thinks she's glad about it. Probably. Lily's a vodka aficionado, and the slurring tells me she's had a festival of her own. She sounds seven shots gone. I feel a wave of affection for her as she apologizes and self-deprecates, but it's followed swiftly by a selfish honk of alarm: does this mean I can't sleep on her red velvet sofa? My head aches sullenly. More paracetamol, it urges, as though it's someone else's head and I'm its slave. Swallow some. You know you want to.

"Wheels. Wheels. *Pick up the fucking phone.*" As soon as I hear the hoarse baby croak, I stop toweling my hair to concentrate. She is calling from an anonymous number that I assume to be St. Swithin's Hospital. "I need you here. You've got to come and get me out. It's happening. It stinks of rotten eggs. We're going to drown. You, me, everyone." How did she get my number? There is a noise in the background. Bethany says "Oh Jesus" and hangs up abruptly. Two psychiatric nurses will be supervising her round the clock. The rules allow her one phone call. I suppose I should feel flattered she has designated me her buddy.

The next message kicks in before I have time to absorb Bethany's call. But in the split second before the physicist speaks, I know it's him. I flinch. Then flare. Flight-fight. I'll opt for fight, every time—but only after a lurch.

"We have to talk. Something's come up. We'll need to rethink things. Just call me right away, can you?"

His voice is low, apologetic, but with a delicate catch, an undercurrent of excitement. So the physicist has had some proper sex, with a woman who can wrap her legs round his back. Whose sudden presence in his life has led to a need to "rethink" things. Good for him. Water deltas down my neck and pools in the hollows of my collarbones. For a moment I am convinced I can't move, that the paraplegia has spread, that my body has calcified, that I am now a quad, a floating brain and no more. In the silence that follows his voice, the physicist's absence throbs in the air, as florid as pain. I press delete.

There's another message, but I can't cope with the possibility of further torture just now, so I call the hospital. The process of getting through to the right department is labyrinthine. When I finally speak to the nurse on duty, she tells me Bethany's condition is stable. She will be kept for a few more days and then transferred to Kiddup Manor. The paperwork is under way. No, they have no knowledge of her having made any phone calls last night. Yes, she has two Oxsmith nurses with her. She's heavily sedated and on painkillers. She has second-degree burns on her hands and arms from the electrocution. She has got hold of my phone number and tried to electrocute herself—but the situation is at least stable, I decide. And she isn't going anywhere for now. I finish drying my hair and laboriously dress. Twice I speed-dial the physicist's number but flip my cell phone shut before it starts to ring.

"Wake up and smell the coffee, Gabrielle Fox," I tell the mirror. I'm applying waterproof mascara and a twenty-four-hour lipstick called Cinnamon Kiss, which like a ship's hull requires a phased application of paint and varnish. "Breathe in deep and inhale the bitter aroma of reality." I stop and consider my reflection and the daily waste of time that is the application of cosmetics, especially those that demand a minute's drying time between layers, and Bethany's astute comment when we first met: why bother with makeup when no one's going to look at you unless they're some kind of perv? "Then go for a swim. And if you drown, don't say Bethany didn't warn you."

Ten minutes later, preparing to leave, I notice that the answering machine light is still winking. I hesitate. A vivid imagination can be as much a curse as a blessing. Today it is all curse. My brain has spent the night conjuring a thousand graphic images and I know that if I hear the physicist's voice again now, twenty lengths of the pool will not be enough for me to process the way his tone has changed to a mixture of apprehension, guilt, and excitement brought on by the thrill of another woman's internal muscles flexing around his penis.

I press play.

"I didn't finish what I needed to tell you the other night," Joy Mc-Coney blurts. I could kiss her. "My husband thinks I'm mad. But I'm not. I need to see you. I have to warn you what'll happen." She leaves her cell phone number. "Ring me when you get this. There's something you have to know about Bethany. It'll change your mind about her."

I recall Joy McConey's paleness as she turned to face us in the doorway of the restaurant. Like those round white paper plates you use for picnics. Blank and honest. She's not just predicting things. She's making them happen.

If humans disappeared from the face of Hadport tomorrow, the botanical species that would most quickly assert itself would be the Australian eucalyptus, a tree that has already made an impressive bid for dominance in the local park where I have suggested to Joy that we meet. Breezes shuffle through their waving silver green canopies, littering the paths beneath with narrow tongues of leaves. If I push hard, I can get there in nine minutes. But today it's seven.

I cross the footbridge of a sluggish stream flanked with burst-open bulrushes, their cottony innards tugged at by the wind. Incongruously, an adult figure is perched on the top of a pyramid-shaped climbing frame in the enclosed children's play area. She sits like a lonely beacon, her pale red hair shining. As I approach and fumble with the gate, she signals hello, then begins to make her way down the wire ropes with a laboriousness that makes me wonder why she climbed up there in the first place. The play area's surface is rubberized; noting its pleasantly soft squish under my wheels I add the sensation to my secret list of life's tiny compensations for all the shit.

"I take the kids here a lot," Joy says, negotiating the last three meters. She squats opposite me on one of the lower metal rungs but makes no attempt to shake hands, which is fine by me because for psychological reasons I want to keep my gloves on.

Before I ask she says, "I have three. Two girls and a boy." She is dressed in jeans and a khaki T-shirt. On her feet, hiking boots. As though she's planning a trip into the jungle, like a modern-day Tintin. "I need to keep fit," she says, brushing something invisible off her knees. "Take care of myself. For the kids' sake. Ronan's only seven. Lots of vitamins, good food, low stress." Her hair swings about her shoulders, glinting with an ethereal, otherworldly shine that belies the combat gear. Her round face is pretty in an understated way but is ghost pale. Apart from a couple of mothers with toddlers over by the sand pit, and the odd dog walker in the distance, we are the only people here. "I can't stay long. I had to sneak out. It's not Nick's fault. He thinks he's doing the right thing. Protecting me from myself, et cetera. He doesn't realize." The words are tumbling out: she could be a teenager exchanging confidences. "My husband's one of those people who have to see things with their own eyes before they'll believe it. And then when they do, they go straight into denial."

The curse of the therapist: reflexively analyzing the behavior of others.

"So tell me what's on your mind, Joy." How I hate the conventions of shrinkspeak. But how unavoidable they are. I can imagine Bethany snorting in contempt.

"When I worked at Oxsmith she wanted something from me that I wasn't prepared to give. I've paid the price and I'll keep paying it for the rest of my life, and I've accepted that." I suggested the park, but the playground was her choice. An interesting one: regression as safety. Joy is clearly in another place—a place so far away from her sane starting point that one must marvel at and respect the journey made. "But I don't want you to be in that situation. That's why I've been following you and why I rang you. I don't want anyone to go through what I have. Especially not you. You look like you've suffered enough." With a sharp twist of irritation, I think: It's not for her to make those judgments. "Bethany's dangerous. Her father knew all about it. I should have realized, it was all there in the notes. Staring at me in black and white. But I had to learn it the hard way, didn't I?"

I ask, "So when Leonard Krall suggests that Bethany's possessed by the devil, you agree?"

"Some kind of force. I don't know what to call it. I was like you once. Not so long ago, I didn't believe in evil. But I do now." Her eyes grow rounder. She seems out of breath, as though her words are exacting a heavy physical price.

"What did Bethany want so badly?"

"She wanted me to help her to escape. I wouldn't, of course. Even though I believed in her. She lost faith in me. And I got scared, and I left."

"You left with nine stars. She liked you. You got along. So what made you scared?"

"When I refused to get her out, she said something terrible would happen to me. It wasn't a prediction. It was a threat."

"What did she say would happen?"

With a single swift movement she raises her hand to her head and, as though removing a hat, lifts off her hair. I stare at the plain white dome of her baldness. Flesh as architecture. I am too shocked to speak. Nor can I think of a single word to say.

She clasps the pale red wig in her hand, its locks trailing like the delicate tendrils of a jellyfish. Her crowning glory. "Cancer."

She tosses the hair to the ground, as if it is of no relevance to her. It lies between us. A piece of evidence, a statement of fact. With extreme reluctance, I pick it up. It's heavier than it looks, and hot inside. I offer it back but she rejects it distractedly. "The doctors have done what they can. But it's terminal."

From the sand pit, a child has materialized. He is about three. He stares at the egg-bald woman on the climbing frame, at my wheel-chair, and then at the mass of red hair curled in my lap, and angles his mouth to form a terrible wail.

For which I do not for one microsecond blame him.

I make it back to the corner of my street in six minutes, shaken to the bone.

I might be forgiven for believing that right now things can't get worse. But then they do. Because in the driveway, chatting to my landlady, dressed in the same crumpled linen suit he wore last night for his blond visitor, stands the very last person I want to see. I approach warily, greet my landlady, and salute the physicist with a curt nod.

He asks, "Where've you been?"

"I was at the park. Not that it's your business."

Mrs. Zarnac's smile falters but her eyes blaze with avid life. Registering tension and perhaps an upcoming clash whose details she can later recount to a gentleman friend, she withdraws only with extreme reluctance into the pickle-scented recesses of her home, prompted by my pointed good-bye. The physicist and I stay where we are, in psychic checkmate. I have no intention of inviting him in. The next move is his.

When it comes, it surprises me. He says, "I need to see Bethany."

"You can't. She's in hospital with burns." Telling him this gives me a perverse satisfaction, as though it is an element of some elaborate punishment that will be meted out to him across the course of his entire life. "She electrocuted herself yesterday. As soon as she's well enough to be transferred, she'll go to another hospital. With a different ethos. Where they'll blast her with every drug known to man. Not the kind of place anyone tends to emerge from."

"Christ," he murmurs. "That's . . . bad news."

"I tried to get hold of you last night to tell you. But I couldn't reach you on the phone. How come?"

He pretends to look puzzled, but when it comes to faking, he is an amateur. His freckles show up like grains of brown sugar, and a little pulse sets up on his left temple.

"I worked late at the office. The switchboard doesn't operate after five. And I must have turned my cell phone off." His left temple is a place that I have often kissed. "I was there till midnight."

I swallow. "And what were you working on, so late, at the office?" I sound like a nagging wife.

"Gabrielle, can you explain why you're interrogating me?" He has not squatted to be at my level, as he usually does. Like a mountain range on the far horizon, or North Korea, he is keeping a strategic distance. I have never heard this coolness in his voice before and I never want to hear it again. If he just bent down now and took me in his arms—

Then I would succumb, and loathe myself even more.

"I don't like being lied to." Folding my arms in unashamed hostility, I let this idea settle.

"I worked late, end of story. I'm sorry I missed your call." Surely I am worth more than this. He looks at me with aggression. "Can I ask what the hell's got into you?"

"For Christ's sake, just tell me the truth. Don't you think I deserve it?" This notion makes him shut his eyes. Perhaps he is hoping I will disappear. Perhaps I am hoping so too. But I am the pigheaded interrogator. "Well?"

He looks down and flushes. "Yes. But you have to trust me." Oh please. I cannot believe that someone I care about—cared about—could allow such verbal dross to pass his lips. How could I ever have— "Anyway, I still need to see Bethany."

"Why?" I snap.

He looks at me levelly. "Take me to her and you'll find out." I'm trying to work out how I could have misread him so badly. He presented himself as being sexually insecure in the wake of his failed marriage. Was that so I would feel I was doing something for him too? "And where have *you* been all this time? You're not the only one who hasn't been able to get through on the phone," he accuses.

Apparently I am a therapist to my marrow because I note, almost with detachment: *anger as a mask for guilt.* "I told you. I was at the park."

"At a time like this? At the park doing what?"

I roll back farther. "Meeting Joy McConey."

"Oh Jesus," he says, lifting his arms in a gesture of dismay. "All on your own? Why on earth—?"

I flare. "Because she asked me to. And I came back in one piece, didn't I?" One broken piece. "Anyway, she's harmless." Why am I suddenly the one defending my actions?

"I don't know why we're arguing like this," he says, finally squatting so that our faces are level. "Look, just tell me what Joy said. It's clearly shaken you up."

If I can't tell him, whom can I tell? I feel horribly alone. And by extension, weak and unloved. I hate myself for caving in to it. "She's got cancer, and she thinks Bethany visited it on her as some kind of . . . retribution. For not helping her escape."

He makes an exasperated noise. "Right. All the more reason to prove there's a scientific explanation for what's happening with Bethany, rather than some pseudoreligious bullshit. Come on," he says, jerking his head at the road. "Let's take your car."

Cooperate with a man who has just betrayed me and lied to my face and has as good as admitted it? *Help* him? But Joy's bald head and the feel of her sweaty wig in my lap has disturbed me in a way I can't allow myself to process without coming to some very sick conclusions. It's eating at me. What if she's right? Despite my rage at the physicist's pathetic, clodhopping, undignified charade, I find myself wanting —vehemently—to find an explanation for all this that does not involve a word as dogmatic and lazy as *evil*. What the physicist needs from Bethany, I need too. If only to prove that Joy's reading of Bethany's motivation is as categorically wrong as it is possible to be.

The self-harm ward of St. Swithin's hospital is an environment of complex despair, of extreme and conclusive failure. Here is where you end up, locally, if you can't even get suicide right. Chastened by its significance and forced into a shaky concord that I can safely bet will not last the hour, the physicist and I enter with due reverence.

In one bed, there's an old man with a mane of white hair who sports a bloody, stitched-up scar across his throat of the variety that only an old-fashioned razor blade or a Stanley knife, brutally applied, will achieve for you. When we enter he sits up as though expecting visitors, then realizes he doesn't know us and swings his majestic head toward the wall. There's a teenage girl not much older than Bethany whose skin is the blunt gray you get when you mix black and white paint. I recognize the most visible symptom of irreversible liver damage, caused by an overdose of paracetamol—which will prove fatal within a couple of weeks unless she is offered a fresh organ. If she isn't, she will turn bright yellow and then she'll die. Her parents sit at their daughter's bedside with a tearful boy of about thirteen. They are blank with disbelief. Or concentration. If they are praying, it's for deliverance in the form of another person's sudden death and a freak stroke of luck with the transplant list. The kid brother is too young for this. They all are. September must be a cruel month because the ward is almost full. In other beds, there are the hunched shapes of people whose eyes are turned inward. The silence of their stoppered, unscreamed pain waltzes around us in invisible currents, fleeting as the shape of wind on water.

The staff nurse is on the phone. "I need the defibrillator," she says. "The new one. Yes. No. Yes. Hold on." Registering our presence, she smothers the mouthpiece with her palm and offers us the valiant half smile of someone doing her best but basically pissing into the wind. Quickly, I introduce myself as a therapist from Oxsmith and my companion as a colleague from Kiddup Manor. We're on a short assessment visit; Bethany's two psychiatric nurses can take a break while we're with her. Perhaps they can be paged and told to come back in ten minutes? When people are embattled in the way this nurse is, they don't have time to suspect others of lying, especially from the moral throne of a wheelchair. She nods, sends a page text, and indicates a door at the far end of the ward, before returning to her call. For the first time in my life, as I watch the two Oxsmith nurses leave, I am grateful for the understaffing of the NHS.

Bethany has the room to herself. She lies with her eyes closed, a negligible mound under the bedclothes, a handful of assembled bones hunched oddly in the manner of an archaeological find. Her newly shaved head barely dents the pillow. Her scalp is a ghoulish white, with a webbing of blue veins pulsing at her temples like a flesh-and-blood section of the London Underground map.

The physicist locates a plastic chair and takes it round to the other side of the bed.

"Wheels," Bethany croaks, her eyes still closed. Then she opens them blearily, blinks them into focus, and flashes an exhausted smile. There's a whiff of chemicals, ointment, sweat. She glances at the physicist, who is now searching in his briefcase for something. She doesn't seem to recognize him. "I heard the nurse say they're transfer-ring me. You can't let them do that. You know what'll happen. I'll kill myself. Unless they give me some volts. Hey, you. Will they give me volts at Kiddup?" she asks the physicist. "I need volts."

"I'm not from Kiddup. I'm Frazer Melville. We met before. You showed me your drawings."

She is wearing a hospital gown. Her arms are wrapped in ban-dages to well above the elbow. Her hands are bound more elaborately, the splayed fingers separated from each other with a thinner gauze, like the webbing of a waterbird.

"He's got quite a sex drive, hasn't he?" she murmurs, nodding to indicate the physicist. "You can smell it on people." Then she sighs, as though the observation has overexerted her. I flush to the roots of my hair. Frazer Melville's eyes meet mine and his mouth twitches in what looks like a small, proud smile, and then he reddens too. The moment is so exquisitely appalling that it could be bottled and sold as a generic life deterrent. Finally, he breaks the sick spell.

"Bethany, you made some drawings that interest me." He fishes some papers from his briefcase and holds one out in front of her. "I'd like to decipher this image. Find out what it signifies."

But Bethany turns her head away as though unnerved by it. Her bandaged hands twitch and scrabble around on the white hospital sheet as though they have an agenda of their own.

"This vertical line," he says, pointing. "Can you tell me what it is?"

Bethany glances at it reluctantly and hesitates. "It's hollow," she mumbles.

"What I need to know is, where does it go to?" The physicist's eyes are intense. What is he getting at? What does he know that I don't?

"Underground. All the way in, like right under the skin." She falters. "It digs its way inside and then explodes and the whole thing cracks open and boom." I flinch and picture Leonard Krall: his canine eyes, his energy, his creepy charisma.

"And if you follow it upwards, instead of down, where does it go to?"

"Just up," says Bethany sulkily. From outside comes the wail of a car alarm, the buzz of traffic, the faint keen of hungry gulls. When I look back at the physicist, I see frustration. He's trying to hide it but can't. I'm torn. I am anxious that this line of questioning is stirring up difficult memories for Bethany. But having come this far, I need to hear something significant, something that will tip the balance back to the rational and as far from the Joy McConey model of interpretation as can be reached. And I'm aware of the time constraint. The two Oxsmith nurses will return from their break any minute.

"OK, Bethany, listen to me," I say, to break the impasse. "Imagine you're at the point where the vertical line meets the ground and then just follow it." She grimaces, as though she is contemplating an open wound. "What do you see?"

She looks puzzled, then aghast. "Fuck, it's water! Everywhere!" Behind her, through the window, the tops of silver birch trees thrash in the breeze, their leaves shimmering like shoals of fish.

"It's OK, Bethany." I say. I nod at the physicist to continue. We seem to have reached a grudging accord, a temporary modus vivendi that will see us through our joint task but no further.

"So this whole thing is underwater?" he asks. "Not on land?"

"I guess it must be. I guess it must be at the bottom of the sea."

"What's the temperature like?"

She shivers and looks scared. "It's freezing. Like there's ice."

"And if you look up?" asks the physicist, scanning Bethany's features urgently. "If you look up toward the sky?" Something seems to have excited him. Even though I don't know what it is, it excites me too and I feel a kind of hope.

"There's something like scaffolding. It's huge." She seems to find the image distasteful.

"What color is it?"

The question throws her for a second. "It's made of iron. It's dripping."

"What else?"

"A crane."

"What color's the crane?"

"Yellow."

"You are sure."

"For fuck's sake. I said yellow."

"OK. Yellow."

"And it stinks. Rotten eggs. Dead jellyfish. It's gross."

I associate a rotten-egg smell with sulphur. But the physicist's face gives nothing away.

"And did you see anything else?"

"Just the scaffolding stuff and a crane on it and some, like, buildings on the platform and some kind of . . . spire. I need some more volts." The physicist is blinking.

"You're sure? Just the crane and the platform and a spire?" She nods. "And the smell?" We sit in silence for a moment. In the distance, a phone rings. "Well, in that case I'll be leaving you," the physicists says abruptly. And he stands up to go. "Thank you both. You've been a great help."

"What about my volts?" says Bethany.

He shrugs. "How long will they keep you in here?"

"Until the people in white coats come and take me away."

He looks at her sharply, as if she has read something going on in his head.

I turn to face him full-on. "Aren't you going to tell us what this all means?"

He heads for the door and opens it. "I will. But just now, I'm afraid I can't."

Does he think I'll let him walk away that easily? "So what now?" I ask. I have followed him out to the corridor but he doesn't stop walking or slow his pace.

"I'm going to Southeast Asia. I'll be out of circulation for a while." He glances at me sideways, uneasy. Now that he has got what he wanted, it seems he can't get away fast enough.

"Southeast Asia? What sort of trip is this? You never mentioned it."

We reach the double doors to the main ward, where he indicates that this is where we part ways. "I'm taking time out. A field trip. Botanical photos. That's all you know. About anything. Today never happened. None of it. Next time you see me, you'll understand."

"What do you mean, today never happened?"

He looks at me with an odd thoughtfulness. I am lured in by the green shard. "Do you trust me?"

A wash of bitterness. I laugh uneasily. When in doubt, joke. "Do you think I'm stupid?"

"No. You're clever, and imaginative, and capable of thinking on your feet. All of which I'm absolutely depending on, Gabrielle. Now go home, and I'll see you when I see you."

He sounds almost flippant—as though he, too, has the right to approach this thing humorously. He does not. Then, sickeningly, he leans as though to kiss me. I swivel sharply away, out of his reach. What kind of kiss was he planning? A friendly peck on the cheek? Or something more intimate, for old times' sake, the very morning after he has stuck his tongue down a blond's throat?

"How can you do this to me?" I whisper. I can feel my whole torso shuddering. The new expression on his face—pity—is as unmistakable as it is appalling.

He says, "Because I have to."

And he pushes his way through the doors and he is gone and my soul shrivels.

No, he doesn't have to. He has a choice.

"What were you thinking, when you put that fork in that socket?" I hurl at Bethany on my return. I am transferring my rage with the physicist onto her, and so what? "You could have died. Look at you."

"I sense negative emotions." She flashes me a metallic grin.

"Swap roles then."

"OK, as your therapist, I'd say you need to steady on. But first, I need to get out of here. You have to help me escape."

Izgoy, izgoy. "You will leave. But only when it's time."

"To Kiddup, right? Come on. Everyone knows about that place. They'll test anything on you there. It's a fucking pharmaceuticals laboratory. If I don't drown first, I'll die in there, you know that. You can't let them do it. And it's happening soon, this thing. I told you. October 12. Maybe sooner. After the thunder comes. It's building up. I saw it. Nothing can stop it."

I take a deep breath. "So why didn't you tell Frazer Melville?" I can barely say his name.

She shrugs. "No point. He already knows."

I flush. Of course he does. I feel dumb, muddled, blindsided. "How could you tell?"

"I felt it in his blood. He and that woman—"

"What woman?" My sharpness betrays me but I'm past caring.

She smiles her mean smile. "I could smell her on him. So could you." I feel a queasy inner slide, like the yawn of a trombone. "They've got something going together. And you're out of the picture." Unsummoned, a graphic image rears: the woman's legs high in the air, his torso above her, his pelvis plunging into hers. Then they roll over, his buttocks working, still doing it. Buttocks I have grasped. Her astride him, rocking. Bethany grimaces theatrically. "Whoa, steady on, Wheels. Porn city."

I blink the image away. "OK, so what's happening at this place you drew?"

"I don't know. Ask him. But we have to get somewhere safe."

"Where would that be?"

"I dunno. Up a mountain. You've got to help me."

"I'm going to find out more. I'm doing what I can."

"Alone? Look at you. You're a spaz. You don't know anyone. And no one will believe you anyway. It's Joy McConey all over again."

Is there menace in her voice, or am I imagining it?

"I'm not alone. Frazer Melville's working on it too," I say. It's as hopeless as it sounds. And his name still sticks in my throat, like something I once ordered in a restaurant and regretted deeply. "You have to trust him." That phrase again. So half-baked you could cry. And soon I will. She looks at me and snorts in derision.

"Jesus, Wheels. You're becoming totally fucking unhinged. Why should I trust him, if you don't?"

I have no response to that. Except to acknowledge that a naïve and stubborn part of me is in militant denial. A horrible truth is star-

ing me in the face. And all I can say to it is, No. Go away. I don't believe you. I can't. I won't.

Dr. Sulieman once gave me a piece of advice that was as powerful as
it was simple: when in doubt, be practical. Deciding to heed this, because it has worked for me in the past, I arrive home with a mission.

The evening the physicist carried me up two flights of stairs to his
office like a sack of veg and we looked at Bethany's notebooks, I saw
her "Moonscape with Machinery" drawings through the prism of
Freud. But I recall now that the physicist was thinking along altogether different lines. He said: *Some kind of mining operation.* What
if that interpretation is closer to the truth than my own, instinctive
one? It's as well to bear in mind that therapists operate within the
same matrix as people who write soap operas. As Freud is supposed
to have said, "Sometimes a cigar is just a cigar." What if the sketch
that I interpreted as a penis invading and ejaculating inside a horizontal, submissive body turned out to be something else altogether?
Bethany mentioned icy temperatures, and scaffolding, and a platform, and the seabed, and a bad smell. What can you mine for underwater that's freezing cold?

I make coffee and switch on my laptop. Within a few minutes I
have encountered the word *clathrate*. Clathrate meaning cage. A
clathrate, also known as a gas hydrate, is a thin coating of ice that has
developed around a gas molecule, forming a shell. But it isn't the unfamiliar word so much as the accompanying diagram in a scientific
paper that snares me. Because unlike most cages you think of, this
one, which is associated with ocean-bed mining operations, bears a
shape familiar to me from Bethany's artwork.

A hexagon.

When I learn what is trapped inside these ice hexagons, I put my
hand to my neck and note its clammy heat.

Methane.

At what point did the physicist make the connection between
Bethany's drawings and the most dangerous greenhouse gas of all?
Many times more powerful than carbon, millions of square kilometers of it are locked frozen onto the seafloor, all around the world, in
the form of a crust. I imagine vast swathes of dirty subzero champagne. Water pressure and cold temperatures are what keep it down
there. Without those, it would shoot to the surface in huge sheets

like polystyrene and burst into flame. It is so volatile that until recently there was no serious discussion about harvesting it for energy purposes. It was too dangerous. I type in "methane" again, but this time—on a hunch—team it with "catastrophe."

There are thousands of references.

I take a sip of coffee.

Choosing the most easily decipherable headings, I swiftly discover that a massive cataclysm involving sudden suboceanic methane gas is not just a theoretical possibility but a dramatic part of geological history. Twice in the distant past, the planet's atmosphere has been microwaved—resulting in the devastation of most of life on Earth. One of the main culprits was methane. The first, and worst, event took place 251 million years ago, at the end of the Permian era. The second extreme warming disaster heralded the Paleocene-Eocene Thermal Maximum. Following a vague instinct, perhaps to do with its relative closeness in prehistoric time, I type this abstruse era in and add the word "research."

At which point, after scrolling through hundreds of links, I come across an image that startles me. It shows a geopaleontologist, a specialist in the so-called PETM, who has worked extensively analyzing foraminifera, fossilized microcrustacea in mud cores hauled from the deep. In the photo the geopaleontologist, who is bundled in a thick anorak and red woolly hat, is proffering, in a gloved hand, a large white lump that resembles a snowball. The snowball is on fire. The flame is pure and orange, blue at the edges. The caption reads, "Frozen methane is known as the ice that burns." The woolly hat, out of which blond strands of hair emerge, is partially covering the left side of the geopaleontologist's face, but you can tell that the sight of the flaming white lump delights her. She could be in love with it.

The geopaleontologist's name is Dr. Kristin Jonsdottir. She is Icelandic.

When I consider Iceland, which I seldom do, I think of geysers, financial meltdown, and fishing crises. But from now on I will think of other things, closer to home.

Because the blond-haired Kristin Jonsdottir, PhD, expert on the contents of prehistoric oceanic mud, has a bone structure, and a tilt to the head, and in particular a pair of legs that I recognize.

I take another sip of coffee and note that my hands are shaking. I lay them flat on the table and wait for them to calm. *When in doubt, be practical.* Returning my attention to my laptop, I shift the focus of my research to the personal. I begin with a potted biography that tells me that the woman I now fervently hate was born in Iceland, has a first-class degree from Edinburgh University and another from Reykjavik, and has worked in the United States, South America, Indonesia, Namibia, and Russia.

Evidence of high intelligence and virulent ambition.

The night I first met Dr. Frazer Melville, he emerged from the banqueting hall of the Armada Hotel in Hadport wiping his face with a napkin because he was hot. He saw I was struggling to reach the guest list on the wall, and he came and helped me. It seemed an innocent coincidence: here was a scientist with whom I might discuss Bethany's case. We abandoned the reception and went for a quiet dinner. And I talked about Bethany. Later, I introduced him to her. But what if he already knew about Bethany and sought me out as a conduit to her?

What if his lover, Kristin Jonsdottir, had sent him?

I skim through the titles of her publications, which include the riveting "Abiotic Forcing of Plankton Evolution in the Cenozoic," "Biogeographic Sedimentology and Chemostratigraphic Recognition of Third-Order Sequences in Resedimented Carbonate," "Recovery after the Cretaceous-Tertiary Boundary Extinction Event," and "Size Distribution of Holocene Planktic Foraminifer Assemblages." Her interests are listed as "Foraminifers and their influence on the global carbon cycle, ocean acidification as a tool to investigate cryptic species, and biotic recovery after extreme events." I don't understand half the vocabulary or know what I am looking for, so perhaps it is no surprise that after printing out one of Kristin Jonsdottir's contributions to *Micropaleontology Today* and absorbing four tightly written pages about the pitfalls of sediment assessment, I decide to take the bull by the horns.

It doesn't take long to trace her, via a friendly man in a research laboratory in Reykjavik. He tells me that his colleague Kristin is currently on a field trip in the UK. Sure, he can give me a mobile number. And he does. I must say hi to her from him. I promise I will.

The phone rings four times before she picks up. The connection isn't good. She says something in Icelandic: it sounds like a question. Politely, I apologize for speaking English and introduce myself as Gabrielle Fox, a friend of Frazer Melville's.

But I do not keep the upper hand for long. Her accent is lilting, her tone gently regretful.

"I'm sorry, Gabrielle. I know exactly who you are. I have heard about you from Frazer. But I have nothing to say to you."

"But I need to know—"

She says bluntly, "Forgive me for doing this, but good-bye, Gabrielle." And she hangs up.

The blood rushes to my face. When I call back, the phone has been switched off. I feel more humiliated than I have ever felt in my life.

But I feel other things too. Because a sick, insistent part of me is visiting a place I thought I would never visit again.

Over the next two days frustration, depression, anger, self-pity, and self-loathing dominate. In the evenings I imbibe excessive quantities of alcohol and in the mornings I feel even more terrible. One night I call Lily; she recounts her love woes and I make friend-and-also-therapist suggestions but don't talk about what is happening with me, because I am not ready, and I am not ready because I am too proud, and I am too proud because I am me. The loss is mine and I know it, and so does Frida Kahlo, at whom I throw a balled-up pair of socks and miss, which compounds my rage. The person I hate most, of course, is myself.

I, too, have been the other woman. Alex always said his wife didn't suspect our affair. She was too trusting, too complacent about her role in his life, too busy with her career and the kids to spot the telltale signs: the late nights at the office, the work trips abroad where alien time zones colluded in the alibi, the scent of fresh soap after a long day. But if she had, and she had telephoned me and introduced herself, I have no doubt about what I would have done.

I, too, would have said, "I'm sorry. I know who you are. But I have nothing to say to you." And I, too, would have hung up.

Bethany remains in St. Swithin's under observation, with two psychiatric nurses in attendance at all times. To take my mind off what has happened, I work extra hours because five staff are off sick. The physicist does not call me, but why should he, now that he has what he really wants, and wanted all along: the information he was after and a fellow scientist he can fuck. I go to Oxsmith at seven in the morning and come home twelve hours later, exhausted. When I have a spare moment, I sleep. One day, slightly drunk, I call the physicist's numbers—all three—but get no reply. His cell phone is switched off. I do not leave messages. I feel abandoned.

But somehow a tiny twist of hope remains, like a persistent virus I can't shake off. *Today never happened.*

What did he mean?

I'm emptying my dishwasher when the phone rings. It's a terse and furious Dr. Sheldon-Gray. I picture him in his righteous pink shirt, the phone clamped to his ear.

"Bethany Krall has disappeared," he announces. "From the hospital. Last night." Something inside me changes pressure at great speed. When I ask for details, the word he uses is *abducted*. "As in, someone got her out."

Today never happened. I close my eyes to steady the vertigo. "How?"

"Whoever took her caught the nurses off guard. Kelly was having a cigarette, Mike claimed he was using the bathroom but was in fact making a long phone call. Someone dressed as a surgeon walked in, woke her up, put her in an overall with a cap and a mask, and off they went. Two bloody doctors, one a child, strolling out to the car park cool as you please. I've seen the CCTV footage. Bethany even turns and gives the camera the finger. It's a disgrace. Any clues?"

I am shocked, but there's a curious heave of excitement too: even a kind of skewed triumph. Bethany must surely be better off with people whose motivation is altruistic than at the end station that is Kiddup Manor. I tell my boss that I am horrified but that I know nothing—nor can I imagine who might be behind it, short of somebody as demented as Bethany herself. Apparently fobbed off for now, Sheldon-Gray says he has more calls to make and hangs up without saying good-bye.

But I have not escaped scrutiny that lightly. Ten minutes later the doorbell rings and I open it to find a young policeman, his fiercely accessorized car parked next to mine. Mrs. Zarnac is leaning out of the upper window in what might be her notion of an erotic nightdress, unable to contain her glee. "I heard it on the radio!" she calls down. "That Oxsmith loony girl, she yours? You hear she run away?"

"Let me give you five minutes to get ready," says the policeman.

"And we'll head down to the station for some paperwork and an interview with one of the detectives on the case. If that's OK with you, Madam."

Somehow, the "Madam" makes it a more serious matter.

A field trip to Southeast Asia. Capable of thinking on your feet.

With the young policeman hovering in the doorway, I search in my handbag for my lipstick. It's one thing to lie—blithely—to one's boss, but perjury and the perversion of justice are a somewhat tougher call, given that they can get you slapped in jail. In the hall mirror, I apply the first coat and check my teeth for smudges. But if I report my suspicion that Frazer Melville is involved, how would the hollow triumph of putting my ex-lover behind bars affect Bethany's fate and that of a world threatened by methane gas? I apply a second coat.

"You ready there, Madam?"

Five minutes is never five minutes.

And less than five minutes—I reckon two—is not a long time in which to make a very crucial decision.

But it's long enough.

NINE

There are certain people who despite being relatively young convey the knowingness of nonagenarians without ever being charmed or moved to tears by anything the world has to offer. Detective Trevor Kavanagh, thirty-something, sits with his legs spread apart because the thickness of his thighs ordains it. I am helping the police with their inquiries in a bare room with a tiny digital tape machine that is recording our conversation for legal posterity.

The story of Bethany's abduction has been on the local radio news all morning. Have I heard it? No: unlike my landlady, I do not listen to Sunshine FM or BBC Southern Counties from morning till night. In that case, for my benefit, Detective Kavanagh will recap. A teenage girl known publicly as Child B., a psychotic minor, was left unattended in hospital for a period of four minutes. The system failure that led to this is an issue that falls in another category and is being "indexed separately." In that crucial period, CCTV footage shows a figure—probably male, age unclear—in green surgeon's overalls and face mask, freeing Bethany Krall. That Bethany left the hospital with this "individual" without a struggle would seem attributable to either collusion or—can I comment on this?—a random symptom of her mental unbalance. Kavanagh does not add that as Bethany's most recent therapist I am an inherent part of this procedural shambles. But the thought hangs between us.

Detective Kavanagh's hands, laid on the desk, are as strong and clean as an orthopedic surgeon's. You could put your life in them. He tells me there were no signs of a struggle, so the likelihood is that Bethany's abductor was somebody known to her.

"Can I ask, how long have you been, er, confined to . . ." he nods at it. I roll a millimeter back.

"One year, ten months, and three days. And it's permanent. I can't walk, if that's what you're getting at. As for where I was last night," I tell him, anticipating where this is going, "I don't have an alibi. At least, not one I can prove. I was at home, alone. Just me and my titanium friend here." I pat a wheel.

The detective tells me that Dr. Frazer Melville's name appears in the visitors' log at Oxsmith. He has taken time off work at very short notice. What is our relationship, what was his interest in Bethany, and where has he gone?

"We're acquaintances rather than close friends. As far as I know, he's away on a field trip."

"Well he *has* gone abroad," Kavanagh says. He presents the information like it's a poker stake. Responding in kind, I do not allow my features to move. "And we're concerned, naturally, at the coincidence."

"Where is he?"

"We have a record of his having arrived in Thailand yesterday."

The detective is reading my face, so I try to keep my shock hidden while I work out the math, and the implications, of what he has just said. If Bethany was taken early this morning, Frazer Melville didn't do it. He was in Thailand. Nothing fits. So who took Bethany? Is it possible that he has actually done what he said he was going to do and is currently photographing nature in Southeast Asia? With a methane disaster unleashing itself in five days?

Today never happened. And nor did Kristin Jonsdottir. I will grit my teeth and play my part in the game. But not for her sake.

"You are acquaintances with Dr. Melville, you say? Rather than close friends? According to Dr. Sheldon-Gray, you met at a charity function here in Hadport which you left early. Missing both the buffet and the prize raffle." It's clear where this is heading.

"I always get indigestion the next day with those buffets. And I'm never lucky with raffles. Dr. Melville showed an interest in Bethany."

"So you told him all about her?"

"I didn't breach patient confidentiality, if that's what you mean." This is not strictly speaking the truth. "He met her once, that's all. At my suggestion. He wanted to encourage her interest in natural science. I didn't realize what it would lead to." I am not much of an actress: my experience as the religiously confused Penny showed me that much. But I tell him anxiously that I want to help find Bethany and that he can—he must—ask me anything.

"Are you aware that Dr. Melville took Bethany's psychotic visions seriously enough to contact scientist colleagues about them, and this caused his superiors alarm on his behalf?"

I nod in shame and tell him I blame myself for that. I should have spotted that Frazer's preoccupation with Bethany's ideas was unhealthy. Especially because my predecessor, Joy McConey, fell into the same . . . here I search for the word and come up with "trap."

"Bethany's very convincing," I insist. "Her delusions seem to be infectious. It's easy to overidentify with a case like hers." I study the floor and take my time before looking up. It feels as though we are both caught in a bell jar. "Dr. Sheldon-Gray thinks I've succumbed to that too." He looks interested. "Though that's something I'd deny." He can't have been expecting this. I wait for him to absorb my flood of honesty, my fervent desire to help the police unravel the mystery of the rogue physicist. "Dr. Melville was going through a very tough time, personally," I venture. "His mother died not long ago, and it distressed him more than he let on. Things got out of hand. And psychologists don't always see the obvious. Even when it's staring them in the face."

"So how do you account for his taking off just before Bethany was abducted? Coincidence?"

"Well, certainly it's no surprise. He needed a complete break. He said something about wanting to go on a field trip. His mother died, he got frozen out of his job, he was confused about Bethany. I said, for God's sake, go. I'm glad he took my advice."

"So have you any idea what Dr. Melville is actually doing in Thailand? On this field trip?"

I concentrate on the table. It's wood laminate. They take a photograph of wood and project it onto plastic. The realism is heartbreaking. The detective shifts impatiently. Men of action do not like being trapped behind desks.

"I'm sorry to say this. But guessing at Frazer's . . . proclivities, I'm afraid that 'field trip' might be something of a euphemism." The detective's eyebrows shoot upward. I am savoring my small act of revenge. "Your field is crime, and mine is the psyche," I continue. "Unhealthy impulses are part of the territory we both inhabit. Personally, I don't like a lot of what I encounter in the human condition. That doesn't mean it doesn't exist."

"Can you clarify that for me, Ms. Fox?"

"Come on, do I need to?" I accuse. Calling my bluff, he thrusts his chin up in affirmation. "OK. Frazer Melville is a lonely, overweight, middle-aged single man who is going through a difficult phase in the wake of his mother's death."

"Mrs. Zarnac, your landlady, seemed to think . . ."

I laugh and shake my head. "Poor Mrs. Zarnac has too much time on her hands and a rampant romantic imagination. She's a devoted subscriber to *True Life* magazine. Which as you know specializes in stories of the fiscally and physically disadvantaged overcoming the mountainous odds stacked against them and discovering eternal love. I'm sorry to disappoint her. Do I honestly look like I'd have a sex life?"

This seems to stump him. "Dr. Melville was married once," he warns, as if I'm about to attempt what he might call "some funny business."

"To a lesbian. You can check it."

With interesting predictability, this seems to put a lid on that line of questioning. Together, in the silence that follows, we picture Frazer Melville buying a ladyboy a fruity cocktail in a Bangkok bar. Do we both see a frangipani flower in her hair, and the sadness of a pair of tilted underage eyes? I make a regretful face, and we allow ourselves a knowing quirk of the mouth, silently agreeing that it takes all sorts but we do not approve. Perhaps we are both regretful, too, that I count a man like Dr. Frazer Melville among my acquaintances—but then I am a cripple and probably can't be choosy. The detective shrugs, shaking off the distaste conjured by our Thai vision.

"What about Bethany's father?" I ask, shifting gear. "I presume he was informed about the electrocution, and he would have known she was in hospital?"

Detective Kavanagh scrutinizes his hands, as though they are be-ings more intelligent than he that require consultation. "Dr. Sheldon-Gray has told me about your unusual intervention with Leonard Krall." He waits for me to speak, but the wood laminate has regained my attention. "As it happens, the reverend has an alibi. But let's dis-cuss your meeting with him. Do you normally visit the parents of your patients incognito?"

"No."

"So why on this occasion?"

"Because Bethany Krall is a highly unusual case. I suppose I thought that her father might hold some sort of clue to her recovery."

He studies his hands again. I can picture them flexed around some weights in a gym. "And did he?"

He looks up sharply and I meet his stare. The flush that spreads upwards from my chest and ignites my face is the real thing because it reflects my definitive and absolute failure.

"He didn't. No."

When I get home, there is a letter from the Regional Authority on the mat along with a huge sprawl of junk mail. Its contents come as no surprise, but I still feel a sharp tug of professional indignation when I read the careful paragraphs of subdivisional personnel administra-tor Ms. Stephanie Buckton. It reminds me of the school reports I used to get from the convent: *Gabrielle is a skilled and insightful pupil but she has a tendency to make life difficult for herself.* Is that what's happened now? Have I pushed things too far yet again?

Apparently I have.

I have been suspended from my post. With immediate effect.

Indignation swiftly gives way to anger. If Ms. Stephanie Buckton were here, she would meet my thunder egg at close range.

I fling the letter in the bin and wheel myself into the kitchen to splash my face with cold water. A moment later I'm throwing out the junk mail with extra fury when I see the postcard. I almost miss it. No one I know sends postcards: they belong to a bygone era of great aunts, paper doilies, coffee thermoses. But there it is, a colorful rec-tangle. It shows Edinburgh Castle with a kilted and sporraned bag-piper in the foreground, his knees proud and hairy, his cheeks bulging comically for the big push. I flip it. On the back, familiar handwriting. Handwriting I first saw in my office, on Joy McConey's leaving card:

Hi Wheels.

Looks like I had to leave without saying good-bye. But stay chilled, I'm doing fine.

Yours electrically,
Child B

Sometimes, an instinct makes you swerve. Blink and it's done. Upon which a new map of the world unveils itself before you, with roads you didn't know about. Roads you might have to stake your life on.

Trusting that my instinct is the right one, I drive to the police station—where, having handed the card to a duty officer, I wait for half an hour to see Detective Kavanagh in a poky cubicle decorated with posters about crime figures, fraud hotlines, and victim support. Far from being relieved at the new development, he seems annoyed, almost to the point of gracelessness. Bethany's postcard from Edinburgh has "thrown a spanner in the works," he tells me severely. "It may be a false lead."

"I suppose in your line of business you are hardwired for mistrust," I say.

"You're sure it's Bethany's handwriting?"

"Positive. But you can have it verified."

His look is withering: clearly that process is already under way. "Did she ever mention friends or relatives in Scotland?"

"Bethany isn't a friends-and-relatives kind of girl. Scotland never cropped up."

"Do you sense there might be some kind of message encoded in this?" I tell him that "yours electrically" is a humorous reference to her ECT, and Wheels is her typically tasteless nickname for me, and Child B. speaks for itself. Apart from that, no. But tell me. How can I help?

He sighs. "I suggest that you just go home and wait. If there's any other contact from her, ring this number." He hands me a card. "If you leave Hadport for any reason, call me first and let me know where you'll be. If she turns up, we may need you at short notice."

.   .   .

Back home, the phone is ringing. I reach it too late to answer, but I can see there have been ten missed calls, all from the same number. Clearly, some hard-core psychopathology is at work. But whose? Seconds later it rings again. It's Joy. She is frantic. She has heard the news about Bethany's abduction. But the word she uses is "escape."

"If you helped her get out, you don't know what you've done. I warned you."

"I didn't help her."

"Don't you see, the whole world's in danger now. Don't you get it?" Her agitation is palpable. "I was like you once. I didn't believe people could be evil. But I do now. She'd destroy the whole planet if she could." Joy's need to cling to a notion that eliminates the random stirs a weary pity in me. But I can do nothing to help her. "If you know where she is—"

I interrupt her and snap, "I wish I did. But the fact is, I don't." Then a man's voice—sharp—can be heard in the background, appealing to her. A second later Joy yells, "Get off me!" There's a clatter in my ear, as though the phone has been dropped to the floor. I can still hear her raging. "Hello?" says the man. Her husband. "Who is this I'm speaking to?

"Gabrielle Fox. We met at the restaurant."

"Oh God. I must apologize for Joy. The drugs she's on—"

I tell him there's no need to explain. Or apologize. That I completely understand. That Joy is blessed to have him. And that I wish him luck.

He will be needing enormous quantities of it.

After the car smash upended my life, I made the assumption that my thoughts would forever revolve around the aftermath and constraints of my injury, that no outside factor would diminish my enforced solipsism, and that this exhausting preoccupation with myself would carry on, like the low-level hum of tinnitus, ad nauseam, until the day I died. That I would continue to wake every morning to the reality of a life chopped down. But now—

It seems I am living in times so charged with grotesque momentum that there are whole minutes in which I forget the mess that I am and, when I remember, can forgive it. When a text message signals itself on my cell phone as I prepare for bed, I know that I have

been waiting for it. It's from an unknown caller: THORNHILL STA-
TION PARKING LOT 10AM TOMORROW. NOTHING TO PO-
LICE. VVG.

Who is VVG? Wary, stirred, and paradoxically elated, I swiftly
pack a large suitcase: clothes, makeup, toothbrush, medical and
wheelchair accessories, painkillers, shampoo. What am I doing?

But I don't stop myself.

When the blood is in charge, logic doesn't get a word in. But hope
does. And it's the fiercest imperative I have felt in a long time.

When I finally fall asleep I dream of whirling black birds.

TEN

There are many things I would like to believe in, because they would accord life coherence. One of them is God. Another is the notion that on the brink of death one's life dances before one's eyes in kaleidoscopic fragments: dramas, traumas, transcendent highs, troughs of gloom, or the crystallized moments that encapsulate a certain mood on a certain day, like—for me—the smell of forsythia blossom at nursery school, or a turn of phrase—*"ça va tourner au vinaigre"*—used by my mother, bitterly, to someone on the phone, or the pop of the dog fleas Pierre and I picked from our terrier and flicked onto the barbecue, or the appalling intimacy of my first kiss, or the body blow of my mother's death, or the chaos of Pierre's wedding, or the aching realization that dawned when my father said "Mesopotamia" instead of "kitchen," or the night I shouted at Alex and he swerved, or the morning the doctors gave me the final assessment of my paraplegia and, for want of anything better to do, I glanced at the clock and noted that it was 11:23.

Or August 22, the day of the Istanbul earthquake, when there was no longer any doubting Bethany, and I crossed a line.

A line now so far behind me that my old life feels surreal.

.   .   .

It's October but so sunny and warm it could still be summer. The popcorn smell of discount biofuel floats on a breeze that sets curled dried leaves rustling across the streets. Out on the horizon the blades of the wind turbines rotate under a blue sky jazzed with threads of cloud. I drive through a Hadport busy with morning ritual: people flocking to work or school, exercising dogs, opening up offices and shops, buying take-out croissants and lattes, queuing for trams, heading for early morning AA meetings or DIY hypermarkets or lovers' arms. Fear and anticipation make for a motivating cocktail, the result being that I am in Thornhill by nine. I park at the station and, with an hour to kill, I head for the town's famous medieval church, negotiating my way through a graveyard freakishly landscaped by subsidence and shored up by crude cement bulwarks. Grit and builders' sand collect in the shallow treads of my tires as I skirt the leaning yews.

Even with the door opened wide, the sepulchre is dark, its chill that of a meat freezer. Above the pulpit, the stained-glass windows hum with complex ecclesiastical matrices of color divided and subdivided by black lead. On one wall, there's a mural depicting Christ pinioned to the cross, head to one side, ribs jutting, speared wound gushing blood, crowds surging around. Shivering, I rummage in my purse and drop some coins into the collection box, inhaling the wax-and-saltpeter mustiness that pervades all houses of God measuring more than a thousand square meters. They're raising money for drought-struck Africa because fresh water has been lost from a third of the earth's surface. Can this be true? Lost since when? If I were a believer I would pray and hunt for a votary candle. Instead, I scrutinize the stained glass in an attempt to decipher a coherent theme linking the panels. Then, at a quarter to ten, I spin back out into sunshine so fierce the colors are bleached clean away, leaving only glitter-edged shapes. Back at the car, I'm dumping my folded wheelchair on the passenger seat when the black-bird dream from last night drifts into my head, perhaps summoned by the lead interstices of the church's stained glass. Ravens?

I feel a sudden, unexpected grin split my face. Praise be to the subconscious. *Wheat Field with Crows.* By VVG.

I switch on the car radio, wondering if there might be more news about Bethany. Instead I get a phone-in about pensions, a subject the nation's overfifties are increasingly obsessed with. It's one of those

programs where people "from all walks of life"—but all, coinciden-
tally, middle class—recount their fiscal woes in a polite but subtly aggressive whine. Just as a financial expert is launching into an analysis
of buy-back mortgages, the door of the news agent's opposite opens
to disgorge a man in baggy jeans and a red and black T-shirt splatted
with a cartoon tarantula, carrying a bumper pack of Haribos. He
crosses the road, scans the car park, and then heads for where I'm
parked, his free hand raised in the casual greeting of an old mate.
He's midthirties, with a tumble of unkempt black hair and wrap-
around shades. He could be a former skateboarder or the drummer in
a band that has not yet lost hope. I switch off the radio and lower my
window.

"Gabrielle Fox?" he asks. I nod. "Then I'll join you in the car, if I
may." Whatever the circumstances, an antipodean accent never fails
to make me smile.

"Be my guest. Whoever you are. You'll have to move my chair."

He goes round to the passenger door, opens it, flings the Haribos
carelessly onto my lap, and with one hand swings the wheelchair
onto the back seat, then settles next to me and fastens his belt. "I
hope these aren't for me," I tell him. "Because I don't like licorice. My
nephews always fight over the jelly eggs."

"They're for Bethany. She likes the black shoestrings. I'm Ned
Rappaport. I'm a climatologist." That invisible question mark at the
end of the sentence: so full of optimism. We shake hands. His grip is
firm, his forearm bronzed, his muscles toned. Further up his arm, below his sleeve, there is a tattoo of a small lizard. In the days before female life died in me, this configuration of characteristics might have
given me an interesting frisson.

"Australian?"

"From Brisbane originally. Went to uni there." Where between
seminars he surely surfed and smoked weed. "But I've lived in the
U.S. mostly, working for the NOAA."

"Which is known to the uneducated as?"

"The National Oceanic and Atmospheric Administration. I quit a
few years back. Got fed up after spending fifteen years modeling climate disaster scenarios and making recommendations that no one
ever listened to. Went freelance after Hurricane Katrina. Let's go for
a drive. Left at the exit, then first right." He sneezes suddenly. "Sorry.
Hay fever." So. Human after all.

"How's Bethany?" I ask, turning on the ignition and pulling out. The agitation has been building despite my efforts to quell it. Anything could be happening in that head of hers, after two years cooped up in Oxsmith. How could a Brisbanian climatologist with a tattoo on his bicep be expected to spot the warning signs?

"Well, her hands and arms are on the mend. I've been changing the dressings every day. And she's mad as a box of frogs. But no surprises there, right?"

"Energy levels?"

"Oh, she's up in the stratosphere."

"I'm not surprised," I say, nodding at the Haribos. "Is someone with her at all times?"

"More or less. Follow the signs for the ring road. She has the run of the house but we keep the doors at night locked just in case. And I've killed the sockets in her room. To be honest, she's been getting pretty out of control. Keeps demanding volts. Not that I know what's normal, when it comes to schizos. You'll see for yourself in a couple of hours' time, if there's not too much traffic. We're hoping you'll exert a calming influence."

I tighten my grip on the wheel as I assess what he has said. "So the reason I was contacted is that you can't handle her?"

His profile changes shape. "I was given the impression you'd be willing to be part of this. Am I wrong?" His concern sounds genuine.

"I never agreed to being kept in the dark."

A sheepish expression takes hold. "I know. I'm sorry. But we discussed it. No one was happy about it, but the consensus was it was necessary."

"A consensus can be an alienating thing, if you're excluded. Which I was. Who's we?"

"Me, Frazer, and Kristin Jonsdottir. She's the—"

"I know who she is," I interrupt, more sharply than is called for. "I looked her up."

He eyes me sideways. "Frazer figured that if you knew we were taking Bethany, you'd have objected. Or if you'd agreed, you'd have been compromised. If Bethany's right, there are a lot of lives at stake."

After Istanbul, I cannot attempt to dispute that. Or diminish the moral implications. Suffocating my selfish thoughts with difficulty, and a certain bitterness, I concentrate on the road.

"Is everything OK?" Ned asks.

"Just about as OK as it can be, considering the circumstances under which we meet," I say lightly, and flash him a Cinnamon Kiss smile, the kind air hostesses use for passengers who hand them a used sick bag. "So were you the kidnapper, or did you subcontract?"

"Guilty. But there was no coercion involved. She didn't object. On the contrary."

I can see how being abducted by a disaster geek who wears comedy T-shirts and takes sugar orders might be Bethany's dream come true. Or one of them.

"So how did you get involved in all this?"

"Frazer and I go way back. He did a stint at the NOAA."

Which he perhaps told me about. And which I perhaps forgot. "So where is he now?" The physicist: the bruise I keep pressing. Even though it hurts. Because it hurts.

"He stopped off in Paris, on his way back from Bangkok. He phoned Kristin last night." He glances at his watch. "He should be on his way."

I am cudgeled by jealousy. The physicist called Kristin Jonsdottir rather than me. Of course he did. Because she's the one he's fucking, and he was using me all along, and now he is using me again, and like a sucker I am expected to collude—for the sake of a world I care about less and less the more I know it.

Behind my ribs, a huge, toxic worm begins to writhe.

We drive on for fifteen minutes in silence.

"Do you think the concept of putting other people first is overrated?" I ask eventually. Being an idealist, he probably imagines I am thinking about all those whose lives will be shattered by the catastrophe that Bethany sees flickering on the horizon like a demented mirage. But he doesn't know about the contortions of my inner worm. I am thinking of someone I know intimately: me. With particular regard to a certain physicist who has so crushed my morale that I fear I will never think straight again. I am thinking of lost love and misplaced devotion and absent wheelchair ramps in waterlogged wildernesses, of dashed hope and practicalities and the helplessness of being left alone with two useless legs in a tunnel with no light at the end.

Ned looks at me sharply. "Are you telling me *you* think it's overrated?"

I fill my lungs and breathe out slowly, as I encourage people to do in my relaxation classes. "Being human, it's a question I can't answer," I say. And stare out of the window at the cornfields. "Van Gogh committed suicide after painting a scene like this."

"We could stop if you need to."

"I'm fine," I say, finally hauling my components together. This man is clearly in the dark about my relationship with the physicist. I shoot him a shaky smile. "Explain the postcard with the bagpiper."

"A diversionary tactic."

"I'm glad to know you're taking Bethany seriously enough to risk a prison sentence. But Detective Kavanagh's no fool."

"He'll still have to have it investigated, and that requires manpower, which is a pain in the ass for him." The climatologist slaps an insect on his forearm and inspects it. "If Kavanagh rings, don't say where you are. Say you'll call him back, and when you do, you'll know what to say because I'll have told you. This visit is just a day trip for you. You'll have to drive back to Hadport this evening."

Although I understand the rationale, and the nonnegotiability of this, the prospect doesn't appeal to me. When I packed my suitcase, I must have thrown in more hope, or foolhardiness, or self-delusion than I realized.

"Where are we going?"

"A farmhouse in Norfolk. Belonging to a marine biologist mate of mine. He's somewhere in the Arctic Circle digging up deep-sea worms. He's one of the world's leading experts on chemiluminescence. Those GM glow-in-the-dark rice paddies they're experimenting with in Asia? That research was done by one of his students. Who defected to the darkish side." Ned gives me a sidelong smile.

"From what I've worked out, this is all about frozen methane. That somebody's been drilling for," I say.

"That's what the drawings suggest. When Kristin first saw them, she was impressed by the detail."

"She was one of the people Frazer contacted?"

"No, not directly. But his mail was passed on to her. She got in touch with him." *And then they became lovers.* "And he rang me and I flew in. Turn right at the next junction. Let's get the news."

He switches on: a tinny blast of music announces it's eleven o'clock. More food riots in developing countries. The mayor of London has pleaded guilty to charges of embezzlement. And the father of Bethany Krall, the psychiatric patient missing after being abducted from a general hospital on Wednesday, has made an emotional appeal for her safe return. Ned and I exchange a glance and he reaches to turn up the volume.

"My daughter is a very sick child," says the Reverend Leonard Krall. His voice is velvety, thick with sadness. "She desperately needs psychiatric and spiritual help. Please, if you have seen Bethany or you know where she is, call the police or take her to the safety of your church. We're all praying for her return."

Ned switches off the radio. Behind the sunglasses, I sense that he is looking at me intently.

"Surprised?"

I think for a moment. "Yes. On two counts. First that they've named her publicly so soon. Second that Leonard Krall's chosen to get involved. He never bothered to visit her once in Oxsmith."

"So why did he?"

"Because I think he genuinely believes she's dangerous. He's a Faith Waver. Satanic possession, creationism, the Rapture, the whole can of worms. Joy McConey—"

"The shrink with cancer?" I nod. "Frazer told us she was a convert to his way of thinking."

"My guess is that Bethany perceived Joy's illness before it was officially diagnosed. When Joy refused to get her out of Oxsmith, Bethany let her think she'd caused it. It would have given her a feeling of power."

"And in the event of a disaster . . ." He doesn't need to finish the question, and I don't need to answer it. My mind has been speeding along the same track. If the forthcoming catastrophe is publicly linked to Bethany, and people like Leonard Krall and Joy McConey give it their spin, we have a witch hunt on top of whatever else we're facing. We contemplate the depressing implications of this for a moment.

"So you've specialized in these clathrates?" I ask eventually.

"No. But I modeled a lot of scenarios at the NOAA. Methane catastrophes among them. Since the energy companies started trying to exploit the suboceanic hydrates, the drilling's increased the threat.

Dramatically. Post-peak oil, everyone's after it. China, the U.S., India. Hundreds of experimental rigs planted off coastlines all round the world."

"How do they access the gas?"

He makes a contemptuous noise. "By playing Russian roulette. You can inject hot water beneath the seabed to destabilize the hydrates. Which will force a pressure change and release methane. The gas moves along the cracks and works its way up. Then you can liquidize the hydrate on the ocean floor and pipe it up like oil and gas. Or release frozen chunks of it from the seafloor and trap them at the surface of the ocean in giant tarpaulins. Exploit the hydrate fields safely, and there's no such thing as an energy problem. Methane's cleaner than oil or coal, if you handle it right. You can power anything with it, and it's there in quantities you can't even imagine. It would solve the whole energy crisis. But it's highly volatile. Which means it may cost more than anyone's ever paid for anything. Ever."

"But with the climate protocols—"

Ned Rappaport gives a bleak grunt. "They were being flouted before they were even established. Never underestimate the hypocrisy of governments, or the selfishness of a tribe." He swats at another insect. He seems to attract them. "And the human capacity to think wishfully. And in the short term. Politicians will say one thing and do another. Or do things that cancel one another out. Don't look for logic."

"So if something happens—"

"Then to put it brutally, Gabrielle, we're fucked."

I drive on in silence.

Having headed north from Thornhill we cross the M25 and travel up to Norfolk. Somewhere between Ely and Kings Lynn there's a sprawl of retail parks and housing estates and processing plants that fall away, leaving the flat countryside gaping at us again: furrowed fields that meld into a horizon pricked with pylons and vanilla-colored sheep grazing under a low sky. We're on a straight road flanked by unseasonal primroses and a brackish, putrescent canal, black as dye. The sun is lurking behind a slur of congealed cloud. There's a smell of silage and burnt vegetation with a chemical undercurrent. After ten kilometers, we turn down a rough track fringed with nettles, briar studded with rosehips, and random patches of mustard. I wind down the window and catch a whiff of diesel and oilseed rape. We round a bend and the landscape opens up again to reveal the shallow slope of a hill and a gray stone house, its garden enclosed by a scrape of herringbone wall. Beyond is a small glistening lake surrounded by clusters of silver birch, a deserted greenhouse, and a huge wind turbine rotating with mournful grandeur.

"It's secluded, but we can't base ourselves here for long," says Ned. Now that we have arrived, he seems tense, as though this morning's visit to Thornhill for our rendezvous was a relaxing interlude in the midst of something prolonged and unbearable. "We'll need to move out again soon. You can park round the back."

I catch my breath as we skirt the turbine.

She is there. Her back is turned, but I recognize her immediately. Her hair is brighter than in the photo. And finer. Like pale spun honey. She is talking on the phone. I don't know how I will handle meeting her.

"That's Kristin," says Ned. I try to look interested instead of appalled. "I'm hoping that the person she's talking to is Harish Modak."

Modak: the Planetarian with the hooded eyes. The ecomovement's éminence grise. "The connection being?" Hearing the engine, Kristin Jonsdottir turns and smiles and points at the phone, indicating she will join us when she has finished her call. Ned waves back.

"His wife, Meera, was Kristin's supervisor and mentor. And a mother figure too, I gather. After Meera died, Kristin stayed in touch with Harish Modak." She is wearing a long sweater but you can see the shape of her breasts and hips beneath it. "Modak is our biggest hope at the moment. If we can get him on board, we'll get the attention we need."

"And if we can't?" I can see why the physicist would want her in his arms.

"I'd like to say we'll find another way. But I can't."

I think: I shouldn't even blame him.

"So what if Harish Modak can't be convinced?" I ask, to distract myself.

"He has to be," says Ned, pointing ahead. "Just pull up here. That's why Frazer's been in Paris. He took Bethany's drawings with him, and just about everything else he could lay his hands on. But Modak's a difficult old bugger. He wants more evidence."

I stop and turn off the engine. "Would he be willing to speak out publicly if he had it?" Ned stifles another sneeze and opens his door.

"There's no telling with Modak. He's seventy-eight. He doesn't have kids. And he has no great affection for Homo sapiens. He thinks we've been hardwired to self-destruct as part of some Gaiac cycle. To him we're just a species like any other. And species come and go. So if he ends up believing us, he may still decide to do nothing. Just shrug his shoulders, say we're getting what we deserve, and enjoy the fireworks."

"How would you propose to change his mind?"

"You're the psychologist," he says, undoing his seat belt.

"Is that the other reason I'm here?"

He flashes me a boyish, winning smile. Even in a foul mood, with my worm wreaking havoc, I can't dislike him.

He opens the car door. "I'll get your chair."

The interior of the house exudes the nostalgic, grandmotherly smell of wood polish. Low ceilings. Darkness, after the blaze of the sun, giving way slowly to a dull ivory gloom as the eyes recalibrate. Thick ceiling beams. From upstairs, the sound of a running shower that abruptly stops.

"That'll be Bethany," says Ned. "Glad to say she's discovered hygiene. She'll be down in a minute. This way."

I follow him along a corridor past an impressive if haphazard collection of art: dark woodcuts, limpid watercolor landscapes, heavier oils, and detailed diagrams of insects, fish, and mollusks. Sometimes you don't realize how hungry your eyes have been. Perhaps it's a displacement urge. But I want to gorge.

Ned Rappaport pushes open a dark door to reveal a cavernous living-room-cum-study fetid with age. The blinds are drawn, but through the gloom I can make out a clutter of old sofas and armchairs, a coffee table, a computer desk, and a collection of glass cabinets packed with specimens of dried fish, fossils, pickled worms and seashells, all carefully labeled according to genus and era. Someone methodical has been at work in this fusty space, diligently categorizing. On two of the walls are shelves full of jars that glow with a pale, ectoplasmic light. Entering the room and drawing closer, I see they're filled with small greenish shrimplike crustaceans with delicate claws, trapped in a liquid suspension.

"What are they?" I ask, pulled toward their luminosity like a moth.

With an enormous hand, Ned pulls down a jar and passes it to me. It's heavy and cool. Clasping it between my palms, I peer in at the pickled, tentacled shape. Around it, small light-filled fragments rise from the bottom and swirl in the cloudy light that emanates from the center of its body, fading at the delicate extremities.

"Myodocopia. Ostracod. They're chemiluminescent. They release a dye as a mating signal. It can go on emitting light waves even after the animal has died. Collective name, *Luzifer gigans.* Japanese soldiers used them in World War II. They'd collect them on the beaches, then crush them up and smear the stuff on their hands. As an instant light source." He takes the jar back and replaces it on the shelf. "Now, according to my research, you won't cooperate fully with anything until you've had coffee. I'll get some in the works." He tosses the Haribos onto an overstuffed green sofa, its upholstery burst at one end, and heads for the door.

"Ned. Wait."

But it has closed behind him.

After driving for so long I'm aware of the need to shift the weight off my pelvis, so I wheel further into the room, negotiating my way around the cabinets. Near a fireplace stuffed with pine cones and dried birch branches, there's a tattered red-striped chaise longue on whose padded upholstery I can imagine myself getting comfortable. Next to it, a walnut coffee table studded with cup rings and, opposite, the green sofa and a couple of sagging leather armchairs of the kind favored by old men's clubs. I maneuver out of my wheelchair and onto the chaise longue, take off my shoes, heave my legs up, and settle lengthways. Thin strips of light filter through the slats of the blinds, dancing with dust motes. My eyes are still adjusting, so I don't see her come in.

Or hear her. Until—

"BOO!"

I jump, and stifle a scream.

"Scared you there, Wheels."

Wet from the shower, her T-shirt blotched with damp, her scalp speckled with a thin growth of stubble, Bethany Krall resembles a manic voodoo doll. The thermal burn marks streaking her arms are a virulent purple leached with yellow, her hands a mess of tattered, blistered skin. Spreading her arms wide, she waggles them at me in a vaudeville gesture. They look like terrible, ravaged starfish.

"Bethany. I'm glad to see you."

"Watch out, we'll be lesbian lovers next."

She comes toward me, too fast, her arms held aloft, as though wielding huge mechanical pincers. Stranded without my chair, I shift to an upright position.

"How have you been?" I ask. I need more space between us. But within seconds, I have it: catching sight of the Haribo packet on the sofa, she leaps over, snatches it up, and starts tearing it open with her teeth. I curse myself for not hiding it.

"How d'you think I've been?" She closes the space again by leaping onto the coffee table, where she stands barefoot, like a vicious elf, her green leggings stained with patches of damp where she failed to dry off, a sickly chemical smell seeping out of the sweet packet in her hand. Fishing inside, she finds a spiral of licorice, unrolls it clumsily, and dangles the end into her mouth, face tipped back. "This place is like a five-star hotel. Want one?" She is on the cusp of something. Glad to be free. And free to—

"No, thanks. And go easy on the sugar." She rolls her eyes.

I shift again. I feel vulnerable without my chair and regret abandoning it. She's still standing right over me, flexing her ruined hands.

"Hey, I've got this weird electric feeling in my fingers."

"It's called pain. It's something normal. Why don't you take a seat?"

"Have you felt how close we are to the sea?" she asks, jumping off the table and moving across to the window. She can't seem to stay still. "It's breathing at us. Can you feel it? Can you smell it? If you want to survive, you've got to go inland." She flicks the blinds further open and daylight streams in. Outside, the road, the bright landscape, the greenhouse, the wheeling white blades of the windmill. "Cabins in the mountains, that's what we need. I'd go there, except I'd miss the grand finale. I need some volts, Wheels. Can you get me some in this place?"

As she is speaking, a gray car comes into view. With a thudding, forlorn dread, I consider who might be inside it, on his way. Then, from behind the greenhouse, Kristin Jonsdottir appears, pocketing her phone and heading for the front door. She is looking worried. Or perhaps simply thoughtful. I wonder how she feels about meeting me. On the doorstep, she stops and turns. She must have heard the car.

"Here comes loverboy," murmurs Bethany, following my gaze. I want to look away. But I can't. He pulls up, parks, and gets out. Kristin Jonsdottir runs toward him. There is no mistaking the look on her face. My face used to light up like that once. And my heart used to—

I blink and swallow as they embrace.

"They've been fucking like rabbits," comments Bethany matter-of-factly. They have pulled apart and Kristin Jonsdottir is speaking to Frazer Melville excitedly, gesturing toward the house. He looks pleased, then anxious. "Look at them. He can't get enough of her." Tipping her head back again, she feeds herself another string of licorice, eyeing me sidelong. "She's a real moaner. She has these orgasms that go on and on." Bethany stops and assesses my face. "And he's noisy too. When he comes, he roars. Right, Wheels?" She grins. "He roars like a lion."

I tear my eyes from the window and shut them, trying not to remember. I am in freefall, hurtling through nothingness. Not just naked but skinned.

"Coffee," announces Ned, entering with a small tray. "Colombian. Frazer told me it was your favorite so I got some in. And I see you found the Haribos, Bethany. Hey, is everything OK?"

No, I want to tell him. Please, get me out of here before I die.

"We were just talking about sex," says Bethany with enthusiasm. "Who's doing what with who." Ned looks at me blankly and I muster a small, noncommittal shrug. But Bethany is on a roll. "You wank a lot, don't you, Ned?" His face tightens and a muscle starts working beneath his stubble. She grins. "I guess you miss your boyfriend. Or should I say your *ex*-boyfriend. You might not guess to look at him, Wheels, but Ned here likes cock." She throws him a triumphant, jackpot look.

I flush. Of course. Ned's jaw moves, as though he's chewing on something, and his Adam's apple strains. I feel a grievous rush of pity for him. He sets the tray down on the table and begins pouring the coffee.

"I don't remember discussing my private life with you, Bethany," he says.

"You didn't," she says. "But I picked up the vibe. I do that, don't I, Wheels? It's one of my irritating skills."

Ned looks at me with a question on his face. I shake my head. The only surprise is that she left it this long.

Just outside, beyond the window, I can hear Frazer Melville and Kristin Jonsdottir talking in low, urgent voices. I must get away or this will kill me. But Bethany, with her feeling for turbulence, intercepts: with a quick movement, she has reangled my empty wheelchair and given it a shove. Silently, it rolls across the room and settles by the door, far out of reach.

"Marooned," she says.

I glance across at Ned, who obliges me by rolling the chair around the back of the chaise longue and settling it where I can rest my hand on it. Outside, the talking stops and I hear a single set of footsteps approaching. When the door opens, I can't look. But I know it's the physicist. I can feel him standing in the doorway, his height filling the frame.

"Gabrielle. Thank God you're here. It all worked out." Frazer Melville sounds excited, unaware of the psychic pain washing the room. "Hi, Bethany. Hi, Ned." I take a sip of coffee, blocking him out, savoring the tiny moment of escape.

"I was just telling Gabrielle about you and Kristin," says Bethany. She grins wide, like a gargoyle, revealing a blackened tongue. "But now you're here, you can tell her yourself." When she electrocuted herself, why didn't she just die?

Flushing fiercely, I glance sideways. He's moving toward me, but when he sees the look on my face—a look I can't hide—he stops in his tracks and his smile fades. Bethany sucks in her breath theatrically.

"Ooh, she's angry, Frazer, I'm warning you! You'd better protect your balls! Catch you later!"

Thrilled with herself, she snatches up her Haribos, runs across to the doorway, ducks under the physicist's arm and out of the room.

Ned, silently sipping coffee on the sofa opposite me, seems absorbed in his own painful thoughts. The physicist and I look at each other. I see the green shard but I won't let it pull me in. I long to be back in my wheelchair, but if I transferred to it now I'd reveal my weakness. Bethany is right. I am stuck.

"Gabrielle," he says softly.

He comes forward—to do what, embrace me? Seeing me recoil, he hesitates, sighs, and settles himself into the armchair next to my chaise longue. He is too big and too close. I ache for him and hate myself for it.

"We kept you in the dark to protect you." His voice is gentle but there's a hint of defiance.

"Like hell." And anyway, I think bleakly, it's not about that.

"It's true," says Ned, topping up my coffee. I breathe in sharply and feel the bile shoot through my blood. "I can see why you'd be angry but Frazer figured that if you lost your job you'd be in big trouble. Personally and professionally. Seriously, Gabrielle. We thought it through."

"I did lose my job."

"Oh no," says Frazer Melville. "God. Oh, Gabrielle, I'm so sorry."

"Don't mention it." I take a sip. The coffee is good. Strong and dark and fortifying. "I'm now officially unemployable."

"Actually, that won't matter in the larger scheme of things, if Bethany's right," suggests Ned. Perhaps he believes he is being helpful.

Ignoring him, I address the physicist. "I may be restricted, physically. But your behavior suggests you think I'm mentally incompetent with it."

"If you were to stay above suspicion with the police, you couldn't know what we were planning. Or what we'd done." Frazer Melville's expression is pleading. "I hoped I'd dropped enough clues for you to guess that I was behind it."

"Which I did when I covered for you with the police and risked imprisonment for perverting the course of justice."

From the next room, the *Simpsons* theme tune blares at unbearable volume.

"Someone wants some attention," Ned sighs, rising. "I'll go and sort her out."

"Get that candy off her," I call after him. "And if you have some, she needs fresh bandages."

When the door has fully closed behind him, I take a deep breath. I can feel the physicist looking at me intently.

"Sweetheart—" He puts a hand on my arm but I shake him off violently.

"Don't touch me and don't call me that!"

"Hey, what's going on with you?" He sounds offended.

"Tell me, what else have you been up to with Kristin Jonsdottir?"

The physicist's face switches from concern to bafflement. "I haven't seen her. I've been in Thailand and Paris, in case you didn't know. Why are you so angry?"

Where to begin? But I can't. It's too humiliating. Whatever I say will sound bitter and self-pitying. I have my pride. I shut my eyes and take a deep breath. When I open them again he is still there. In the next room, the TV noise stops, and Bethany protests. I hear "bastard" and "asshole" and some quiet remonstrations from Ned.

"Well, if you won't tell me . . ."

"Do I have to spell it out? OK, I'll spell it out. I know about her. OK? *I know.*"

"Get the fuck off me!" Bethany shrieks from the next room. "Cocksucking asshole! I can do it myself!" Then Ned's voice, sharp with alarm: "Hey! Look what you've done! Jesus!"

The door opens and Kristin Jonsdottir walks in, smiling.

She comes toward me, her hand outstretched. She has one of those faces you'd look at twice without quite knowing why. A broad forehead and calm eyes. A serenity.

"Gabrielle. I'm so pleased to meet you at last."

In the next room, Bethany has begun a new tirade.

"Gabrielle," says the physicist, ignoring the noise. "This is Kristin."

Reluctantly, I take the hand she offers but drop it again as swiftly as possible.

"Kristin Jonsdottir, with a soft *J,* pronounced Y," she says smiling. "I am Icelandic." There's a catch to her accent that might make you want to hear more, if you were in love with her. It strikes me that she seems to feel no embarrassment about meeting me. She even looks happy. Because—I flush as it dawns on me—the physicist never even told her we were lovers. Just as he never told Ned. I am no threat to her. And never have been.

"I looked you up," I say. "But the soft *J* wasn't mentioned." If she hears the irony in my voice, she ignores it. She is still smiling, taking me in with her calm, friendly eyes. The world of women is divided between those who can be bothered with makeup, those who can't, and those who don't need it in the first place. She's the latter: a fresh-air woman who offsets her carbon emissions.

"I've been looking forward to this. Encounters with art therapists aren't normally on the agenda of someone specializing in the world fifty-five million years ago."

What about encounters with your lover's cast-off girlfriends? I flash the physicist a furious look and he replies with a shrug, as though aggrieved. Ned comes in, looking shaken, greets Kristin, and slumps down gratefully on the sofa opposite me.

"Whew. Jesus."

"All sorted?" I ask.

"She scratched me." He shows his forearm, striped with beads of blood. "So, Kristin. What did Harish Modak say?"

She takes a breath. "He's still reluctant."

"I'll go and call him," says the physicist, rising to his feet. He probably can't leave fast enough. "Ned, perhaps you and Kristin can fill Gabrielle in some more?"

"Sure thing," says Ned, lifting a laptop from the floor and booting it up. "Just give me a minute and we'll do a visual."

"So, Kristin. Geology," I say, when the door has closed behind the physicist. I pull the thunder egg from its pouch under my seat. I feel like hurling it at her, but instead I hold it out. She takes it, and a smile of great beauty illuminates her face. Her eyes are a delicate grayish green. She weighs it in her hand, then shakes it. "Solid. You've never been tempted to crack it open?"

"I'm waiting for the right moment. It's an heirloom."

She smiles. "Where's it from?"

"Nevada."

"If it's from the Black Rock Desert, it probably has a lovely opal filling. Some of them are agate. Or a mixture." So she can identify a piece of rock as fast as I can diagnose a loony. I hate her with a hate that I fear may be deeper than the deepest love. Handing the thunder egg back, she clasps her other hand over mine, enclosing it around the stone.

"You're upset with me. And you're right to be. I owe you an apology."

I shrink into myself. She is looking me in the eye with a terrible calmness. With a sharp movement, I tug my hand back. The last thing I've expected is candor. It might be more than I can bear. I take an inward breath. I, too, must be candid.

I say, "Yes. I think you do."

Ned is watching us with interest. A spot of red has appeared on each of Kristin Jonsdottir's cheeks.

"The way I handled things when you rang me out of the blue like that was unforgivable. I'm afraid I panicked. It never crossed my mind that you would find out about me and then call. It threw me totally."

"I bet it did."

"You must be quite a detective."

"Not really. I just followed up a few clues."

Ned interjects anxiously, "I told you. None of us felt good about keeping you in the dark." Heavily, he rises from the sofa and begins hanging a white bedsheet from some nails above the fireplace. It seems he is constructing a makeshift whiteboard.

Kristin says, "I can only apologize. Again. When Frazer showed me the drawings and told me about Bethany's ability, I wanted to talk to you. But he insisted that if we were going to intervene with her, you mustn't be involved, because you'd be compromised professionally."

"*Intervene* is an interesting euphemism for what you did. So tell me. At what point did you decide to kidnap my patient?" From the corner of my eye I register Ned's increasing unease.

"When we learned she was being moved to another facility. Where there'd be no access to her. The fact that she was in a public hospital made it easier."

Kristin looks down at the dark wood floor with delicacy, as though she is considering whether to polish it and what product she might use to achieve maximal results. She is so patently unaware of the damage she's wreaked, and so obviously pained by my hostility, that it almost hurts.

Ned steps back and contemplates his handiwork, then shifts the position of the laptop on the coffee table so that the screen is projecting onto the whiteboard and adjusts the focus. Kristin Jonsdottir leans forward on her chair earnestly, hands clasped together. Despite her good skin and fine, intellectual-looking bones, she probably never spends time gazing into mirrors. She doesn't need to. She doesn't need to because she knows who she is. Her sediment has settled, I think enviously. While mine is still moiling about. Perhaps that's why Frazer Melville found her irresistible. Perhaps it isn't a rejection of my paraplegia after all. Perhaps it's a hundred thousand times worse.

"When I saw Bethany's drawings I was intrigued by the way in which these images occurred. These projections, these . . ." Her Icelandic lilt trails off.

"Visions," I finish. "Psychotic visions." For some reason I want to call a spade a spade. I want to be blunt and charmless and graceless. Despite the gloom, I can see the red of Kristin Jonsdottir's cheekbones intensifying. Perhaps it has sunk in that my feelings toward her are neither benign nor sisterly. "Bethany says 'visions.' Just so you know."

How empiricists—and I include myself—disdain anything that smacks of the supernatural, of manipulative TV series, of low-budget believe-it-or-not, of strange-but-true.

"Sorry to interrupt but I'm going to close the blinds now," says Ned quietly. "So I can project these images for you. And we can move on a bit?"

We both nod at him distractedly and the room darkens.

She says, "It's not my field, so I can't presume to comment on the genesis of the, er . . ." She elegantly replaces the word "visions" with a hand gesture indicating something ephemeral being flung outward from the temples. "But with respect to the actual *depictions*—"

"What Kristin's getting at is, we need more information in order to locate the site of this possible disaster," says Ned, clicking his mouse. "Take a look at this." One of Bethany's drawings appears on the sheet. He adjusts the contrast. "It's got a lot of detail on it. Not the kind of detail you'd be aware of. Unless you knew the mechanics of rigs." He points to the platform and the line that works its way down beneath the sea. "Images like this are what make us concerned that she's seen the beginnings of a submarine landslide triggered by activity at one of the rigs. But we don't know which one. They're all fairly distinctive." He shoots me an amused glance. "The people who discover the sites are allowed to christen them, so they've mostly got quite fanciful names."

Kristin gets up. "I'm going to get Frazer. I think he should be in on this." Something has finally got through to her. Good.

"You were pretty tough on her there," says Ned, when she has gone. "Tougher than you were with me. And I was the one who kidnapped Bethany."

I don't answer. If he's blind and stupid, then that's his problem.

As Ned Rappaport scrolls through a list of images, I shift my legs into a new position on the chaise longue. I will need all my strength to face the physicist again.

"OK. Here are all the offshore rigs that we know are already experimenting with exploiting methane, plus ten that we suspect are converting from oil or gas production." With a click, the whiteboard is filled with a patchwork of images of ocean rigs, their platform scaffolds and spirelike derricks rearing from the sea: bleak constructions of iron and concrete, pounded by stormy seas or blanketed with snow or parked in sunlight in the iridescent turquoise of tropical waters, seemingly far from any coast. "The derricks are all bare metal but, as you can see, the lifting cranes come in all colors, just like cranes on land. I gather Bethany says the one we're after is yellow, so . . ." He shrinks the patchwork to several tighter images. On each of them stands a canary-colored crane, several new-looking, but most with flaking paintwork. "Of these eight here, the three off the coasts of China, India, and New Zealand are closed for machine refits, and one of the Russian ones hasn't been operational for the past year. That leaves us with four suspects. He clicks again, quartering the whiteboard. "*Buried Hope Alpha* in the North Sea, *Mirage* in Indonesian waters, *Lost World* in the Caribbean, and *Endgame Beta* off the coast of Siberia. For various reasons to do with chronic mismanagement, my hunch is *Endgame Beta.*"

Frazer Melville and Kristin Jonsdottir are talking animatedly as they enter the room.

"Any luck with Harish?" asks Ned. They look at each other and make a joint decision.

"Some. But let's talk Gabrielle through this first," says Frazer Melville.

He and Kristin Jonsdottir position themselves on either side of me, he on one edge of the chaise longue and she on a chair to my left. Trapped, I give the whiteboard my full attention. Until this moment I have not paid offshore rigs a single thought.

"They look heroic."

"They are," responds Frazer Melville, as though my remark is the correct answer to a secret, unuttered question. "All that human ingenuity and ambition. All that aspiration." It is almost like the beginning of the kind of conversation we used to have, in the days when we talked. "Until Bethany can give us more information we have to assume it's any one of them. Now if the submarine crack Bethany saw—"

He shifts closer to me on the edge of the chaise longue. I lean away. But he is still close. I can feel the heat of his body.

"That's what she drew?" I ask. I'm barely able to concentrate but I need to sound normal, for the sake of my pride. "A crack?"

"A fissure and a flash point," says Kristin Jonsdottir. "To free the frozen methane from the ocean floor, they'll have drilled beneath it horizontally and forced a pressure change. But if they've miscalculated what's down there and the interference has widened the gap that's already there, the pressure will build up. When it reaches a critical point, there's a risk that huge amounts of this frozen methane—far more than they ever intended—could be unleashed."

As she speaks, I am aware that Frazer Melville is trying to make further eye contact with me, but I resist. I wonder if Kristin told him about my hostility toward her, or whether other matters—like the phone call to Harish Modak—took precedence.

Ned says, "The sediment will destabilize and trigger a submarine avalanche. Possibly leading to the release of the entire methane reserve buried under the explored hydrate field. Thereby removing vast amounts of sediment above and adjacent to the methane. Creating further cascades across the whole area. In the case of any of these rigs, we're talking about thousands of square kilometers. Followed by a huge tsunami. Which is likely to destabilize more sediment packages, leading to more massive landslides."

With their scientific knowledge, the three others here can no doubt picture the whole delta-shaped flow chart of the disaster's repercussions. But I am unable to. Instead, I envisage an oil painting in the style of Turner: a vast and magisterial canvas that depicts a churning miasma of water and wave and cloud, of pale, mother-of-pearl light that transforms into rose, then tangerine, then blood red as the spume froths and bubbles and explodes into flame, while in the foreground the matchstick scaffold of a rig is toppled by the force of colliding elements.

Which is not much use, except as an aesthetic comfort.

No: the information I am getting isn't sinking in the way it should.

"Which in turn is highly likely to trigger a further cycle of landslides and more tsunamis," says Ned. "With more of the hydrate field being dislodged and releasing more methane. Methane is ten times more powerful as a greenhouse gas than CO_2. If the whole thing spreads and escalates, we get runaway global warming on a scale that's beyond anyone's worst nightmare. Everywhere will be radically hotter. It used to be called the clathrate gun hypothesis. Back when it was only a hypothesis."

The physicist is looking at me intently, as if trying to gauge how much is getting though. Not much is. "Last time, geologically speaking, it happened as fast as the flick of a switch," he says.

They all have their eyes on me.

"So we have to do what we can to warn people," says Kristin Jonsdottir. "There'll be huge coastal flooding. Not just locally. With the domino effect, within a very short time we're talking about the whole globe." She blinks. "Scandinavians call it *Ragnarok*."

"Chaos," says Frazer Melville. "A kind of hell." My heart shrinks to a tiny hard marble. What does he want: my approval? Ned flicks to the next image, of the earth, spinning slowly and transmogrifying with each turn.

"The last time it happened, glaciers melted, huge areas were flooded. There were mass extinctions. This time, whether it's triggered off the coast of Siberia or Indonesia or Florida, or in the North Sea, it won't just be that region that's affected. It'll flash heat the whole planet. Imagine a cataclysm on a scale that humans have never seen before."

I can't. Not even with the earth spinning in front of me, its white and blue and green patches shifting and melding into one another like a giant ball of plasticine.

"But wouldn't the energy company that owns it *know* about it?" I can hear my own stubbornness. Denial, for now, feels like an appropriate response. They are all being absurd. It's science fiction. The fact that there are precedents for such a catastrophe is irrelevant. These things may have happened in prehistory, but they can't happen in the age of man. Nature can't just destroy civilization. We've come too far. We can cope with things on this scale nowadays. We can prepare for them.

Ned says, "There might not be any visible signs at this stage. But even if the company does know, it might not want to publicize it. Especially if it's corrupt and mismanaged. There are plenty of those, believe me."

"It might try to contain it," I say. But even I can hear the absurdity.

One side of my face feels hot, as though my body is registering what my brain is failing to. A moment passes. Kristin Jonsdottir walks over to the window, reangles the slats on one of the blinds, and stares out. Ned is clicking at his laptop, and the physicist, perhaps finally taking the hint that I want no more to do with him, is staring fixedly at the images on the whiteboard. Outside, a plane scrapes a white arc across the sky, leaving a delicate snail trail of vapor.

"So what now?" I ask.

"I spoke to Harish Modak," says Frazer Melville. "He still doesn't share our sense of urgency. But I persuaded him to travel over from Paris tonight." He stops and glances at Kristin. She nods her head. There's more. Something that neither of them is keen on conveying. "He's coming on the understanding that we'll have something new to show him by then. If not proof, then a compelling piece of support-ing evidence."

"Why on earth did you say that when you can't guarantee it?" I'm baffled. Kristin gives me a strange, supplicant look.

"Because it was all I could come up with. I was hoping that, with your help, Bethany might be able to remember some more."

Sharply, it becomes clear. "So this is where I come in, right? This is why I'm here?"

"Gabrielle," says Kristin gently, "we do need your help. You have already gone further than anyone could have expected in this. But we can't do this without you."

I sigh, sickened. "If we want more information from Bethany, she has to have more ECT. Do you realize that? It's the only way."

There is a silence. Yes, they do realize.

"It's what she's been telling us," confirms Kristin quietly. "It's what seems to work."

"And I have to supervise it," I continue, thinking aloud. "And if it goes wrong I take responsibility."

The physicist reaches out and rests his hand on mine and gives it a small squeeze. If I had any pride left I would shake it off but I need his touch. I can feel its heat. I can remember the time when a gesture like that would have flooded me with joy. He says softly, "You remem-ber how we felt after Istanbul. That night, when we heard the news and—"

No. I don't want to.

My phone rings. I should leave it—it's not the moment—but I am relieved to have a distraction, an excuse to emerge. I flick it open—and instantly regret doing so.

"Detective Kavanagh here. Where are you exactly, Miss Fox?"

"At home," I lie quickly. A reflex. But the wrong one. "Let me call you right back," I say, thinking wildly of ways to right what I've just said and signaling to Ned that I've been caught unawares. But he is shaking his head. It's too late. I have blown it.

"No need for that," says Kavanagh evenly. "If you're at home, you can just open the door. I'm right outside. I've been ringing the bell. But no joy. I'm surprised to hear you're in there, to be honest. Because there's no sign of your car out here." I say nothing. "Have you heard of the term 'perverting the course of justice,' Miss Fox? A dangerous minor's been abducted. Bethany Krall is a known killer. That's quite heavy stuff. I don't know what kind of disabled facilities they have in a women's prison like Holloway. But you can be sure there will be, er, *art therapy*. So if you'd care to—"

But he doesn't get any further because I've shut my phone and turned it off.

"Well, forget about going back to Hadport tonight," says Ned. "You've just become a criminal."

The three of them are staring at me. From the next room comes the theme tune of *Friends*. I am a natural, deep-rooted pessimist, but somewhere along the way I trained myself in optimism, learning reflexes that I incorporated, as the years went by, until positive thinking came to dominate my mental landscape like an enforced code of conduct. But the bizarre rush of relief that I am feeling in the wake of Kavanagh's call does not come from that. It's not manufactured. Despite the renewed misery I have encountered here, it's real. And I must trust it. I must trust it because perhaps, all along, I've had an intuition that this moment would come. A stowaway, furtive knowledge of where I have been headed, without knowing it, from the day I arrived at Oxsmith to meet Bethany Krall, from the evening the physicist and I fled the Armada to order poppadoms in an Indian restaurant, from the afternoon he lit the bulb inside Bethany's short-lived globe and the planet was illuminated, from the day Christ the Redeemer fell and Istanbul shuddered to dust, from the moment Kristin Jonsdottir appeared on my computer screen with her red woolly hat and her chunk of flaming ice.

"You questioned your involvement earlier," says Ned. "But given the sudden change in your legal status . . ."

I look at him, and at Frazer Melville and his lover. I try to think of the world. Its innocence. The children who will die. But for now, suddenly, all I can think of is me. My pain, my jealousy, my double loss of womanhood. My lack of any future.

I am not ready for any of this. I will never be ready.

If I shut my eyes tight, I can blot it all out.

ELEVEN

"Problem sorted," announces Bethany, striding in barefoot. She is brandishing a red plastic bucket. "Cereal, milk, one apple, an omelette, and fifteen Haribos—thank you for those, Ned. Puked up the lot in three goes. So now my stomach's empty for the anesthetic and Wheels here has one less thing to fret about. Care to inspect?"

We don't get the choice. Having done our duty, Ned and I exchange a glance that turns into a smile. You can't help admiring Bethany's commitment to her fix.

If I'd been told a few weeks ago that I would find myself in a creaking farmhouse unpacking medical paraphernalia with an Australian climatologist in a room where illegal electroconvulsive therapy would be shortly performed on a matricidal teenager I was suspected of abducting, I'd have had trouble believing it. But here I am with Ned Rappaport, in a small, damp parlor, surrounded by boxes and bubble wrap. Before dark descended, I looked outside at an apple tree, its fruit littered across an overgrown meadow shaking with teasel brushes and the flat, shimmering coins of dried honesty, and I thought of my father's garden, and then my father, and missed him so fiercely that I was ready to leave on the spot, drive to the care home, haul him out and bring him here, for no other reason than that I am the flesh of his flesh and I am lonely. The ECT machine is a small box similar to the one Dr. Ehmet used at Oxsmith. Under my instructions, Ned has made up a low sofa as a bed.

"Thank you, Bethany," I tell her, nodding at the bucket. "Now please go and empty it. Preferably down a toilet rather than over someone's head. We'll call you back downstairs when we're ready."

Apart from worrying about Bethany's food intake, a problem now neatly resolved, my main activity over the past couple of hours has been avoidance of the physicist. Savoring the relief and the pain of his absence, I gaze out of the window.

Autumn Evening with Approaching Headlights.

"That," says Ned, "will be the man."

When we reach the front door, a tall, skinny man in jeans is being greeted by a reluctant-looking Kristin Jonsdottir and the physicist, whose eye I still refuse to meet.

"Let's not bother with names," says Ned quickly. "Less grief all round."

The anesthetist looks young enough to be straight out of medical school. His long, pale hair is parted in the middle and hangs to his shoulders in a way that exaggerates his narrow, penciled features, and his skin bears the sullen pallor of long hours exposed to fluorescents and halogens. There's a vulnerability about him that's familiar but that I can't immediately place. He tweaks his mouth in a generalized hello. There's a subdued atmosphere. Kristin, in particular, looks as though she would rather be anywhere—perhaps at the bottom of the sea with her frozen ice molecules—than here. I almost pity her. In an upstairs room, a clock chimes six.

"We'll get out of your hair," Frazer Melville says. "Just call if you need us."

"And you're the one responsible for the patient?" asks the anesthetist. I nod. "Then I'll need you there with me. As soon as we're done with the procedure I'll want to get going. And—no offense, but I want to forget I ever came here."

"Is this guy safe?" I ask Ned when Kristin Jonsdottir has melted discreetly upstairs and Frazer Melville has led the medic to the parlor.

"Yes. But he doesn't have to like the situation."

"So how did you persuade him in the first place?"

Ned looks evasive. "We're living by new priorities. Not·all the choices we make are going to be of the finest moral quality."

"I can tell you've hung around with politicians. Are you going to add that the end will justify the means?" He doesn't answer. I sigh. "I'll need the pictures of all four rigs ready so we can look at them immediately afterwards. I'm hoping she'll spot a detail that clinches it. We'll need good definition. Some new angles, if you can get them."

"Right. I'll go summon the princess."

When Bethany comes downstairs, barefoot, rebandaged, and unkempt, she's hungry for action. Grabbing the handles of my chair despite my protests, she pushes me at high speed down the corridor and into the parlor, where she greets the medic with a "Yo, doc" and a blazing orthodontic grin. He returns it with a baleful look and eyes her as she settles herself on the low sofa, humming tunelessly and picking at the scabs on the exposed parts of her arms.

I have often wondered what draws anesthetists to a profession that requires one to so finely judge the line between the conscious and the unconscious self, the living state and the dead. Their high suicide rate is ascribed to the ready availability of the means, but something about the way this young man carries himself makes me speculate there's more to it than that. As for Bethany, a stranger is about to blast her brain with electricity in a medical procedure whose effectiveness has never been understood—and she is ready and willing. The trust involved, the inevitability of a massive power imbalance, and the paradoxical absence of intimacy between Bethany and the anonymous doctor make for an emotionally lurid contract, I reflect, watching him adjust the position of the small machine on the coffee table. He inserts a rubber wedge in her mouth: she opens wide to accept it with uncharacteristic docility. Her bare feet are smudged with what looks like mud. The medic takes it all in but doesn't inquire about how Bethany became injured. Or indeed, why she is here.

"Ready?" he asks. She nods. For both of them, it's a familiar routine. He puts the anesthetic bag over her nose and mouth, then wipes her temples with a wet sponge.

A few moments later, Bethany's eyelids have closed and she has succumbed.

I hold my breath. The medic flicks the timer on and applies the electrodes to her temples. He presses them in place, but after a few seconds he frowns as though dissatisfied.

"Her brain's built up a resistance," he murmurs. The seconds tick by. Five, six.

"How do you know? I thought the point of the muscle relaxants and the anesthetic was to make sure that, whatever happens, it's confined to the brain."

"There are small signs. And I'm not seeing any of them. I can tell you now, the machine's working fine, but it's not having an effect."

The ten seconds are up. He removes the electrodes. There is still no movement from Bethany, not even the curl of toes that I saw when I watched this before, like bracken unfurling. In the distance, a phone rings.

"Can you do it again?" I whisper. "And give her longer?"

He presses his lips together in a line of disapproval. "Unsafe to do it twice in one day."

"You said her brain's built up a resistance. There must be variations anyway. Aren't there?"

He looks annoyed. "I'll wait for her to come round and then I'll make a decision."

Within two minutes, Bethany's eyes have flickered open. I remove her mask. It leaves a faint red suction mark around her mouth, like the unhappy grimace of a clown.

"Didn't fucking work," she slurs through the rubber mouth guard. The muscles of her face have gone slack and distorted, and she's sweating. Even her hair looks greasier, as though the volts have somehow ravaged her and spooled her life through years rather than seconds. She spits out the guard. "Give me more of it, you fuckwit. A proper shot this time. Give me thirty seconds."

He blinks and addresses his answer to me. "I'll give her twenty," he says, rolling up his sleeves, picking up the mouth guard, and wiping the saliva off it with a paper towel. As he does so I notice the puncture marks on his arms. The stark fact of his addiction, which should have been obvious to me from the start, now shoulders its way into the equation.

"Twenty's not enough," Bethany protests, as she succumbs to the anesthetic. "What kind of doctor are you anyway?"

He plugs her mouth with the rubber guard and she is silenced.

"One who's worried about being struck off?" I suggest to him, when her eyes have closed.

His smile is dry. "Too late for that. I lost my license to practice a year ago."

I should have worked that out too. "You'd better tell me why."

"Sure," he says, checking the dials on the metal box. "I killed someone."

Oh Christ. "With a machine like this?"

He considers. "Nope. A more up-to-date version."

"Performing this procedure?" I can hear the panic in my voice, the shrillness.

He looks at me. "I can't imagine what other procedure you'd perform with it. Yes. But I'm not prepared to do that again. I won't go over twenty seconds. I made that clear from the start." *And if it's not enough? What then?* "Want me to stop?"

"No," I say, detesting us both for it. "You're here now. Just get it over with."

He presses the switch and we both hold our breath. Only a slight twitch of Bethany's toes indicates that anything has happened, until at the end of twenty seconds, a tiny noise escapes from her: a high sigh like the start of a groan.

"Do you think it's worked this time?"

He stands up, checks his mobile, and pats his pockets, then heads for the door. "I'm not staying to find out."

"Stop," I tell him. "Look. I don't know your name. As far as I'm concerned, I've never met you. This equipment isn't traceable to you. If it hasn't worked, can't you try again?"

"I don't think you heard me the first time," he says from the doorway. "I told you. I killed someone. I have to live with that. But I don't have to repeat it."

"Please, can't you even wait till—" But he has left the room. I know there's no point chasing after him, that he has made up his mind, that this was the deal he struck with Ned or, more simply and more importantly, with himself.

After five minutes, with the sound of the medic's car starting in the background, Bethany's eyes flicker open and I remove the mask from her face and let her spit the guard into my hand. I pass her a glass of water, which she gulps down sloppily. She looks even more destroyed than before. It's almost obscene.

"Hi, Bethany."

She looks at me fuzzily and speaks from the side of her mouth. "Hi, Wheels. It didn't work."

The disappointment is like a strong, ugly taste. "He's gone."

"Why?" Her lower lip seems to be in spasm.

"He had reasons I couldn't argue with."

I find the others assembled in the kitchen, deep in gloomy discussion.

"Harish Modak rang," says Frazer Melville, looking up. "He's on his way."

A vile heat flashes through me. "So what do we do now?"

He shrugs. "I don't know."

Our eyes meet. But I cannot bear it. My failure has left me with a weariness that presses on my shoulders, turning me into a yoked beast dragged in endless circles, its hooves clogged with earth. Sensing my misery, Frazer Melville touches my arm in sympathy, but feeling me stiffen, he withdraws his hand.

"Let's talk to Bethany," I suggest. "Maybe some of it got through."

Wordlessly, the others follow me back to the small parlor, where she is sprawled on the settee inspecting her blistered hands, the long bandage unwound and strewn around her on the floor like a giant strand of fettuccini.

"He could see I could take more but the little fucker wimped out!" she rails. "And you let him go! I told you, Wheels. I need thirty seconds. If I'd had that long it would've worked."

"You're sure you didn't see anything?"

"You know I didn't!" she explodes. "Because I didn't get enough volts!"

"There's nothing we can do now," I say. I feel flattened and helpless and oddly distanced from my own body. I could be watching myself from the far wall. Or from outside, in the darkness.

"Of course there is," she says, lifting herself higher on her elbow and wincing from the pain. "How dumb are you guys? Look, we've still got the machine. You know how to operate it. So go for it."

Kristin Jonsdottir's eyes widen, and Frazer Melville shoots me an uneasy glance. Ned strokes his stubble.

"You must be joking, Bethany," Frazer Melville blurts. "It could kill you."

"It won't. Go on," she says, jerking her head woozily in the direction of the little machine. "A two-year-old could work that thing. So can Wheels here. So can any of you. Just do it. I need thirty seconds. The professor guy's on his way, right? So do it now. While you dare. Don't think about it, just do it."

Kristin takes a step back. She seems suddenly smaller, as though ready to shrivel her way out of the room. Frazer Melville stands motionless. He opens his mouth to say something, looks at me questioningly, then closes it again. I know what he's thinking.

I say, "No."

"Jesus!" spits Bethany. "You fucking coward. If you can't do it for me, then do it for the sake of all those people you think are worth saving, you dumb cow!"

She is quivering with rage.

I ask, "Do *you* think they're worth saving? Would you risk your life for them?"

"You're such an idiot. It's not about other people. It's about me. And my life's fucked anyway. So just do it."

"Assisted suicide? No thanks."

"OK," she sighs heavily. "Let's tell Wheels what she wants to hear. I *love* life. Can't get enough of it. I want to celebrate this glorious fucking world. A certain spaz has made me see just how mind-blowingly wonderful it is, with her miracle psychobabble. I can't wait to see the future. Bring it on. Just do it, for fuck's sake. It's my final wish, OK?"

And before I can think, she has shoved back the mouth guard, reached out shakily for the face mask, applied it to her nose and mouth, and administered a pump of gas. "Do it now," she says, groggily, her eyes sliding shut. "Or I'll never forgive you."

You may not be alive to, I think. I am so terrified I could puke. Ned Rappaport, Frazer Melville, and Kristin Jonsdottir are staring at me aghast. Outside, there's the sound of a car approaching.

"That'll be Harish. I'll go," murmurs Kristin Jonsdottir. Noiselessly, she slips out.

People used to tell me I spent too much time thinking, analyzing, reflecting, hunting for hidden meanings when perhaps there just weren't any. When something huge is at stake—something so big its sheer size could blind you—you can't waste time speculating.

Sometimes, you just have to take a leap in the dark.

A big, ignorant leap. To a new place, where nothing is the same.

It could be the worst choice I ever make, but in that instant, it's done. Swiftly, I wipe Bethany's forehead with the sponge, grab the electrodes, flick on the timer, apply them to her temples, and shift the switch. I hold my breath as the clock ticks and the electricity floods her brain.

Cold, factual thoughts take hold. I must not pass out from fear. If she dies, they'll call it murder. They will be right to.

I keep the electrodes clamped to her temples and watch the seconds pass.

There's an uncanny silence. Bethany's face is so impassive she could be dead. The longest ten seconds of my life pass, but nothing terrible is happening. Then twenty. Twenty-five. Twenty-six. Twenty-seven. Still no movement from Bethany, no sign that the current is having an effect. How should I interpret this? What am I looking for? I don't even know. I won't breathe till it's over. Twenty-eight. I hear Ned gulp. *Cuando te tengo a ti, vida, cuanto te quiero.* Frazer Melville puts a hand on my shoulder and squeezes it. I shuck it off because I loathe myself even more than I loathe him.

Then at twenty-nine seconds, catastrophe.

With no warning, Bethany's head jerks up with a violent epileptic spasm and her legs and arms start jerking. The electrode pads crash to the floor and the mouth guard goes flying, but the frantic break-dance continues, unstoppable. Frazer Melville shouts to Ned to take her legs and grapples with her flailing arms. Barely thinking about what I am doing, I heave myself out of the chair, and with immense effort—I can feel the adrenaline whipping through me—I throw myself across her on the settee, pinning her convulsing torso down with my weight. Her head, freed from its strap, butts me in the mouth and I taste blood. She's still convulsing. Despite my weight on top of her, she's half off the settee. There's more blood, Bethany's or mine—I can't tell. I think: *She's bitten off her tongue.* Then she flops still.

Ned stands back while Frazer Melville lifts me bodily off her and settles me back into my chair. I am aware of his immense strength. He could be picking up a rag doll.

Bethany, covered in blood, skewed at an awkward angle, is now completely motionless. Her chest was heaving before, but now there is no rise and fall.

The world drops away beneath me.

Kristin appears at the door, open-mouthed. With her is Harish Modak.

The old man is frailer in the flesh than in the photographs I have seen: a small, shrunken figure with iron gray hair and the dark, hooded eyes of a bird of prey. Eyes that flicker across the room, widening as they take in the carnage.

Everywhere is streaked with red. Bethany is twisted oddly, as though she has tried to turn herself inside out. Blood drips from the corner of her lip.

She has stopped breathing.

Harish Modak's legs buckle as he registers what has happened, and he reaches out to support himself on the door frame. Kristin grabs his arm and settles him, gray-faced, in a chair by the window.

"I'll do mouth-to-mouth and you work her heart," I tell Frazer Melville.

"I'll count," says Ned, hastening over. I take a deep breath, clamp my mouth over Bethany's, and exhale into her lungs.

The next few minutes are a blur. I taste blood and snot. *If I can die in her place, I will. I'll find a way. Bethany, come back. Come back.* My lungs are weak with the effort of shoving air into hers. I'm working on her like a machine, all my reflexes kicking in. At one point I pull my head back from Bethany's mouth and think, This isn't Bethany anymore. It's Bethany's dead body. But I carry on forcing air into her lungs anyway, peripherally conscious that Ned has handed over to Kristin Jonsdottir, and is now making a phone call.

"Ambulance," he says. "Child having convulsions. Yes. Mouth-to-mouth, yes, and . . ."

"Sit her up," I tell Frazer Melville. With a huge movement, he hauls her up and slings her across his chest so that she's semi-upright in his arms. Kristin jumps back to make way for him as he topples then regains his balance. I thought I had been through the darkest times of my life. But I had not counted on this moment.

"What now?" Kristin asks in a whisper.

"This," I say. And slam Bethany on the back with all my force.

There's no reaction. "Gabrielle," says Frazer Melville quietly, restraining my arm, which is poised for another thump. "Gabrielle, can't you see? It's too late."

"She's gone," says Kristin. "She's dead." A low sob escapes her and her face crumples. Harish Modak is sitting completely still, as though mummified.

"No!" I free my arm and slam her on the back again. "Come back, Bethany!" As though she can be yelled into life. Which she cannot. "Come back!"

Ned, who has been talking urgently into the phone, suddenly stops. He's staring at me. No. Not at me. At Bethany. I can't see her face from this angle. But he can.

"Sorry, false alarm," he says quietly into the phone, and snaps it shut.

A groan escapes me. But something odd is happening. Ned's face has broken into a bewildered, ecstatic smile. I look at Harish Modak: the old man's expression mirrors Ned's. Kristin's gray green eyes widen, then narrow, and I realize that she's smiling too. They are all deranged. When Harish Modak speaks, his voice is like a creaky wheel.

"Well, Miss Bethany Krall," he whispers. "We meet at last."

Then Bethany coughs, and my heart flips about like a landed fish.

Quickly, Frazer Melville sets Bethany down and we both see what Ned, Kristin, and Harish Modak saw first: her eyes are open and she's blinking. She's alive. From deep in her chest, she draws in a raucous breath and coughs again. A huge red chrysanthemum of blood splats onto the floor.

I burst into tears. Harish Modak comes over to me stiffly, as though hampered by pain. My breathing has become awkward: heaving and uncontrollable. I'm on the edge of hysteria. From the corner of my eye I see that Bethany is shuddering.

"It's over now, Miss Fox," says Harish Modak. "You can relax." The voice is hoarse, the Indian accent stronger than I had expected. He is old. Frail. Perhaps also very ill. He may be cynical about Homo sapiens' use to the earth's system, but he is kind. I can tell from the gentleness with which he touches my shoulder. "Let us go and clean off this blood. I don't know exactly what went on in here just now and I don't think I want to. But the young lady will be OK. Now, if you will permit me, Miss Fox, I have brought with me a selection of alcohol and foodstuffs. Let us see if we can improve your morale." Frazer Melville turns away from Bethany and comes forward, apparently to accompany us, but Harish Modak puts up a hand. "Miss Fox and I

will be fine, my boy. You see to Miss Krall here and we will all con-
vene shortly."

And with an old-world flourish, like a servant waiting on a seated
monarch, he positions himself behind my chair, spins me round, and
wheels me out of the room.

TWELVE

'm nursing my second whisky and Harish Modak is installing himself in the living room, emptying a camel-hide briefcase of various
packages that he unwraps and arranges on the coffee table. I've returned from a visit to the bathroom, where I indulged in a fierce private bout of crying, the most intense since I lost Max. My blood is
calming, but my legs still vibrate with pins and needles, like the flickering of a shoal of tiny electric shrimp—an infuriating reminder that,
although unresponsive to any demands I make on them, my lower
limbs have found a way of registering mental disturbance and causing their own, parallel form of havoc.

"There we are. Disaster relief," says Harish Modak, gesturing at
the food. I take in the display of odorous French cheeses, the block
of pâté de foie gras, the tiny samosas, the box of Belgian chocolates,
the bars of Swiss Lindt, the bag of lychees, and the Turkish delights,
and readjust my image of Harish Modak as an ascetic. "I will be offended if you refuse."

"Then I'll have a café cognac truffle," I say, helping myself from
the box. "Followed by another." I discover I am starving. A sugar rush
would be just the ticket right now.

"How do you feel?"

I'm wondering whether he heard me crying in the bathroom and, if he did, whether it matters. "It's normally my job to ask that kind of question. Or it was until recently. I feel like asking you how *you* feel. As Bethany keeps reminding me, it's what I do. It's how I get to know people. I know no other way."

"Fair enough," he says, returning my smile. The chocolate is working, warming and cosseting me from within. "*Fair enough.* I am fond of that expression, aren't you? So evenhandedly British!"

"So how *do* you feel?"

"Now, specifically?" he asks. I nod. Amused, he applies his mind to the question, his brow furrowing slightly. "If we're discussing the current situation, I would say alarmed and fascinated. But cautious."

"And more generally?"

"Aha, a larger question. Are we talking about the world?"

"I can't think of a more pressing matter right now."

"Alarmed and fascinated again. But more than that, I feel cheated not being able to see fifty years ahead," he says, settling in a straight-backed armchair. He moves in the manner of those afflicted with chronic rheumatic pain. "I would like more than anything to see the future. I would like to see in what way life develops."

"That's quite a claim, coming from a leading proponent of the idea that it isn't going to," I say, taking another gulp of whisky and letting the glow spread through my rib cage.

"Not for most humans, in all probability. But the collapse of Homo sapiens as a dominant species means the dawn of a new era for a million other life forms. These interest me." If this is the man's small talk, I wonder what his big talk is like. From the breast pocket of his jacket, he reaches for a horn-handled pocketknife, opens it up, and pares himself a modest wedge of Pyrenean goat cheese. "We've been here a mere instant, in geological terms," he says, inspecting it as he might a slice of brain on a slide. "My wife was one of the leading experts on the end-Permian. Back then, life on the planet was nearly wiped out altogether. But within an era or two, it had regenerated most efficiently." He pours himself a whisky and gives it an amber swirl. "Millions of years ago, a reptilian ancestor of the pig, *Lystrosaurus,* was the king of the hill. A catastrophe species, like fungi. Perfect for the aftermath of a high-stress event because they thrive on decaying organic matter. Two hundred and fifty-one million years ago, fungi had an orgy. So did the hagfish. Arguably the ugliest creature of the sea, but a successful scavenger."

"The point being?"

His smile is an unwilling one, as though wrought against his better judgment. The shadowed eyes glint like ancient marbles. "That in terms of the life of this planet, blink and you will miss Homo sapiens altogether. We'll be an irrelevance." Having uttered it, the notion seems to please him. He cuts himself a second slice of cheese and slots it into his mouth.

"We weren't sure you would come."

The hooded eyes edge sideways. "Nor was I."

His discomfort suggests that the decision came from an urge born somewhere in the complex substrata of his psyche, an urge he cannot or will not name. I won't insist. It will emerge on its own or not at all. "And now that you're here?"

He points the tip of the pocketknife at me. "I have seen with my own eyes the dramatic seriousness with which you take this interesting child. One cannot be unimpressed. I only hope that the experiment has paid off."

"If Bethany comes up with something definitive . . ."

"I came here on the understanding that she already had."

"It doesn't change my question. How will you respond?"

"I will consider crossing the bridge when I have seen what kind of bridge it is. And have judged whether it is crossable." From somewhere else in the house, we can hear Ned loudly cajoling Bethany. She tells him to leave her the fuck alone. A doubt is hatching. Why is Modak really here? Ned hinted that, even if convinced, he might prove hard to persuade to do anything. He mentioned his curiosity. Could that alone be what has brought him here? If so, how far will it take him? If he proves stubborn, what leverage is there?

"What was Meera like?" I ask. His response is a defensive, troubled glance. "You were married a long time. You must miss her."

"May I ask you something, as a psychologist?" His tone is still playful but I sense a shift. I nod. "She wanted her ashes to be thrown in the Ganges but I kept some aside because when the urn arrived back from the crematorium I had the strangest urge to eat them." Ah. The mud has finally stirred. I wait for more. "Is the ingestion of one's other half a known syndrome?"

"I've read some of the literature on it. It's a surprisingly common urge."

"Do you regard it as a form of cannibalism?"

"Do you?"

"My internal jury is still out on that one."

"It's not a crime to want her with you. I imagine it's a comfort. A way of being one flesh, even after death. So. You followed the urge."

He smiles, revealing teeth the color of old piano keys. "Dr. Melville told me you were good." I flush. He reaches into the leather briefcase and pulls out a small jam jar of granular ash, which he holds up with reverence. Then he grins. "Essence of Meera."

I have a sudden, avid urge to discover whether he sprinkles her on his food condiment-style or swallows her like medicine, but diplomacy is called for.

"I imagine she was a formidable woman."

"Like me, she believed that our only afterlife is an organic one. I'm not afraid of death myself. Of the change of matter, animal to mineral. You are not at my age."

"So you have achieved all you wanted to?"

"I came to certain conclusions about our species and its fate. Conclusions to which most people chose not to listen."

"You spawned a whole movement. With self-sufficient settlements all over the world. I get the impression a lot of people listened."

"Not hard enough." His old mouth forms a rigid line, like a turtle's.

"You and Meera didn't have children. I imagine that was a private response."

"Why create hostages to a future whose shape one could so clearly see? The decision was to avoid grief. For oneself but also for others." From habit, I note the telling use of "one" instead of "I" or "we" and store the observation. "The world is too full. But the childless are always punished. It's a great irony that one gets called selfish for making what is essentially an altruistic choice."

Since my father's brain dissolved, I have missed the company of elderly men. But Professor Modak's presence is causing unsettling questions, rather than a daughterly affinity, to germinate. If, with his blithe nihilism and his jar of edible marital ashes, he truly believes the world will be a better place without humans and sees time in terms of epochs rather than days and hours, then yes: why should he bother to save a few random millions?

Why on earth?

At the sound of footsteps on the stairs, Harish Modak replaces the jar in his briefcase and turns his head to the door. Bethany enters first, followed by the physicist.

"Hi, Wheels."

I look Bethany up and down. Our absent host, the expert in chemiluminescence, is a man of impressive physical proportions, to judge by the size of the toweling bathrobe she is wrapped in. Drowned in its red tartan folds, she settles in a corner of the sofa opposite mine, with her bare feet tucked underneath her. Frazer Melville greets us somberly and comments to Harish Modak on the impressive display of food. I can feel him looking at me searchingly, but I have now fully mastered the knack of avoiding his eye. Bethany has been cleaned up and somebody—I guess Ned—has rebandaged her arms and hands. Her face is ashen and her bitten tongue lolls on her lower lip, its tip a chunk of hacked meat.

"I told her to do it," she says, nodding at me but addressing Harish Modak. She emits the words with care, working them past her ruined tongue. "I made her give me thirty seconds." She sounds proud. Ned and Kristin come in quietly and settle in chairs. All six of us now form a circle around the coffee table opposite the fireplace.

Harish Modak nods. "And was it effective, Miss Krall?"

Silence stiffens the air around us. Enjoying the attention of five pairs of adult eyes, Bethany grins, then winces with the pain and sucks in a breath.

"I was right in the middle of it. It was like being struck by lightning. It was so cool. I got this huge charge."

Harish's stillness has an intense, reptilian quality. "Take your time. Describe everything."

Ned is positioning his laptop on a corner of the coffee table to project the rigs onto the whiteboard.

"It's like a giant cover being lifted off a bed. Bubbles and stuff are just, like, pouring out from the edges." Frazer Melville and Kristin Jonsdottir exchange a private glance that hits my guts like the fist of a thug. "These stinking bubbles. And it breaks up and there are these huge white sheets just tearing off and shooting up. It goes on and on. As far as you can see. Then there's fire on the water, the sea's just, like, glowing in the dark. Yellow and orange. Blue in some places. Just flickering on top of the water." She tells it with the lull of a fairy tale. "Then this giant wave swells up. It's like a wall in the sky. Higher than the clouds."

The old man does not move, but I'm aware of embers beginning to glow.

"We have to know where this happens," says Kristin Jonsdottir. "We have to identify the rig."

I roll closer to Bethany. "The drawing you did. You were underwater and you imagined traveling up the pipe and you saw the platform and the yellow crane. Did you see it again?" Bethany nods, squints, and dabs at the tip of her tongue. When she removes her hand, there's fresh blood on the bandage that wraps her finger. She spits on the floor, then closes her eyes and lolls her head back. "Can you remember the crane? Could you see inside it?"

She sighs and screws up her eyes. A moment passes. "There was something. Ouch. It hurts to talk. Something pink. It looked like a . . ." Although her eyes are still closed, it's clear she's trying to focus. "God. It was a cunt," says Bethany. She bursts out laughing. "A woman's cunt! Shaved!" Her eyes flip open and meet Kristin Jonsdottir's and she smiles lopsidedly, uncertain of what she's remembered. Then she laughs again, delighted. "It was a naked muff! You could see her asshole too. Ew, gross!"

"Bethany," I say sharply. "This is serious. I nearly killed you earlier. There isn't time for games."

"It's not a game!" she laughs. "I tell you, I saw a vag!"

"Er, if I know anything about rigs," Ned Rappaport intervenes, "she may well have done, and there's actually no mystery."

Harish Modak looks fleetingly amused. "They allow prostitutes? Most enlightened!"

Kristin gives a wan smile. "The next best thing," she says, tightening the blinds.

A second later the images of the four rigs have reappeared on the wall screen. The blue of the water in the fourth image is a virulent turquoise but in the others it's darker.

"These are the main suspects. They're all drilling for methane. They're located off Siberia, and Indonesia, in the North Sea, and in the Caribbean south of Florida," says Ned. "We've ruled out the rest for various reasons to do with their operational mode. These four all have yellow cranes."

"These are good-quality pictures," comments Harish Modak, looking quizzical. "Better than anything from a satellite."

"The sort of thing spies kill each other for," murmurs Ned, adjusting the focus, clearly pleased that Harish has noticed. "They're from the military." He clicks and three of the rigs disappear. "This is the Siberian one. *Endgame Beta*," he says, zooming in first on the spire of the derrick and then on the yellow crane, which is perched to one side of the rig.

"Go in closer," commands Bethany. We're suddenly confronted by the broad, spilling stomach of a middle-aged man sitting at the controls of the crane's cabin. His mouth hangs open, as if he is singing or yawning. He has no idea he has been caught on camera.

"See anything you recognize now, Bethany?" asks Ned. "This bloke here? Anything familiar?"

Bethany shrugs and points at the family photographs on the wall of the man's cabin. "No intimate flesh. No *pew-denda*. I'd say Mr. Clean from Siberia is sitting in a fanny-free zone."

Ned moves to the next image: nothing. On the next, *Lost World* in the Caribbean, the crane is unmanned—but on the inside wall of the cabin, to the left of the joystick and controls, is a rectangle of pink. Ned tightens the picture and adjusts the focus. Then, too suddenly, the slur of flesh has taken on silhouette and texture and we're staring at a pair of hugely swollen breasts with dark, saucerlike nipples. Perched above them, the smiling face of their brunette owner.

"Pass the sick bag!" Bethany guffaws. Ned scrolls down the image but stops just north of the jewel-studded belly button.

"No mons veneris. So shall we rule out Miss November in the Caribbean," says Ned dryly, "and move on?"

In the next image, the windscreen of the manned crane has sunlight on it, making it hard, initially, to distinguish much beyond the outline of the operator's head. But Bethany is pointing excitedly.

"Let's see the top right. Behind his left shoulder and up a bit." The fair-haired man is lifting a can of Dr Pepper to his lips with a gloved hand. "Higher," commands Bethany. Something pink and glistening comes into lurid focus. Ned pulls out until the entire girl materializes. She is Chinese.

Her legs are spread wide.

Between them, a slick, meaty confusion.

"That's the one," says Bethany, noncommittally. She seems to have lost interest. Ned flicks the screen off, engulfing us again in the room's gloom. When he speaks, his voice is constricted. "It's *Buried Hope Alpha*."

"Christ," says Kristin Jonsdottir. "It's in the North Sea. A hundred kilometers off the coast of Norway."

"Norway," repeats Harish Modak. He breathes in deeply and exhales in silence. I think: Mountains. Cruises in fjords. But then stumble, stuck. Looking bored, Bethany rummages about in the chocolates, mews in disgust at the cheese, and settles for a lychee.

"*Buried Hope Alpha* belongs to Traxorac," says Ned. The color has abandoned his face, making his dark stubble stand out. It strikes me that he feels as lonely as I do.

"Can you get the exact coordinates?" asks Frazer Melville. Kristin Jonsdottir is biting her lip.

After a false start, a geological map fills the screen: a huddle of thin concentric rings intersected with lines of latitude and longitude, with a small red dot indicating what I assume is the rig. Bethany is now yawning widely, frustrated at no longer being the center of attention.

"I see. Well, this is not good," says Harish Modak. He has become as somber as the others.

"I told you," says Bethany casually. We all look at her. "I kept saying it was close. I told you we'd be drowned. I said all along. But no one listened. Story of my fucking life."

"Can someone explain?" I ask.

Frazer Melville removes his exhausted face from his hands. "Have you heard of the Storegga Slide?" I shake my head, still unable to respond directly. It is all too raw, too agonizing. I want to leave this place and never come back. "It's a massive package of sand and mud off the continental shelf that stretches for eight hundred kilometers, from Norway to Greenland. It's the result of the biggest submarine upheaval we know of, eight thousand years ago. It generated a huge tsunami that washed over most of the British Isles. This rig is sited on the edge of Storegga."

But somehow he can't continue.

If I loved him I would feel sorry for him. I would want to take him in my arms and kiss his cheekbone. I glance at Kristin Jonsdottir. She seems too busy with her own reactions to be concerned with his. Her delicate eyes have become glassy and perturbed.

Harish Modak clears his throat and takes over.

"It seems, Miss Fox, that we are faced with the interesting prospect of a disaster which will begin very, er . . . *locally*. A huge underwater collapse anywhere in the Storegga region will cause a tsunami that will devastate the entire area. Norway's coastline is the closest to Storegga but the sediment package will push the water into the basin in the other direction to begin with, projecting it faster east than west. Making your country the first to be hit. It will be amplified in the river estuaries and in the funnel of German Bight." There's a gape of quiet, as though the air's molecules have squeezed into a new shape and sucked out noise. "Norway and Denmark will be hit next, and the rest of northern Europe. The tsunami will certainly reach Iceland and, if it's big enough, the United States."

"And the date?" asks Frazer Melville. His breathing is ragged. "Bethany, are you still sure about the date?"

"The coming of the dragon and the false prophet! The battle of Armageddon!" Bethany chortles, peeling off the shell of a lychee.

"Bethany," I say. My throat is bunching up. "You said October 12."

She is rummaging around in her tartan robe for a piece of lychee shell, dropped during the peeling process. "Did I? I don't know. Maybe before. There's a thunderstorm. It's after that. But this thing's different from everything else." She fishes out the piece of shell and flicks it across the room, then returns her attention to the fruit.

"Miss Krall has been correct before," says Harish Modak, watching Bethany intently. "For the sake of argument we should perhaps assume that she is correct again."

"Too right you should. You know," Bethany murmurs, holding up the pearly orb of her lychee to the light. "These things look like eyeballs."

For a long time there is a pensive silence, broken only by Bethany's tuneless humming. It's Kristin who breaks it. "Harish, it's the tenth. You must help us."

He turns to her as if in pain. "Must? *Must* is an interesting word. It belongs with *should* and *ought*. I do not trust it." Bethany looks interested.

Kristin flares. "You mean you came all this way—"

"My dear Kristin. You know me well. So you know the question I shall ask. The same question I have spent half my life asking. To what end?" Kristin shoots a hopeless look first at Frazer Melville, then at me. Harish smiles. Bethany is nodding perkily, as though egging him on. "To what possible end, when the world that remains beyond this disaster will be unrecognizable?"

"Have you heard of moral duty?" Ned speaks calmly enough, but he looks ready for violence. "Have you heard of nonassistance to people in danger?" He gets to his feet and starts pacing the room, stroking at his stubble.

"Speaking personally, I would always prefer to know my options," says Frazer Melville. "So that I could make my own choices. We don't have the right to deny that to others."

Harish Modak does not look impressed. "I am glad to be this old," he says, sighing. "I would hate to be young."

"It completely fucking sucks," agrees Bethany, sticking her finger in her ear and tilting her head back carefully, as though it contains liquid that might spill.

"Harish," I say. He swivels his head and frowns.

"My dear Miss Fox."

"Whatever the future's like for most people, it's going to be even harder for me. But I don't want to die. I want to live." I sound more sure of this than I feel.

"There is living and there is surviving."

"Are we back to the avoidance of grief?" I notice Kristin stiffening.

"In a way, we are," says Modak. "And is there anything wrong with that?" *The decision was to avoid grief. For oneself but also for others.*

I turn to Kristin. "You knew Meera well. What would she say now, do you think?"

Modak looks stung at the mention of his wife's name. Good. If Meera is forbidden territory, then trespassing will have an effect.

"I tell you what she'd say, Gabrielle," says Kristin. She's addressing me but her words are for him. "She'd be ashamed to hear her husband talking like this." Harish's face tightens and he lets out an exasperated noise. "She didn't see the world the way Harish does. She never did. She sacrificed too much for him." His eyelids close to shut her out. But she won't stop. "She wanted children. But you wouldn't agree, would you, Harish? She'd have risked grief for the sake of some kind of future. If she were here now she would tell you that if it's the last thing you do—"

Kristin breaks off and looks away, too furious to go on.

"I agree with Professor M. here," says Bethany with a grin. "The world sucks. Humans suck. We don't deserve to live. None of us. Let something else take over the planet. Some kind of scorpion or whatever it's going to be. Toadstools. Hyenas. Those glow-in-the-dark creepy crawlies. So what if a load of idiots get swept away?"

"That is not what I am saying, Miss Krall," he says, standing up, his fists clenched. "You are misrepresenting me."

"How?"

"In every way possible."

"You don't agree then?"

"The present universe has undergone innumerable deaths and rebirths."

I grab his clenched hand, pull him down next to me and force his face to meet mine because I need him to witness my fury. "Whatever you feel about the Great Cycle and Gaia and the futility of the species is irrelevant, Harish! The issue is about the people who are alive now, who will die if you don't help us warn them!" He wants his hand back but I won't let go. "Look at me. I felt like a murderer after Istanbul. So did Frazer. If we fail to act now, none of us is any better than any war criminal on trial in the Hague. Most of all you, because you're the one with the power to do something."

Kristin moves over and stands behind him, resting her fingers lightly on his shoulder. Abruptly, Ned leaps up, grabs the tray, and heads for a side cupboard. He returns with six glasses and unscrews the Laphroaig.

"We all are. Let's drink to your health, Harish. And your moral courage."

"But I haven't—" Harish begins.

"Yes, you have," I say. "And we salute you for it."

He draws away from me and stands up. We're all looking at him. He sighs. As though drained of energy by the conflict, he sits down again with a small, hard thud.

"I will say one thing to all of you. And I will say it to anyone thinking beyond this disaster. Be careful what you wish for." Then, blinking, he reaches for the jar in his briefcase. It is too intimate. I look away.

Determined to keep the momentum of Harish's forced decision, Ned clinks glasses and proposes a further toast to Bethany. "A Coke for you, Bethany? Fruit juice?"

It might be the first time in her entire life that anyone has proposed a toast in her honor, but she shakes her head sullenly. The look on her face, as she rolls another lychee between her fingers, disturbs me. She is working up to something.

"If my wife were here, she would remind us that there's a common misconception about the Chinese character that represents the word *crisis*," says Harish Modak, sipping his whisky. With the moral decisions behind him, he seems to be rallying.

"Crisis equals danger plus opportunity," says Frazer Melville.

"So Western business gurus and life coaches would have you believe. They'll show you how the strokes break down, and say: Look. Danger and opportunity. But the Chinese will tell you that is in fact a myth."

"The moral being?"

"That a crisis is simply a crisis, nothing more and nothing less."

"For Traxorac, this is going to be about pride, self-image, about face," I say, thinking aloud. "We're dealing with the emotions of institutions, with herd psychology. And herds are unwieldy and tumultuous; they have mood swings, they go through phases in their thinking, they get idées fixes."

"No one likes to admit they screwed up," agrees Ned. "But it will apply to governments too."

"Our job is to warn the maximum number of people in the most efficient and convincing way about what's coming, whether or not Traxorac admits the danger and whether or not the authorities listen," says Kristin Jonsdottir. If I didn't hate her, I would like her. And I hate her for not letting me like her. "I'll bet that once they recognize it's happening, they'll be more preoccupied first with a cover-up and then with looking for a scapegoat than with tackling the logistics."

"She's right," says Ned, reaching for a notepad. "I've seen it from the inside. The first instinct will be denial, but then they'll flip into blame mode." He is jotting something down.

"If a horizontal crack's forming and loosening the sediment package where they've been drilling, there will be proof of it somewhere," says Frazer Melville, taking a slug of whisky.

"Yes. One piece of evidence would do it," says Kristin. "If it were uncontestable. If it's visible anywhere, it'll be in Traxorac's latest seismic logs of the drill site. If you compare them over time and there's a discrepancy, it means there's been movement. That would be proof."

"Harish," says Ned bluntly, looking up from his note making. "We'll be needing your clout there too."

"I feel a thousand years old."

"Once we have the logs, we hold a press conference and present the facts and the public can make its own decision. Which is what we owe them. Then we get somewhere safe, fast."

"Who's we?" says Bethany. The room goes still. "I said, who the fuck is *we*."

With a huge effort, she tries to stand up. But it's too soon: she's weak. She sways on her feet and looks ready to topple. "You listen to me, fuckwits." She seizes hold of the sofa arm and manages to right herself. Frazer Melville moves to help her but she shakes him off. She has our attention. "I'm the one who saw it happening. So don't even fucking think about handing me back to those wankers at Oxsmith. Or Kiddup Manor. You know what'll happen there." No one speaks. Ned shifts uncomfortably. "Well?" she says, accusingly. "Well, Professor M.? Ned? Frazer? Kristin? Wheels? Are you going to dump me now you've got what you need?" Her eyes are having trouble focusing. Spotting it, Frazer Melville pulls her firmly back down to the sofa. "Flush me down the fucking toilet, you assholes? Is that your plan?"

"We're obviously a team," begins Ned hesitantly. But he can't follow through. Being more pragmatist than diplomat, he's thinking the obvious thought. She's a loose cannon. A danger to herself and others. A mad girl. A liability. The police are looking for her. There is no way she can be involved. Kristin is eyeing Bethany with a mixture of dismay and profound distaste. The physicist is inspecting his hands.

"Wheels," says Bethany. Her eyes are glittering and her mouth has turned down at the edges. I feel a faint, high buzzing in my ears, like a pressure change on an airplane.

When I swivel to face the others, an ache spreads across my shoulders, pressing me down. I shift and straighten. "This is also a moral decision."

The éminence grise sighs wearily. "They seem to keep coming."

"Yes, Professor M.," snarls Bethany. Angry tears are tracking down her face. "And you're supposed to be good at them. Your reputation's kind of based on that idea, right? I Googled you."

Harish Modak closes his eyelids and exhales quietly. "I had not expected quite so much pressure to be exerted on me today concerning my status in the world," he murmurs. "But one must be consistent, I suppose." I breathe out. I had not expected this much relief. He opens his eyes and scrutinizes me. "As for your role in this, Miss Fox . . ."

I shrug. "You don't stop doing your job just because someone fires you. I'm doing my job."

Ned shifts in his seat but says nothing.

I think: I am doing my job because Bethany is my job.

And Bethany is all I have left.

THIRTEEN

Having established the principle of her freedom, the human hand grenade disappears into the next room to watch TV, while the others begin an intense technical discussion, orchestrated by Ned. The first priority, he says, is to obtain Traxorac's seismic data, the second to ensure that the warning they issue at the press conference reaches the maximum audience. "I have a stunt lined up involving the marine biologist mate whose house we're in and a team of his in Greenland. But in the meantime . . ." He clicks the laptop to reveal a screen filled with eight columns of bullet points over a map of the North Sea. "Here's the way forward as I see it." I understand why Frazer Melville recruited him. He is a strategy machine. But there's an item he has not yet factored in. While Harish Modak stops Ned with a question about the tonnage of *Buried Hope Alpha* and Frazer Melville and Kristin Jonsdottir reach for their notepads, I leave the room unnoticed and roll down the corridor.

Huge and somber, the farmhouse kitchen has low beams and a dark oak table, varnished to a high gloss. On it sits an open laptop. I set the kettle to boil on the range, locate teabags, cups, and milk, boot up, and check the news online. Sure enough, the story I have been dreading ever since the phone call from Kavanagh is one of the main headlines.

Teen Abduction: Disabled Therapist Suspected. I flush with irritation at the word *disabled*. As I read on, the flush spreads: *The hunt for the teenager abducted from a hospital ward last Wednesday has intensified following the disappearance of her former therapist, Gabrielle Fox, who now joins Dr. Frazer Melville, a research physicist, as a prime suspect in the case.*

The photo is unflattering and doubtless chosen to suit the story: it shows me looking vengeful. I recognize the occasion from the shapeless outfit I'm wearing, an unhappy hybrid of track suit and dress. They held a small party when I left the unit in Hammersmith. It was Dr. Sulieman's idea. Perhaps he thought it would cheer me up. But it didn't. I got drunk and someone had to ring for a taxi. The image of the physicist is smaller: an anodyne corporate shot in black and white. The BBC online article, which describes us, mortifyingly, as "the couple," continues with a quote from Leonard Krall demanding the immediate return of his estranged daughter for her own safety and that of others. This is followed by a statement from Detective Kavanagh, another from an Oxsmith spokeswoman, and a defensive comment from the senior administrator of St. Swithin's hospital. Joy McConey is quoted only toward the end of the article: "There's something I believe that her kidnappers haven't understood. Bethany Krall is damaged, dangerous, and very angry." I picture Joy's homeopathically pale eyes. "She has killed before. She's quite capable of killing again. Whoever is sheltering her should know that, unless she is safely contained, lives are at risk. The best way to help Bethany is to return her safely to the professionals."

I presume that the BBC, along with the main news agencies, will not run its interview with Joy in full because it has a reputation to maintain. But the rest of the Net is free of such scruples. Within a few clicks, I have located a video clip of Joy McConey, extracted from a longer interview. I turn up the volume and press play. She has worked hard on herself since our meeting in the playground. Gone is the combat gear. Her pale red wig is coiffed into a feminine chignon, while discreet makeup and a sober business suit provide a professional gravitas she must be credited for mustering at such short notice.

"When she was an inmate at Oxsmith, Bethany Krall foresaw several disasters which all then happened on the exact dates she predicted," she says. I remember Joy's voice when she called me on the phone, shrieking at her husband while he battled to restrain her.

Now, levelly and reasonably, she runs through the list of catastrophes Bethany foresaw, starting with Mount Etna a year ago and ending with the Istanbul quake. "My biggest concern isn't that Bethany Krall can predict events like these." She pauses to emphasize her point. "It's that she's somehow able to cause them. I don't say this lightly. I myself have personal proof of how powerful the forces within her are. When I contracted cancer two months ago . . ."

The kettle is boiling but I have given up on tea. I pause the clip and hurtle back to the others.

"Right, this'll mean a change of plan," says Ned when I have conveyed the news, to which he and the others listened with evident alarm, though if any of them now regrets the decision to allow Bethany to stay with us, the cavil is not voiced. "Gabrielle. Instead of coming with us to London, you, Frazer, and Bethany will need to stay here. We can't risk you being seen. Especially not with us. After the press conference, we'll collect you by helicopter." He flips open his phone and punches in a number. "But I'll organize alternative transport for you, just in case. He looks at his watch, sandwiching his mobile between his cheek and shoulder. "Kristin, Harish: we'll need to leave here within the next couple of hours. Hi, Jerry. Ned again. Another car, untraceable . . . yes, today."

I glance at Frazer Melville, the man who showed me a new world, then smashed it. If the morose expression on his face is related to the sudden prospect of staying here with me and Bethany, instead of going to London with his lover and the others to warn the world about the catastrophe on the horizon, then I share his gloom.

The others have left, and it is late. Frazer Melville has prepared a Marks & Spencer microwave dinner, which we eat in the kitchen around the oak table, largely in silence.

The food sticks in my throat. Even Bethany is subdued.

"I'll be sleeping on the sofa in the living room," I say, when Bethany has left the kitchen, announcing that she is going to bed.

"We need to talk," says the physicist.

"There's nothing to say. I'll clear the dishes, if you check on Bethany and lock the doors."

By the time he returns, fifteen minutes later, I have settled on the sofa with a blanket over me. Like a coward, I am faking sleep because I cannot face him. I'm too tired and too forlorn and I know that the conversation we will have will make me feel even worse than I already do. I'm aware of him coming in, approaching the sofa, and squatting next to me. I stay immobile. He kisses my forehead and I feel a huge wave of sadness.

He whispers, "Gabrielle. I know you're awake. Please stop being angry. You have to forgive me. We have to talk again. We have to move on."

But I don't shift.

I long for him to kiss me again, to touch me. But he doesn't.

Instead, he sits a little longer, then gets heavily to his feet, and leaves the room. What is he feeling? Pity, guilt, remorse?

A moment later I hear his tread on the stairs and the sound of him talking to someone on the phone. He must miss her, because it's a long conversation.

Unlike lovers who betray, those who die remain forever constant. If I could erect a No Trespassing notice to prevent Alex's creeping into my dreams at night, I would do it. Whenever he infiltrates, I awake with reluctance, knowing that surviving the day ahead will require an act of faith, a pledge to optimism that I will have trouble summoning. Another hour's sleep and my perspective might change, but now the dream—an unsettling one in which Alex twisted my hair into bewildering shapes—is too recent for that to be an option. And reality is too penetrating.

"Come on, Wheels. Let me show you the lake." She's flapping a white towel in my face. Through the blinds, there is already a striped glow of light. Eight o'clock, at a guess. "Come on! Get moving! Let's get some air!"

The day stretches ahead: a day of stress, of waiting for the phone to ring, of avoiding the physicist.

"Give me five minutes," I say and pull on a T-shirt.

Wheelchairs and mud do not get along well, but there's a concrete walkway that takes me close to a waterline fringed with reeds. Bethany has run on ahead and is stripping off.

"What are you doing? Bethany, you'll freeze!"

"It's great!" she yells, balling up her towel and flinging it at me.

I understand her urge because suddenly, with a rush of blood to the head, I share it. I, too, would love to strip off my clothes and swim. The sunrise is a delicate tangerine, the air so warm it could still be August. There's a faint breeze. Gulls and starlings wheel above us and hop about in the mulch. Just a few years ago, being able to swim outdoors in Britain in October would have seemed as outlandish as the arrival of seahorse colonies in the Thames or commercial papaya orchards in Kent. Now, warm autumns are just another in a long list of pill sweeteners as we descend into the ninth circle. Bethany has hurled her clothes onto the narrow sloping beach. Naked, she is a pitiful amalgam of skin and bone: thin rib cage, negligible breasts, concave stomach, gaunt thighs studded and criss-crossed with the scars of cuts and cigarette burns, a fuzz of dark hair between. She has abandoned her bandages but the wounds on her hands and arms are still raw.

"Be careful!" I call out, but she has plunged into the lake and is prancing about in the shimmering water, oblivious. If it is stinging her, and freezing cold, she doesn't let it show.

"Come on in!" she screams, ecstatic. "This is fucking amazing!"

My first instinct is the sane one: to refuse. There are no nurses to restrain Bethany should she attack me, and leaving my chair requires a level of confidence I don't feel. But having chosen to enter a territory with no rules, I am perversely tempted. I have missed the physical routine of my daily swims: my muscles yearn for movement, for something that edges toward punishment, and the serotonin rush that follows. I'm more mobile and free in the water than anywhere else. And it's not far to the edge.

Sometimes I think too much. Today I won't. I lower myself out of my chair and shuffle a few meters along the cool mud to get closer to the gap in the reeds where Bethany entered the water. Near the lake's edge I discard my skirt, keeping just my T-shirt and knickers. The compressed soil is cold and firm against my palms. When the slope sharpens, I turn sideways and roll, using gravity to propel me. It's an unexpected, stolen, and absurdly sensual feeling. In this moment, the refusal of my legs to cooperate with the rest of my body is forgiven. Irrelevant, even. If the slope were longer, I could roll forever. I could roll to the edge of the world. When I reach the scummy froth I am shocked by the slap of cold but don't let my momentum slow, merging into its chilly suck. Once submerged, I paddle a little way out, then float on my back, working my arms, savoring the harsh bliss of the water. Bethany stands chest-deep, facing the horizon, her arms held high above her, shivering and swaying.

" 'And I stood upon the sand of the sea and saw a beast rise up out of the sea,' " she shrieks to the sky. A seagull swoops past and disappears toward a hulked mass of trees in the far distance. " 'Having seven heads and ten horns, and upon his horns ten crowns, and upon his heads the name of blasphemy!' "

The lake is soft and benign as amniotic fluid, the creeping daylight seductive as a whisper. The world could almost feel like a good place. Unexpectedly, the sight of Bethany cavorting in the ripples with the giant wind turbine rotating on the hill beyond provokes a strange, painful wash of tenderness.

You could care about her, and the world we live in.

Perhaps you already do.

I close my eyes and float. After a while Bethany quiets down, bored with herself, and I listen to the sound of birdsong and the rustle of the wind in the reeds. In the distance, a tractor starts up. It's October 11, and I would feel anxious were it not for a vague but persistent feeling that Bethany has got it wrong and that whatever happens tomorrow—and I do not doubt that something will—cannot affect us here. It's too unimaginable. This country, with its patch-worked farmland, its hills and cliffs and valleys and gorges, its woodlands of oak and birch and beech and pine, its rivers and cattle pastures and bright swathes of hemp and rape: there is no room for catastrophes in such a world. They cannot gain entry.

Dr. Sulieman would have a thing or two to say about such fantasies of denial.

Lost in them, I don't hear Bethany's approach.

When she speaks, teeth chattering, her voice is right in my ear.

"I suppose Frazer'll want to fuck you again, now Kristin's gone." Her tone is conversational. She could be commenting on the weather. I don't want to open my eyes, but I must if I am to face whatever comes next. She's treading water next to me, with only her head visible. On top of it, perched like a fright wig, is a filthy clump of chickweed. "So are you going to let him? I guess you can't be choosy." I start working my arms, heading for the lake's edge. But she doesn't let up. "He's into tits, isn't he? Yours are better than Kristin's, so you've got that going for you, Wheels. Shame about the rest." I must get away. Not just from Bethany (did I catch myself, just seconds ago, caring about her?) but from everything here. This is no place for an *izgoy*. I'll go back to Hadport, explain the whole thing to

Kavanagh. "Hey, you didn't really think Frazer was humping you for the fun of it, did you? You didn't think he was in love with you?" My arms are aching now, and the chill has penetrated my bones. I battle toward the shore, gulping in water. "Why would anyone want to fuck a spaz? I told you!" she yells. "He's fucking Kristin! You know it! Stop pretending you don't!"

If I drowned now, I wouldn't care.

But I don't. I swim to the edge, fighting back the sobs, while Bethany explodes into ugly, high-pitched laughter and splashes her way to the opposite bank. Scrambling out and grabbing her towel, she runs, stark naked, toward the house.

I drag myself out of the water to the safety of my chair and strip off. Bethany's cries grow fainter in the distance. *You're being manipulated,* her father said. *And you can't even see it.* Now I do. I know she is insane but I still feel betrayed. Just a moment ago, I thought we might have edged into a new realm. My teeth are chattering and there is steam coming off my skin as my heat mingles with the cold air. Laboriously, I towel myself off and squeeze out my wet clothes. Transferring from the ground into my chair is something I mastered long ago, in rehab. But here, with the chair perched at an awkward angle on the concrete platform next to the mud bank, the maneuver seems impossible. I fail twice. By the third attempt I am in tears.

N'abandonne pas! says a voice in my head. Whenever I fantasize about Maman, I am eleven again. But I'm not listening to her. Or to my father, who's here too, not as the man he is but as the man he was, with his kindness and his gentle jokes and his cultivation. The word that best summed up both him and the things he appreciated in life was *civilized.* He is saying, *This is not civilized.*

No, Dad. And I'm sorry about that. But this is the way things panned out. Lying naked in the mud, I imagine my body dissolving to become a part of the earth's crust, my flesh rotting and my bones fossilizing to rock.

I hear a shout. Frazer Melville is calling my name. Wearily, I look up. He's running toward me from the direction of the house. He looks desperate. Trying to summon some dignity, I haul myself to a sitting position and cover up with the towel.

"What happened? What did she do? Did she hurt you?" He squats next to me, panting, and takes hold of my arm. "My God, you're freezing!"

"Let me go!" I shuck him off violently.

"You've had a shock. Calm down. It's OK, I'm here." He looks wild with alarm. I draw a line in the mud with my finger, gouging deep. He'd better not cross it. "You have to tell me what's going on!" he pleads. "What are you doing out here? Why are you acting like you hate me?"

"Because I do hate you!" And now I need his help to get into my chair and I hate him for that too. He looks astonished, slapped. Confounded. Then horrified.

"But why? What have I done?"

"Well, you tell me!" I lunge for my chair and miss. He repositions it, hauls me up by the arms—I succumb for practical reasons but despise myself for it—and seats me in it. Free to move, I roll back sharply but miscalculate the edge of the concrete platform. The chair tips; catching it just in time, he pitches me back.

"I haven't done anything!"

"Yes, right! And I'm supposed to believe that? When I saw you with her?" I spin on my wheels and propel myself as fast as I can along the walkway. He grabs my chair by a handle and jerks it to a stop, planting himself in front of me at eye level.

"When you saw me with who?"

"With Kristin!"

"Kristin?"

"In your house. It was evening. You drew the blinds. And the next day you lied and said you'd been at the office."

"Yes, Kristin came to my house! I showed her Bethany's drawings and we talked and that's all we did. Oh, and I drew the blinds. Which is now obviously one of the classic signs of infidelity!" he shouts. "If you think that, then you're as crazy as Bethany! I didn't tell you about her because we realized we'd have to abduct Bethany and I didn't want you to be part of it. For your sake. I did it for you. How could you think—"

"I came to see you and there she was and so of course I thought what I thought!"

"There's no 'of course'!"

"There is if you're me! And Bethany said—" But I can't say it. The tears and the rage are in the way.

"*Bethany?* You're trusting *her?*" he shouts.

"We're both trusting her! It's why we're here, remember?"

"But you believed her? About me and Kristin? Doing what? Having an affair? How could you?" He is furious. And it's genuine. "How could you insult me like that?"

"So tell me it's not true!" I yell. "Go on, I dare you to tell me."

"Stop it. Stop this. Look at me. I love you. Can't you see that, Gabrielle? I love you!"

But I can't let it go. Not yet. "No! I can't see it, how could I? How could anyone? Look at me! I can't even feel it when you're inside me, do you understand? *I can't feel anything down there!*"

"I don't care! Do you hear me? When we make love I'm making love to all of you! Not just the bit that can't feel, don't you get it?" He's grabbed me by the shoulder and he's shaking me. I struggle to free myself but he won't let go. We grip each other. I am fighting him off even though I feel the truth and I should be ashamed, because my anger is on its own, unstoppable roll and it's in control of me, roaring its way through until finally the tears burst out and I go limp, and he lifts me up in his arms and kisses my hair and my face and my neck and tells me he doesn't care, he doesn't care, he doesn't care. He would never even look at another woman. He loves me. Every part of me, now and forever.

Frazer Melville has lit the fire in the hearth, and we are watching the flames throwing shadows across the walls and ceiling. Every now and then a log pops or some bark bursts open and releases a fizzing drool of sap. I could stare at it endlessly. Earlier, in the downstairs bathroom, I managed to bathe and wash my hair and I let him dry it for me, which took a long time because every two minutes he stopped to kiss me and tell me I was a fool. Now, with coffee inside me and an Indian shawl wrapped around my shoulders, I am finally warming up. After a furious altercation in which I overheard Frazer Melville threaten to return Bethany to the authorities if she ever, ever pulled a stunt like that again, she is keeping a low profile upstairs. But I do not kid myself that it springs from remorse.

"Low self-esteem can wreak the worst kind of havoc," I say in conclusion.

"I never guessed you suffered from it," he says sadly. The green shard in his eye flickers and I realize how much I have missed it. And him. "I should have. But you're so sure of yourself. So incredibly sexy." He leans in to me and buries his face in my cleavage. "I want you all the time. I can't get enough of you. I want you now."

I want him too. But I still can't let go of the cruel truth I met in the lake, the truth I have not articulated before. The truth about the depth of my insecurity, the intensity of the hurt. The realization that whatever I may have told myself, I have not even begun to heal.

Frazer Melville is adding more wood to the fire when the phone rings. I pick up; it's Kristin. If she is surprised at the warmth with which I greet her, she doesn't let it show. But I feel the need to make amends.

"I have an apology to make, Kristin. I was rude to you. There was a lot going on and I—"

"Forget it. It was understandable. But listen." She's speaking in an excited rush. "Harish pulled some strings and got hold of the seismic logs from *Buried Hope*. They have some geophysicists who do some research for them and get the data regularly. I had two other experts study them. They confirm what Bethany said. There's a horizontal crack beneath the hydrate field that will lead to a huge methane blowout. We don't know when it developed but it showed up on the data from September so it has been going on for a while. The company must know about it."

"So now you can announce the press conference?"

"Yes. We're doing a big stunt to publicize it. Keep an eye on the news. By the way, the forecast says we're in for those thunderstorms Bethany mentioned. They'll sweep across northern Britain this afternoon and move south. Can you pass me to Frazer? I need to run something past him."

Interesting, how easily I can do that now that I know she is not, and has never been, my sex rival. Now that I am free to like and admire her, I find that I do. Intensely. I hand over the phone and she and Frazer Melville begin a technical conversation about the series of graphs that have just appeared on his laptop. While they speak, I pull my wheelchair across and transfer into it. I have not seen Bethany since she ran out of the lake, but if I am to be in any way professional I must reopen the dialogue.

I only wish I felt readier.

When Frazer Melville finishes on the phone, I say, "I'd better talk to Bethany. Alone."

"You're sure?"

"I have to."

"I'll make some tea, and get her to come down."

Ten minutes later Bethany, engulfed in the tartan bathrobe, has flung herself on the sofa opposite me. She's scowling.

"I accept your apology," I say.

"I didn't apologize."

"I know. So I offered it on your behalf, and then I accepted it on mine."

"How the fuck does that work?"

"Magic. Don't knock it."

"Harish Modak calls me Miss Krall."

"And you like the sound of that?"

She nods.

"In that case, you can stop calling me Wheels and call me Gabrielle. Deal, Miss Krall?" She blinks, considering, but doesn't speak. Frazer Melville enters with two cups of tea and places them on the table between us. "Lapsang souchong," he announces, closing the door behind him. "I'll leave you to it."

There is a silence. Then Bethany says, "She used to do that."

"Who used to do what?"

"My mum. She'd bring me a cup of tea."

I am immediately alert. I misjudged her mood. This is the first time she has mentioned her mother unprompted. She's on the brink of something.

"She brought you cups of tea, but what kind of person was she?" She shrugs and looks away. "Something went very wrong between you. What was it like, that evening?"

"I don't know."

"How can't you know?"

"You can forget stuff."

"Sometimes you need to forget. Because it can make things easier. Like feeling that you're dead. But the ECT can bring memories to the surface. Perhaps that's what's happening. You had a big dose."

She reaches to bury her fingers in the rug and flexes them. I think of the photo of the Krall family: the handsome father, the girl with a broad smile and braces on her teeth, the mother a bloodless, ineffectual mouse. When Bethany speaks, her voice is barely audible, carried on her breath like an exhalation.

"I was never good enough for them."

"In what way?"

"Even when I believed in God, the Bible, Genesis, the whole bag of shit, I wasn't good enough. So I tried being bad."

"Sex?" I ask, remembering the case notes. A boy at school. But I feel there's more, something bigger and more fundamental.

"Have you ever tried burning a book?"

"No. How do you go about it?"

"You have to pour white alcohol on it first."

"And why would you want to burn a book?"

"Because it's full of shit. Right from the beginning." She looks at the fresh bandages that Frazer Melville has wrapped around her hands, having swabbed them with antiseptic.

"The beginning is Genesis. 'And the earth was without form and void, and darkness was upon the face of the deep.' It's beautiful," I say.

"It's beautiful shit. And they expect you to go on believing it even when you know, you *know*—" She stops. She stares out of the window at the turbine wheeling its arc, the tilt of birds in the far distance. To migrate or not migrate? More and more, they are having trouble deciding. How small Bethany looks in her big, stupid tartan bathrobe. It swallows her up. I reach under my seat for my thunder egg and hold it out to her.

"This is millions of years old. From the time before humans, before dinosaurs. Before fossils, before life. What happens to someone who burns a Bible because she thinks Genesis is full of shit?"

She takes the thunder egg and cradles it in her scabby, wrecked hands. "The big bang."

"That sounds more like the beginning of something than the end."

"It's both."

"What happens to Bethany, during the big bang?"

When she starts talking it comes in a flood that catches me unawares.

"She gets tied to the stairs. They try to get the devil out of her and then they tape up her mouth so the devil can't curse them and they keep shaking her but the devil won't come out so they tie her up and the next morning the devil's still there so they shake her some more and that goes on for three days and they won't let her eat or sleep and she's tied up the whole time and the devil won't come out." She stops abruptly and turns the thunder egg in her palms. I'm aware of the grandfather clock ticking. Of the sky outside darkening to a bruised gray. Of birdsong and the taste of whisky in my mouth.

I say, "So that night, when your father was away, it was just you and your mother."

"I'd got one hand free. But as soon as I get the other one loose she comes in from the kitchen and starts screaming at me. I run for the door but I can't do it—I'm dizzy. She stops me and she's going on about the devil and she won't shut up, and she blocks the door, she won't let me past, and then she grabs me by the hair and starts shaking me and screaming at me that I'm an ungrateful evil freak and why don't I just die. I'm on the floor, doubled up. There's a screwdriver just lying there. Like it's waiting for one of us to use it." She laughs. "Like God put it there."

I nod. "Go on."

"So I grab it and jam it into her." I try not to picture it. And fail. "In her throat. But it doesn't stop her. She won't let go of me. So I jam it into her again. When she falls down it's easier. I just hold her down and keep shoving it into her. Everywhere. And it feels so fucking good."

Her face has gained color, as though ignited by the memory. Then it drains away as quickly as it came and she looks at her hands. There is another long silence, yawning out into the space between us. A bird screeches. Then she turns to face me, her eyes vivid with pain.

I roll closer. "Your mother's job was to protect you. That's what parents are supposed to do. What they did to you was wrong." I remember Leonard Krall's frank, open-faced conviction: "Terrible things happen. And God seems to let them happen. . . . Things that don't make sense to us make sense to him." Does torturing your own daughter make sense to God? Somehow, Leonard Krall and his wife, Karen, must have convinced themselves it did. "If someone's done something monstrous to you, I can understand how you'd feel that the rules had changed." My heart is hammering. If Karen Krall were standing in front of me now, perhaps I'd want to kill her myself.

"That's what happened," she says. "The rules changed."

She slumps back in the sofa. Time and thought settle into a solid mass within me, condensing like a cast. Her face is wet. I reach out and dab it with a tissue. She doesn't resist.

"Gabrielle." She is whispering, as though she fears someone is listening. "I saw us." It's the first time she has used my name. But her voice is faint, like distant wind receding to silence. I wait. There are so many things she could mean. "I saw us. I saw you and me."

"Where did you see us?"

"Up in the sky." I wait some more. "But we went different ways."

"Where did we go?"

"After the thunder we went to the golden circle. Then we were caught up in the air. But you went to one place and I went to another place."

"Look at me, Bethany." Slowly she lifts her face and our eyes meet. Hers are glittering. "Bethany. We won't go different ways. I won't leave you."

She shakes her head slowly, as though it is an immeasurable weight. "It doesn't work that way. But I just want to tell you, it's OK. You mustn't feel bad."

"About what?"

She seems to be looking right through me, at something on the other side of my head.

"About the way it ends."

FOURTEEN

I enter the kitchen feeling dazed. "I just spoke to Ned," says Frazer Melville, looking up from his laptop. I have left Bethany on the sofa, staring catatonically at the wall. "How did it go with Bethany?" When I give him a condensed account, he sighs heavily. "Jesus. Poor kid. No wonder she's screwed up."

"What's the news from London?"

"The seismic data's been published on the Web. The good news is that some prominent scientists are getting on board."

"Who?"

"Kaspar Blatt, Akira Kamochi, Walid Habibi, Vance Ozek." I can't put faces to anyone except Kamochi, but the names are all familiar. "The bad news is that Ned says the other lobbying they've done has hit a brick wall. No one wants to believe it. But the rumor's spreading on the Net and the data's out there. By the way, he says to watch the news." I flick on the TV and zap to BBC World. Another failed assassination attempt on the president of Iran: three bodyguards dead. They show some bloodstained paving. More food riots in South America. But it's the third, far more outlandish headline that grabs our attention.

It concerns graffiti in Greenland.

The local correspondent's report thumbnail sketches a territory of

Inuits with huskies, snowmobiles, alcohol problems, and, more recently, livelihoods collapsing owing to climate change: a Danish-administered enclave that from June to August is bathed in nonstop, hallucinogenic sunshine. But during the winter months, like now, it's a land engulfed in darkness, illuminated only by electricity, the moon, and the night sky, with its canopy of stars and the magic swirls of aurora borealis.

And now, as discovered within the last hour, graffiti.

Giant graffiti. A jumble of numbers and letters. Some sort of code. It straddles fifty kilometers of ice cap, far from anywhere habitable. And it glows in the dark. Frazer Melville's face is breaking into a grin. A satellite image has appeared: a pale blue tracery of semilegible numbers and characters—seemingly meaningless—etched on the night-darkened landscape. They're impossible to make out clearly but each cipher, says the reporter, measures at least ten kilometers high and across. I can see the number three, and the letters *E* and *B*, and what looks like a hyphen, and an *N*. Out there in the darkness, on the Greenlandic ice, somebody with a monstrous ego has been determinedly expressing himself. Or—

"Ned must've tipped off a local camera crew," murmurs Frazer Melville. "Just watch."

The camera lights create a halo around the Greenlandic reporter's head, broadened and flattened by the TV's wide-screen function. It's minus twenty degrees and he's trembling with cold beneath the fur-trimmed hood of his parka. Against the velvet Arctic sky, there's a pulsing light show of red, blue, and green, a swish of color that makes it look as if the scene has been filtered through the gaudy wing of a giant insect. "The characters on the ice are so big you can see them only by satellite," he says, shivering, the northern lights pulsing behind him. "Space shots show they weren't there yesterday but there's no mistaking them today. They're calling it the world's biggest-ever publicity stunt. I'm standing here on the down stroke of the number four. Now this line forms a ridge that stretches all the way over to the horizon, as far as the eye can see."

The camera pulls back to show it, at the same time revealing the reporter's female companion, whom he introduces as a local biologist. Bending down, she uses a small ice pick to detach a chunk of whiteness tinged with a pale mauve glow that she holds out to the camera. She pronounces it to be a phosphorescent liquid that has frozen on contact with the ice. The notion seems to please her profoundly.

"The dye appears to be organic and to contain shards of what seem to be the crushed shells of some form of crustacean. We don't know exactly what it is yet, but we've sent samples to be analyzed." It's bluish green with a touch of mauve: a color Picasso liked. A color I have seen before. In this very house, in a row of jars.

I laugh. "How do you liquidize them?"

"Cement mixer, at a guess," says Frazer Melville, grinning. He couldn't look more thrilled if he had laid a thunder egg. A beleaguered-looking man from the Kennedy Space Center materializes.

"A man rang in. He didn't give a name—he just said to take a close look at Greenland. Then he gave the coordinates and hung up. We zoomed in and saw some faint light traces. We sharpened them up and realized it was a message."

Now they're reshowing satellite pictures of the thin stitching of ghostly ciphers. It's the kind of writing you imagine a spirit scrawling laboriously across a Ouija board. "The ice cap, shrouded in the darkness of winter, has been used as a giant blackboard," says the anchorman back in the studio. "But who's playing teacher? And what's the lesson? Well, here's where the geo-graffiti phenomenon gets interesting." The camera focuses on the mystery ciphers, with a red graphic creeping across to delineate them more clearly. BH63N–05.24ECH4. "To anyone with a background in science, this isn't even a code. The central ciphers, 63N–5.24E, are geographical coordinates of latitude and longitude, and the final three characters, CH4, are the chemical symbol for methane. The location is a rig a hundred kilometers off the coast of Norway known as *Buried Hope Alpha*, so we can assume that's what the letters *B* and *H* stand for. Now, the rig's owned and run by the energy giant Traxorac, who are drilling for frozen methane. We'll be speaking to them shortly. But first, here's what Greenpeace had to say."

"We like our stunts, but this one isn't ours," says the spokeswoman emphatically but with what might be a hint of regret. "I'd say that the message is probably an environmental one and that this rig needs investigating. Methane hydrates are highly volatile and if someone's decided to draw the world's attention to the dangers of exploiting them, we're glad."

"*Bingo!*" whispers Bethany hoarsely, from the doorway. She's huddled in a duvet, her face still flushed, as though she has woken from a nightmare. "Look." She points at the screen. "There's our rig. The one with the cunt in the crane." Frazer Melville pulls up a chair for her and she settles in it heavily. She clutches her bandaged arms to her chest and fixes her eyes on the TV.

Evidence of human endeavour in a hostile natural setting can be a noble sight. Shot from the air, Buried Hope Alpha looks like the ambitious, life-enhancing piece of engineering that it was no doubt conceived to be. "Traxorac has absolutely nothing to hide here," says the rig's site controller, Lars Axelsen. The Norwegian stands on the vast platform wearing a hard hat which reflects the morning sun. Behind him, overalled technicians come and go, clutching tools and palmtops. Far below them, the sea is a restless skin of dark blue, close to black, its high waves battering the struts. When asked his reaction to the message on the ice cap, he expresses puzzlement. "We've sent down a remote-controlled vehicle to assess the picture, but the first reports indicate that everything's as it should be down there. Security is obviously our number one concern. If there does turn out to be some kind of malfunction, we wouldn't be able to rule out some form of sabotage. Or hostile intervention. With the terrorist threat being ever-present . . ."

"Where would we be without Al Qaeda," says Frazer Melville.

Axelsen furrows his brow. "I'm not denying accidents do sometimes happen on these rigs, it's a risk that comes with the territory. But we have all the security systems in place and a system of checks and balances to ensure that . . ."

"Blah, blah," says Bethany, stretching theatrically. She seems to have made a dramatic recovery, but I am still anxious about her state of mind. She wanders over to the fridge and flings the door open wide. "I'm hungry. I'm going to make an omelette," she announces, dropping the duvet to the floor and reaching for a pack of eggs.

"Isn't methane one of the most dangerous greenhouse gases?" the anchorman is asking.

"Sure, if it's not handled correctly," responds Axelsen. "But we're extracting the hydrates under controlled conditions, liquefying the gas on the seabed and piping it up. I emphasize that we have nothing to hide. Come and see for yourselves. We're inviting members of the media here today, to take a look."

While I zap channels, Bethany swiftly cracks six eggs into a huge Pyrex bowl, flinging the shells into the sink. On CNN a marine biologist has appeared, with the verdict that the "organic dye" is seawater in which the ground-up remnants of the phosphorescent crustacean *Luzifer gigans* are suspended. "It may have been spread from a vehicle on the ice cap itself or off-loaded from a helicopter on a carefully configured flight path." An Arctic pilot and a cartographer appear in the studio to discuss the logistics of the airdrop method. I flick over to Euronews, where a weather map shows storms heading for Britain. Bethany pours an alarming amount of salt into her egg mixture and starts whisking manically.

"Our last normal hours on earth," she says, lighting the gas. She scoops up a hunk of butter with her fingers and flings it in the pan. When it starts to sizzle, she sloshes in the beaten egg.

"I would dispute the word 'normal,' but what do you mean, 'hours'?"

"I mean it might all happen sooner than I thought." She sounds hopeful. She fishes two nectarines from the fruit bowl and begins to juggle them. "The smell's getting stronger. I can feel it coming. I'm getting headaches." She tosses the nectarines back in the bowl, grabs the remote control, and starts zapping. "Hey, *The Simpsons*!" Lisa and Bart are in a tent. A monster appears. Marge scolds it and tells it to go away. It obeys. "Maybe it'll even hit this afternoon. Can't you smell it? I can. Rotten eggs." Her face has a dark, riotous look. "It happens everywhere. Here and in the golden circle. 'And there came a rushing as of a mighty wind.' The sea catches fire. I saw the end of the whole fucking story." The omelette starts to bubble. "I saw Bethanyland. I saw it with my own eyes."

The phone rings. I pick up and press the speaker. It's Ned, his voice urgent.

"Gabrielle. I'm sorry. But you have to leave, now." Frazer Melville draws a deep breath and pinches the bridge of his nose, as though summoning his thoughts to an internal muster station. "They raided the anesthetist's flat. It's quite possible they've traced him and he's told them where you are. Take the Nissan that's outside. The keys are in it. And a mobile. Don't stop anywhere for long. Keep an eye on the news: you've got a TV in there. Head south toward London and we'll send a helicopter. Find somewhere we can land and send us the co-ordinates."

He hangs up. Claustrophobia engulfs me. I force myself to concentrate. "We need to avoid the worst of the traffic chaos," I say. "Because once the story's out, if other scientists start backing it publicly, which they will when they've seen the data, then there's going to be mass panic. We should head for the Thames estuary. Everyone else will be leaving it."

"Helicopters need space," says Frazer Melville. "It's got to be a playing field. Or a car park."

"The golden circle," says Bethany, poking at her burning omelette. The smell of the smoke makes me want to retch. "That's where we get caught up in the air. I saw it."

"But where is it?" asks Frazer Melville sharply, snapping off the gas.

Bethany is rummaging in a drawer for a fork. "How the fuck should I know? It's golden. It's a circle. A great big circle." She begins shoveling the steaming egg mess into her mouth, straight from the pan. "Christ, I could eat a fucking horse."

"We need a satellite map," I say. Seconds later, on Frazer Melville's laptop, we have the British Isles, seen from space. "Now find it," I tell Bethany.

She plonks the frying pan on the table, perches on a chair, and points her laden fork at the screen. "There," she says, indicating a section of southeast London. Frazer Melville zooms in.

"But that's the East End," he says, staring blankly. That's the—"

"Yes," she says noncommittally, still eating. "That's it. That's what I saw. That's the golden circle." She wipes her mouth on her sleeve, leaving a greasy trail. "That's where we get caught up in the air."

Frazer Melville zooms in further, until there's no mistaking it. I should have guessed. The Paralympics were held there three months after my accident. I watched some of the games on TV in rehab with several other newly injured patients. We were all cheered and energized by the stream of wheelchairs racing around the track at dizzying speeds—though no one warned us about the slump that would hit afterwards, when we were struggling with floor-to-chair transfer techniques and failing over and over again. We christened it Post-Paralympic Inadequacy Syndrome, which allowed us to joke about something that wasn't funny. A necessary condition of psychic survival.

"You could land a helicopter there easily," says Frazer Melville. He has been Googling. "There's a concert next week, but nothing listed before then. It's empty."

Hard to imagine, though I read that after the 2012 Games they dismantled half of it and sold the seats.

A depth charge of fear vibrates its way up from my smashed vertebra. My breath shakes as I exhale, as though I've been punched in the chest. It's odd, and new, to want so fiercely to live. But the smell of burnt egg has got to me. Hurtling to the bathroom, I throw up the entire contents of my stomach. I throw up until my head is spinning furiously on the axle of its own emptiness. When I breathe in again, a weird, self-disgusted despair has engulfed me. It's a despair that's intimately connected to my Alex dream. I don't know how or why. But the knowledge is rooted too deep for me to argue with.

When I come back, Frazer Melville is heaving bags out of the back door and into a gray hatchback. Everything looks different. As though this is a place I am remembering rather than seeing, a place I am looking back on from a time in the distant future. There is an invisible line across my abdomen beneath which I feel nothing. But now, above it, in the section that has nerves, a muscle clenches like a sea anemone. I spread the flat of my palm across the bare skin and I can almost feel an alien growth burgeoning like a parasite that has a knowledge I don't possess, a brain of its own, a will.

It's screaming no.

FIFTEEN

In the thrum of Norfolk traffic, banality confers invisibility. A gray hybrid Nissan with a small pseudofamily inside it, a middle-aged patriarch at the wheel, heeding the speed limit and heading for London via the not-so-scenic route: we could be anyone. Which effectively and reassuringly makes us no one. To our left, a sour, metallic sea; to our right, the dun of plowed agricultural land, interrupted by a sporadic urban sprawl of industrial zones, caravan parks, office blocks, and food outlets advertising coffee, hot dogs, Coca-Cola, and Internet access. I've programmed the satnav to guide us along minor roads to Great Yarmouth, then down the coast past Lowestoft, Aldeburgh, and Felixstowe, and west toward Stadium Island parallel to the Thames estuary. With a psychotic teenager to factor into the mix, there's no telling how our unexpected road trip might play out, but mercifully Bethany has colluded in our escape so far. When Frazer Melville stopped at a service station for supplies, including the jumbo pack of popcorn she insisted on, she slipped into the toilets with a fistful of makeup and emerged as a darkly whorish Goth. No one gave her, or us, a second glance. So far so good. But I won't make the mistake of trusting her. Sprawled on the backseat confettied with exploded caramel grains, her eyes flitting to and fro, her shaved head now sprouting a ghostly helmet of stubble, she resembles a chained beast awaiting its glory moment. Occasionally she reads out a bill-board advertisement in a cracked Marge Simpson voice ("Need a loan? Call 0870-101101 now for a free consultation. Pagoda Emporium, all-you-can-eat breakfast!") But otherwise it's a silent drive. We're all cocooned in our disparate thoughts.

I'm finding no comfort in mine. When I roll the window down, there is a fetid smell, as though the moon has rotted and exhaled a candid lunar foulness across the ocean. It feeds my unease and reminds me—more than I care to be reminded—that an island is a prison. If we did somehow make it to safety, what kind of safety might that be? How does a paralyzed woman go about surviving in an overheated, flood-swamped, ransacked world with wrecked communication, diminished resources, and no readily available supplies of food? Will we be looting supermarkets for bottled water, sugar, and canned sardines? Planting cabbages? If we require guns, will we know how to fire them, and at whom? Perhaps, deep down, if I've assumed anything, it is that the disaster won't happen. Or that if it does, we'll die, quietly and efficiently and without pain, via the application of an inner delete button that permits us to be here one second and gone the next. Until now, the thought of my own demise hasn't scared me—perhaps because I have already kissed death long and hard enough to feel a sick intimacy. But now, with the specter of catastrophe massing behind the stacked clouds, I discover I am not ready to kiss it again. Apart from anything else, I have a healthy fear of pain.

"What kind of people live on these Planetarian settlements?" I ask Frazer Melville in an undertone. I have been trying to picture such a place, but all I can conjure are the images I have seen in magazines: humped rows of solar-paneled ecoshelters, wind turbines, beet and hemp fields, fish farms, indoor vines, and muddy toddlers in Wellington boots. Beyond that, and my acquaintance with Harish Modak's pessimistic assessment of Homo sapiens' prospects as a species, I don't have a clue.

"Like Harish said. Farmers, doctors, engineers," replies Frazer Melville, his eyes fixed on the road. I envy him something to focus on. "The people you'd need."

"Physicists, paleontologists, pessimistic old farts, gay climatologists, fucked-up shrinks," Bethany offers from the backseat. "And teenagers. For breeding purposes, right?"

I should probably cry at this point, but I find myself doing the opposite. If a little hysterically.

"I visited one in Canada once," says Frazer Melville. "You have to get into a whole new way of thinking."

"In a good way or a bad way?"

He shrugs. "In the only way." He glances at the satnav. "We'll be at the stadium in two hours." His face is rigid with concentration.

"Injured at work?" inquires Marge Simpson. "What's your case worth? Call now and talk to an expert. Office Sense: financial planning redefined."

Some time ago, Ned called to say they would fetch us by helicopter from the center of the stadium sometime after the press conference. In the meantime, if need be, we'd stay in touch by phone. We should keep an eye on the news on the dashboard TV. But he warned us to be careful: if a link is made between Bethany and what is about to happen, things will get ugly.

As if they aren't now.

After I woke from my coma after the crash, the "one day at a time" principle of coping ruled. Though often it was one minute or even, in times of extreme pain, ten seconds. Drugs helped. The rest was down to self-delusion, a skill I'd previously scorned. Now, with the long-term definitively lost from the radar and the future stretching no further than the conceivable handful of hours we have left, that principle reigns again. In World War II, during the Blitz, down in the bomb shelters men and women shagged like rabbits. In this moment I have an exquisite understanding as to why.

We've entered a wilderness of low-cost housing, burger bars, and wreckage yards piled with picked-over vehicle carcasses and defunct scaffolding. When I roll the window down again, it isn't for long. Bethany squawks "What the fuck?" and Frazer Melville coughs in protest. The reek has taken on a putrid, ferrous edge. I close the window swiftly and gulp, fighting back a volcanic sensation of nausea. This is new psychic territory. We should get visitors' badges. As the kilometers pass, the odor intensifies. At eleven o'clock we switch on the news on the tiny dashboard TV and discover the reason. Tens of thousands of jellyfish have been washing up and disintegrating on the beaches of Britain, Scandinavia, and northern Europe. Pictures from space show vast shoals moving toward the coasts like subsea clouds, while terrestrial images reveal whole armadas bobbing darkly against the shoreline and gathering in concentric ridges, as though a manic giant has garlanded the coastline with bubble wrap. Frazer Melville's hands tighten on the wheel. "They've sensed it," he says. Moments later, when we skirt the shore again, we see it for ourselves. Illuminated by a fierce shard of sunshine, the beach glitters. For a moment we say nothing, absorbing the freakish dazzle of jelly and mucus. Then Frazer Melville points up at the sky, where a flock of black birds is circling. Soon the air is dark with them.

"They're leaving," he says.

"Where to?" I ask. "Where can they possibly go?"

"Same place we're going," murmurs a cracked voice from the backseat. She laughs dirtily. I glance back at her. The black kohl around her eyes is beginning to smudge. A glue-on metal stud on her upper lip hangs loose, and her sooty lipstick has faded to the unearthly gray favored by zombies in slasher movies.

The TV news continues with a report about unusual dolphin and bird activity across the entire east coast of Britain and into the Channel. A map zooms out from the UK to cover the whole North Sea region: a series of animated graphs shows how the disrupted shoaling and flocking is spreading outward from the Norwegian coast. There, marine biologists have speculated on a link with Buried Hope Alpha. Bethany, unimpressed, yawns wide and closes her mouth with a clack. "Meanwhile the environmentalist Harish Modak, who has claimed responsibility for this morning's geo-graffiti, will be holding a press conference at one o'clock to explain why he's drawing attention to Traxorac's methane rig in the North Sea." I try to envisage Harish, Kristin, and Ned confronting the global media in a hotel conference room. The cameras flashing, the bouquets of microphones tilted in their direction. And the aftermath: traffic snarls, road rage, fighting, looting, the crude, vicious scramble for safety. At a traffic light on the outskirts of Lowestoft, I picture a reef of destruction. That woman over there struggling to heave the plastic shopping bags out of her car trunk, the chubby little girl in a violet sweatshirt that says Mean Bitch, her hair divided into a hundred tight braids, the man in the suit carefully removing a blob of chewing gum from the sole of his shoe, the woman in the hairdresser's window flicking elaborately customized fingernails through the pages of *Heat* magazine, the entire staff of that SUV dealership offering incredible one-year finance packages. The overweight child from Lowestoft in a T-shirt that says

Mean Bitch does not represent the glory of mankind. But nor, in this moment, does she diminish it. She is simply herself. Just as I am me, sitting in a car sipping bottled water and scaring myself sick. The TV news has segued into another weather report. We drive on, out of town. The skies have broken over Scotland, bringing heavy rain. Storms are sweeping rapidly south. Commercials for life insurance and weight loss clinics kick in, and the rank air darkens, taking on a mineral chill. I feel a wave of claustrophobia, as though we've been plunged deep into a reeking hole.

"Can we stop?" I say, tightening my grip on Frazer Melville's thigh. "This isn't very romantic, but I need to throw up."

There is an age past which a woman should have stopped caring about chattels, objects of sentimental value, bibelots. But clearly I have not reached it yet, because in the rushed departure from the farmhouse, I left my favorite Frida Kahlo book on the table and now that I have vomited out of the opened door and recovered what dignity I can, its absence is gnawing at me. It's as though I have betrayed someone who matters, and I can never make it up to them. To quell the creeping paranoia, I gaze on what comforts me. The cheekbone I love to bite when we make love. His strong nose. The stubble reappearing, the red of oxidized soil. He wiped my mouth, he gave me water, he hugged me tight and kissed my face even though I had just puked. I put my hand back on his thigh, where it belongs, and he covers it with his own. I feel infinite gratitude. But it doesn't stop the fear sliding back. If now were a time for escapist fantasies born of sheer blue funk, I would put us on the shore of a river. Let's say the Severn, somewhere near Bristol. It would be late spring. There would be dragonflies, kayaks, long, lazy filaments of weed. The meadow behind us would be dotted with poppies and Michaelmas daisies and buttercups. Perhaps there is enough telepathy between us that unsaid things can be left unsaid.

"Name the first river that comes into your head."

He smiles tightly. "The Nile."

Incorrect answer. That means we'll die. "What's wrong with the Severn?"

"Nothing's wrong with the Severn. But I thought of the Nile. Now it's my turn to be ridiculous. Name a lake."

"Titicaca."

"No. Lake Powell. Which straddles Utah and Arizona, in case you didn't know."

I didn't. I have never heard of Lake Powell. *So that's it. We will definitely die.* "This can't be the first time people have believed Armageddon was approaching." My voice sounds fake and chirpy. "Think about Carthage. The great plague. The Lisbon earthquake in seventeen something or other. Hiroshima."

"Noah's flood. The birth of survivalism and an object lesson in the advantages of forward planning." His voice sounds fake and chirpy too. Which means he is playing my game. Is that good or bad? "Isaac Newton believed the world would end in 2060. But when people say 'the world,' they really mean, *our* world." Yes: he's concentrating on sounding normal. But like me, he's failing. "The world as we know it. Geologically speaking, it's just business as usual. One era comes to an abrupt end, the biosphere takes a severe knock, and a new era begins."

"The reign of the Antichrist," belches Bethany from the backseat. "The dominion of the Beast."

The storm begins with a smatter of rain on the windscreen and a wash of freezing air bearing the dark, organic stench of enzymes attacking proteins, of fish innards, of kelp and mud and bladder wrack. Pewter clouds wheel in from the horizon. The sea has turned restless and choppy, and in the distance a white yellow flash of lightning breaches the sky, silhouetting radio masts, telegraph poles, and the spectral skeletons of trees. Seconds later comes a gurgle of thunder. We're now somewhere north of a residential suburb of Felixstowe where the plane trees have been pruned into arthritic fists. We're still more than a hundred kilometers from London. Raindrops thwack at the windscreen and dribble sideways. Bethany rolls her window down and thrusts her head out to inhale the loaded, stinking air. It punches its way into the car like something alive.

"I can feel the volts!" she calls. Then addresses the sky. "Hey, bring it on!"

"Close the window!" roars Frazer Melville. Ignoring him, Bethany starts rocking on the backseat, humming loud and openmouthed, the way a baby will test its voice for rowdiness: an experiment in noise production.

"Storms agitate her." I'm remembering Oxsmith. "We need to park somewhere and calm her down." The stench is so dense I can taste it on my tongue. In the backseat, Bethany's eyes are glittering darkly, as though she is watching a dangerous stage show beyond an invisible curtain.

She leans out of the window and yells into the gusting rain: " 'And there shall come a rushing as of a mighty wind! And there shall come electricity! And the righteous shall be caught up together with them in the clouds to meet the Lord in the air!' "

"Hey, Bethany, shut the window, I'm trying to drive a car here!" snaps Frazer Melville. A line of sweat is running down the side of his face and into the collar of his shirt. I glance back at Bethany. She is fighting the buckle of her seat belt.

"Pull over right away. Bethany, it's OK. You'll be OK," I say.

But she won't be OK. There was never going to be a time when she would be. She unstraps her belt and flings it off. Then with an ecstatic cry, she has yanked open the door and hurled herself out.

Frazer Melville twists the steering wheel and swerves the car into the pavement, where it stalls, skewed half on the road, half off. My mouth is wide open so I must have screamed. Bethany's door gapes open to the pavement and rain lashes in, darkening the seat. Cars honk furiously as they swerve past. Ahead, there's no sign of Bethany. Then, in the side mirror, I see an outline and something fights in my throat. She's spread-eagled on the pavement behind us, motionless.

With forensic clarity, I picture her broken spine. Specifically, the smashed vertebrae. The break is at T3 level. Maybe T4. The nightmare springs to violent life. My heart volleys with blood.

But a second later—the relief is disorienting—she has jumped to her feet as though nothing has happened, and she's running past us and up a side street across the road to the left, her giant black T-shirt flapping loosely. I wonder vaguely if someone might have called the police. And whether, in this moment, it might even be a blessing if they came. Up ahead, fork lightning divides the sky, followed immediately by a ferocious thunderclap, shockingly close. The storm is right overhead.

"I'm going after her," mutters Frazer Melville, flinging open his door to another blare of horns. In a second, he's out. I call after him but he is gone, swallowed into the storm's murk.

The rain is still whipping in through the open back door, flooding the seat. I reach over to the controls and turn on the hazard lights. A young man curses me in Urdu before revving off into the storm. Out of reach of my wheelchair, I am helpless. I can't even close the back door from where I'm sitting. The wet air seethes like a putrid stew. To my left, I can just make out Bethany's tiny black silhouette. Frazer Melville is running after her. They've taken a side street flanked with planes, where three young children are splashing in the downpour. There's a blond man, perhaps their father, in the covered driveway, fixing his car. He straightens up to watch the stubble-headed Goth kid rush past at full tilt, followed by the big man in shirtsleeves, soaked to the skin, shouting wildly.

Then I see where Bethany is headed. There is a horrible logic to it.

On a patch of wilderness beyond the road, the steel electricity tower stands tall as an eight-story building.

I roll down the window and honk the car horn until the blond man turns. He's in his thirties, wearing an oil-stained sweatshirt with a hood. Chest hair sprouts out of the top. "Please come here, I need your help!" I yell through the whipping wind. He glares at me accusingly, then glances back at Bethany and Frazer Melville, who are now halfway to the tower, and shouts at the kids in a language that sounds Slavic. They ignore him. He shouts again, more brutally, and they run inside the house. Another lightning flash splits the sky in two. I try to indicate I can't move, grinning at him desperately, as animals do when cornered by a predator. Finally, with reluctance, the man ducks his head into the rain and runs over. The next thunderclap resounds with a series of crashes like hurled crockery.

"You got a problem?" He shouts over its dying reverb.

"My wheelchair's in the trunk! I can't walk! I need your help!" Coming closer, he peers at my legs with clear skepticism. "I'm paralyzed," I insist. "I can't use them. If I could I wouldn't be asking you for help." He's wearing a crucifix round his neck. His eyes are pale and mistrustful. "Our daughter just went crazy on us. She's a drug addict. We're taking her back to rehab. We thought she was clean for the trip, but she's taken something and now she's suicidal." The man looks wary. "She's on drugs, do you understand what I'm saying? We nearly had an accident." The rain smashes at my face, my arms, my lap.

"This is a quiet neighborhood," he says. I recognize the accent as Russian. "You call the police. They deal with it."

His shirt is soaked through, showing big, hefty muscles, not the
bodybuilding, gym-born variety but the kind farmers and workmen
have. Muscles I desperately need to borrow. A flare of sheet lightning
turns his face into a flash photograph. Then more thunder, like the
slow ripping of canvas.

"There's no time. Please, just get in the car and drive. We have to
stop her. She's violent."

The Russian clamps his mouth closed, locking it with a resolute
shift of his jaw. I realize just how tired and hungry I am. And then
how furious. "Listen to me!" I'm shouting now, right in his stupid,
stubborn face.

"Hey, calm down, lady!"

"My daughter is about to climb up that tower over there and electrocute herself! And you're just standing there. We have to stop her.
Come on! Get in the car. The keys are in the ignition. So for Christ's
sake, just drive!"

We reach the base of the tower just as Bethany hurls herself at it.
The Russian stops the car and throws himself out, leaving the engine
running and the windscreen wipers on. I peer through the misting
glass. Bethany grips a section of the huge scaffold leg, then tips her
head back to assess the tower's height, and starts to scale it, agile as
an insect. Frazer Melville is calling at her through the rain, approaching at a run.

"Help him! Do it!" I yell at the Russian, who is speeding after him.
But my voice is lost.

Nimble and determined, Bethany is now balanced on the lowest
rung, five meters up, and is stretching to get a grip on the next. But
it's too far for her to reach. The wind is whirling in all directions and
her feet are slipping on the wet metal.

I curse my useless legs.

Shouting as he goes, Frazer Melville heads for the thick base strut
and throws himself at it, grabbing a rung with one hand. He hangs for
a moment, dazed. Then, hauling his weight up, he shuffles precari-
ously across to where Bethany is now hunched, a tiny bundle of wet
black clothes. Through the rain, I can hear her screaming at him to
fuck off. He signals to the Russian to get directly underneath: he
must be hoping to dislodge her. The Russian obeys, but when Frazer
Melville reaches Bethany to prise her away, she lashes out at his face
with her nails and he yells in pain. Seizing her upper arm he tugs at

her, but she has wound her lower limbs around the metal strut and locked them fast.

"You have to go up there!" I yell at the Russian. He can't hear me. I watch as he hesitates. Then, deciding on the other strut, he starts to climb. After slipping a few times he gets the hang of it and approaches Bethany from behind. She doesn't see him closing in. Frazer Melville, on the other side of her, still has her by the arm but his balance looks precarious. With a forward lunge, the Russian manages to seize hold of Bethany's right leg. She screams and kicks out at him, knocking the side of his face, but he keeps dogged claim, prising her foot away from the strut. Both men have a grip on her now, one at either end, but I know she's resisting with all her force. I can hear her banshee screams and the two men shouting back in fury. It's Frazer Melville who loses his balance first. But he doesn't let go of Bethany. And nor does the Russian.

The moment has a horrible slow-motion inevitability. Clinging to one another in a writhing tangle, still fighting, the three of them tilt and fall, crashing to the ground five meters below.

Bethany has been hyperventilating, but her breathing has finally calmed. There's an ugly graze on her forehead. Her hands, still bandaged, are a bloody mess. Frazer Melville's cheek sports a huge scratch, running with dark red blood and smeared with rust. The Russian landed badly. He is limping. They are all wet through and the rain is still hammering down. Both of the back doors are gaping open: the Russian holds Bethany down on the rear seat while Frazer Melville secures her wrists behind her with a scarf from my handbag.

It belonged to my mother, and came from Liberty's. Somehow, remembering this incongruous fact makes me feel immensely sad, as though she is watching over me with appalled concern.

"The sea's going to catch fire," Bethany gasps, directing her kohl-smudged eyes to the Russian. But she can't seem to focus. She's breathing oddly. "Do you get what I'm saying? Everyone's going to drown. In a giant wave. You too. You're going to die."

"I don't know how to thank you," says Frazer Melville, pressing a wad of cash into the man's hand. Nodding in acknowledgment, the Russian inspects the money, then stuffs it in his back pocket.

"No trouble, man." His elbow is bleeding profusely.

"He's not my father, you know," slurs Bethany, wiping her forehead and inspecting the blood. "And she's not my mum. But they fuck their brains out. True story."

Repelled by what he has saved, the Russian slams Bethany's door shut and turns to leave.

"Listen," I say urgently. "It's true about the tsunami. They haven't announced it yet. But it would be a good idea to leave before the roads get completely jammed. You won't regret it."

"You've got a head start," confirms Frazer Melville, turning the key in the ignition. "Take your family and drive inland. Go for the highest ground you can find. Or if you know anyone with a boat . . ."

A thousand questions are forming on the Russian's face but we don't have time to answer them. Frazer Melville shoves the car into gear, spins the steering wheel round, and propels us onto the road with an abrupt jolt.

Bethany remains defiant about her escapade. She needed some volts, she said. It would take more than a tower to kill her. She got a buzz just from the air. A yellowish bruise is developing around the graze on her forehead. There's a first-aid kit in the glove compartment. After attending to the deep scratch down Frazer Melville's cheek, I persuade Bethany to lean her head forward, and twisting awkwardly in my seat, I get rid of her remaining makeup, wash her wound with more violence than is called for, and smear on some antiseptic. Her wrists are still tied with my mother's Liberty scarf and no one is about to free her in a hurry.

The storm has receded to a smatter of rain as we approach London. A pale light, brittle as tinfoil, glints off warehouses and office blocks. Now, as though invigorated by the sun, Bethany upgrades her tuneless humming to a full-throated rendition of a repetitive hymn about "the love of the lamb." Aware of my blood pressure, I try to breathe calmly, but the tension is almost choking me. The lamb is becoming a creature I'd happily throttle with my bare hands. Frazer Melville, still fuming after the tower episode, pleads with her to stop, but as I could have warned him, she is as unreachable as a far-flung galaxy. She laughs and switches to a new hymn. This one's about "power in the blood."

"Remind me why we let her come," I murmur. We are still at least forty kilometers from the stadium.

"Some bollocks about ethics. Regretting it?" Frazer Melville checks his watch. "Two o'clock. Let's catch the news. The story should be out."

I flick on the BBC to a blare of theme music announcing the bulletin. When the dashboard screen fills with an aerial shot of Buried Hope, Frazer Melville thumps the steering wheel in delight. "Scientists warn of a disaster in the North Sea set to strike Europe." The image switches to the press conference, where Harish Modak, Ned Rappaport, and Kristin Jonsdottir sit on a raised stage in a vast hall packed with journalists. "They're claiming it's a crisis on a global scale . . ." Now that the news is out, relief pulses through me, as welcome and sweet as a dose of morphine. Bethany, apparently indifferent, continues her off-tune singing. I turn up the volume to concentrate. "In the past hour, leading environmentalist Harish Modak has warned of a tsunami in the North Sea which could devastate northern Europe and submerge much of Britain. He says the event has already been triggered by an accident at the North Sea methane rig *Buried Hope Alpha*."

"Would you be free-hee from your passion and pride?" warbles Bethany. "There's power in the blood, power in the blood. Come for a clea-hensing to Calvary's tide. There's wonderful power in the blood!"

"Professor Modak, whose team claimed responsibility for the Greenland graffiti that first drew attention to the Traxorac site, says a series of massive subsea avalanches . . ." Bethany stops singing abruptly and announces, "My head hurts." On the TV, another view of *Buried Hope Alpha* appears, the arm of the yellow haulage crane cocked at a forty-five-degree angle. "While the North Sea Alliance has strongly refuted the professor's claims, unusual marine activity has prompted speculation." An animated map shows the North Sea alive with arrows charting the mass movements of marine life. Harish Modak, Kristin, and Ned reappear in front of a map of the ocean floor and what I assume to be the seismic logs of the site. Our friends from the Norfolk farmhouse have cleaned up well. Clad in a suit, Ned is barely recognizable. He has shaved the stubble from his jaw and his wavy curls are gone, replaced by a sober, corporate-lawyer crop. Kristin, her hair in an elegant chignon, is wearing a dark green jacket and cream shirt, while Harish Modak looks sharp, alert, and less frail than in the flesh. If Kristin is feeling nervous, she shows no sign of it as she explains the science, illustrated by figures, maps, and graphs. She makes a clear, succinct case. Frazer Melville flexes his hands on the steering wheel, reenergized. Ned is next. He, too, has prepared efficiently.

"In practical terms this means that if you live within ten kilometers of any coast, leave now. Pack food, water, and medical supplies and move to high ground," he finishes. "Expect a domino effect."

If the British public is anything like I was, the warning won't sink in at first, I reflect. They'll go into denial or worry about peripherals like toothpaste and dog food. When Harish speaks, it's with the regretful air of someone forced to disappoint a child. "Sudden global warming, with an increase of average global temperatures by four degrees or more, will be the most devastating result of the oncoming catastrophe. It has happened twice before on Earth in the distant past. Now we have every reason to believe it is happening again. We fear it will begin in this part of the world within a matter of hours."

I think of my father in the nursing home. How fast do chalk cliffs crumble when submerged by a wall of water traveling at the speed of a jumbo jet? How long does it take for an old man's lungs to fill with liquid?

Harish Modak is speaking again, this time over a wash of agitated voices. "Many won't believe us. And that is their choice. But my associates and I believe in the right to know. Now that people have been warned, they can decide for themselves what to do. And I wish them luck."

The anchorwoman appears again over running images of the press conference, where reporters continue to bombard the panel with shouted questions. "Traxorac has firmly refuted Professor Modak's claims, denying there's any unusual activity at *Buried Hope Alpha*. The government has dismissed the alert as wholly unfounded, insisting that the evidence is not credible and the public should not panic. But while the chief scientist has yet to make a public statement, leading figures in the scientific community—among them Kaspar Blatt, Akira Kamochi, Walid Habibi, and Vance Ozek, who have all seen the Traxorac data—are supporting mass evacuation. They say the unusual behavior of marine life, particularly off the Norwegian coast, is further confirmation that an instability on the seafloor could soon become critical." On the backseat, exhausted by her hymn-induced headache, Bethany is staring blankly out of the window.

Ahead of us sprawls the cluttered, uneven skyline of London's periphery. A second later, her eyelids droop.

On the satellite picture we looked at back at the farmhouse, the geography of southeastern Britain—the hump of Norfolk and Suffolk, the gray brown dotting of urban conurbations, the chiseled roads, the snaking gut of the Thames—seemed dreamlike, its obliteration a hypothetical scenario you might idly fabricate on a screen if you had the software and the destructive urge. But here at ground level, with the sun's glint giving the air the translucency of a troubled onion glaze, amid the rearing high-rises and paint-flaking retail outlets and towering cranes, the pornography of disaster springs all too readily into vivid Technicolor: the flagellated trees, the crying children, the splintered road signs, the human bodies, bobbing like swollen tubers. Once upon a time, I think, kings would plant oak forests for wood that could be felled in a hundred years to make ships to attack their enemies. They knew they would never live to see the resulting armadas but it wasn't about seeing: it was about vision. What has happened to us? How is it that we, the inventors of devices that fly across oceans, hurtle to other planets, burrow underground, and kill from a distance—we, the atom splitters, the antibiotic discoverers, the computer modelers, the artificial-heart implanters, the creators of GM crops and ski slopes in Dubai—have failed to see five minutes beyond our own lifetimes?

The storm has rinsed the air but there's still a cloying smell of decay. Has a whiff of rotten eggs crept into the organic reek, or has my imagination been hijacked?

" 'In case of the Rapture, this vehicle may be unmanned,' " says Frazer Melville, pointing to the bumper sticker on the car ahead of us. To our left, the Thames has darkened to black, its surface flecked by quills of white foam. He looks pensive. "Turn to the God Channel." I fling a blanket across Bethany and zap until I hit *The Worship Workshop*, a studio discussion in which it's clear from the aggressive way the guests are eyeing one another that a ferocious argument has erupted in response to the news. A thickset man in a well-cut suit is speaking animatedly, waving a Bible at his neighbor, a rangy preacher with sunburnt features and a great-outdoors look.

"The answer is in this book! It's called the Holy Bible and it's all in here! So with respect, to refute your argument, Marlon, and I appreciate your sincerity and don't doubt your love of Jesus, I say this is a time for Bible study and for a careful reading of the word of the Lord as it is laid down here. Let's not go making interpretations on the fly, in response to all this! Let's stick to the basics. Let's not get swept up in this 'is it or isn't it' until we have studied exactly what the scriptures say! And that's going to take time—"

"Which is exactly what we don't have!" explodes a young black woman, splaying her hands wide. "I don't know what your clock's doing, but mine's ticking very loudly right now!"

Another man, older, cuts in. His voice is slow and measured. "We're forgetting something here. There will be no warning. Jesus told us *it will come like a thief in the night*. That's the beauty of the Rapture. We do not know when it will happen. We cannot know, Christine. *We cannot know!*"

"True words, Jerry," agrees the craggy-faced man. He, too, is clutching a Bible. "But what about saving our brothers and sisters? We have a Christian duty to help these people. If what we've heard here today on the news is true—"

"And who did we hear it from? Planetarians! Atheists!" protests Marlon.

"Their facts are confirmed by other scientists who are *not* Planetarians. Kaspar Blatt among them, and he is a man of God whom I respect. Frankly, Marlon, I can't imagine, short of all-out nuclear war, what could be a clearer signal of the end times being on their way, apart from the *other* very clear signal we already have, which is the war in the Middle East! This is a wake-up call. We're not just talking about one tsunami in the North Sea, my friends. We're talking about sudden global warming of up to four or even six degrees. Let me quote to you Zechariah, chapter 14, verse 12: 'Their flesh will be consumed from their bones, their eyes shall be burned out of their sockets, and their tongues consumed out of their mouths while they stand on their feet.' I say we should all be taking action here. Think of your loved ones who have not yet found Jesus! Bring them to the Lord before it's too late, so they may be raptured too!"

The black woman opens her arms wide, as if embracing the whole studio. "Yes! We should be rejoicing! We should be rallying people to celebrate this event in God, because the hour is coming!" She breaks into a glorious smile, and tears fill her eyes. "What's up with you guys? I mean, I've waited all my life for this day! I feel so *blessed*!"

The panel's mediator interrupts. "Well, there's one congregation that agrees with that sentiment. We're going live now to Birmingham, where the Temple of God has already decided on its own reaction."

The image switches to a young preacher addressing a crowd of worshippers, many still arriving through the doors. A choir in long, shiny blue robes is swaying behind the preacher. "We're celebrating, people!" he roars, thumping the air with his fist. "We're mobilizing!" The crowd roars back its applause. There are wolf whistles and cheers. "We're celebrating the good news which the elders here have interpreted for us! We're celebrating the triumph of the Faith Wave and the coming of God's Rapture! Long have we waited! But now, praise God, the hour is at hand! Let's have all you people back home head on down to your neighborhood church, just like we've done here!" The congregation whoops its support. "You know what we're doing here in God's name? We're staying and praying! So join us! Stay and pray! Join the stayers and the prayers, mobilize alongside the righteous!" He addresses the camera. "Bring your loved ones to God today. Tell them it's not too late to find salvation. Come and get blessed, hand your soul over to Jesus and be part of the Rapture!"

"OK," says Frazer Melville heavily. "I think we get the picture." I switch off the TV. The cars ahead of us have slowed to a crawl.

When we stop at traffic lights a few kilometers from Stadium Island, the streets are beginning to vibrate with activity. Animated groups have gathered on corners. Young men predominate. Stores are closing their doors and locking up, and it's soon apparent why. From our left side comes an abrupt smash, followed by a tinkle of glass, as a youth lobs a brick through a huge windowpane and ducks inside. The looting has begun. On the pavement ahead an overweight middle-aged man in a track suit is waving his arms, trying to flag down a car, his features frozen in a grimace of anxiety. We drive past him and on, using the satnav to weave through back roads, avoiding the chaos of the high streets as much as we can. The business districts are quiet, almost dead. But in all the commercial and residential zones we pass through, men and boys are heaving laden rucksacks out of stores or jerkily shoving shopping trolleys piled high with plundered goods— not just food but plasma TVs, microwave ovens, DVD players, golf clubs. Every now and then we swerve to avoid someone rushing across streets littered with thrown rubble and smashed glass. In a side alley, two drunken girls in short skirts and impossibly high heels stagger out of TGIF clutching each other and shrieking with laughter. They stumble past an elderly couple struggling to load three battered leather trunks into the boot of a white Renault, and disappear into a subway, their hoots reverberating from the stairwell.

On the backseat, Bethany sleeps on, oblivious. The TV news reports that the government has repeated its condemnation of the scare, calling it "a cynical hoax designed to disrupt the entire country." The home secretary has appealed for calm. The prime minister will address the nation shortly. There's speculation that a state of emergency will be declared within the hour. The mayor of London has insisted he will stay at his desk and "stay sane." But in Norway, where the alert is being taken seriously by the authorities as well as the population, whole communities have evacuated the coasts and headed into the mountains. Denmark, northern Germany, Belgium, the Netherlands, and the Atlantic coast of France are in gridlock. Still heading east into London, we pass squat malls, tattered trees, ransacked food outlets. Everywhere, buildings are emptying. The TV news bursts at us in disjointed fragments. Some of the images mirror what we can see with our own eyes from the car, while others reflect the flow chart of chaos that Ned drew up back at the farmhouse: inundated airports, violent skirmishes and arrests, cities hemorrhaging people, traffic jammed, sailboats hijacked, ferries and airplanes changing course. I can feel my breath becoming more shallow and strained. I need all my concentration to keep full-blown panic at bay. But I'm losing the fight, because as we drive on through thickening traffic in the direction of the stadium, a new fear has been massing energy like a geyser about to blow.

"Are you wondering what I'm wondering?" I ask Frazer Melville. I'm looking at the cars around us. He nods miserably. His hands are clutched tight on the wheel, his profile pale and strained.

I zap through the channels, then stop and freeze when I see Bethany's face grinning back at me from the family photograph that I saw in her file at Oxsmith. The cheesy smile, the braces that fill her entire mouth. The image zooms out to show her parents. "In a new development, the abducted teenager Bethany Krall has been linked to the disaster alert." We exchange a look of dismay. I glance at the backseat: she is still curled up in the blanket, fast asleep. "Her father, the Reverend Leonard Krall, and her former therapist Joy McConey say the teenager predicted the catastrophe that Professor Modak says is imminent. They're urging anyone who sees Bethany to treat her with extreme caution. They're also asking the public to look out for her two abductors, Dr. Frazer Melville, a research physicist, and Gabrielle Fox, a former employee at the high-security facility where Bethany was confined." Abruptly our faces—unflattering portraits from ID cards—fill the screen.

"When it comes to sixteen-year-old Bethany Krall, there are more questions than answers at the moment," says a young female reporter. She is standing outside Oxsmith. Sheldon-Gray's rowing machine, Newton smashing Bethany's globe, the parched institutional lawn, Mesut's striped hot air balloon hanging from the ceiling in the art room: mental snapshots from a lifetime ago. "First, could it be that the young killer, until recently an inmate here, is behind a huge global hoax? Some charismatic church leaders have expressed the belief that she predicted the massive global disaster that Harish Modak's team have warned of. Her father, the Reverend Leonard Krall, has even declared he believes his daughter is the embodiment of a satanic force. Bethany's so-called prophecies have been uncannily accurate in the past, according to her former therapist Joy McConey. But is the teenager really a modern-day Nostradamus? What are her claims based on? As for the girl who stabbed her own mother to death: where is she now?" Around us, the traffic is slowing down. But it shouldn't be. It doesn't make sense. We're not heading out of the capital but into it. Then Leonard Krall appears. He's standing in front of a huge outdoor screen flashing the message *Are You Rapture Ready?*

"As a Christian, I'm praying for Bethany," says the man who tipped me out of my wheelchair and left me helpless in a church parking lot. "I'm a father as well as a believer. I love my child. And I love the Lord too. And when two great loves are not compatible . . ." His lip quivers, his eyes shine with passion. But a corner of my mind is preoccupied with something else: why are so many other cars headed in the same direction as us? "If our church elders are correct in believing that this is a sign the end times are here, I am praying that she, too, will be raptured along with the righteous," continues Krall. "But I fear that will not happen." He shakes his head, as though too upset to continue, then regains his grip. "My daughter has chosen another kind of future." And why do these cars have no roof racks or trailers? No obvious luggage? Why do the families inside them look thrilled with life, instead of scared out of their wits? "If Bethany were here now I would say to her, stop doing the devil's work and return to your true family, which is the family of Jesus Christ. I will be praying for her here today, along with many thousands of others, as we await the glory that shall be ours."

And why do so many of them have Christian bumper stickers?

When the camera pulls out and we see where Leonard Krall is standing, Frazer Melville says quietly, "Oh fuck."

Which more or less sums things up.

I turn my head away from the screen and blink. It can't be.

But it is.

The Olympic stadium has been transformed into a huge, impromptu worship center.

I whip round. Bethany is still sleeping. Did she know all along that this would happen? Did she engineer it?

"Leave her. It doesn't matter. We'll find another place," says Frazer Melville. "Quick. Call Ned and tell him."

I punch at the phone in mounting panic. But there's no connection. I try again. And again. The line is blocked.

"If the government's declared a state of emergency, the phone lines will be down," says Frazer Melville. He has seen my panic and probably shares it. But he's hiding it well. With cruel efficiency, a plughole opens up inside me and hope drains out.

A tiny brown spider is making its way along the dashboard. Sometimes, as a young child, I'd squash small creatures, from a mixture of boredom, sadism, and curiosity. Following its stumbling progress toward the air filter and contemplating what I could or could not do, at this moment, to radically alter the course of its tiny, unaware life, I realize the extent of my mistake in accepting the grandiose notion that Earth's plight is man's punishment. That all we have wished for in modern times, and engendered in the getting, is an affront to some invisible principle of ethics. Nature is neither good nor motherly nor punitive nor vengeful. It neither blesses nor cherishes. It is indifferent. Which makes us as expendable as the dodo or the polar bear.

"Drive one kilometer to destination," says the GPS.

"Did you know your father would be at the stadium?" I ask as levelly as I can manage when Bethany wakes, her face plastic with sweat. Despite the huge bruise and her tied wrists, she looks oddly serene, as though she has slept for hours rather than minutes. She inhales deeply and breathes out slowly, as though somehow, along the journey, she has studied yoga and it has nourished her.

"Sure," she says, smiling. Her voice is measured, almost thoughtful. "Along with thousands of other people. All expecting the Rapture. I saw it."

A current of fury sweeps through me. Frazer Melville swings round, his face red.

"So you led us—deliberately—to the worst place we could possibly go!" he yells. "And we can't change the plan because we can't get hold of Ned!" He thumps the wheel.

"The helicopter's landing there," I say quietly. My mouth is dry: I have to force the words past my tongue. "Right in the middle of it. And there's nothing we can do but go there. Did you see that, too, Bethany?"

She smiles sweetly. "Yup. Into the lion's den."

I'm remembering my calamitous meeting with the Reverend Leonard Krall. Paranoia is like a fast-growing crystal. Blink and it has sprouted a whole new section. *You're being manipulated, Ms. Fox,* he said. *And you can't even see it.*

"Hey, there it is!" yells Bethany. She is pointing ahead, her whole face alight with excitement. She looks almost innocent. "O come all ye faithful, for the Lord himself will descend from heaven with a shout! Halle-fucking-lujah!"

I stare.

It's like contemplating a mirage.

The colossal ziggurat rears up from its man-made island, the shiny, tilted cliff of its outer wall dwarfing the crowds that swarm across the footbridges and filter inside, sucked through the porous skin of its flank.

We have arrived.

SIXTEEN

'd forgotten its epic scale, its amalgam of practicality and grandeur, its seemingly endless capacity for absorption. A stadium is a shell into which human flesh must be poured before it can spring to life. Fathoming that complex, unassailable dynamic was part of what shocked me out of my misery when I watched some of the Paralympics in rehab with a group of fellow patients, all of us spinal injured, all in mourning for what we had lost. The neuropathic pain that racked my lower back and my dead limbs was so violent I knew it would tip me over the edge if I didn't get a grip. That, and the open wound of my grief—for Alex, for Max, and for my legs—was vivid enough to turn every day into an inner conference on suicide. But during the few hours I spent watching other wheelchair users barreling along the track in a shining spin of metal, something happened to eject the pain from my consciousness. Afterwards there was a cruel reflux of anguish, and the days returned to their routine. But the experience led to an inner shift. Those athletes had offered some kind of hope, an idea to aspire to, concrete proof that the unimaginable was possible and that life could continue in some wholly different form. That the spirit might thrive. I knew enough to grab it like someone drowning and cling on.

Somehow, that day changed me.

As for this one . . .

If I believed in God, I would request his help at this juncture.

As we enter the east parking lot, thin shafts of sunlight pierce the clouds and glitter on the roofs and hoods of a thousand vehicles, refracting off them in kaleidoscopic fragments. From the distance, the acoustic thrum of prayer music emanates from the stadium's deep cradle, relayed on the giant screens illuminating its exterior walls. Droves of smartly dressed worshippers are surging toward the wide footbridges that cross the waterways encircling the island, their chatter lending the atmosphere the geniality of a friendly sports tournament. There are smiles and winks, whoops and waves, shouted blessings. A pretty woman in a yellow uniform with navy epaulettes directs us to follow a line of cars to a distant bay of the car park and calls out after us, "May Christ be with you!"

We park, and I glance back at the concourse: the screen shows the banked tiers of seats within the stadium are filling steadily while five or six white-clad preachers, working as a team, are engaged in a vigorous warm-up on a raised white stage at one end of the stadium. On another screen nearby, BBC News 24 is running images under the heading "Britain in Chaos," scenes that are duplicated in miniature on our car's dashboard TV. I pass Frazer Melville the bottle of water. He takes a slug and hands it back.

"If we want the helicopter to reach us, we have to go in," I say. The sensation of confinement has been building like a slow torture. If I don't get out of the car soon, claustrophobia will win. Frazer Melville is still pale. I can see the journey has taken its toll on him too.

"Our names and faces and crimes have been broadcast to the whole nation. With your wheelchair and the size of that news screen over there, I don't imagine we'll stay unnoticed for long."

"So let's stay here and drown!" offers Bethany cheerily. "We could all die together, like a family!"

I snap open the mobile. "I'll try Ned again. If we can get a connection, we'll know where they are, at least. And we can tell them we've arrived. They'll have left the press conference by now, right?" Frazer Melville nods. I dial but can't get through.

All around us, yellow-uniformed ushers are shepherding people toward the footbridge that leads to the wide concourse and the stadium. As I punch at the phone again, the TV shows more images of traffic and air chaos, then rejoins a live link to *Buried Hope Alpha*. In the pitch darkness of a North Sea afternoon the platform stands in a pool of light, its brightness pulsing outwards into the sky and across the churning ocean. An enchanted stronghold. The site controller, Lars Axelsen, is taking questions from a cluster of journalists in raincoats who have flown out for a hastily arranged press briefing. It's clearly freezing out there. Far below them, the sea shifts blackly. I dial again: still no connection. Axelsen and another Traxorac official say there is no indication of unusual activity on or below the seabed. The questions continue. I turn the volume down and clamp the phone hard against my ear. I'm failing to connect, but I can't accept it. Lars Axelsen is showing the subsea robot Traxorac used to bring up underwater pictures of the drill pipe and indicating that the pictures it took show everything to be normal.

I'm dialing again when there's a gasp from the backseat. I swing round. Bethany is shuddering, her eyes and nostrils flared wide. "It's started!" she whispers. "I can feel it!" Her breathing is odd: labored and ragged. She's struggling to gulp huge mouthfuls of air.

"Bethany?" But she's elsewhere. She has doubled up sharply as though something has jabbed her in the stomach. Her wrists are still tied together, but she grabs her head in both hands as if to protect it while her body bucks in frantic spasms. "Oh God," I murmur. "Please, Bethany. Not now."

"I'll get her," says Frazer Melville. He leaps out. Bethany's head jackknifes back and she emits a high, unworldly scream, like the hiss of a pressure cooker, her eyes rolling upward to reveal the bloodshot whites. Then she buckles again, rocking the whole car with her convulsions. I'm aware that Frazer Melville has pulled open the back door and is trying to pin her down with his weight. That they're struggling on the backseat, half in and half out of the car. From the corner of my eye I see one of the ushers noticing the car's movement. Signaling to his colleague, he points in our direction, then starts making his way over, weaving his narrow body between the parked vehicles. He's young and big-boned, but as skinny as a colt: his uniform hangs loose. By now Frazer Melville has somehow managed to push Bethany's feet to the floor and wrench her into a sitting position, then shove himself in next to her and slam the car door so they are trapped together on the backseat.

"Quick, undo her wrists," I urge. The young usher is closing in. Swiftly, Frazer Melville frees them.

Peering into the car, the youth calls anxiously: "Everything OK there?"

Bethany's spasms have now quietened to a tremble. Opening her mouth in a wide O, she takes a huge gasp of air and swallows it down.

"Fine," I say, rolling the window down a fraction. "Just one excited girl!" But he looks wary. He can see something's wrong. Maybe he's recognized us from the news.

Bethany's lips, which have turned completely gray, start to move. She's trying to say something. She coughs.

"I felt it start," she chokes. Her voice is so faint and distant it could be a ghost's.

Frazer Melville is staring past her, at one of the huge TV screens on the stadium's outer concourse. "She's right," he says, almost to himself. "Look."

On *Buried Hope Alpha*, the journalists are getting to their feet and shouting in alarm. Something has unsettled them. Something we can't see.

"I'm Calum. I'm on the stadium team," says the young usher. He isn't giving up. "Do you need a doctor?"

"She's fine, thanks, Calum. We're just watching the news," I say weakly, pointing at the screen. "Something's happening."

And it is. Suddenly the whole picture trembles, as though being vibrated. Lars Axelsen grabs a chair to steady himself, but he's jolted viciously in the other direction, hurled out of view like a flung cushion. The camera zooms out to a wide shot, judders epileptically, then somersaults. It must have crashed to the floor. You see inverted feet, running. There are incoherent shouts. Then there's a thud. Calum's eyes widen.

"A preshock," murmurs Frazer Melville.

A new image, taken from the air, now shows the entire lit-up rig bouncing furiously from left to right. Then it's motionless again. But a second later, slowly and languorously, the angle of the whole edifice shifts, tilting sideways until it's at an impossible, gravity-defying pitch. Then with the delicate, almost balletic elegance of a camel getting to its knees, the huge structure begins to sink into the surrounding sea. There's a fierce flare of orange and then the lights extinguish one by one. After that everything happens almost too rapidly to register. Within the space of two seconds the entire rig has vanished, sucked silently beneath the waves.

Then darkness. It's as if it had never been.

"I told you," whispers Bethany. "I told you. It's started."

The link lost, the screen flutters and goes blank. Before I can stop her, Bethany has seen her opportunity. She grabs Calum's uniformed arm through the window and pulls him close, bringing his ear up to her mouth. He recoils from her grip, but she clings onto his sleeve. "Your big day's arrived!" she croaks hoarsely. "Are you *rapture ready?*" And she breaks into a foul laugh.

In that instant, I can see he has recognized her. Wrenching himself away, the young usher darts off through the parked cars, shouting into his headset.

"Well, thank you, Bethany," sighs Frazer Melville. "I guess there is no plan B."

He's right. Yellow-clad ushers are appearing from all directions but there's nowhere to run. Especially for someone who can't even walk. It isn't even worth discussing.

"If that was a preshock, how long have we got left?" I ask him, trying to keep my voice level. The pins and needles seethe in my legs.

"No telling. But I'd say an hour at most. It will move at the speed of a jumbo jet." His voice is so quiet and calm that it's almost reassuring. "From what I've seen of the structure of the hydrate layer, and what's beneath, the next landslide will be catastrophic. A tsunami's propagation velocity is equal to the square root of the acceleration of gravity times the depth of the water."

I swallow. My throat is parched. "Is that how a physicist says good-bye?"

He shuts his eyes and doesn't speak. I can feel a long, desperate howl welling inside me. Seconds later five ushers have formed a ring around the car. From behind them a woman's voice calls out, high and shrill as an alarm system. "Over there, in the gray Nissan! It's that girl they're looking for! Bethany Krall! She's got the devil in her, I saw it on TV!"

A throng of people is gathering around us. Most are men, the expression on their faces ranging from fear to rage. Some are shouting abuse. Swiftly, I clunk the doors locked. Terror makes a clenched fist of my throat: I try to swallow but I can't. Frazer Melville is staring straight ahead. "This way!" someone yells. More faces peer in, some thrust right up against the front windscreen. Hands hammer on the roof of the car, clamoring for us to open the doors.

"Over here! The girl's in the car!" "Bethany Krall." "Leonard Krall's daughter. Abducted."

A tall security guard with a broad, handsome face materializes and signals to the onlookers to stay clear of the car. Reluctantly, they move back. The guard positions himself in the empty parking space next to us, legs apart, arms braced, but makes no eye contact. It seems he's waiting for backup. He looks confident and professional: a man who enjoys his job because he's good at it. Not that Bethany's aware of him. She has netted her fingers over her stubbled head and she's rocking back and forth like a distraught baby trapped in the prison of its cot, her face and neck sequined with sweat. Frazer Melville exhales in resignation.

"It was a pit," murmurs Bethany, uncoiling herself but still clutching her head in her hands. Something about the dreaminess of her voice makes me feel alert to what she's saying. "They threw him in and put a stone over and sealed it with wax."

"Who are you talking about?"

"Daniel. They threw him in the pit with the lions. But the next morning he was still alive."

My heart starts thudding fast. Too fast. Something needs deciphering. I put my hand to my chest to quell it. "Why, Bethany? Why didn't the lions eat him?"

Her smile is almost languid. "Because they weren't hungry for meat."

Outside, I'm aware of a man parting the crowds. He's fiftyish, silver-haired, dark-suited. Some kind of authority. A stadium official, or a preacher, at a guess. He's flanked by four or five younger men, all black or Asian, in sober suits and bright ties. "Why weren't they hungry for meat, Bethany?"

"I guess they wanted something else. Something you couldn't eat."

I'm still watching the man. A preacher, I'm sure. After a brief exchange with Calum, who points in our direction while conveying his story in a hectic rush, he stalls for a second. Then he strides over to the guard and questions him, gesturing at the car.

I look at Bethany urgently. "What was it the lions wanted, then?"

She shrugs. "They were all trapped in a pit. Daniel was trapped but the animals were trapped too. What would *you* want? The lions didn't eat him. He survived." She coughs and blinks.

"So what are you saying, Bethany? We go into the den, is that it?"

She gives a tiny nod. "What's happening?" asks Frazer Melville.

"We're putting smiles on our faces," I say, opening my door. "And getting out."

By the time the preacher has finished talking to the guard and is coming over to confront us, I've reclaimed possession of my wheelchair and transferred into it. People stare openly and without shame as I effect the maneuver. But I don't care. What the lions wanted was what I want now. And will do anything for.

I roll forward and greet the man with a smile, offering him my hand. He doesn't take it. "I'm Gabrielle Fox." But it's not me he's interested in. He wears his revulsion for Bethany on his sleeve, like a badge of honor. His eyes are blue, piercing, and oddly triangular. "We've brought Bethany Krall."

"So I see," he says. "She's a child we've heard a lot about in this community. A child we've prayed for." Bethany hangs her head, and Frazer Melville puts a fatherly hand on her shoulder.

"In that case I'm sure you can guess why we've brought her here today." I keep smiling. He lifts his well-groomed face in question. "As you probably know, I'm her therapist. Bethany and I have done a lot of talking. She's been doing some soul searching, as you can imagine." His appraising glance flits between me, Frazer Melville, and Bethany. "She knows what she's done. She isn't denying her past. But she wants to ask her father's forgiveness. We heard that Leonard was praying for Bethany here, so we came." This seems to throw him. He opens his mouth to speak but thinks better of it. Taking advantage of his confusion, I press it further, trying to engage him. "She wants to come back to God, don't you, Bethany?" She looks blank for a moment. Her pupils are dilated and her eyes unfocused and shuddering, as though the recent convulsions have cauterized the optic nerves. But she nods in affirmation. "She wants to be part of the Rapture." I lower my voice. "She was just telling me the story of Daniel in the lions' den. That's how she's feeling right now. A bit nervous. Aren't you, Bethany?" She inclines her head and I force my smile further. "Understandable. But she's a brave kid. She's ready to face up to what she's done. I'm proud of her."

" 'Behold, I show you a mystery,' " says Bethany mournfully. " 'We shall not all sleep, but we all shall be changed. In a moment, in the twinkling of an eye.' I want to see my dad."

The preacher says nothing, but I sense inner machinery working at speed.

"As a man of God, you can't deny her this chance," I urge loudly. "Not today of all days."

A murmur spreads among the ushers and seeps back through the hanging crowd.

"Can you confirm this?" the preacher asks Frazer Melville. He seems determined not to address Bethany directly, as if any communication with her might infect his soul. I can sense Frazer Melville computing the situation.

Like me, Frazer Melville pitches his voice to reach as far as possible. "Yes. So I understand. Bethany and Gabrielle have done a lot of work. Covered quite a bit of ground." He has judged his tone well: man-to-man frankness. "Emotionally and spiritually." He nods, as if judging and then confirming his own words. "Yes. I'd definitely say they'd done a lot of spiritual work. Bethany's genuinely after forgiveness. I mean, why else would we be here?"

We all look at the preacher. He's hesitating.

It's Bethany who breaks the silence. She is addressing the crowd as much as the preacher. "Let me ask you what you think Matthew meant in chapter 6, verses 14 and 15." A small shiver passes along my shoulder blades. Her voice is different: persuasive and assured. She is unmistakably Leonard's daughter. "Can I remind you what he said? He said, 'If ye forgive men their trespasses, so your heavenly father will also forgive you.'" She pauses. "'But if ye forgive not men their trespasses, neither will your Father forgive your trespasses.'" Her smile is disorienting. It belongs to someone else, someone who is not the Bethany I know but another Bethany, a sane, sweet, ordinary girl who once shopped for clothes in the high street and went on Facebook and giggled in the cinema over a tub of popcorn and believed what she read in the Bible. "Now what do you think Matthew had in mind there, Reverend?"

They are escorting us out of the car park. It seems we're heading toward the east footbridge that leads to the stadium. Bethany is a few meters ahead, flanked by two minders. Frazer Melville and I follow, with a bulky, resolutely silent usher assigned to each of us. Frazer Melville's is almost as tall as him, while mine is female, squat and healthily plain, with the hefty rump of an ox. The sun has disappeared behind roils of gray black vapor that hover on the horizon, stacked like geological strata. I breathe in deep and exhale. Despite the ominous security presence, it's a relief to be outdoors again after the claustrophobia of the car and to have the steel rims of my wheels in my grip. I even feel a small nudge of affection for my chair. I have met others who see their wheelchair not as a hated symbol but as a natural extension of their body, an object of love. I never saw myself becoming one of them. But in this moment, I no longer consider them deluded.

As we forge on, it becomes evident that the crowd's mood has curdled into an uneasy brew of ecstasy, desperation, and despair. As the fall of the rig and the phrase *high tsunami risk* is processed in a thousand brains, some sections of the crowd seem coshed by the news of *Buried Hope Alpha*'s spectacular fall, standing with the dazed expression of abruptly woken sleepwalkers, while others are openly rejoicing, their children laughing and clamoring as they flood across the wide footbridge. Some young police officers are attempting to calm the drivers who want to leave but who are hampered by the incoming flow. It's a hopeless task; the police are outnumbered and overwhelmed. Beyond the growing pedestrian bottleneck on the bridge, people are fanning out on the concourse in front of the stadium and congregating near the huge pebble-shaped retail booths, exchanging hugs and kisses. Some, bearing the panicked, haunted look of refugees, seem intent on gleaning information. A group of Iraq-veteran types has gathered near a fountain, where they argue and gesticulate vigorously. In the meantime whole families are scaling the giant concession pods and settling on the curved roofs, hauling their belongings with them. Picking up on the simmer of human stress hormones, dogs that have been cooped too long in vehicles bark frenziedly. And through it all, an electronic bell tolls, summoning the faithful. Ahead, at the foot of the stadium's outer wall, people are filtering through the hanging strips of plastic sheeting that separate the inside of the structure from the outer concourse. The litter bins are overflowing and there's a smell of fish and chips. All around, families are ingesting food with a concentrated urgency, as though determined to fill their stomachs before whatever journey they envisage embarking on. Next to a rowan tree dotted with clusters of berries, an elderly woman with a blank, soulful face stands hugging herself and swaying rhythmically in a weird, solitary dance. A dark patch of urine stains her skirt. Nearby two square-shaped men are fighting, bashing at each other with monolithic industriousness. On the outer edges of the concourse, next to the waterways, groups of adults and children stand watching the news on the giant screens.

I lose sight of Bethany for a while, but when I see her again I realize she must have tried to make an escape because her two ushers are now on either side of her, gripping her elbows. A blond teenage girl spits as they bundle her past, darkening the back of her T-shirt with a splat of bubbled saliva. Fury roars through me. Unaware, Bethany keeps going, her gait uneven and puppetlike, as though she is concentrating on keeping her spine straight. When we catch up with the blond girl, I abandon all pretense of professionalism and grab her arm.

"How dare you behave like that," I hiss. "Bethany's sixteen. She's a kid. A damaged kid."

"But she killed her own mum, right?" counters the girl. The crucifix around her neck flashes at me. "And she made this whole thing happen."

"No. That's wrong. She's here for good reasons."

"No, she isn't," says the girl, looking down at me with the kind of scorn that only teenagers have the confidence for.

"How do you know?" I snap. My nerves are so frayed I could scream.

"Because I'm sixteen too. I saw the look on her face. She's taking the piss."

"Come on," says Frazer Melville urgently. "Let's not lose her."

Grabbing the handles of my chair, he gives me a sharp shove forward. Our two ushers are now fully engaged in clearing a way for us in the throng so that we can enter the stadium unimpeded. Frazer Melville's force is propelling me on through the surge of bodies cascading through the plastic strips that form the structure's porous wall. It's like being filtered into the cavernous stomach of a whale. I'm aware of the sheer, impossible quantity of flesh and molecules around me and of my own insignificance in the moiling throng. "She's up ahead," Frazer Melville shouts, leaning down so I can hear. "I can see her. Let's just keep going and hope we can catch up."

Despite the post-Olympic downsizing of the stadium, it seems even more immense in its present form, too large for one set of eyes to absorb. Its far end is unlit, so that the effect is that of entering a dark-throated cave whose mouth is a pool of brightness. At the near end, ringed by the running track, the stage is a white floodlit disc, its center dominated by a gigantic fountain of blinding white lilies. Where did such a spectacular creation come from? Who organized it at such short notice? Nearby, beyond the microphones, stands a collection of giant white blocks of staggered height, clearly intended for a choir. The warm-up team is still at work, but perhaps to cope with the shift in the emotional current, the preachers have split up, with each now addressing a different section of the lit space from the outer edges of the stage. Our ushers pause for a hurried discussion and I scan the rows of seats, looking for Bethany. But there's no sign of her. On all sides, we are surrounded by people, some sitting, others milling about in the wide aisles. Even before my accident, I felt uneasy in crowds, aware of the inherent danger of shoaling masses. A shudder works its way through me and I feel Frazer Melville's hand pressing on my shoulder. He squeezes. Does he need me as much as I need him? I tip my head back and he leans down and kisses me hard on the mouth. Then he is jostled by someone and pulls away sharply and I am left with just the taste of him.

"This way," says the female usher, directing me toward a row of seating at the front of the stage. "Stay there," she indicates woodenly. Frazer Melville seats himself at the end of the row and I position myself next to him in the aisle, while she speaks to someone on her headset. I strain to catch what she is saying. "Yes, Reverend. As I understand it, sir, yes . . . She quoted Matthew. Forgiveness . . ." Out of the blue, her blunt face is lit by a smile whose beauty surprises me. "Just give the signal . . . We certainly will, sir . . . God bless you and your family too, sir! We will meet again in God's kingdom!"

Frazer Melville's minder seems to have disappeared during this discussion, but a moment later I see him on the other side of the stadium, directing people up stairways into the rows of seats around the structure's nearside rim. But it's at ground level that the biggest crowds are congregating. And it's here, all around us, that the unease is most palpable. Some people, unashamedly panicking, are barging against the surge of those still entering, forming a hysterical counter-current. Others are on their knees, eyes tight shut, praying intensely. A bottle-blond woman in a pink bathrobe has climbed onto the top of a giant loudspeaker and is mouthing a prayer, or perhaps an elaborate curse, incoherently and at great speed. She's holding some kind of package up as though pleading with the grubby cauliflower clouds that are ruching the sky. Her husband is shouting at her to *come the fuck down, Trish*. But he may as well be speaking Chinese.

"Where's Bethany?" I ask the usher.

"We're taking care of her."

"She wants to see her father! That's why we came!"

"Don't worry," she says. "She's on her way to him right now."

Frazer Melville and I exchange a miserable glance. Never have I felt so helpless.

"Welcome, people!" A young, energetic preacher, tracked by a moving spotlight, has bounced to the edge of the stage in front of us, hands aloft, white blond hair backlit. Behind him, beyond the rim of the stage, pure blackness. "Hard times—some of the severest times ever seen by man—are about to be witnessed on the shores of our nation." His voice is gravelly with reverb. "Our elders confirm, and the Bible confirms, that we are now on the threshold of the end times." There are a few thrilled shrieks and some raucous cheering. One of his shoes has a white lily petal stuck to it, and for some reason this makes me want to cry. I picture the huge greenhouses in which those flowers were forced into blossom, the rows of hydroponics, the harsh artificial sunlight, so bright the workers must wear sunglasses. People with livelihoods, passions, cars, track suits, allergies, lovers, children, favorite brands of cereal. "May they feel a heart change and come to the Lord! That's what the Rapture's all about! Salvation! Redemption! I believe in it. Do you believe in it?"

There's a surge of assent: whistles, hallelujahs, and catcalls. A perverse thought—*What if they're right?*—sprouts in my mind. I'm aware of the pink-clad woman on the loudspeaker nearby screaming something, holding up her lumpy bundle to the sky like an offering. When she tilts it at an angle, I realize it's a baby.

From behind me comes a wash of words: "murdered," "kidnapped," "devil," "pre-Trib." Like me, Frazer Melville is scanning the stadium for Bethany. But there's still no sign of her. I squeeze his hand. When our eyes connect, something deep and private is swiftly exchanged. A feeling that cannot be doubted. A knowledge that in other circumstances would cramp up my heart with bliss, not pain. *Cuando te tengo a ti, vida, cuanto te quiero.*

But we're circling the drain.

When Kristin Jonsdottir and Harish Modak talked me through the various stages of rapid climate catastrophe back in the farmhouse, it seemed too theoretical to be terrifying. But now the knowledge is visceral. Out at sea, the jolt that shook *Buried Hope Alpha* giving way to further violent spasms. Ships sucked down, subsea cables destroyed. The seafloor erupting, caving in on itself, tons of sediment avalanching in a second earth shock. The first giant wave triggered, and then building, and then sweeping in. Then the domino effect. One subsea landslide leading to another, each releasing millions of tons of trapped hydrates. A vicious chain of tsunamis barreling through the linked oceans. Everywhere, methane that lay buried for millions of years suddenly freed, roaring to the surface and combusting on contact with the oxygen. The ocean on fire, pulsing gas high into the atmosphere. As the days and weeks pass, the air and water growing ever hotter. The heat dislodging more hydrate fields. Until continent after continent and sea after sea have joined the paroxysm. The vicious cycle creating within only weeks, months, and years a world where the sun's glare roasts the planet. Climate change gone psychotic. Glaciers melting, the warmer oceans expanding to drown coasts and cities and forests, crushed by the pressure of salt water and mineral froth, sunk under a deep blue whose surface bears the poignant relics of human endeavor: hair curlers, oil drums, condoms, empty Évian bottles, plastic Barbie dolls in sexy outfits.

As if to quell my mounting panic, some gentle music has crept into the hubbub, alluring and narcotic. From all directions, the stage is filling with choir members in long white robes. Frazer Melville's big hand rests on my shoulder, and I lay my cheek on it for comfort. On either side of us, huge screens flicker to new life. An image of the stadium seen from above, one end plunged in darkness, the other throbbing with light like a crescent moon. Close-ups of the audience. Wide shots of the choir from different angles. The beaming faces of the white-clad preachers. Then, as the members of the choir assume their places on the raised blocks, I catch sight of a face I know.

"Look," I say, pointing. Joy McConey is sitting in a row of what look like VIP seats, a hundred meters away from us. She is clad in a robe of flowing white. Her eyes are closed, as though she is deep in meditation or prayer. She's holding a candle. Her pale red hair, decorated with a single lily, glimmers in its light. A frail, fading creature wrapped in a death shroud. My heart goes out to her. I wonder where her children are. I see no sign of them or her husband.

On an invisible signal, the five warm-up preachers turn to the choir and start to clap in rhythm. Taking their lead, the audience joins in as the music swells and spills across us like lapping water. Then, humming at first, the choir begins a wordless song, the men's voices buzzing low, the women's clear and warm. It's as soothing and graceful as morphine. On the giant screens, you can see into their eyes and their moving mouths. It's only when the lyrics start that I recognize the hymn that Bethany sang in the car.

Would you be free from the burden of sin?
There's power in the blood, power in the blood.
Would you over evil a victory win?
There's wonderful power in the blood.

The elderly woman next to us starts up a high, quavering vibrato and the service at Feniton Acres comes back to me: the sense of belonging, of shared aspiration, of the fellowship of good people, the seduction of belief. The music pours and slides, a pure, organic embrace. People rock and clap and sway about me. I would like to be whisked from the brink too. Or failing that, I would like to believe I will. I look at my watch. Where is Bethany? Where is the helicopter?

Believe, I think.

Next to me the old lady stops singing and turns to me abruptly, her eyes brimming with joy. "Yes, my darling. Believe! Believe in him and you shall enter the kingdom!"

Would you do service for Jesus your king?
There's power in the blood, power in the blood.
Would you live daily his praises to sing?
There's wonderful power in the blood.

As the music builds to a crescendo and dies off, swallowed in clapping and whoops, I'm aware of a new, more urgent tone entering the clamor. Heads are turning. I almost don't recognize Leonard Krall when he comes bounding along the aisle nearby and up to the raised stage. Like his fellow preachers, he's dressed entirely in white and

sporting a discreet microphone headset. There are high fives and catcalls as he lifts his long arms skyward in greeting. His good-looking,
honest face is reproduced on the huge screens all around. Ten giant
Leonard Kralls, radiating identical energy and faith. If there is power
in anyone's blood today, it's running in this man's veins.

"People, welcome to the Temple of Praise, and welcome to the
greatest day of our lives!" His voice reverberates through the huge
space and up into the darkening air. The worshippers cheer and wave
their arms in delight. There's a hectic buzz, a whir of joyful laughter.
I feel the envy again. *If only.*

"The Rapture is upon us, the Lord be praised!" Showmanship is a
talent. He has it. The commanding bulk, the confident body language, the electric energy, the unassailable conviction. There is clapping and whistling from the hard core. But I begin to sense a more
muted and anxious reaction elsewhere. "This day is a day like no
other!" declares Krall. "This day is a day of joy, the day all true Christians have been waiting for and praying for. Remember what Jesus
promised us: 'Since you have kept my command to endure patiently,
I will also keep you from the hour of trial that is going to come upon
the whole world to test those who live on the earth.' Revelation. 'After this I looked, and there before me was a door standing open in
heaven.'" People are joining in, mouthing the words with him. "'And
the voice I had first heard speaking to me like a trumpet said, Come
up here!'" There's wild applause. Next to Frazer Melville, a large
black woman in a red dress is rocking to and fro. Her companion, a
young boy with Down's syndrome, closes his eyes and hums dreamily. "Yes, folks. We shall be caught up and enter into the kingdom of
heaven! We shall enter that door! I am one of many who'll be repeating that good news in this temple today." Krall pauses and his face
shifts into regret. "But today is not all about us and our joy. First of all,
we grieve for our loved ones, those who have not found God and will
be left behind to endure the Tribulation. Yes, we grieve for them. And
we ask for strength. Let me tell you something else." He looks up,
and turns slowly. His expression, caught on the giant screens, is now
one of intense thoughtfulness. "Today, God has handed us the privilege of an extra task before the time of deliverance unto him. Yes. Today, God sent a challenge to us." He draws in a deep breath, then
exhales slowly. "And I will confess it to you now, folks. A particular
challenge to me." There's a ripple of interest. Catching its wave, Krall

stands expectantly, then with a half smile points to the opposite side of the stadium. Frazer Melville takes my hand and grips it in his. "Praise be to the Lord!" Krall shouts, his smile transforming. It's the transcendent, replete expression of a man in love.

"Hallelujah," breathes my neighbor.

"Oh no," says Frazer Melville, nodding at the giant screen. Bethany.

She's climbing the steps to the platform. I glance about but can't place her in the flesh, so I return to the projected image. Her gait is still jerky and stiff, as though she isn't fully in charge of her body. Her two guards are hanging back, fingers pressing their earpieces, awaiting further instructions. She is tiny, dwarfed by the colossal amphitheater. Then the shot tightens. Blown up on the screen, her eyes are deep and dark, their pupils dilated wide.

"It's Bethany Krall!" shrieks a woman from somewhere behind me. "It's his daughter! She killed her own mother! She has the devil in her!" From elsewhere come similar cries of alarm.

"At least we know where she is," I murmur to Frazer Melville.

"No!" yells a voice over to our left. Joy McConey is on her feet, stabbing her fist in the air. "Don't, Len! Don't! I know her! It's a trick!"

But Krall appears not to have heard. Or he does not want to listen.

The flower falls from Joy's wig and she sits down in sudden defeat. She drops her candle and her face crumples.

The choir members raise their arms and hum the chords of the hymn we have just sung. *"There is power, power power, wonder-working power . . ."* The worshippers are pointing Bethany out to one another with a mixture of curiosity, horror, and high, coiled panic. From behind me come incoherent shouts, urgent disputes, and cries of alarm that mirror Joy's outburst. Two women in front of me have got to their feet. Swaying in unison, they emit a bubbling cascade of noise—neither language nor song—and raise their arms in the air, as if to ward off evil. Anxiety swarms across the hall. But Leonard Krall stands tall. With an outstretched hand, still smiling, he gestures at the audience to hush.

"Have no fear, people. Welcome, my darling Bethany. My beloved daughter. My blessed child."

Bethany smiles back at him, and her smile is so beautiful and unexpected and pure it stalls us all. I didn't know her to be capable of such an expression. It's that of a loving daughter.

Her voice chokes as she utters simply, "Dad."

There is a brief pause, then a collective exhalation of breath. Then a rush of voices all talking at once.

Krall raises his voice. "Yes. This is my daughter, people. My daughter." He is beaming.

"My darling Bethany. We were separated by evil. But now to my great joy, she has cast out the devil and expressed the wish to return to God!" He lifts his voice to a shout. "Praise be!"

Agitated murmurs swill around the amphitheater like liquor in a glass, releasing new flavors. There are triumphant exclamations but more hostile undercurrents too. Not everyone, it seems, is ready to celebrate the news. Bethany's smile widens as she lifts her face upward, as if to heaven. On the huge screen, she looks unexpectedly and insanely pretty. Her eyes gleam.

"Tell them, Dad," she says. "Tell them why I'm here."

Hushing the crowd with his hand, Krall breathes in deep before he speaks. "Folks. Many of you have heard about Bethany's fight with evil, and with her own demons. Many of you here know what she has done in the past." He pauses. "And I know it all too well. To my sorrow." Heads are nodding. "I know some of you will be skeptical. But we all have loved ones who we hope will be saved today and who we pray may be part of the Rapture." At this, there is a heartfelt swell of assent. "And today, a father's wish has come true." His smile is genuine. "My Bethany has chosen to ask for God's forgiveness! And our Lord is a Lord who listens!" Bethany's hands clasp together in supplication and she falls to her knees, head bowed. On the screens, all that's visible in the close-up shot is the stubbled top of Bethany's skull, but then she looks up. Her eyes are glittering with tears. She raises her hands high above her head. Excitement and unease flash through the crowd. "I hear disbelief from some of you," continues Krall. "But let me remind you that the Lord our God is merciful and forgiving, even if we rebel against him! My daughter is proof that it's never too late to banish the devil. 'Repent therefore and be converted, that your sins may be blotted out, so that times of refreshing may come from the presence of the Lord!' Bethany, do you repent your sins, truly, before God and before us who witness you here today?" They must have met and talked before they came on stage. But how did she convince him? Was that strange, angelic smile enough to lure him into this bizarre public folie à deux? "There are those here who want to hear it from your mouth. Has the devil left you? Speak!" He raises his hands in the air. "Tell them, Bethany. And tell the Lord! Tell everyone! Let them hear it for themselves!"

There's a huge cry of enthusiasm, mixed with yells of warning.

Slowly, Bethany gets to her feet and faces her father. Her eyes are still wet. She speaks quietly.

"Thank you for letting me speak here today, Dad. I know what I put you through."

There are noises of sympathy. A girl who killed her mother is asking her father and God for forgiveness: can that be anything but a miracle, fitting for a day such as this? A man standing near me frowns and nudges his wife; they exchange a concerned nod. But other worshippers are beginning to soften: the two women in front of me are whispering to each other gently and holding hands. Bethany spreads her skinny, scarred arms wide, pivoting slowly around until she has taken in the entire floodlit crescent. She is her father's daughter; I can see it now more than ever. She has his gift.

"It's true I had something inside me," she says. There's something new in her voice I haven't heard before. There's confidence. But there's also something you could mistake for humility. "And it was something terrible." She nods vigorously and hangs her head in an aspect of misery. Around us, there is a flurry of whispers. "Something so ugly and evil that most of you wouldn't believe it." More chatter: intrigued, doubting, supportive. Bethany starts pacing the stage, glancing about sadly as she speaks. She has their full attention. "Mum and Dad kept trying to get rid of it. But it wouldn't leave me, no matter how much they prayed. They tried over and over again. They did everything. And they tried harder each time. Isn't that right, Dad?"

Leonard Krall's face is still luminous, but a shadow crosses it. He nods warily.

"Yes, my love. We did our best, your mother and I. God rest her beloved soul."

"In the end they had to strip my clothes off and tie me to the stairs for three days instead of just a couple of hours." The woman next to me catches her breath. "Now I can see some of you are shocked, but it was for my own good, wasn't it, Dad?" Leonard Krall steps forward, clearly horrified, but she raises a hand to stop him. "No, Dad, let me tell them what you had to do to try and save me from myself! Let me tell them what you and Mum did, in the name of the Lord!"

"Yes, let's hear it!" shouts a man's voice.

Bethany is in her stride now. Her voice is getting firmer and louder, her pacing faster, until she's skipping about the stage, almost dancing. "You had to leave me there for three whole days, shitting and pissing on the floor. You couldn't let me eat or sleep. That's how strong your love was, and I admire you for it!" Krall is gesturing vigorously for a technician to disable her microphone. There is some crackling and then the siren of howlround but she keeps talking through it. "You had to get rid of the devil in me because the devil doesn't believe in the earth being without form and void and darkness on the face of the deep and all that shit. But the fact is, the devil believes what she's told at school *because it makes fucking sense, Dad.*" There's a collective gasp. A man shouts something incoherent, and the security guard next to me clenches his fists. Krall is staring at his daughter, open-mouthed.

"Bethany, you know it wasn't like that!"

"Yes, it was. That's what happened, Dad, you know it did. And—" But with an ugly electronic squawk followed by a series of crackles, Bethany's microphone is cut off. She continues yelling soundlessly for a few seconds, then with a sharp, swift movement she flings herself at her father and yanks his headset off. Too stunned to react, he stands motionless while she dervishes about him, as though on hot coals, shrieking into the headset clutched in her hand.

"Yes! It was! But it didn't work, did it?" Her face is bright with rage. "So you and Mum started shaking my head, do you remember that? That's how you get the devil out, right? You take turns grabbing your kid's head. And you shook it so hard it felt like my brains would spill out. But you still couldn't get rid of the evil thing! It's still in there, Dad! You know why? Because it's not the devil. It's me! It's Bethany! I'm Bethany all the way through. There's no devil in there and there's no God. There's me and that's all. There's just fucking *me.*"

With a loud crumpling sound the microphone is abruptly unplugged. Bethany stops in her tracks, facing her father with rigid defiance. The audience's lull gives way to welling declarations of outrage, then desperate shouts. Several men in the front rows jump to their feet, then look around questioningly, unsure of what to do because it seems that all of a sudden there is no one in charge. Least of all Leonard Krall. The woman next to me fans herself furiously with her hymn sheet. Our usher rushes off toward a group of yellow-clad staff. I should have guessed that, if faced with the temptation, Bethany would be unable to resist. That she would have done anything to secure this confrontation. But looking at Leonard Krall now as he steps back from her, his face chalky, unable to believe the scale of the betrayal, I realize it wasn't even that difficult.

She told her father what he wanted to hear.

And in his narcissism, he believed.

No wonder her face has now broken into a grin. Bethany has sensed the size of the audience and the scope of her power, and it has given her a charge. I can see it. Joy McConey has too, because I hear her scream, "No!"

Finally, as though her cry has released them from a spell, the preachers mobilize. Three rush up to Krall and there is a swift, urgent exchange of words as they gesture at the smiling Bethany. On Krall's shocked nod, two security guards come and grab her by the armpits, hefting her tiny frame with ease. Krall motions to keep her there. But with a sharp movement—so sudden that a woman behind me lets out a cry—Bethany has started to squirm. She escapes the men's grip and breaks into a run. Then with no warning a violent muscle spasm halts her as crudely as the slam of a bullet, throwing her to the ground. She is having another fit. She is on the floor, her body jerking epileptically. As her flailing limbs relax, Krall grabs a microphone, energized.

"The devil is still in her!" he shouts. "We must get him out! Pray for her, people, pray for my daughter!"

Instinctively, I reach for my thunder egg. But Frazer Melville grabs my arm. He's indicating something with an upward jerk of his head. I crane my neck at the sky. I can't see anything, but I can hear it in the distance, growing louder. The pulsing whir of a helicopter.

Krall continues to speak, his voice building in volume and control, while Bethany lies spread-eagled on the stage like a tribal sacrifice. The convulsions have stopped but she is still twitching. "Do not fear, people! Remember, fear is the devil's weapon!" Krall scans the audience, gauging its new mood. If the expressions of those around me are anything to go by, it is one of confusion, mutiny even. The mistrust and fear have metastasized. He'll have to work hard. "This moment in history which we have the privilege to live through now is God's judgment on man!" His tone is doggedly optimistic and upbeat.

"We here in this stadium today and in churches around the country are blessed that the Lord recognizes our devotion and our love and we shall be spared!" He punches the air. " 'Therefore hath the curse devoured the earth, and they that dwell therein are desolate: therefore the inhabitants of the earth are burned, and few men left.' " Bethany lies motionless.

My heart skips a beat. In the furor, the ushers seem to have abandoned us. If we're going to make it to the helicopter, we have to move now.

"You go and get her," I tell Frazer Melville. "It'll land at the far end of the stadium. I'll catch up with you."

He nods. "I love you, Gabrielle."

"I know. And I—" But he has disappeared into the crowd.

"Yes, Earth will be a terrible place for those who remain!" Krall is insisting. "Let us pray for them, as we pray for my Bethany. Let us rejoice in the eternal kingdom that we shall so soon be entering!" Hands aloft, palms outstretched, he raises a scattered cheer. But there are hoots of anger too and cries of "shame!" "We await your Rapture, O king of kings, O mighty one, O loving God! In the name of Jesus!" Sensing the shift, he quickly nods to the choir; seconds later comes an ear-splitting blast of music. More preachers pour onto the central platform, followed by a second wave of white-clad choristers, who swell out the harmonies. People get to their feet, dancing and swaying and singing at full pitch, while others barge past them in a human maelstrom, rushing toward the outer edges of the stadium and disappearing through its porous sides like water through a colander.

Grabbing my wheels, I shove my way forward.

Bethany is still sprawled on the floor of the stage near the flower arrangement, which shelters her like a huge white parasol. As I come closer, I call at her to get up but it's pointless. She hasn't the strength to move and my voice is lost in a cacophony of music, shouting, and engine noise. I am at the far side of the stage now, still heading toward the empty end of the stadium, where the helicopter is circling to land, its propellers a blurred silver radius. I keep going doggedly toward it, my wheels fighting the turf. Stopping to catch my breath, I glance back to see that Frazer Melville has finally reached Bethany. He's cradling her in his arms beneath the lilies, scanning the crowd for me. I gesture at him: *Take her. Go. Now.* Has he seen me? I have no idea. He hesitates. "Go!" I yell. He heaves Bethany up and stabilizes himself. Two security guards are racing over. For a second he stands rigid, as though unable to muster movement. Then with a violent outward kick, he rams his foot into the base of the floral decoration. It sways tantalizingly, then rights itself like a skittle, but he is ready with another kick, higher up, which topples the whole structure. In an instant it has crashed to the stage, smashing colossally apart, spilling blooms and petals in a gushing river of water and debris. The security guards swerve and one of them stumbles; the choir screams and scatters in disarray. Taking advantage of the confusion, Frazer Melville hoisks Bethany higher in his arms and breaks into a heavy, awkward run.

I'm knocking past people as I pick up speed but I don't care. I scream at them to get the hell out of my way, can't they see I need some space? With a fierce engine roar and a rush of hot diesel wind, the helicopter is settling on the turf like a huge unwieldy dragonfly. To my left, far ahead of me, Frazer Melville is stumbling toward it, weighed down by the comatose Bethany, battling his way through the oncoming rush of air. Lit up like a beacon, the aircraft is the size of a house, its open side revealing a chaos of people and equipment and crates within. Five or six men, two brandishing guns, jump out. I recognize Ned. I scream at him to come and get me. Behind him is Kristin, her face pale and tight. Ned hasn't seen me in the gathering gloom, but I keep him firmly in view as he seizes Bethany from Frazer Melville's outstretched arms, then lifts her up to one of the men inside, aided by Kristin. She's yelling something at him and pointing toward me. I shove at my wheels with all my force but I'm losing the fight. Behind me I can hear the thump of feet as the crowd surges in.

"Over here!" My voice is drowned out by the engine noise and the sound of shouts and music and screams, but Frazer Melville has seen me and is running toward me, gasping. Propelling myself with all the strength left in my arms, I struggle across the bumpy grass. When he reaches me, we collide. There's no need to speak: we both know what to do. He turns and sinks to his knees, his back facing me, so I can fling my arms around his neck. I grab on tight and he hoists me up and I am hanging on his back with his hands under my rump. Ducking the fierce cyclone that whips our heads, we stumble toward the helicopter.

I'm hauled up bodily by three of the men inside, who land me like a sack. I thud to the floor and realize vaguely that I have wet myself.

"My chair!" I need my chair!" No one seems to hear me. Frazer Melville is lying on the floor of the helicopter, collapsed and panting. He shakes his head. He can't. "Someone, please! I need it!"

I let out a wail of grief because I cannot live without it.

Too late, I know that love and need can be the same thing.

The helicopter shudders and through its gaping open side everything comes at me at an angle. From the floodlit end of the stadium people are streaming toward us, waving their arms imploringly. The bottle-blond woman in the pink robe is there, carrying her baby. Her grime-streaked husband. Flagellated by the propeller wind, people are shouldering one another aside to climb in. Then I see my wheelchair and I scream for it.

In a single movement, Ned has slung it in. It skids on its side, then slams against a crate and stops. Flattened against the shuddering floor of the aircraft, I watch its wheels spinning and spinning and in that moment, as I weep with relief, I feel I could watch them forever.

The aircraft shifts and from outside a woman screams: "No! Wait for me!"

There's a wide lurch and then we are rising jerkily, as though pulled roughly from above. I see the woman's face—plain and round as a ball—and see her terror and her baby and know they are imprinted on me forever. Then another upward tug and the strangely angled ground is dropping away beneath us. We've taken off. Everything is lopsided and the engine is straining. The face of the woman shrinks to nothing, her scream inaudible against the snarling rev.

With a surge of vertigo, I see the stadium and the pebble-shaped concession booths on the outer concourse shift in scale, then spin and tip as the aircraft executes a sharp turn over the flashing water of the canal and river system below.

Then I see a tautened rope on the floor and a pair of rough, square hands gripping the open side, scrabbling for purchase. Somehow, someone is hanging from the edge. An elbow appears. Two men sitting near me shout at each other, then shuffle across, grab the arm and the rope, and heave a body in. Exhausted, the man lies sprawled, groaning with the pain of a dislocated arm. Then comes an explosion of yells and shouts: impossibly, there are more hands grappling at the edge. The helicopter is veering off balance. Three more men, all hanging from the same rope, are hauled in. Others lose their grip and fall. There's a single appalled scream as the last one is lost.

In the belly of the aircraft there are people everywhere: on benches or squatting on the floor amid sacks and trunks. Kristin is sitting with Bethany's head in her lap, her face so pale and rigid with concentration she seems cast in wax. Behind them is a tiny, frail figure whom I don't recognize at first. And then with an inner pop of shock, I do. Harish Modak clutches his open jam jar of ashes, a dribble of gray saliva emerging from the corner of his mouth. He's making swallowing movements. I try to catch his eye but he doesn't see me. His whole body is shaking. Awkwardly, I shunt toward Kristin, heaving my legs behind me. She's yelling something I can't hear, eyes wide. The helicopter's engine is still straining, a wild metallic shriek. A man next to me vomits. Kristin is pointing outside. I freeze. The sky has marbled and darkened.

Then comes a deafening, unworldly boom.

Its sound vibrates across the horizon, spreading in a languid, reverberating crescendo. As if it has all the time in the world. From deep beneath the seafloor, something has spoken. With sudden, colossal force, a series of jolts buffets the helicopter from side to side, then up and down. We're being rammed from all directions. There are screams as people grab at one another for support. Somehow, the pilot manages to right the aircraft. But the engine is laboring.

I look across to the open mouth of the aircraft. Beyond the lit crescent of the stadium, the sea is pulling back in a ferocious sucking rush of spume, exposing hectares of glittering sand and rock and flipping silver creatures that must be dolphins or whales, stranded by the giant drag of water. Then on the horizon, a wide orange flare flickers and pulsates beneath the dome of the sky. As we struggle to rise higher into the air, the flare swells and changes shape, flattening itself to meet the sea.

At first it looks like a glassy mountain ridge has shot up from the exposed sand of the recast shoreline. But it's a sheer wall of water. It blots out the clouds. Its base is dark, almost black. It's topped by plumes of dancing, spritzing white.

The giant wave, more beautiful and more terrifying in its generous grandeur than anything I could dream, is hurtling toward us.

Then all around, there are new shouts and screams. With a lurch

I understand why. We're flying too low. Even if the wave doesn't reach us, the air currents it will generate will suck us down.

"Try and get some more height!" Ned yells to the pilot. The helicopter whines and balks, battered from side to side by the residue of the shock. The pilot yells something back. "Tip out one of the crates!" Ned shouts across the stewing cavern. The word goes round, and ten men—Ned and Frazer Melville among them—stagger to their feet and strain to shove the largest wooden box to the edge. Kristin hesitates, then joins them, leaving Bethany with her head propped on a sack. It's heavy, and there's no floor space. There's a wild, animal scuffle as everyone else presses against the walls of the helicopter. I have to get to Bethany. As the massed bodies push at the crate, I begin to haul myself in her direction.

Like a giant wheel, the future rolls in with all its murderous force.

I've nearly reached her. She blinks rapidly and musters a pained mouth twitch of recognition. Shuffling myself up, I rest my head next to hers on the vibrating floor of the helicopter. I can feel her breath hot on my face. It smells faintly of bubblegum. With a jerky movement, she reaches over and places her hand, bony as a bird's claw, on my belly. As long as I can keep her anger going, that Bethany rage, she will be OK. And so long as she can, I can too.

"I thought we didn't do touching, Bethany." I am whispering into her ear, the only way to be heard above the roar.

"It's not you I'm touching." Her voice is strangled, as if she can barely breathe.

"What do you mean, not me?"

"It. I just felt it. Inside you. Our little friend. How's that for bad timing?"

I don't get it. I glance across at Frazer Melville, still straining against the crate, his face drained of all color. And in that instant I realize what Bethany has said. The truth of it. Of course. How could I not know what the things we have done have led to? How could I not?

Oh Christ. Not now. My heart free-falls.

And then, for no good reason on earth, lifts.

"You know where you're going with that baby?" Bethany whispers hoarsely in my ear. I nod. In that tiny glimmer of time, I feel that I have known all along. Her mouth is straining. Behind the distortion of pain, there's something that you could mistake for ecstasy. She's looking out into the bleached-bone nothingness of the air outside, a throb of dizzying white.

"Get back, everyone!" yells a voice. The bodies are pushing rhythmically at the crate, inching it closer to the edge, until with a final concerted heave, the giant rectangle, now shunted halfway out, hesitates, then tips and plummets. Then it's lost to view. There's a sickening sideways swing as the helicopter struggles to right itself. It seems to be failing. We're jolted sideways again. I grip Bethany's shoulder and close my eyes.

When I open them again, I see Harish, Frazer Melville, and Kristin clutching one another and swaying near the far wall of water—filthy, frothing, black, heaving with cars and trees and rubble and human bodies—that's rushing at us with the speed of a jet plane. With a vicious mechanical jerk, the helicopter lifts vertically, the pilot slamming at the controls as the wash below ignites. The fire spreads greedily as though devouring pure oil, yellow flames bursting from the crest of the liquid swell, triggering starburst gas explosions above. With a deep-throated bellow the wave gushes across the landscape, turning buildings and trees to matchwood in an upward rush of spume. As the force catapults us upward, the scene shrinks to brutal eloquence: a vast carpet of glass unrolling, incandescent, with powdery plumes of rubble shooting from its edges, part solid, part liquid, and part gas—a monstrous concoction of elements from the pit of the earth's stomach. There's a gentle, pliant crunching as far below buildings buckle, plowed under, then vanish in the suck. Only a few skyscrapers stand proud of the burning waterscape as the land is relentlessly and efficiently erased. The heat is unbearable, as though the sun itself has plunged into the water and is irradiating us from below. It's almost impossible to breathe. There's a stench of burnt wood, melted plastic, of meat and seafood boiled to the bone. Tiny rainbows dance across the open side of the helicopter above the pulsing floodwater. It is the most terrible thing I have ever seen.

"It's wonderful," whispers Bethany in my ear. She is staring at it, mesmerized. "You'll remember it forever. You'll remember me too. I know you will." The strange light makes her face look as translucent and ghostly as rice paper.

"We'll get out of here, we'll land somewhere safe, we'll get you treated," I'm saying. But then, as the helicopter begins to swing in a new direction, I realize I have misunderstood her. Utterly and completely and—

"Bethany, no!"

I slam my arm out to stop her but she has started to roll. It's an almost languid movement. Balletic and calm. A smooth, considered rotation. Her eyes are wide open. She knows what she is doing.

I scream but no sound comes out. Then I scream again, aloud. But against the shriek of the engine, no one hears me.

Bethany keeps rolling, until she has rolled to the very edge of the world.

And then over it.

The crest of the giant wave has sluiced on, leaving in its wake a sheet of glassy, liquefied flame, bobbing with charred bodies and black detritus, a foul, fizzing stew of water and gas and heat. My eyes trace the arc of the falling girl silhouetted against the blinding brightness below. As its furnace blasts upward, scorching my skin, I see her cartwheel down through the vapors. The motion is slow, almost graceful.

Down and down. First she is a comma and then a speck.

And then a burning shard, gulped into the abyss.

And then nothing.

Then Frazer Melville has understood what's happened. What I failed to understand in time. The granting of the death wish evident in Bethany from the moment I saw her, a wish whose force I so fatally misjudged: that dark, calculated single-minded mission to end it. He's shouting to Ned and Harish and Kristin. There's commotion as the word spreads that she has gone. With a lunge, Frazer Melville has shot across and grabbed me. He grips me to his chest so I am trapped in his arms, squeezing a great wail out of me, a cry that will echo across the rest of my life, because I know already there will be no green fields in Bethanyland, no safe place for a child to play. Nothing but hard burnt rock and blasted earth, a struggle for water, for food, for hope. A place where every day will be marked by the rude, clobbering battle for survival and the permanent endurance of regret, among the ruins of all we have created and invented, the busted remains of the marvels and commonplaces we have conjured and built, strived for and held dear: food, shelter, myth, beauty, art, knowledge, material comfort, stories, gods, music, ideas, ideals, shelter.

And there will be no Bethany.

From the crush of Frazer Melville's arms, I look out onto the birthday of a new world. A world a child must enter.

A world I want no part of.

A world not ours.

ACKNOWLEDGMENTS

Although the disaster that takes place in *The Rapture* is within the realm of possibility, the likelihood of extreme global heating happening so suddenly is small. However, in reality we face a far more potent and immediate threat. If climate change continues unabated, the consequences will be more devastating than most of us would care to imagine. Several books influenced me during the gestation of this novel, in particular *Six Degrees* by Mark Lynas, *Heat* by George Monbiot, *The Revenge of Gaia* by James Lovelock, *The Weather Makers* by Tim Flannery, and *Notes from a Catastrophe* by Elizabeth Kolbert. And for anyone wishing to explore the science further, I recommend the Web site RealClimate.org.

I am deeply grateful to my agent, Clare Alexander, and to Lesley Thorne and Sally Riley at Aitken Alexander Associates, as well as to Gail Campbell, Polly Coles, Matti Coleman, Gina de Ferrer, Humphrey Hawksley, Carsten Jensen, Kate O'Riordan, Lisanne Radice, Kitty Sewell, and Morgan Todd for their insightful feedback on the manuscript at different stages. I am indebted to Bill Thomas at Doubleday for putting faith in me and to the wonderful Jennifer Jackson for her astute and visionary editing.

While all the mistakes are my own, I owe a huge debt of gratitude to the people without whose encouragement, specialist input, and respect for the imperatives of poetic license this book could not have been written. Nicholas Guyatt, author of *Have a Nice Doomsday!* shepherded me through the world of Christian evangelism, while Rod and Cathy Sheard gave me an early glimpse of the Olympic stadium. Dr. Mary-Jane Attenburrow gave invaluable advice on medical matters, while Anne Luttman-Johnson generously provided me with insights into wheelchair use and was a huge influence and inspiration throughout the writing of the book. And through the Web site SciTalk I made contact with Dr. Daniela Schmidt at Bristol University's Department of Earth Sciences. Her passion for a fascinating subject and facility to convey its complexities lit the creative fire and kept it burning.

And thank you, Carsten, for being the love of my life.